3/5

Advance Praise for Petru Popescu's *Girl Mary*

"*Girl Mary* brings the people and settings of Biblical antiquity to life with compassion, vivid storytelling, and an unerring eye for the Rightness of the world's greatest story. It will speak to anyone who cherishes the essential humanity of our foundational spiritual traditions."

—Deepak Chopra, author of *Perfect Health*

"In this novel Petru Popescu's literary imagination will stimulate the reader's interest in religious and historical events."

—Elie Wiesel, author of *Night*

"With deep research and masterful storytelling, Petru Popescu brings the worlds of Augustan Rome and Judea to triumphant life. As for the heroine of *Girl Mary,* she is an exquisitely nuanced creation: scrappy, inquisitive, lovable, and, yes, very much an adolescent (in the best sense). An unforgettable story."

—Blake Bailey, author of *Cheever: A Life*

"Petru Popescu has written a remarkable and compelling novel about one of the most enigmatic and revered figures in history: Mary, the mother of Jesus. . . . Popescu has given us a Mary with an earthy and sensual presence thick with the religious and political realities of her day. . . . *Girl Mary* is a marvelous and inspired read."

—Dr. Jeffrey S. Siker, Chair of Theological Studies, Loyola Marymount University

"A powerful book, in which history, legend, and the contemporary world merge in the best tradition of Mikhail Bulgakov."

—Radu Ioanid, author of *The Ransom of the Jews*

"Petru Popescu provides a moving, vivid, and psychologically astute look at the events leading up to the birth of Jesus. . . . This book is a triumph."

—Dennis Palumbo, author of *Writing From the Inside Out*

Girl Mary

Petru Popescu

Simon & Schuster Paperbacks
New York   London   Toronto   Sydney

Simon & Schuster Paperbacks
A Division of Simon & Schuster, Inc.
1230 Avenue of the Americas
New York, NY 10020

First Simon & Schuster trade paperback edition September 2009

SIMON & SCHUSTER PAPERBACKS and colophon are registered
trademarks of Simon & Schuster, Inc.

For information about special discounts for bulk purchases,
please contact Simon & Schuster Special Sales at
1-866-506-1949 or business@simonandschuster.com.

The Simon & Schuster Speakers Bureau can bring authors to your live event.
For more information or to book an event contact the Simon & Schuster Speakers
Bureau at 1-866-248-3049 or visit our website at www.simonspeakers.com.

Designed by Davina Mock-Maniscalco

Manufactured in the United States of America

1 3 5 7 9 10 8 6 4 2

Library of Congress Cataloging-in-Publication Data
Popescu, Petru
Girl Mary / Petru Popescu.
p. cm.
1. Mary, Blessed Virgin, Saint—Childhood and youth—Fiction.   I. Title.
PS3566.O6267G57 2009
813'.54—dc22   2009002304

ISBN 978-1-4165-3263-7

To Iris, Chloe, and Adam

O woman, uniquely to be wondered at . . . by you the elements are renewed . . .

Anselm of Canterbury

A girl, I do not know by what caresses, passions or promises . . . she seduced . . . and wounded, and enraptured the divine heart . . . the wisdom of God . . .

Bernardino de Siena

Her hands were long, and her fingers also.

Epiphanius

She was tall, with large eyes and dark, wheat-colored skin.

Nikos Kazantzakis, *The Last Temptation of Christ*

She's not the statue in the parlor. She's something inside of you.
Do you understand what I'm telling you?

Sue Monk Kidd, *The Secret Life of Bees*

Contents

Part 1

The Girl
in the Desert

He spurred his horse, which pulled behind it another horse, loaded with water skins and bales of hay.

Five nights in a row, the young Roman, King Herod's envoy, had chosen a campsite in the desert, poured water from the skins into a bucket, and watered the horses, then broke hay and spread it on a tarp of flax before them. He ate heavy barley bread and ripe cheese and figs. Then he tied the horses' front legs two palms above their ankles, as if handcuffed. If they spooked and took off during the night, the hooves banging on the sand would awake him.

When jackals approached, the horses whinnied and awoke the envoy, who bolted and waved his arms and shouted until the jackals withdrew. He lay back to sleep. When the dawn cracked the dark open, he was in his saddle already, horse leading horse. Each day, he rode the horse he'd spared the day before. The sunlight scalded his face. His cape fluttered behind him, like an angry flame billowing off his shoulders. Scanning with narrowed eyes the shadows of the dunes, and riding against them, east.

On the third day of riding, bones started cracking under his racing hooves. Skulls, hidden under shallow sand, exploded under his passage like blasts from catapult shots. The man stopped the horses, jumped off his saddle, and hunkered down. He dug the ground with his ornate Roman *pugio*. In an instant, the short heavy dagger revealed more skulls, with hair mixed with shreds of striped fabric still clinging to them—the dead had been wearing *tallits,* male prayer shawls. The hair was dark. Those slaughtered men were young.

The Roman grinned at the desert's fiery air; he was on the right course.

He would find the Jews of the Desert, and there would be enough of them to bring back.

Hope swelled inside him. He got on his horse and rode on.

AHEAD OF the Roman man, hour after hour, the desert dried up more. It looked like a moon face, as in that old tale whispered before the writing of the Torah:

God made the earth, fertile and wet he made it. Then, just to play, God made the moon, but it came out barren. God slammed it to the ground, where it broke into a thousand shards.

God made another moon. Again, it came out barren. God flipped it with the back of his hand, off into the sky: Hover up there, and light up the humans' night, or what good are you? Obeying God's wish, the second moon shone silently in the sky. And the first moon, God let its shards mix with the earth, and they became the earth's deserts.

The envoy knew many stories of the Jews, even some not written in books. In the few months before sailing from Italy, he had learned so much about God's chosen people.

Across that shattered moon, he rode until he glimpsed palm trees. The oasis was no mirage. Had he not found it, he might have lost his way, using up his supplies until he died in the desert. But here he was. The awe of being alive twinned him with those unknown desert dwellers. He rode into that cluster of trees.

THE WATER WHEEL was moved by a capstan, whose bars were pushed by girls walking in a circle, like donkeys toiling on a farm. Clay pots tied on the rim of the wheel brought up the clear flow, emptying it into a cistern large enough to water a caravan. The Roman counted the desert girls: eight, in wet robes of unfitted flax, treading that muddy rut. Small and malnourished, they urged each other on with brief, guttural cries. As the Roman hissed, *tsstss,* to slow down his horse, a girl jumped into the wheel and walked inside it, like a hamster in a cage.

Amused, the Roman stared at the camp beyond. A jumble of tents patched with rags. Rock walls, beehived with puffing holes. *They live in those holes,* he marveled. *That smoke is from cooking pots.*

The girl in the wheel started to run. The spokes creaked, the pots splashed water onto the other workers. The impatient girl flicked the hair off her face with a tanned hand. Cries of "stop," "slow down," made her run faster—until the visitor sat up in his saddle and called out, "The rabbi, who is the rabbi here?"

The girls stopped pushing the capstan. Halting abruptly, the wheel threw out the prankster—she flew to the ground, landing by the visitor's horse. Dizzied, she looked straight at him. *Ite me dei,* the man swore softly in Latin, *so help me, gods!—I've seen her before!* Though he knew he had not. But since for five days he'd seen only barren sands and the flanks of his horses, maybe she reminded him of all that was nurturing and feminine. She was tall and wore the *istomukhvia,* the all-purpose shift of flax of women from Galilee. It was old and worn-out, likely handed down from her mother. Looking at her, he imagined a body without an ounce of fat under her shift.

He took in her face. So baked by the sun, it had the tint of ripe carobs. Freckles dotted the sides of her small, straight nose, a few above each delicate nostril. Her eyes seemed lilac in the shade, but when she stood up against the late sunlight, her eyes were brown. When she spoke, he felt that he knew her voice.

"My father's the rabbi here, and who are you to ask?"

"I am an envoy with a message from your king."

"Orpa!" the tallest one called out to a girl even darker and wirier. The one named Orpa nodded, then both of them whistled, while the other girls pulled out the capstan's ribs. In a blink, these children were armed with bats. The Roman's hand went to his sword, but he caught himself. *Easy,* he thought. The lips of the freckled girl were thin, but so finely drawn. "What's your name?" he asked her. His voice, thank the gods, was calm.

"Mary-amneh," she replied, a little defiant. But the Roman guessed that she blushed, as her skin started to shine under her tan.

A shadow drew close: a jackal, low-bodied, brightly fanged, followed by three more. The Roman gasped—tame jackals! One of the animals put up its muzzle, and the girl stroked it. Were they trained to attack? If they jumped him, he'd be easy prey . . .

Seized by fear, he blurted out, "Herod the Great sends word to the tribe of Joachim ben Ahaz ben Matthan . . . Are you his tribe?" The brown-eyed girl nodded. "The king forgives you all! You're no longer in exile, you can return to your homes in Nazareth!"

They gaped at him. The silence dripped with the water from those pots.

Then Mary-amneh threw her head back. She gave a high, ululated call, like a desert bird.

There was a rush of voices from people lunging out of tents and caves.

The Roman jumped off his horse. Dizzy. He'd been in the saddle since dawn.

A crowd was hurrying over. Older men and women, boys with fuzz on their upper lips, a gaggle of children. They wore old clothes, discolored from use and washing; only one tall, gray-haired woman wore an apron smeared with bright color stains— that's the girl's mother, and she's a dyer, the Roman remembered. The mother did not look much like Mary-amneh except for her height, but the bearded man running next to her had the girl's nose, her thin, expressive lips, her freckles even. *Casus patris certi, unquestionably her father by blood,* the envoy thought, silently enjoying the Latin words. He was lonely for home. He spoke Latin to other Roman soldiers in Jerusalem, mostly when they banded together to visit a whorehouse outside the walls, in the Kidron Valley.

The pale old man and his wife surged at the fore of the crowd. Here they are, he thought, Joachim and Anna. He was informed of these people's names, and alert for anything they would say—*speculator vigilans semper,* a spy is forever at work. He glanced back. By the cistern, the girl pulled a hair slide from a fold in her shift and forked it into her rich hair. The crowd yammered in Aramaic, with harsh *khh* sounds, as if spit boiled in their throats. How many of them had survived King Herod's wrath, fifty, eighty?

He remembered those skulls in the desert, cracking under his passage. The tribe's young males had all been killed, but some boys had been spared—he spotted them in the crowd now, grown, with fuzz under their noses. But who had fathered these wailing infants? The visiting camel drivers? *I'll find the answers to all those questions,* he told himself, when Rabbi Joachim, pale, his beard grainy white, stopped right in front of him and gazed at him suspiciously.

Civil, the Roman said, "My name is Apella, special servant to the king. You may have guessed that I'm not Judean or Galilean though I speak your language and know your customs. The king's message is that you may return to Nazareth, as of right now."

Joachim and his wife looked at each other; the crowd looked at each other. It seemed that this message, once so desired, was coming too late. Then Joachim asked, "You have a writ from the king bearing out your words?"

"Of course." He walked to the stamping horses, unbuttoned a leather holster, and pulled out the king's scroll, tearing the bone clasp that sealed it.

Joachim lifted his arms. When his sleeves fell back, Apella cringed—Joachim's hands had been beaten severely. Fingers knobby and crooked, nails missing, he gestured with a maimed hand that the wife should hold up the scroll before his eyes. Then he read like a learned man, quick, without glancing twice at a word, and shook his head. "It says here that we've been amnestied, but of what offense? We were never tried in a court."

Apella shrugged. "It's the king's will that you return to your homes. You should take advantage of his generosity."

Joachim turned to his daughter. "Mary-amneh?"

The name was common in Galilee. King Herod's late wife, his one Jewish spouse among a harem of ten, was also called Mary-amneh. Herod's other wives were Greek or Phoenician. But Queen Mary-amneh was Jewish and the king's favorite until he had killed her in a drunken fit of jealousy. Allegedly, she had stared out her window at a young captain of the guards. Herod had snuffed her with a pillow. He had also killed Aristobulus and Alexander, the two sons she bore him. Everyone knew about Herod's crimes, but Herod was kept on his throne by the Romans precisely because he was cruel. That made him an *optimus rex socius,* an excellent client king, and client kings did the will of Rome all around the world.

The girl named after the murdered queen stepped closer to her father. Joachim whispered to her. She nodded and whistled again. Now a dozen jackals scurried out of the bushes, and two of the water girls ran leading them up the path, back into the desert.

Good, Apella thought. *They would scour the dunes and find that I've come alone. After that, they will trust me. The girls particularly must be dying to leave this hole.*

Mary-amneh turned to the cistern, scooped water in her palms, and washed her face. Apella stepped up. "I'd be thankful to wash, too."

She grabbed her shift, wiped her forehead and cheeks, then swung her bare arm at the cistern: Be my guest. She wasn't going to pour water, or wait on him with a towel. "You unscrubbed brat. Who needs your favors?" he grumbled under his breath, dunking his hands, forearms, then his face into the water. Flies and wasps floated where she had rippled it. He splashed them away, noticing that the cistern was built of freshly fitted planks. Wood was expensive in Galilee, earmarked for Roman ships; trading with the caravans, the Jews of the desert had done well. He was thirsty but fearful to drink from where camels drank. But the girl had just washed her face in the cistern. *To hell with it.* He drank with long gulps.

He stood up, stocky, his hair short and curly, his eyes

piercingly brown, his nose strong, prowlike. Handsome, he rated himself.

"Mind the flies," Mary said. A cloud of them rose from the rippling water. He peeled off his *subucula,* his vest, revealing a gut swollen from eating barley bread, and slapped the flies away. The girls tittered. Having just turned twenty-five, Apella had never felt old or unfit in front of females. Scowling, he pulled his vest back on.

"Has the king arranged for our homes to be returned to us?" Mary asked. "When we were chased here, the clan of Shalafta and the clan of Aaron stole our homes, our herds, all we owned." Apella frowned as if this were the first he had heard about that; but he knew about those clans. "They joined the king's Syrians, to drive us to our deaths—our own cousins. If we go back, they'll jump us and kill us."

"They won't. I'll stop in Nazareth on my way back, and convey the king's wish." He turned to Anna, "You dye clothes, yes? My mother was a dyer, too. Dyers pass their secret recipes to their children, yes?" She nodded curtly. He pointed to a purple stain on her apron. "I thought purple could only be drawn from Red Sea shells."

"That's true, but the caravans bring us shells," said Anna. "And we get colors from desert flowers, crushed with water."

He beamed at her. "You people made the well into a good business; you'll know how to bargain for your houses."

"Sweet-talking, aren't you?" said the girl Orpa, surprising him with her daring. "Tell the king to give us our homes back, otherwise this is meaningless." And everyone yelled, "Our homes, yes! Amen! Amen!"

Amen. That word which the Jews used so often and with

such passion—it really meant "I believe." The Romans felt excluded when they heard the Jews say it. Some Romans belched or farted when they heard it.

"What do you know about us?" Joachim asked. And the crowd became deeply silent, eyes drilling the stranger.

Apella answered softly, "Only what I heard at the court. I've been in the king's pay only a year. When you people still lived in Nazareth, the king's oldest son, Aristobulus, hired you, Rabbi, to build him a prayer chest, yes? You were renowned as a carpenter, yes?" Joachim nodded, suspicious but flattered. "But Aristobulus was scheming to seize his father's throne, so the king had him killed. Then he banished everyone who knew the prince, including your tribe, Rabbi Joachim, and that's all I know. After Prince Aristobulus was killed, Queen Mary-amneh drowned herself in the palace pool, but before she did that, she sent a letter to Rome telling Emperor Augustus that her husband had gone insane and Augustus should remove him from the throne . . ."

"The king was always insane!" someone yelled. "He's like the lame old lion who eats his cubs!"

"Why are you serving the king?" a teenager shouted, cocking his scrawny neck at the well-fed visitor.

"What's your name?" Apella asked.

The boy cleared his voice. "Shimon," he muttered, less hotly.

"I'm a soldier of fortune, Shimon. A good one, too, as long as the kings pays me, and that makes the king less suspicious."

"Less crazy, less rabid!" many voices shouted.

"Maybe so," Apella replied. "But just now the king's in a tight spot. He's old and sick, and must rein in his sons by his youngest queen, Malthace the Phoenician. So he hired new servants, me included, to put a new face on his rule. And I told him,

'Your Majesty, you have too many discontents. Pardon the Jews of the Desert, write the scroll, I'll take it to them . . .'"

Joachim's cheeks surged red. "*You* told him to do that?"

"Yes, that was my suggestion. He agreed so easily, maybe the conjunction of the stars two months ago was unusually favorable . . ."

"Two months!" the crowd marveled.

"I'm sorry it took that long. The king keeps me busy."

"It's not like Herod to forgive," an older man shouted. "This is a trap."

"Then it's your choice to stay here," Apella said. "But I give you the word of the *urbs* of Rome, I'm not putting you in harm's way! I am a *vigil Asiae*, a supervisor of these lands, it's my duty to maintain peace here. The king is sixty-nine, and his memory's slipping. I don't think he remembered who you were when he signed the scroll."

"So, we'll go home and no one will harm us?"

"Yes. You have nothing to fear."

The people crowded around Apella. The closest ones touched his vest and his tunic of platelets, while the children scurried to paw his boots. Dizzied by so many breaths and odors, he yelled, "It is as I said, amen!" Hearing "I believe" from the lips of a Roman made them laugh, and he laughed with them. "If you start on your way back tomorrow, I'll get a writ for your homes, too, and we'll meet outside Nazareth's gates."

"We can't leave tomorrow, we must decide what to do with the well," Mary said.

Her father nodded. "Yes, the lives of travelers and their animals depend on our water."

The daughter's the key, Apella concluded. *If she trusts me,*

13

everyone will. I must try to speak with her alone. He gave her a quick bow. "Show me around, so I can tell whoever asks how you survived here. You could use some friends." She was silent, though she undoubtedly heard him. "Mary, don't waste this chance. Don't you want to go home?" He smiled at the other girls, folding his arms as if lullabying an imaginary baby. "Girls, don't you want to get married, have children, know the pleasures of *neshikot ve reerim* [little kisses and slobbers]?" The girls laughed, all except the tall one. She leaned toward him and whispered, "Why did you lie about the queen's death?"

"Huh?" The sun stabbed between two trees. He raised his hands to shade his eyes.

She whispered again. "Or maybe you didn't know?"

"Know what?" He turned to avoid the glare, right into her eyes.

"The king killed Mary-amneh *before* he killed Aristobulus. So Aristobulus wanted to avenge his mother. He told me that when he came to Nazareth to see my father's work. If he failed, he knew that his father would kill him. It was just a matter of who would be quicker."

Apella gaped, without faking. "He said that to you alone?"

"No, he said it at my father's dinner table, for everyone to hear. He was drunk. Before the night was over, the king raided Nazareth. I saw him kill Aristobulus, while his Syrians whipped us out of our homes and into the desert." Her words conjured images of torture and murder. Meantime there was something about her that was so peacefully female, the arc of her lips, the appeal of her still-unripe body. Apella knew that with the special emphasis Jews put on virginity, the caravan masters called her *betoola*, "unopened young woman," "virgin." But Prince Aristobulus had been a terror with women, seducing so many of them, then forsaking them all. In the time he had spent in Nazareth, had Aristobolus tried to seduce the rabbi's daughter?

Molliter, molliter. Gently, gently. I'll find out all those answers.

The girl stood on tiptoe, turning toward the desert; the tamed jackals were trotting back. Behind them, tired, walked the two water girls. The jackals plunged into the crowd to be petted, drooling cheerfully, they'd found no hidden killers in the desert.

Mary turned to Apella and smiled. "Lucky for you, you didn't lie about coming here alone. I'll show you the camp."

Mary called Orpa and Shimon. All three surrounded Apella as he uncinctured his sword and handed it to Mary, who handed it to her mother, who stored it under her apron. Orpa whistled for the jackals. Under escort, Apella was steered around the oasis.

Behind him, his horses were being cared for. Buckets of ripe dates were put under their noses, while two boys sponged them first with water to cool them off, next with vinegar to snuff the ticks on their hides, then again with water. The presence of vinegar, too, Apella noted, indicated that the tribe was decently supplied.

They passed vats wafting the sweet stench of ripe dates, which older women mushed with their hands. The older women wiped their hands on their shifts and started following the little group. Apella was now convinced that these people were not witches; no matter where he stared, he saw no statues to pagan deities, or snakes or lizards hung on sticks for spells. A jackal hurried ahead of him. Watching its touchingly mangy rear, he couldn't imagine it as a witch's familiar.

Mary headed for a flight of steps carved in the rock wall. She climbed up, and the Roman man followed, thinking, *If I strike the right tone with her, my mission could become pleasant.* Mary's heels blew dust in his face. He tried not to give in to memories, but it was impossible. Rome, one year ago. He was following another girl back then, a Roman girl.

A jackal slunk up past him, agile like a circus animal. He called to Mary, "How, by the gods, did you domesticate these beasts?"

"Fed them," she replied over her shoulder. "The pups die, their mothers don't have enough milk for them. So we raised a few pups."

"But they should've run off when they grew up."

"And starve?" She laughed. "Ever seen hungry jackals jump after flies?"

"No." He laughed with her.

Behind him, the old women climbed the steps, too. Vigilant aunts. After a Jewish girl showed her first bloods, her *dameem,* she was monitored ferociously, as if a dome of unbreakable glass had descended over her. The way out of that imprisonment was into marriage. There was even a profession of checking if Jewish girls were virgins before they got married. An experienced woman, usually a former midwife, could make nice money as a *yavesh zaken etsba,* literally a "dry old finger," paid to palpate a girl's hymen before her wedding night, and hopefully confirm that it was intact. There was a whole street of such dry old fingers in Jerusalem, where the honor of noble families was counted in thousands of shekels if a girl had not been deflowered before the vows. Barbaric, and fascinating. Broad-minded Roman girls couldn't wait to get rid of that flap of skin—the rich ones had their hymens removed by doctors, the easier to join the *ludi carnales,* the flesh games. The rich can afford progress, Apella reflected, feeling how much he missed Rome.

The rabbi's daughter stepped onto the desert top and into a tiny wheat field, perhaps twenty yards across. Tubes made of hollowed palm saplings sprayed it with water from the cistern. Next to the wheat, he saw patches of cucumbers, dill, parsley, and onions.

"Marvelous," he exclaimed, pointing to the pathetically small harvest. "Who brought you the seeds?"

"The caravan masters. It's all doing well, except for the wheat. But we feed it to our goats. Now we get good flour from the caravans."

The old women stopped at the edge of the gulch. They watched, shading their eyes from the dying sun. *Which one's the dry old finger?* he joked to himself. In the desert, he glimpsed goats grazing on nearly invisible vegetation, guarded by jackal mutts with tongues hanging out. He drew a chestful of hot air, and it seared his lungs.

"How do you purify here?" he asked, to show the girl that he knew her people's customs.

"There's a hot spring there, in a cave." She pointed between two dunes.

He looked, reckoned that it might take an hour to walk to it. He felt ready to faint. "You trek that far, to bathe in hot water?"

"It's running water," she said sweetly, infuriating him.

"I know," he snapped. "Jews only purify in running water. River, brook, hot spring: *running*. Lake, sea, desert well: *not running*. The most wonderful bath, if its water's not running, it can't cleanse Jews. But if Jews have running water, and their temple in Jerusalem, they're God's people!"

She pressed her lips together. "There's more to our law than that," she said carefully. She had tied a scarf over her hair. So low, it brushed her eyebrows. Her face against the red-hot dunes seemed like an actor's without make-up: Lips and nose, *hmm,* pretty ordinary, why would the audience fall in love with them? And yet . . . How could she know that she's pretty, traipsing around here among goats? He smiled at her. "Your father values your advice. He and everyone else."

She shrugged, as if replying, I help my people, and they help me. What is, is.

"How did he get maimed like that?"

"Are your hands strong?"

He grinned, boastful of his muscular body.

"Feel the sand, down here," she said. Apella lowered a knee, placed his hands on the sand. How could she walk barefoot on this skillet?

Mary jumped onto his hands. He uttered a throttled cry. She stepped aside.

"The king did that to my father. He broke into our house with his Syrians, they held me and my mother so we would watch, and the king jumped on my father's hands with his boots."

He winced from the pain in her voice. He knew Herod's boots, he stared at them every time he was called to the palace. Herod liked to dress Roman, and despite Judea's hot climate he wore double-soled hobnailed *caligae,* Roman assault boots. Herod was deathly afraid of the evil eye; he killed servants who dared stare at him. When speaking to Herod, Apella studied his boots.

Joachim's daughter completed her story in simple words. "We're afraid to be grateful to you. Even if you are honest with us, maybe the king still isn't. Maybe he's drawing us into a trap." A teardrop broke out of her delicately drawn lashes and slid down her cheek. Apella's heart beat slowly, as if timed by that teardrop's movement. She wiped it with the back of her hand.

"Did your father speak to the prince about *Mashiah*?" Apella asked, light, as if it were one topic in a hundred.

"My father told him that Mashiah would come soon. He believes that."

"When is he coming, then?" Apella asked naïvely. She shrugged, how would she know? "Does your father know what others don't know? Your father's a seer and diviner, isn't he?"

"No. He's just well read, and he listens to people."

"That's all?"

"That's it."

He repressed his other questions. He had his own theory about why Herod had killed his eldest son and heir. Shortly before traveling to Nazareth, Aristobulus had sent word to one of the temple's high priests that he wanted to be circumcised—and Herod had seen that request as a move toward the throne. Herod had not had any of his sons circumcised, he had raised them as Romans, and there was a law against mutilating Roman citizens—*non mutilatur*, the law was known as, and it included circumcision. Aristobulus had contacted the priest in secret, but the priest had betrayed him to the king.

Maybe the girl knew nothing about that. Her lips were moving, as if whispering.

"Are you speaking to yourself?"

She laughed, and her voice broke. "When you walk alone around here, and the goats stray in the desert, and you lose your way . . . I got lost so many times, when we didn't yet have the dogs . . ."

"So what did you do?"

"I put my shift over my head, and prayed for the sun to set faster. When it got dark, I lay down, slept a while, then got up and followed the marks of the caravans." She pointed under their feet. Frittered camel prints were beginning to fill with the evening's shadows. "At night, the moonlight brings out the prints."

"Really."

"That's when I learned to talk to myself, to be less afraid." She sounded so friendly now.

"You talk about Mashiah?"

What had he touched? She drew her lips in, with that blue of held-back tears filling her eyes. Her upper lip shone with perspiration so fine, he felt like touching it, with the curiosity he'd had as a boy playing with puppies. Little marvels of *simplicitas naturae* . . . "Mary . . ." He gripped her hand; her palm was callused, but it felt so impatiently alive. She jerked her hand free, almost losing her balance.

He raised his voice. "Herod knows he is old, and his sons by Queen Malthace are not popular in Rome. He must make peace here, or we'll turn his kingdom into a colony!" What was he saying? Was he discussing Rome's policies with this dusty little vestal with hempy hair?

Just then Orpa dashed past them. Running, teasing Shimon, who tried to catch her but wasn't fast enough.

Apella evened his voice. "We, the urbs of Rome, want your tribe to survive for our own vested interests. We lack one thing that binds your people together, faith. Our own gods lost their appeal to the crowds." The girl listened, round eyed. "We need a new belief to get excited about . . . Emperor Augustus, a very busy ruler, believe me, took the time to read the books of the Jews, and that story of renewal heralded by Mashiah piqued his interest."

He was telling the truth now, and making one blunder after another. She replied, her eyes shining with worry. "Woe to the Jews when the Romans take a liking to their faith. I don't know when Mashiah will come or what he will look like, nor does my father. Is that why we're being forgiven, to provide those answers?" She sounded so concerned that Apella grumbled, confused: "No, *puella* . . . you don't have to provide any answers . . . Augustus thinks that Mashiah is a real person, but his curiosity is . . . philosophical. Will you gossip about what I told you?"

She shook her head. "I won't gossip. There's nothing to talk about, is there?"

"Nothing at all."

"Don't worry, then." Almost ready to reach for *his* hand now—but her modesty won. She pressed her palms together and agonized until he smiled again. He wasn't angry at her. *What could be tickled more sweetly than a girl's mind?* the poet Ovid had written, the one poet Apella had ever read. The air was slightly cooler now; on the ground, her shadow and his met, and parted again . . . "Puella, I can be your friend. Trust me." *Because you are that tribe, the one from the prophecy. That's Rome's intelligence on you!* But he couldn't say that.

Her fingers touched his wrist, so quickly, they felt like a fluttering wingtip. "You must be starved." She called out to Orpa. "Go tell my mother to get the food ready . . . Wait, I'll go." Turning back to the Roman: "Will you eat mutton, flour cakes, and dates? Sit on this rock, take off your boots or your feet will swell. When you're done eating, stick the plates in the sand, so the lizards and scorpions won't smell them."

"What about water to wash and drink?"

"We'll bring you everything. But we can't keep you company."

"I know. Jews don't eat with the unclean."

He undid his platelet tunic, letting the air dry off his sweaty chest. He would eat a cooked meal for the first time in five days.

"Your young mothers can't trek back home on foot," he told the girl. "I'll lend you money to buy a few donkeys for them from the next caravan."

"Thank you, but we have a little money. We'll manage." She started toward the lip of the gulch. He stepped after her. "Were you in love with the prince?"

"No. And you're prying," she replied, soft, uninsulting.

"I'm prying, because I like you. I suppose you guessed that?"

She seemed amused. "A woman always knows about a man, for the woman was inside the man at the start." She shook her head, pleased that he seemed baffled. "Don't you remember? The man was made from dirt, but the woman was made of the man's flesh."

"Oh, yes," he grunted. "I see."

"You don't see, you're a man."

"Indeed." He laughed. But then a strange vision emerged in his mind. He himself was the first man, lying on his back, deep in that sleep which God threw over him, so he could remove his rib. He awoke and glimpsed that rib being pulled out of him. Red, palpitating, loaded with a future that the man could never experience by himself. That rib carried such secrets. But he, the man, would never guess them; the secrets were now hidden in the woman.

"Very clever."

23

She was standing so close, he could have pulled her to him. "I'll see about the food."

She whirled down the steps like a little fury. He watched from above as she ran into the gulch, under hanging palm fronds. He glimpsed the back of her neck, untouched by the sun, creamy white.

Part 2

The Roman Spy

SITTING ON that rock in the desert, the Roman reviewed the turns of fate that had brought him here. One year ago, in Rome, gritty cake of a city, under a watery snowfall. The girl he was following then wasn't barefoot like the rabbi's daughter; she wore tall, stylish *coturni,* which only an aristocrat could afford. She was Octavia Minima, the niece of Emperor Augustus.

He had followed Octavia into an unassuming vineyard off the Via Appia. Past vines wrapped in straw, so the winter would not freeze them, they arrived at a dilapidated brick storage.

They entered through a creaking door. Pink tufa steps descended into Triclia, Rome's largest and deepest catacomb. Octavia led the way sure-footed, she'd been here before. The fruity smell of wine casks was replaced by an odor of old graves. Rome's catacombs had been dug as graveyards for the rich. Rome had always been overpopulated—even in death, the Romans competed for space. A *loculus,* a narrow cubic storage for one sarcophagus, could cost hundreds of *aurei,* gold coins, for just one month of maintenance.

Octavia produced two masks of black woven felt, with slits for the eyes. She put one on, handed the other one to Apella. They stepped into an atrium lit by torches affixed to the walls. Masked guests lined up to be frisked for weapons. The lookouts who frisked them wore masks, too—giggling nasally, they sounded like boys and girls from the aristocracy. *By the gods, I won't go unarmed into this,* Apella decided, and while a masked girl fingered the crack of his buttocks for hidden weapons, he pulled a short knife out of his belt, a knife to repair harnesses, and tucked it into his sleeve. The masked girl missed it.

She turned to pat Octavia. "Who did you bring with you?" she asked her. "A slave?"

Octavia laughed. "Worse, a commoner. My riding instructor."

The orphan Apella knew horses. He taught riding at the stables of Senator Marcias, who networked with other rich Romans by running his own riding school. At Octavia's last lesson, as she stepped off the horse into Apella's hand, which he held as a step, she had asked him, "You want to meet my uncle?"

She meant the emperor.

She was a fleshy, snotty teenager with a grating nasal voice. Each time he had sex with her in the stables with horses stamping nearby, she detachedly observed his body, his movements, his expression. He loathed her, but . . . *penis stupidus sed promptus,* the penis is stupid but responsive, went a Roman saying. He, whose parents had been pushed off the Tarpeian Rock as enemies to Caesar's rule, got his doubtful revenge by mounting Caesar's niece. And now . . . she would introduce him to his parents' murderer. *How can I be so excited?* he wondered.

The masked guards waved them along, into a crowd streaming downward. Many of these people knew each other; they chatted and laughed.

He felt the knife in his sleeve and thought, *Caesar, beware, I might be your only armed guest tonight!*

The stench of tombs and drainpipes eased off, replaced by a damp mist. Unseen ventilation shafts freshened the air: *luminaria,* they were called by the robbers who used them to crawl down to that bottom level where the graves lay. The corpses buried in Triclia, rumor had it, were loaded with gems and gold. Apella passed under a doorway with a word chipped on a stone slab: FIDES.

"Fides" meant loyalty, a virtue so admired in earlier times. It also meant faith; lately, the Romans used that meaning in association with the emperor. The letters were jagged, as if carved by a dying hand.

Apella began to lose his nerve. He grabbed Octavia's elbow. "I don't like this."

"Are you scared? Others would kill to be here, and meet *him*."

Apella had only seen *him* from a distance—a silhouette on horseback, a distant icon at the Coliseum. But he'd heard so much about him, especially about one strange anatomic feature: the eyes of Augustus Caesar Octavianus had irises half the size of ordinary ones. Because his eyes were so small, the Romans joked that Caesar saw the world in miniature. The empire was the banana peel of "Pinprick Eyes," and its citizens the flies on it.

The stairway ended. As in a temple, pillars divided the place. The walls were dug with lows doorways for loculi, those gravesites for the superrich. An unmasked boy stood by a pillar, distributing pinches of white powder to the arriving guests. Most likely an aphrodisiac. Octavia held out her palm, the boy sprinkled powder on it, and she licked it.

"I won't need that," Apella grumbled. The boy threw the powder in his own mouth and laughed—"Heeee!"—like a homunculus in a nightmare.

Octavia pushed Apella into one of those loculi, and he stumbled on a sarcophagus. "Come on!" she hissed, parting her clothes. He heard bare feet rapping the ground and cracks of whips and strangled cries. "Don't mind them, they're *servi!*" she whispered. Slaves. Apella, too, had grown up with slaves. "What's going on?" he asked, as she palmed his member, which had shrunk from nervousness.

"What's going on with you? Go get some of that powder."

Apella peered back into the nave. A throng of masked men were walking in. Leading them, one man stared out of his mask with tiny eyes. *Pinprick Eyes,* he thought. "Caesar!" Octavia confirmed, in a moan suffused with adulation, and she pulled Apella to her again. Panting arose from the loculi, while the unseen slaves started to scream hideously. Then, out in the nave of the sunken temple, a voice asked thickly, "Which of you is Caesar?" Voices began to squawk. "Guards, where are the guards?" The same thick voice threatened, "Step aside, or we'll stab you all! We want Caesar! Caesar, which one are you?" Then a screeching voice, like a parrot's: "I'm Caesar! Here I am!"

Apella shoved Octavia aside. Gripping his knife, he lunged out of the loculus, and froze.

He saw two unmasked men, armed with swords, methodically stabbing Caesar's entourage. They were middle-aged but bulky, lifelong athletes, and though they didn't hide their faces, they looked strangely anonymous. *Hired assassins,* he thought. *Swisshh,* their swords sliced into layers of body fat. "Caesar, remember the Rock?" one of the assassins called out. "I'm here for all the Romans you pushed off the Rock! Step in the clear, Caesar, I want to stab you and watch you die!"

Apella dashed away, meaning to race up the stairs and flee, and bumped into . . . Caesar, standing alone next to a pillar, his pinprick eyes glaring out of his mask.

Apella turned to run the other way, and felt that he was hallucinating. Another Caesar, same hair combed sideways to hide his baldness, same small jaw and recessed lips—a body double, he realized—stepped in the path of those swords, squawking, "I'm Caesar!" He looked so identical to the emperor, except for his eyes, which were not like pinpricks.

As in a dream, Apella dived with his knife, stabbing one of the assassins. Deep in the side of the neck, severing the jugular vein. He plucked the knife out, stabbed the other assassin in the neck, severing another jugular. Blood spurted out of them both, as they collapsed and writhed on the ground. "I'm Caesar! I'm Caesar!" the body double kept screeching. He sounded drugged.

Fate, guide my hand! Apella thought. Then he slashed that parrot's throat, side to side. "I'm Caesar . . . rrr . . ." The parrot collapsed.

The real Pinprick Eyes had not moved one step. But his entourage had scattered, running back toward the stairs, while the reek of feces filled the temple's vaults—some of those older men had loosed their bowels. Clothes undone, Octavia staggered out of the loculus and saw Caesar still by the pillar, staring at Apella with his bleeding knife high in hand. "I brought this man here," she shouted. "I saved your life!" Pinprick Eyes glanced briefly at his niece, then back at Apella, as if asking him why.

Then guards with torches rushed in at last.

Caesar took off his mask. Speaking nasally, he ordered, "Take him and have him questioned!"

WHAT WAS THE emperor doing in the catacomb? What was the meaning of that saturnalia of sex and death?

And why did I not kill him? Am I coward?

While those questions racked his mind, he was beaten with wet ropes, with studded gloves, with sacks of sand thudding on his horribly bruised body.

"Who are you?" his interrogators kept asking. "Why did you want to kill our emperor-god?"

For years, it had been rumored in Rome that Augustus would declare himself God. One time after Apella and Octavia had had sex, the imperial niece had made Apella swear secrecy, then produced a freshly minted aureus, the highest Roman coin, and showed him that it bore the face of Augustus encircled by AU-GUSTUS DEUS. Augustus God. She had made it stand on its thin side between her breasts. Millions of aurei like this one would be put in circulation the day Augustus made his deification public.

"That rumor's been out for years. What's he waiting for?" Apella had asked, snatching the coin off her damp skin.

"He's looking for a ritual to help him do godly feats," Octavia explained. "A god would have power over procreation and death. Augustus doesn't want to shortchange Rome with the wrong ritual."

Apella couldn't tell whether she was serious or joking.

Julius Caesar, Augustus's predecessor at Rome's helm, had also minted coins to his own divinity, though a little more restrained: *filius dei,* son of a god, their inscriptions read. Julius Caesar had spread the rumor that his mother was impregnated by the god Apollo during a swim off the island of Capri.

Now, being beaten savagely, Apella remembered the youngsters in Triclia, panting in multiorgasm. To symbolize a god's power over procreation. He remembered those slaves' heartrending screams. They were being killed, right then, to symbolize a god's power over death. The shame of it all. How could he miss his chance to rid Rome of that maniac?

He fainted from the beating and woke up to more beating. Seized by an irresistible desire to live, he wailed that, like a good Roman citizen, he'd rescued Augustus with his pathetic little knife.

"Then why did you kill the lookalike? That makes no sense."

They forced him to drink gallons after gallons of water through a wood funnel shoved down his throat. His gut would burst; it was only a matter of time. Vomiting bile and blood, he cried that he'd meant to disorient the killers, that's why he stabbed the lookalike.

Then Octavia was allowed inside. She was dressed with care, wearing perfumed sandals that broke the stench of the jail, and her hair was done up in a three-tiered cake of curls. She knelt by him and whispered, "Tell them that you did want to kill Caesar, but when you came face-to-face with him, you were overpowered by the aura of his deity."

She glanced back quickly, as if checking something behind her. High up in the wall of the questioning room, there was a tiny window of bronze, an *oculus* with a sliding cover. Like an eyelid, it blinked open, blinked shut . . . Someone was watching.

"Tell them," Octavia whispered hotly. She stamped her sandal on the filthy floor. Even now, her commanding manner was grating.

A jailer called, "Time's up." Octavia turned away and left.

Apella groaned. "I had nothing to do with the other killers. I acted on my own, I wanted to avenge the murder of my own parents." The oculus slid open again. He yelled with his lips spongelike from swallowing so much water. "But when I faced Augustus, I saw the aura of his deity, and it stayed my hand!"

He was now part of that deification sham. The disgust made him want to vomit, but he only heaved dryly, his flushed gut was empty.

They stopped beating him.

HE WAS CARRIED to a brightly lit higher floor, where he was hoisted onto a wooden platform. Smeared in shit and piss, he tried to stand up and slipped. Someone held him up. Other young men dressed in short square tunics, pants fitted onto their muscular legs, and leather boots climbed next to him. They fanned out into a lineup.

They were *vigiles,* free men serving in the *politia,* that institution of public watch that Augustus had invented, Rome's first police. Its name came from a word that meant the people, the republic. An empty word now.

A man, hunched over and graying, stepped up on the platform, looked closely at Apella, then slapped him on his bruised arm. Apella's arm jerked up in a tired reflex. The old man grinned. Apella saw four little tattoos on his right cheek. Apella had grown up near a synagogue. He was familiar with the look of Hebrew from the board outside the synagogue door that announced upcoming services. The little man's face was tattooed with Hebrew letters. Free Roman citizens were rarely tattooed; Apella wondered if he was a slave.

If so, he behaved with unusual authoritativeness. "I choose this one." He indicated the naked prisoner. The groomed vigiles started protesting, but the little man cut off their voices with a tough swipe of his hand. "He has nerves of steel. He has endurance and character, he's the one."

"The emperor wanted him dead," someone interjected.

"I'll take care of that." Not squeamish, he gripped Apella by his dirt-caked arm, pulled him off the platform.

Moments later, two vigiles scoured the dirt off his body with rough brooms of spruce, then rinsed him with pails and pails of cold water. They threw a blanket on him, blindfolded him, and shoved him into a wagon.

He was driven to a place that felt like high altitude; the air was thin and cold. He was ordered out of the wagon. The ground under his feet was soaked by one of those Roman snowfalls that melted within the hour. He heard slaves talking to each other in a foreign tongue and smelled pine trees. He guessed that he might be in Colli Albani, a mountain retreat for the rich. Augustus owned a summerhouse in Colli Albani. He became excited. *I'll see Augustus! The man-god wants to speak to me! I rocked the empire, with my pocketknife!*

Inside a building, his blindfold was removed.

He winced. He was face to face with a full-size Babylonian winged lion. The place was packed chaotically with sculptures of exotic gods, snakes with hissing tongues of alabaster, Egyptian hawks, giant scarabs. Deities of all times, interspersed with likenesses of Augustus carved in wood, stone, ivory, bronze. There were even jewels shaped like Augustus—earrings and necklaces hanging from pegs. And a few Roman gods, Jupiter, Juno, Vulcan, looking naïve and second-rate. For the last two centuries, since Hannibal's armored elephants had invaded Italy, the Romans' trust in their gods had dived steadily. "We pay to have temples, that's our faith," the Romans grumbled.

Petru Popescu

"Advance," a man's voice ordered.

The man-god? The emperor?

Apella shuffled ahead, into a room loaded with scrolls, rolled-up papyri, heaps of wax tablets. There was a giant map of Europe and the Mediterranean, painted onto an entire wall. It was beautiful, its rivers, mountains, and verdant plains so expressive, they seemed alive. He felt a flash of regret that he'd never been a good student.

Eastward from Rome, a route drawn in red curled around the Greek islands, landed on the tan shore of Judea, paused in Jerusalem. Then it braved the desert to the border with Persia. Augustus had traveled to Persia twice to sign and then to renew a celebrated peace with the world's other great power. Apella guessed that the riches in the anteroom were gifts from the rulers Augustus had visited on his way there and back.

The graying old man stood by the map, clutching his woolen *lacerna* over his sunken chest.

"Where is the emperor?" Apella mumbled.

"In Rome, at the helm of the state." The aging man stepped aside from the map, allowing a better view of how vast the empire was, and by sheer size, how vulnerable. Twenty-eight legions, each marked with the symbol of a helmeted soldier, were spread along the most turbulent borders: the Danube, Dacia, and that bottleneck between Syria and Egypt, the land of Israel, Herod's kingdom. One legion averaged six thousand soldiers. Adding the cavalry, the navy, and the auxiliaries, the Roman military rose to three million able-bodied men.

The old man spoke. "You are at Caesar's private library. Ascanius is my name. I'm the emperor's oldest slave and the organizer of his vigiles." He bowed with implicit sarcasm. "Yet I was

36

born a slave and half a Jew. The poet Virgil was born a slave and half a Jew—don't believe his official biography—he is Caesar's house poet. Anyway, Caesar liked your confession. He wants to adopt you in his house, and make you a vigil Asiae because you saw his halo of godliness." Apella weakened from the knees; the old man pushed a stool toward him, and he collapsed onto it. "Now, between us, did you really see it? A little cloud floating above his carefully combed thinning hair? He likes haloes—they hide his baldness." He waited. "I didn't think so. But don't change your story, it saved your life. I'll be your tutor for your mission. Wipe your mouth."

Apella had bitten his lip. The old Jew handed him a napkin. Apella dabbed his bleeding lip. "What's my mission?"

"How shall I tell you this without overcooking your brain? Augustus promised Rome a big renewal—instead of an unstable republic, an unassailable empire. Instead of our old freedoms, the inspired leadership of a man-god. But with that, he boxed himself into a corner. He spread rumors that he'll produce a theophany—you know what that means?"

"No."

He'd never heard the word. It sounded Greek.

"It means, a direct manifestation, a physical act of being God. You know? God brought on the flood, he turned Lot's wife into salt, he plopped a goat from the sky to save Isaac from being sacrificed—all theophanies, acts of God. Gaping in ignorance, you big-boned, white-skinned Roman boy? Never heard those stories? Well, how can a mortal man do God things, except for masquerades like what you saw in Triclia? And time is pressing." He tapped his finger on the legions quartered along the Danube. "Caesar's rival Tiberius, commander of our troops in Germany, is looking for godliness, too." He curled his lips in scorn. "He crawls into caves with Teutonic shamans painted with mud, to invoke bear-gods! Augustus is in a pickle. He can't kill Tiberius without causing a big crisis for he is married to Tiberius's mother, Drusilla." Apella knew who Drusilla was; before Caesar married her, Drusilla had been Rome's wealthiest, best-connected widow. "So, Tiberius is technically Caesar's stepson. What a mess. Now Caesar wants to send *you* to the land of the one true God," he tapped his finger on Judea's sun-parched shore. "To spy for a theophany and bring it back to Rome."

Apella was speechless. He wondered if he should pinch himself.

"Why me?"

"I had several vigiles ready to go," the old man pouted. "I myself trained them." Apella remembered the clean-cut young men in that lineup. "But this morning, the emperor wanted to see if you were still alive, so he peered at you through that oculus. You were raving about his deity. He ate it up. He said to me, 'That's the man, this is heaven-ordained!' So the job's yours. Don't bungle it!"

"Why doesn't Augustus go to Judea himself, to learn his magic tricks and bring them back?"

"He can't leave Rome for any length of time or his opponents will crown Tiberius. So you'll go to Judea and bring back the theophany. What better choice do you have? The Rock?"

"Listen . . ." Apella could not decide what scared him most, to accept the mission, or not accept it. He felt man's oldest fear, the fear of what cannot be seen. "I know nothing about God and less about the Jews . . ."

"I'll teach you," the tattooed man said optimistically. "You have a quick brain, in three months you'll be ready. If you accomplish your mission, you'll become as powerful as I. Don't I pack lots of power for a slave?"

For an instant, Apella considered trying to flee. But he was exhausted, and even if he escaped, Augustus would set the vigiles after him in every corner of the empire. He'd be tracked and killed like a dog. "Some food might help my resolve," he muttered. Ascanius smiled and clapped his hands. Agile servants rolled in a table with bread, roasted chicken, raw honey in a large goblet, and a pitcher of water. Food that was rich, yet stoic. Apella tore a drumstick, dipped it in honey, stuffed it in his mouth.

Eating, he listened to the old man describe the land he would be sent to. An ancient kingdom, a land of mythical feats and people, fallen to the tyranny of an Arab pretending to be a Jew. Herod was an obscure Idumean-born chieftain whom Mark Anthony had appointed governor of Galilee. Herod had ruled Galilee with an iron fist and squeezed it of copious taxes to be paid to Rome. Then Augustus and Mark Anthony had fought each other for who would be emperor. Herod had betrayed Mark Anthony and sided with Augustus. The winner had made Herod king in Jerusalem, the holy city where Apella would be stationed. Still munching, Apella rolled his eyes. What had he gotten himself into by claiming to glimpse Caesar's deity?

The old man smiled. "I know what you're feeling, *puer* [boy]. From an unbridled young stud, you are to become a most cunning, perfectly disciplined spy—yes, I'd be shuddering, too. But you'll be history's agent, and you'll *understand* . . ." He made the word "understand" sound delicious.

"Why did Augustus pick the Jews?" Apella asked, tipsy on that mixture of meat and sugar. "Why not the Parthians or the Egyptians?"

"The Parthians have many gods. The Egyptians, too. Many gods smack of a republic all over again. The Jews have one god— that to Augustus means one empire led by one emperor. Oh, before I forget. Augustus said that you should propose to Octavia. She sleeps around a lot. An official fiancé would come in handy if she gets pregnant."

"Do I have any say in the matter?"

"Of course not. I'll send her a gift of fruit and flowers, with a love poem by Ovid—your official proposal to her. If she gets pregnant, she'll accept your proposal. You'll be the father of her child, is that understood?"

"Yes." His cheeks blazed. The vigiles entered quietly, took away the lowering braziers, and brought in fresh ones.

"When will I meet the emperor?"

"What for? He doesn't need to meet you. When he asks me, I'll tell him about you. Come, I'll show you your room."

The library was built like an *insula,* an autonomous rectangular building with three stories. On the top story, Ascanius opened a wooden door and invited the new student in. The room was as plain as a gladiator's *carcer* but freshly whitewashed and with a wooden pallet for a bed, a wooden table, and chair. The shutters were open. Ascanius pointed to a dozen rolled-up papyri, placed upright on the bare floor.

"These are the Jews' books of faith. These are Aramaic and Hebrew grammars and conversation manuals. And these"—he indicated more papyri—"contain the family trees of Herod and his wives."

Emboldened, Apella pointed to the letters on the old man's cheek. "What's the meaning of that?"

Ascanius touched his tattoo and smiled with memories.

"They're the first letters of *El baruch gadol deah.* 'God the blessed, so great and understanding.' My father was branded with these letters when he was bought as a slave by Augustus's father. He was the only Jew slave of the house. Mocked by his master and the other slaves. When he died, I had the same letters tattooed on my face. I was twelve years old. Augustus, who was six at the time, asked that I shouldn't be whipped for the tattoo, though it made me harder to be resold. A flawed slave, you know. From then on, I served Augustus. Here I am. Second most powerful man in Rome, I can't buy my own freedom, Augustus would kill me rather then let me go. Now choose your secret vigil name so I can tell it to Augustus."

The old man took a stylus and a wax tablet and waited. Apella shrugged.

"Call me anything you like. No one knows my real name, not even Octavia."

"You're from the clan of the Pontii. Don't deny it, we vigiles know everything."

Apella shrugged. "Yes, I'm the last Pontius. Augustus had all my clan killed."

"What's your given name?"

"Pilate."

Ascanius whistled, amused. "Pilate? *Pilatus?* Meaning armed with the *pilum,* the spear? Named so in honor of your lineage?" Apella nodded. "They were fierce warriors, the Pontii," Ascanius muttered, impressed. He took a tablet, wrote on it in big legible letters: PONTIUS PILATUS. Pontius Pilate shrugged. He'd been hiding under the nickname Apella for so long, his own name no longer felt familiar to him.

"For right now, you'll remain Apella, but you'll sign your letters to us 'Pilate' so we'll know that they're authentic. One day, you'll use your real name openly again."

"Very well." Disclosing his true name, using it freely one day felt unimportant. The young man, Pontius Pilate, was grateful to be alive. "So, what kind of tricks of God am I to look for?"

"Anything that signifies renewal in a grand and majestic way. The world commencing anew. The Jews were always great at such tales—the flood is only one of them. They even have a prediction of a child king, born from a virgin; we'll study those passages in their Book. Caesar likes the one with the virgin. Caesar may be insane, but one thing he understands: sell the crowds on a rebirth, you'll have them in your pocket." Ascanius spun around. Octavia stood in the doorway.

The old slave smiled. "I'll go out and count to a hundred," he said and left.

Octavia was dressed strikingly. A spotless white tunic of wool and over it a fur coat with a bristling collar, smoky gray against her pink cheeks. Wolf fur was very Roman; Romulus and Remus, Rome's legendary founders, had been suckled by a she-wolf. Octavia's dress was a suggestion of possession and killing. She whispered to Apella, "You can't tell anyone that I'm here. Caesar is still wondering if I knew of that conspiracy."

So, she, too, had been a suspect. Had the old slave saved her? Had she saved herself, by begging Caesar, by reminding him that she was the one who took Apella down into Triclia? Without her, there would have been no man with a knife down there, to see Caesar's aura and stab Caesar's assassins. How clever! And now, scared and yet sexually stimulated, Octavia whirled around in front of Apella. "Make Augustus God," she urged in an inarguable tone. "Do it. Ascanius will teach you how. You'll teach Caesar, and then you and I will be the power in Rome."

"Augustus will be the power. We'll be the tools."

"It's the same thing!" She stamped her feet in irritation. "And you were my best lover yet, don't forget that! Now Caesar is so taken with the Jews—no wonder . . ." She pointed to the door beyond which the old Jewish confidant was pacing. Her expression betrayed her jealousy. "He should send *me* to Judea to bring back magic powers! If you marry me, you can still have all the women you want." The perfume she wore smelled musky against the austere whitewash of Apella's new home. "Are you in love with anyone I don't know about?" she asked. "I'll give her money while you're away."

"Thank you, but I'm not in love with anyone."

"Lucky. The one I'm in love with, I can't touch." Apella wondered if that man might be Caesar himself.

The old slave's voice cut into his feverish thoughts. "Love, power, God: One can't have them all." Ascanius had walked back in. "It's been a hundred. You," he addressed Octavia, "you already chose what's best for you."

She averted her eyes from the slave, turning them to the man who would pierce godly secrets. "I'll burn cypress sticks in offering for you. *Fortuna juvat,* luck bless you." She hurried out.

In Apella's mind, three words played hide and seek with each other: Love, power, God. Power, God, love. God, love, power.

Ascanius allowed Octavia's footfalls to fade. Then he turned sternly to his new student. "By the way, you will be a recluse during your training. No women at all, or I'll have you whipped over your *tubulus vitae,* your hose of life. And when you're in Judea, you'll be wise not to spill secrets to whores. Your mission before all else, understand?"

WHAT FOLLOWED WERE months of intensive training. Classes in Aramaic and Hebrew. Days and days of chaste study of the Bible, under Ascanius's guidance.

And so, *Eques* Pontius Pilate, whose clan had been killed by Augustus, became Augustus's superagent in Judea.

NOW HE WAS sitting on that rock in the desert, while Mary led toward him the little group bringing his food. She carried an overflowing plate of meat. Orpa brought the mashed dates and a basket of flat bread. The mother managed two water pitchers, one to wash with and one to drink. The boy, Shimon, stepped along slapping two palm fronds, to keep the flies off the food.

Mary kneeled on the sand, took a knife and spoon, and placed them by that mound of meat. "I'll cut your food," she offered.

"And not serve me?"

"We're not allowed . . ."

"Spare me. I brought you your freedom. Your Torah has exceptions for this kind of situation, and hospitability is a mitzvah."

She glanced at her mother as if pleading: What shall I do? Shimon stared sarcastically at the strong-minded girl. Now deal with *this,* tough one. But then Mary said something he did not catch, and Anna, Orpa, and Shimon strode back toward the gulch.

Left alone with him, Mary ladled dates next to the meat,

added slices of bread, put the plate by him, reached for the pitcher and towels, and stepped so close she breathed in his face. He held his hands up. She poured water on his hands, spout close to reduce the splashing. She seemed eager to get it over with. As he took the towel from her, their hands touched. Then, picking up a bread crumb, she popped it in her mouth—here, I'm eating with you, are you content? He ate a spoonful of awful grilled goat and overripe dates. He reached for the pitcher and drank straight from it, feeling the chipped spout. He gulped more food, sucking his teeth and burping.

"So you're a betoola?"

She gave him a quietly dark look: And what about it?

"That's not rude to ask. I could take you into my house as a servant."

Upon his arrival in Jerusalem, he had gone out with a *tesserarius,* a Roman rationing officer, to shop for a house servant. The tesserarius told him that there were no servants paid by the day or the month in Judea. He had a choice between a regular slave or a girl he could rent from her parents for a negotiated time, paying a lump sum, a bond. Bond girls were preferable to slaves, the tesserarius advised, because they worked extra hard to win "parting money," which would be their dowry to attract a husband. It was understood that they would not come back virgins from their service, so they needed that money to wash away their dishonor, else their odds for Jewish husbands would be nil.

The tesserarius had taken Apella into a showroom with some forty girls standing on wooden auction blocks. Stark naked, some as young as ten, they wore plaques around their necks marked with their names, ages, virginity or lack thereof, and prices. The few girls marked not virgins had very few browsers.

Greek and Roman merchants, Arabian caravan masters, and Jewish slaves running households sized up the virgins, told them to bend, kneel, raise their arms, spread their legs. They peeked in their mouths, or up their buttocks. Often, the girls' parents were on hand, vouching for their cleanness, lack of hidden diseases, and hard work.

"Look at their prices, it's a buyers' market," the tesserarius had laughed.

The prices were stunningly low. As stunning as the prices were the girls' bodies—tiny like children's, nipples like little dark seeds. "But they're ready for you," The tesserarius laughed. "I had the devil's time reselling my last one, and the bastard son she gave me."

"She made you a child?"

"A ruddy boy." The tesserarius scratched his moustache with pride. "I'm glad I don't have to see him."

I'll hire a hag with grown kids to serve me, Apella told himself. Must protect my mission.

He'd ended up using a young Roman soldier as orderly. For female comforts, he went to the whorehouse in the Kidron Valley. He had not seen Octavia again after that one time in Colli Albani. He had sailed off engaged to her and looking forward to that letter that would read Yes, I'm pregnant, now I'll marry you. He didn't feel shamed by the arrangement, it was the Roman way. "But what if the letter gets lost?" he had worried. "Highly unlikely. Our postal service is the world's best," Ascanius had smiled, parting from Apella at the side of a ship with three rows of oars. Good luck." Ascanius had hugged Apella. Eight days of sailing to Caesarea, then on to Jerusalem, to bow to Herod as the skilled interpreter from Rome, Augustus's personal gift to Herod.

He conveyed a verbal invitation to Herod to join Caesar in Rome twenty months later, at the next Olympic Games.

Herod was flattered by the invitation. "I'm a born Roman citizen, too," he told Apella. He was a cruel, childish, philandering, greedy ruler. He believed in sorcery and astrology. He bragged incessantly. He liked Apella, though undoubtedly he suspected that Apella was a spy.

Reminiscing about all that, Apella eyed the girl. She became self-conscious from his stare and knocked the plate as she refilled it.

"Mary, listen. We Romans believe in *do ut des,* I give, so you give, too. I'm helping your people. What are you going to give me for it?"

She answered tightly. "The elders would agree on half the money we made from the caravans this year . . . which we already spent on seed, wheat, and cooking and candle oil, so we'll have to reborrow it . . . to pay you for your goodness."

"You think your elders would agree to that?"

"If my father agrees, I think they would."

"What about coming with me to Jerusalem? I have an easy household. Wouldn't you like to live in Jerusalem?"

"Wouldn't money be more useful to you?" She lifted the pitcher, turned it upside down to show him it was empty. "I'll bring more water." She started toward the gulch.

He jumped up, caught up with her. "Wait. I apologize for being abrupt, I have so little time. I must rush back to Jerusalem, pick up the writ for your homes, then I'm off to Caesarea to welcome an important visitor, a Roman surgeon traveling here at the king's expense." All that was true. "But I'll meet you, shall we say, in ten days? You'll need at least a week to trek back. We can time it so we meet before Nazareth's gate, and I'll give you the writ for your homes in front of those thieving neighbors."

She lowered her face. "I'm sorry. I'm not a good servant, I wouldn't keep a good house for you. Besides, if we're going home, my parents will want me to get married—they deserve to have grandchildren. And I don't want to live in Jerusalem."

"Why? Did you not like it there as a little girl?"

He knew that her family had lived in Jerusalem for a year when she was nine or so, knew even why Jerusalem was a painful memory for her. She whispered quickly, "Does it matter why I didn't like Jerusalem?" Then she laid the dirty dishes on the sand, took sand in her hands, and threw it on them. He knew the custom—you make soiled dishes kosher again by burying them, God's earth will clean them.

"Tell me," he asked, "did anything ever happen to you, that only God could have done? I mean . . . I'm not speaking of magic tricks . . ." He smiled. *My warm unwavering gaze,* he thought, *don't let me down now!* It didn't let him down; the girl looked right back at him, and nodded. "Yes, the well."

"The well?"

He glanced back toward the wheel that drew water, showing above the sandy rim. No one had been working the last few hours, so the wheel was still.

"What do you mean?" he mouthed.

She took a breath. Then she told him how, after the Syrians had chased them for days, they finally arrived at *this place*—she pointed to the surrounding dunes, identical to each other. They had been without water for maybe five days. She and her friend Orpa decided to crawl on ahead, for if they crawled on, the sun would eventually set, the heat would diminish, and maybe they

48

would live 'til the next dawn. As they tumbled down the gulch, they saw the trees, then the well. "The wheel looked like it hadn't moved for a hundred years. But we started turning it. It gushed mud, then water . . ." He felt her emotion as she remembered those moments.

"We drank water. We took off our shifts and tried to hold water in them, but it seeped right through. By this time, it had gotten dark, we couldn't see where our people were. We prayed hard that they would have heartbeats 'til dawn, and we'd bring them here. I prayed"—she leaned her head back, facing the sky to show him how she prayed—"God, you gave me this amazing proof that you exist, please give it to my kin, too . . ."

She cleared her voice. "Then we slept. In the morning, we found the others, and brought them here."

"You mean, no one knew about this well?"

"No one. After we drank and ate dates and rebuilt our strength a little, a caravan trekked by. We waved, they entered the gulch, and the camel drivers knelt by the well and cried and marveled. This old Arabian, Jibril, who became our regular customer, had been trekking the desert for forty years. He never knew of this well or of anyone else who did."

"You mean, God made up the well and put it in your path, complete with wheel and pots that look like they watered Moses?"

She shrugged. "You asked me, I told you."

He could hear the soft, homey murmur of the hearths below. He glanced around, but didn't see those chaperoning old women; they'd gone back down. He was totally alone with the girl now. He stepped toward her.

"I won't take your money. But I want you in my house in Jerusalem."

She looked him straight in the eyes, replying quickly. "Why me and not some other girl? And why is Rome so mindful of us, all of a sudden?"

"Because there are those who think that your lineage is special. The Jews are God's people, but especially . . . one tribe, the tribe of the promise . . ." He raised his hand toward that homey murmur of people. ". . . you might be the ones from whom Mashiah will arise . . ."

"Our king thinks that?" Her body tightened like a string.

"I'm talking of the one above your king, my emperor. He'll be benefited if he protects you—if you're invested with some godly promise, that is. You're from a noble clan of priests, the very priesthood of Nazareth, is that not so?"

"The king told you that?"

"Actually, I told that to the king."

"Be wary of helping us," she said with sudden coldness, almost with a touch of threat. "Our faith is between God and us, he'll save us from this waste if he wants to."

"But he already saved you once." He pointed to the well that no one had found before. "Your God put the well right in your path. Isn't that enough proof"—he chose his words carefully—"that you might be the tribe of Mashiah?"

"Of course not. God may do whatever he wants. He saves so many unfortunates every day, why not us?"

Was she playing with him? If he jumped on his horse and rode away, would she run after him, begging him to stay, confessing that the rumors about her tribe and lineage were true? But what if she didn't run after him? *Be gentle,* he told himself. *Win her trust.* "I think you're right, you're not cut to be my servant, and your family needs you more than I do . . ."

"*Todah la El!* Thank God," she breathed, so grateful, her eyes became shiny. "You're a good man, then?" Surprised to be so pleased by her praise, he grumbled: "Oh well. Bring me more water to mix some ink. I'm going to write a letter about your people."

"Right away." She throbbed, as if having averted a great danger. "To whom?" she asked, deliciously curious, touching his arm with her palm. The feel of her hand aroused him bizarrely, by its unlewdness, by its lack of invitation. "A letter to the emperor."

"And you'll say that we are good people?"

"Of course," he rewarded her.

She danced toward the steps, to bring water, while he reminisced again.

His first days in Jerusalem. Collecting information about her tribe, from Rome's stool pigeons in Jerusalem.

AMONG THOSE STOOL pigeons, there was a Jerusalem-born Greek named Xilos. Xilos owned a nonkosher catering business, providing prawn and pork to the Greeks and Romans of Jerusalem, Greeks and Romans who built roads and military machines and maintained the aqueduct that wound across the city like a dragon with a bricked-up spine. Xilos had been married once, but no one knew the whereabouts of his wife. He was in his forties, a heavy drinker with a face red like a lantern. He kept scores of street urchins in his pay, to soak up rumors and put out new ones.

Xilos came to bow to Apella on the Roman's third morning in Jerusalem; the new king's interpreter was carrying his valuables from Fortress Antonia to his own rooms in the king's palace.

Xilos approached him in the street and offered his catering services.

Apella asked Xilos why he wasn't in his kitchen preparing meals. Xilos replied that the number of resident Greeks and Romans boomed under Herod, so his business boomed, too, and he had plenty of hired help. For himself, he preferred the freedom of the streets. The Romans and Greeks purchased gossip, too; here he was, harvesting it.

"Anything you want known about yourself?" the Greek inquired, walking along with the Roman.

"No," Apella laughed.

"I suppose the king has been waiting for a superspy from Rome?" the Greek said. He waited. Silent, Apella kept walking. "After Queen Mary-amneh sent that letter to Augustus, what else could the king expect but a superspy to keep an eye on him?"

Arms filled with a sack of clothes and toiletries that included his steel razors, Apella glared at the red-faced Greek. He had to pretend to be annoyed by the Greek's directness. "Don't be too smart for your own good," he grumbled.

The Greek beamed as if from a compliment. "We're in a cauldron here. We all learned how to swim in it."

"I swam in Rome," Apella countered.

"This is harder. Rome's a cesspool, Jerusalem is a wild river with venomous eels in it."

A noisy crowd of children formed just a few steps from them. Homeless boys in rags. They clashed pieces of metal—fragments of Roman armor, even rusted priestly breastplates—like cymbals. "Anything new?" Xilos asked them importantly. The boys laughed but shook their heads. One boy cranked a primitive musical instrument, a barrel-shaped box with a swivel. When he turned the swivel, it moaned barbarically. Xilos threw coins at the boys. "Go to Ge Hinnom, there's blood on the trash heaps. Look for gold bangles in the trash, find out who Herod killed last night, and put the news on the street. Go!" They turned and ran away cheerfully, as if headed for a game.

"Why is there blood in Ge Hinnom?" Apella asked.

Ge Hinnom, or Gehenna, a sprawling wasteland to the south of the city, had been used as a sacrificing area by the pagan Jebusites. Malformed infants were killed there and fed to clay ovens shaped like giant open mouths, to appease the hunger of the pagan god Moloch. When King David had conquered Jerusalem, he had chased away the Jebusites. But although the cremating ovens had been razed, fires kept springing up in that grisly valley. They were doused with the city's trash, carted out through the "dung gate" by a breed of beggar untouchables who lived outside the walls. The fires still sprang from the trash, earning the place the name Gehenna, hell on earth.

The Greek explained, "The Hasmoneans, the late Queen Mary-amneh's clan, ride past Ge Hinnom on their way to their summer palaces. They get robbed and killed on the way, and their jobs at the court are filled by the clan of the new queen, Malthace."

"You mean Herod kills the Hasmoneans?"

"Yes. They're the last Jews in the royal family. Malthace's kin are Arabian. Herod is now without one Jewish queen. He killed Mary-amneh and her sons, and now he kills the servants who witnessed their deaths, and that's why the demons and witches are so rife in the air. Can you smell the demons and witches?" He opened his arms. Apella shrank back from the reek of an old drunk's skin. Xilos scooped in his pocket, brought out a stick of sandalwood. "Chew this wood when you walk in the palace, it keeps the bad air away and scares the witches! You need anything else—slaves, guard dogs, a bathtub of marble, a pet monkey?"

"No, thanks. But I'll be sure to order my pork from you."

He vowed to himself, *I'll never use this fool to spy for me.*

He didn't run into Xilos again until one day, after he persuaded the king to forgive Joachim's tribe, when Xilos sent word that he was waiting for him outside the palace.

Apella went out to meet him, and Xilos said, "You want to see where they lived when they were in Jerusalem?"

"They?"

"The leader of the tribe you asked forgiveness for. And his wife and his betoola daughter."

Apella became scared. Xilos knew what Apella had asked from the king, the very next day! While Apella had talked to the king, had someone eavesdropped from behind a curtain? A guard, a servant? Xilos himself, maybe? Did Herod pay Xilos to spy on Apella? *It's a wild river with venomous eels in it.* But there was nothing he could do but smile and answer. "Certainly. You want to take me there tomorrow? I'll come prepared."

Meaning that his belt would be filled with coins.

They met the next day on a public stairway leading from the lower to the upper city. The pilgrims' crowds were thick. There was no wind, the smoke from the offerings rose above the temple like a solid pillar. Xilos's street urchins were following Xilos, who told Apella to throw them coins, then ordered an urchin to run to the palace and tell the guards where he had last spotted Xilos. The child dashed off like an arrow. Apella grabbed the Greek by the collar. "What are you doing? Letting the king know where we are?"

"Of course. That's business as usual." Xilos grinned, pushing off Apella's hands.

He headed off again, toward the temple. Apella controlled himself. He followed the Greek. It rained briefly. The rain flattened the smoke from the offerings, griming the faces and clothes of the pilgrims.

On clear days, Jerusalem shined white and golden, as cool winds cleaned its streets like magic brooms. On such days, Apella roamed the city, marveling over the feelings it brought up in him, the pagan visitor. Shaped like an arrowhead whose tip was the temple, Jerusalem seemed in motion, journeying into the cosmos. It was the "city of Yahweh of Hosts," as the psalm said. Rome, though laid out on seven hills, seemed ugly by comparison, aggressive, and rank with debauchery and brute sports. Here, the desire to live close to God was tangible. The Jerusalemites had so many sects boasting ordainments from God. The Essenes occupied a large quarter south of the house of Herod's appointed high priest. They denied that priest's authority and refused to worship in the temple. They did not marry unless their numbers were so low that their tribe was endangered, and were the butt of crude jokes for living as holy wankers. Yet they could recite the Torah word for word. Yea, indeed, if Israel would live through *two utterly perfect Sabbaths,* the world would be saved. Yea, and Mashiah would reveal himself, *and everyone would know him, even though they never saw him before.* Wondrous was this city of God by day, but even more wondrous at night, when thousands of candles and oil lamps glittered in humble homes, their flickering seeming like a mute whispering to God, a twisting, spiraling flame . . . a passionate whisper . . .

Apella felt it. He felt the city's feeling of God.

Yet, like an insult to that feeling, right by the temple rose the symbol of the Roman invasion, Fortress Antonia.

Herod had named the fortress after his first protector, Roman general Mark Anthony, who had made Herod tetrarch of Galilee. After marrying Cleopatra, who was enormously unpopular in Rome, Mark Anthony had warred with Augustus and lost the war. Herod had switched his allegiance to Augustus, who had placed Herod on the throne of David, elevating a non-Jew, though a circumcised convert, to supreme leader of the Chosen. Safe in his power, Herod had not removed Fortress Antonia, the most hated symbol of his alliance with Rome. Even though, as the enlarging of the temple continued, the Jerusalemites moaned: The temple is now only ten steps from Antonia! The Roman sentinels can piss from the watch tower into the women's courts! Herod must remove that sty in the eye of God, he must! So prayed the people of Jerusalem, fiercely desiring to see that abomination removed. And yet, they were also fascinated that Herod didn't do it! Would God punish Herod, and how, and when? And if he didn't, what message was God sending out? That most reviled ruler was also the one who had rebuilt the temple. Why?

Trekking after Xilos, Apella could now see the temple.

As always, the instant that he glimpsed it, he held his breath. The new marble platforms covered thirty-five acres. Herod had vowed to build something bigger than anything else in the known world. The holy area was twice as large as Rome's imperial forum. Rome's largest temples, to Astarte-Venus, to Castor and Pollux, and to Saturn, could have stood together in the new court of women. Even the area for animals to be sacrificed, a tethering stand with fifty tying posts and dozens of skinning tables, was larger in foundation than the Roman Senate.

Six years earlier, Rabbi Joachim ben Ahaz ben Matthan, from Nazareth, Galilee, had arrived in Jerusalem with his wife, who knew how to dye, and with their one child, a girl nine years old. Joachim had been drafted to work on the temple as a carpenter. Herod would not stop the services during the rebuilding, for he took a cut from all worshipping taxes, so he drafted all the rabbis in Judea and Galilee who knew how to shape stone or wood to work on the temple. According to the intelligence revealed to Apella by Ascanius, Joachim worked on the temple less than a year. His daughter was ten when the king had sacked Joachim and sent all three back to Nazareth.

Joachim's tribe was banished to the desert three years later. Three more years after that banishment, Apella had arrived from Italy. Fulfilling Ascanius's secret instructions, he had made himself useful to the king, then he had wrested the tribe's forgiveness from the king. He was to ride to the desert soon, to inform the tribe that they had been forgiven. The girl should be seventeen by now. Almost too ripe for marriage.

So, Apella thought, *now Xilos will show me where she lived when she was only nine, when her carpenter father worked on the temple, and her mother dyed dresses for Jerusalem wives.*

He'd never thought so much about a young female he hadn't even met. He found that fact mysteriously pleasant.

He imagined the girl's eyes. Dark, glowing Jewish eyes, perhaps shaded by a demure veil. Fearful of men's stares, but all the more enticing.

Xilos pointed Apella to a wooden ramp veering away from the steps of the temple. It led down into a street sloping along the temple's western wall.

They followed the ramp down. The Greek walked to a row

of hovels of sun-baked bricks propped against the temple, each stealing a piece of the temple as their back wall.

All of those homes looked miserable, yet so alive. Linen hung to wash flapped everywhere. Plants in chipped pots filled every windowsill. Women in black stepped out of wooden doors and emptied washbasins in the street. The smell of the washbasins' loads hit Apella in the face—it was strong, sour, sulfurous. A wedding party walked past Apella, led by a little girl with her hair done in twists knotted around a rosebud each—the bride. She looked to be under ten years of age. Her parents and siblings, in white shifts, accompanied her to a doorway. One woman emptying a washbasin seemed to recognize them—she gestured, inviting them inside. The thin shoulders of the girl with rosebuds seemed to shake as she stepped over the doorstep. The door closed. The Greek rushed to the door, which had a viewing hole covered with thinned-out goat hide.

"*Etsba!*" the Greek called, scratching the taut hide, and winking lewdly at Apella.

The word meant "finger" in Aramaic.

The door opened. A woman whose face was narrow as an ax blade showed up. The Greek whispered to her. She nodded and closed the door again, and although he'd glimpsed no one else, Apella felt the wedding party, standing tensely behind that door. He imagined the preteen bride being stripped and examined.

The hovel had two stories connected by outer steps. Xilos beckoned Apella to follow him up to the second story. Xilos explained that the upper story was the one Joachim's family had lived in. He led Apella into a square little space without furniture or domestic implements, except for the darkened hole of a fireplace in the middle of the floor. "Want to rent?" Xilos joked. "Right here, in the midst of the finger business?"

Apella smelled the Greek's breath. Xilos had dropped a couple this morning.

Xilos pointed shakily to the room's back wall. "That's the temple wall."

Apella examined it in silence. The temple wall loomed like a huge home altar—the yellow sandstone blocks, bright as if storing sunlight, showed their perfectly aligned edges, and in between the slabs' cracks there were tiny creeping plants. Little angels of sewn rags were stuffed in the cracks. Their wings hung wilted. Apella pictured them as the dolls of that nine-year-old girl. She lived, ate, slept, and played here.

"No one touched that girl's toys," Xilos commented.

He waited. Apella silently stared at the wall. The wall was hypnotic. He could not look away from it.

Xilos slurred, "The people in this street are crazy, they say that the rabbi's daughter could summon angels."

Apella looked up. He was standing under a skylight of glass chips held together with dried mud. The sky of Jerusalem, the world's clearest and bluest sky, smiled on him through the glass chips, refracting into the room and glowing on the temple wall. Through the day, the wall would shine golden, until the sunset would turn it bloodred. That redness would still linger on the wall through the night, because limestone stored light. Waking up at night, the girl would see the glowing of that mystical altar, never dark, never extinct, undying. Until the morning would turn it golden again.

He felt the girl's presence. Her frail body, pushing against the air as it turned this and that way.

Outside, there was a rapping of departing feet. The bride had been tested. As he could hear no women crying and no men shouting insults, Apella concluded that the terrified girl had been found intact. The rental room's door rattled open, and the woman with the blade face stepped in. Xilos gestured that Apella could ask questions.

"You remember Rabbi Joachim's daughter?" Apella asked.

She looked at him inexpressively. Apella held up five silver shekels.

She took the money, and spoke. Yes, she remembered when Mary-amneh and her family lived in this room; she herself lived in the hovel's other room and worked for her mother, one Zohra, who checked virginities in this street after having served as checker of virginities in the king's palace, no less. Zohra had died of a weak heart two springs before. At the time that Joachim was looking for a place to live in Jerusalem, this hovel was falling apart, so Zohra offered Joachim the room rent free if he rebuilt the place, which Joachim did in his spare time from working on the temple. Zohra paid the rabbi's daughter one shekel a month to cook and clean the floors and the stairs. Joachim's wife had brought her dyeing bench from Nazareth, and the family of three lived off her dyeing, because the king did not pay salaries to his temple workers.

"Those stupid men of God," Xilos laughed. "The king told them that building God's house should be their pay, and they were happy to do it."

"No one complained?" Apella asked.

The woman hesitated. Xilos glanced at the Roman, who scooped in his belt and gave her another five shekels.

The woman explained that Joachim was the one known worker who had challenged the king to pay salaries because the

60

workers' children went hungry every day and they turned to begging and stealing. "The king is stingy, he hardly pays his palace servants, so the news of Joachim's request went all over Jerusalem, and the work at the temple stopped. Even the Essenes came out of their holes, ran to the temple, although they denied the temple's holiness, and stood chanting on the steps of Nicanor's Gate." That gate, Apella remembered from Ascanius's trivia, was built by the architect Nicanor of Alexandria, who drew blueprints without seeing them, because he was blind. "They chanted Joachim's name, and asked for the king to come out and confront that righteous man of God, Joachim. But the king locked himself in the palace and waited, and after the three days of protest, Joachim asked the Essenes to go home, because that third night it was Sabbath," she concluded, with regret.

"Was that the only clash Joachim had with the king?" Apella asked quickly.

She was silent. Apella took one gold aureus from his belt, handed it to her.

"He also challenged the king not to enlarge the court of the gentiles."

Apella knew about that issue. The king was trying to attract more gentile pilgrims to add to the revenue of the temple from which he took a large cut. But he didn't know that Joachim had taken a stance on that, too.

He saw a pattern emerging. Joachim had challenged the king at least twice. The king's prestige was tied up in the temple—opposition to his decisions was a crime, and the king was not squeamish to kill. He had killed people from his immediate family. Yet Joachim he had not killed, only banished him from the city. Why the special treatment?

"There was a stoning here, right about that time," Apella said to the woman. "An accused bride was stoned. Joachim's daughter tried to save her, isn't that so?" He took another aureus from his belt and held it up.

"The bad bride ran up those stairs." The woman pointed in the direction of the outer stairway. "The little girl was sweeping the stairs. But she was such a mighty little witch already. She summoned angels to pick up the bride and lift her off, but . . ."

"But what?"

"It had rained. The angels flew down slowly, with rain in their wings. The bad bride was already on the roof, but she slipped and fell into the street before the angels could help her. And the crowd caught her."

"That truly happened?" Apella asked.

The woman shrugged. "Maybe people made up things. They felt bad that only that little girl, the rabbi's daughter, had the guts to help the bride."

"How did the little girl help her?"

"She took her by the hand, and they ran from roof to roof. People saw them. If they kept going, they could've fled. But it had rained, and the roofs were slippery. The bride slipped and fell."

Xilos muttered in Latin, "That bad bride was from a Hasmonean family. Queen Mary-amneh's blood. The king feared Mary-amneh's kin. He gave money to the old bag, this woman's mother, to testify that the bride had been penetrated. I know that Zohra accused the bride, I had spies in this street back then. Give her a whole purse. We're done here."

Fitting a jingling purse into a palm crevassed from dipping in hot water, Apella asked the woman in Aramaic, "Why didn't the bride's family sell the tainted bride, instead of having her killed? Why spill blood?"

The ax-faced woman spewed angrily, "When the blood of Israel is being raped by foreigners, a girl's duty is to hold on to that skin, which God put in her with a purpose, for girls are not cats! Defilement robs Israel of its cleanness, brings strife among tribes, and weakens Israel! If a girl lets herself be spoiled that way, stick an ember where she sinned, then crush her skull, and make all others take heed! The rabbi's daughter shouldn't have helped that strumpet, but she was only nine at the time, she was a soft-hearted, ignorant child!"

Then, with the purse clasped in her hand, the ax-faced woman flounced out.

The two men were back in the street a moment later, while another family in white, accompanying a tiny, flower-bedecked bride-to-be, headed to the etsba's door. Apella asked how those women learned their trade. Xilos laughed. "They say that they were midwives before, but I say, most of them were prostitutes. They should know their stuff, huh?"

"How could one trust them with one's daughter?"

Xilos laughed. What trust? These women inserted their fingers, and if their fingers came out "dry," a girl was intact, but if their fingers came out "flowing," the girl had been stretched by a lover—which the checkers proceeded to prove by measuring that up-down opening with a fixed length of string; too open, the girl had lost her virtue. For that, they were paid. Sometimes the groom's family hired them for a second examination; thus, by casting doubt on the bride, they drove down the bride's price. Sometimes a bride was known to be easy, but the checkers pronounced her intact, for they'd been paid off. If two families wanted a match, lack of virginity never foiled a wedding. "It's a business," Xilos insisted. "Don't you know that the Jews make everything into a business?"

"Wait," Apella said. "If I am to believe you, these hags should be making a lot of money—where is it?" He swept his arm at the impoverished-looking neighborhood.

Xilos shrugged. "Maybe they give it in trust to the priests of the temple? They're all in it together, the 'fingers,' the priests, the king even. You want to buy a virgin girl? Lie down with virgins, you'll never ail from gout or dropsy."

"Can these hags make a girl back into a virgin?"

Xilos whistled. "And how! They put astringent leaves in broken hymens, and make them narrower than the real thing. They gather blood from a chicken, sew it up inside the chicken's craw, slip it in a girl—if it breaks at the right time, the etsba gets more money." Tipsy and lewd, the Greek put out his palm. "How much is this worth to you?"

The Roman threw a purse at Xilos. "Out of my way," he blurted, shoving him and darting back to the ramp toward the temple. Xilos trotted after him. "Hey, wait! Rabbi Joachim, trust my old nose, he's a powerful witch!"

"Shut up!"

Gasping, insulted, Xilos fell behind. Apella ran past the stream of pilgrims, feeling that those strangers had good reason to be here, and good reason just to be. They *believed.* Did he believe in anything?

He hurried to Antonia and met the tesserarius he was friends with. The man was getting out of a dusty sedan chair, returning from Nazareth. He'd traveled there on Apella's orders, masquerading as a tax collector, to reconnoiter the betoola's village.

The tesserarius summed up what he had found in Nazareth. "After Joachim's people were chased into the desert, the two clans who plundered their homes and herds warred over the spoils. A lot of blood was spilled. Now there are ditches and armed palisades between the neighborhoods. Even the building of the local synagogue was stopped. You want to see what that famed daughter looks like?" He undid the ties of an army sack, took out a sculpted piece of wood. "This face was carved on a pillar of that unfinished synagogue, one of the Greek merchants showed it to me. I cut it out, and brought it with me."

It was the face of a young woman, sculpted in clumsy high relief. The tesserarius held it up.

"The synagogue faces Mount Barak, which is the tallest peak near Nazareth. Mount Barak, the mountain of lightning. People say that lightning starts flashing on its peak when God is displeased with people's sins. There's a lot of lightning on that peak, it rains up there even when the drought starts fires down below."

Apella examined the carved face.

It was slightly smaller than life-size and seemed hurriedly carved. The knife that had cut it in that pillar had not lingered long. The oval of the face, the straight nose with one little dent to one side, a scar or maybe a freckle, were still emerging. But the wide-open eyes and the dip of the upper lip and the mouth were fully carved. The face leaned out of the wood, alive.

"Who made this?"

"Some Nazarene with a gift for carving. I was told his name, but I forgot it."

Her eyes were looking out, but also glancing inside her. As if so aware, so intimately connected with herself that she knew precisely what went on in her unseen body. Apella noticed that despite the sculptor's apparent speed, the wood was shaped with a kind of velvety fineness, lightly scratched here and there, wood that was wood, but felt like flesh. *I am* was the feeling of that flesh. So undeniably alive and present, it made Apella's cheeks warm with thoughts he couldn't describe.

"I need to think. *Vade*, go away," he ordered the tesserarius.

ALONE, HE LOOKED at that sculpted face and let his thoughts wander.

He remembered Ascanius introducing him to the Book of Creation. Quizzing him, discussing the hidden meanings.

When Eve had first known the man, Adam. When she lay down with him. That piece of the woman's anatomy that held history's future in it, the Book of Creation did not name it. The Greeks called it hymen. The Jews had not called it anything, yet what importance they gave to a bride's virginity. There it was, in the beginning of the Bible, the woman's little door of flesh, shut between childhood and maturity, between innocence and experience. It was not named, but creation depended on it, for without its first tearing, mankind would not continue and God's plan would not be completed.

Said the Book, . . . *and the snake said to the woman, though God told you that you would die from eating from the tree of knowledge, you shall not die . . . yet your eyes should be open, and you should be like gods, knowing good and evil . . .*

After reading aloud that passage, worded so bafflingly simply, Ascanius had speculated on Eve's quandary: to know or not to know? "It was all left to her, to the woman," Ascanius philosophized. "It didn't even cross the man's mind that the fruit of knowledge might benefit his children. He did not reach for the forbidden fruit. He'd been eating of all the other fruit, and would have not known the difference. It was left to the woman to make that exploration, to assume the danger and the responsibility. And she was the one punished harshest. *'In pain you shall bring forth your children,'* God said to the woman. God punished the man by sentencing him to hard work, but onto the woman's womb he heaped his greatest wrath—aren't we lucky to be born men, eh, puer?"

Remembering his teacher's words, Apella realized how he missed him.

"But what say you, Pilate," Ascanius had continued, "about the third party to that first union, the snake? Isn't it fascinating that the snake is shaped like a male organ? When the snake insisted to Eve that she would not die of the fruit, was the snake really saying, you shall not die of *me,* for I am shaped like your mate's manhood—don't shrink back from manhood, woman, don't be terrified of it, *enjoy it*! But why does the snake know so much? Why is he so daring in encouraging the humans to *know*? Is God himself speaking through the snake? Is God leaving to the snake what he didn't know how to teach to his children, yet it needed to be taught, so that life continues on?"

How inspired the old teacher's words sounded.

"Leave it to the Jews, puer, to be carnal without even seeming to be," Ascanius added. "But then, from Eve's loss of virginity, maybe the story is fated to come full circle?" He tapped on the spread-out scrolls and smiled to his wide-eyed student. "For listen to this: *God shall give a sign, behold, an unmarried young mother*—does that mean a virgin, eh, puer?—*shall bear a son, and call his name Immanuel, God is with us.* Hinting that God is inside us, perhaps? That he's inside that virgin, too, that God is her seed? What say you, Pilate, renewer of the Pontii's clan? A virgin birth! Could that be? Is that a less glorious feat than making Caesar a god?"

"It's an impossible feat," Pilate had replied.

Ascanius had nodded. "Of course. And yet . . . as a renewal story, as a marvel of meaning, wouldn't that be wonderful?"

"Maybe so, *magister,*" mumbled Apella, who had been chaste for months while instructing himself in writing Hebrew, so simple in appearance yet so deep it made Ovid's *Ars Amatoria* seem vacuous and silly.

Now, at Antonia, staring at the girl's carved face, he wondered about what he didn't know. What were a woman's true feelings about being a woman? What agony did a woman endure as a virgin, then as a lover and bedmate, then as a mother? God put virginity in Eve, yet not in any other breed of female animal. Girls are not cats, that checker of virginities had said it bluntly. God, who had been father and mother to Adam and Eve, had shaped them with tools of procreation, yet he had denied them the knowledge, the easy access, the pleasure— but in forbidding all that, had God himself driven them to *find out?*

Maybe I should take Xilos up on buying me a virgin. *Usus cognitio,* practice is knowledge, as we Romans say.

He tried to quiet his thoughts, but they were so many—a storm of thoughts inside the breast of one ignorant man. Would he ever love a woman not with his penis but with his heart? How binding would it feel to marry a woman not as a means to success, but as a truly beloved bride? How would that first night be etched inside him, who had always dreaded love, for it turned men into children? And who would be the woman to tame his wild nature, yoking him to Eve's womb, forever?

You will understand, Ascanius had told Apella.

He wondered if he was beginning to understand.

IN AMAZEMENT HE thought, *In the past hour, I remembered Rome, then my first days in Jerusalem. I plunged in my mind to man's beginning, then woke up in this desert again. Time's moving roundly like the wheel of this well!*

Here and now, he took papyri out of a case and spread them on the flattest rock top he could find.

He arranged to the right of them two reed pens and a vial of dry ink powder.

The ink powder was made of black soot collected with a fine brush from the walls of a special marble furnace that was fired every week at Fortress Antonia, fed with special pine pitch from Italy. Mixed with water, the soot of the Italian pine pitch made for the finest Roman ink. Apella had taken a box of soot to the king's palace when he had pleaded with the king to forgive Joachim's tribe. Herod had liked the gift. Herod never wrote letters in his own hand, but he loved things Roman.

The girl reappeared on the lip of the oasis, carrying a pitcher tipping full of water.

She poured water for him to drink. He sipped a mouthful, dripped water in the inkstand, then used a reed pen to mix the soot into the water. It became fluid ink.

Looking up, he caught Mary staring at him.

She sighed. "When we return, maybe my father will teach me how to write."

"He should, you're a smart young woman. So, you'll be starting back tomorrow?"

"Not tomorrow. Jibril's caravan is due." Jibril . . . *Ah yes,* Apella thought. *The one who never saw the well in forty years.* "We'll turn the well over to him and his people. Then we'll round up the sheep, and sort out the tents, what to take, what to throw away. We need three or four days at least."

"So we'll meet in Nazareth in ten days' time? I'll bring the king's guest with me."

"If you wish." She didn't care about the king's guest. But about him, her people's savior, she was brimming with hope. She gestured to the stretched-out papyri. "You'll really write that we're not a threat to anyone?"

"Yes."

"Maybe you should also write . . ."

She was so attractive, he thought, *when she tried to find her words—words to her were precious and intimate. She'll make me proud when she'll discuss issues of faith and history, while reclining on my left, at a Roman dinner . . . But . . . I suppose I'll never educate her, or take her out, or fondle her when I bring her back home, in reward for how she shined. Oh well . . .* She spoke, the flame of her mind flickering in her eyes. "People wonder why we, the Jews, are the chosen, of all nations. The truth is, God chose us *because we chose him.* Our enemies passed laws forcing us to stop believing, but we believe, no matter what. That's what makes us Jews." She sang out those words, *ma'aminim,* we believe. "We don't give up. It's frightening, it's paid in blood—but we don't give up, we choose God, we believe."

She smiled at him again. Now that she didn't fear him, she gave him a truly bright smile, with lips wide open. Inexperienced, voluptuous curiosity lit her features as she put her hand over her throat, choking with feelings. Her hair waved to her shoulders, hungrily dark. With rounded lips, she blew off an unseen mosquito and laughed.

Then she was gone.

He wrote in code.

> To Caesar, *Augustus Princeps, Urbi et Populi Tribunus, Dux Imperator.*
>
> Caesar, I am with that tribe now. There is no doubt about their lineage. And they were saved from death miraculously. The appearance of a water well in their path could itself rate as a theophany. I'll monitor them, to see if they can work miracles *manu propria,* with their own hands.

He stopped, turned the pen in his hands. He could erase what he had written.

He did not erase it. He added more.

> Caesar, give some thought to this: Virginhood is a firm part (*facetia,* pun, not intended!) of these people's customs of marriage, but there's more to it than the male pride of being first through an unopened door. Virginhood has power in these people's faith. Why was it written with such emphasis into the first encounter between man and woman? Is virginhood connected with some ability to do godly things, or *to be* godly? I shall keep investigating.
>
> I am . . .

He heard himself titter, alone under inscrutable stars. The reed shook in his hand. Maybe all this is insane. Maybe I am insane.

71

He disciplined his hand, and resumed.

. . . I am very close to finding answers to these
questions. And I'm surer than ever that you'll be
revealed as God, Caesar. I've gained such expertise
with these people, it would help you if you appointed
me the next procurator of Judea. My deepest respects
to Octavia. Signing now with my true name,

Pontius Pilate

He breathed. He waved the papyrus in the air to dry the ink,
rolled it shut, set it aside. He started chuckling to himself, as he
wrote a second papyrus, in a different code.

Salve, Ascanius, carus magister, beloved teacher.
Tribe found, just informed emperor of it. *Idiota
Maximus* eats up raves mine. Moon full tonight. Back
in palace, Herod stable *in sanguine.* Out here, special
agent calm.

Big-boned

He laughed again, as he wrote on a third papyrus:

Caesar,
Maybe I found the girl of the prophecy—she does
act like a sweet lunatic, but she loves her people. And
even in this filthy pit-hole, she acts as if she had God
inside her. What do you have inside you, Caesar? Your
love for yourself? What if the true God exposes you as a
fraud—what a laugh for the world. But, with your
vigiles watching, no one will dare laugh loud. Too bad.
Your plan to deify yourself is absurd and ridiculous.

The one who should have killed you
in Triclia catacomb

He smiled. Then his hands tore the last papyrus into unreadable bits.

The other two papyri he'll send to Italy by the army boat sailing from Caesarea. Arriving in Italy after eight days of fierce rowing, ten in case of storms, those papyri would be handed at the port of Brundisium to a special courier who would break his horse under him to take them to Rome in two days—one message to Pilate's teacher, the other to the emperor.

Part 3

Virgo Amans
(A Virgin in Love)

The oasis in the desert, three days after the Roman's visit.

So, THIS is hope again. And hope is a busy time.

The Roman left, and it's been three days now. Throughout their waking hours, our elders have been in prayer. Sprawling in the dirt, hitting their heads on rocks that face Jerusalem. They didn't put on *tefillin,* they had no chance to take their tefillin or scrolls on that dreaded night when the king exiled us. So they speak the prayers as they remember them, and when my father hears them go wrong, he corrects them.

Our boys pray, too. Most don't know the prayers, but what a good trick, to stop working and start mumbling and swaying back and forth. We women keep the work going, as usual.

We clean, care for the infants and the goats, cook, and put the food on covered plates near the men. Flies and worms crawl toward the food and gather at the plates' rims. We wave off the flies. We set water buckets for washing behind the praying men.

When they have to ease themselves, they traipse behind a dune, where, if two men cross paths, they pull their tallits over their faces, not to see each other. They come back, stop at the washing buckets, then pick up the prayer again, in unbroken purity.

I'm busily spinning about, telling the youngsters what to do. I'm done with whatever's in my hands in no time, and lunge for something else, or I'll choke from sheer elation: I'm going home!

All over the gulch, fires flicker in pits. We've kept them lit day and night since the day when a caravan master gave us our first fire—a burning rag dipped in sunflower oil. We ripped clothes and lit them from the burning rag, and we dug fire pits among the tents and trees. I remember my hands fighting the sand, I remember the grains of sand, cutting me under my fingernails. I was so eager to feel pain in my body, so I wouldn't feel my other pain—*where was Joseph?*

He wasn't with us. He hadn't made it to the well.

Was he alive?

Had the king's Syrians killed him?

The fire did go out many times our first week here. I told the girls to tear up rags and stretch them on rocks in the sun, until the rags were so dry they caught fire from the sunrays. We cradled a flame in each pit. Gobs of camel dung—we dragged them from the caravan trails, stacked them by the fire pits, and everyone kicked dung into the flames when we walked past. Pushing the water wheel, I kept glancing over my shoulder—if smoke curled thickly above the pit, dark against the bushes and leaves, I rushed and fed that fire back to life. I taught the other girls to do it, too. The fire never went out again—three whole years.

In Nazareth, we young girls walked barefoot. When we worked in the fields, to protect our feet from brambles and roots left after reaping, our mothers packed grass and dried it up, cut it to the sizes of our feet, and tied it with donkey hair. Grass sandals. We would walk in grass sandals until we started to have our bloods and young men started asking us in marriage; if the parents agreed on a bride price, the wedding was fated to be, and then we would soak our feet in warm goat milk for a few days, to soften them. So we wouldn't scratch the floors of our new homes with our flinty feet, so we wouldn't put off our husbands with the unsightliness of corns and bunions and cracked skin on heels hardened like hooves! But there's no one to ask us in marriage in the desert—and no goat milk to spare and no grass to make sandals, either. My feet became unfeeling, I kick the flames and feel no pain. I can walk on embers.

I'm so happy just now, I take the fire pits at a run, stepping in three flaming pits, one after the other.

"Mary?" my mother snaps from inside our tent. "What are you doing? Have you gone insane?"

Our tent is so frayed, she sees me through its sagging tarp.

"Yes," I shout back. "I've gone insane! I'll go home insane! Yes!"

END OF A DAY of praying. The elders call out to us girls to wash their faces, arms, necks, and feet. I wash Akam, a worthless old drunk who tries to pinch me. But my skin doesn't clump up in his fingers—I'm so skinny, nothing to pinch. I slap his hand. Then we serve the men their food and step back. They eat sitting by themselves, arguing, loud. "What are we to do? Send back a few of us only, to meet with the Roman when he brings the second writ? Or all of us go back?"

"All of us, yes," those old cowards yell. "If we are to die, let all of us die!"

"No, no!" Orpa's father yells. "If the Roman's not there,

and the Nazarenes see us outside the gates, we'll be sitting ducks!"

"All of us go back," shrieks Akam, the cowardest. "We're one tribe, one family."

"And if the Roman doesn't return?"

My father moves around the men, touching them with his hideous hands. I stand nearby, to hear what he's saying. "Shalafta and Aaron are our blood cousins. They'll see us before their gates, their hearts are not of stone."

Oh, El Gibbor, God, my hero, forgive me for what I think. Shalafta and Aaron, who robbed us and killed us more eagerly than the king's Syrians, they're made of stone from top to bottom! Take them to you, Hashem, that'll be no loss to the world. Forgive me, forgive me. And he forgives me on the spot.

Akam slurs, "Let the men with young daughters go back first, with their daughters!" He just finished praying, when did he have the time to drink? "Joachim has young meat to trade, let him give Mary to Shalafta, to soften him!" He makes himself a brew from ripe dates, disgustingly thick and inebriating.

A young voice jumps into the hubbub. "We should bust the gates of Nazareth, and take back our homes! And kill the ones who tried to kill us!"

The boy, Shimon. Oh well, he's fourteen.

"It's better to bargain," my father says. "No blood spilled. We'll offer to work for them."

"Be their slaves, you mean?" Shimon scoffs.

"Work is the best trading value we have," my father says gently.

Akam snickers. "Joachim cut his deal with the Roman. He bargained Mary to him."

"I did no such thing," my father replies. But Akam creaks on happily. "I snuck up to the lip of the pit and watched Mary feed the Roman. They whispered to each other." The dirty old roach, God forgive me! "The Roman was leering, like so." Akam hangs out his tongue. The Roman's healthy lips and shiny teeth flash in my mind. I glance at the water girls; they heard Akam. They giggle, and Orpa winks at me. *When I dole out the food for the trek back, I'll make sure you get enough for a rat, Akam!*

I hear the sand crunching. The women creep closer, to hear what the men are deciding.

"I had a dream," my father says. "God changed the king's mind. The king stepped into the temple, and from behind the curtain hiding the holy of holies, God wafted out at him like a cloud of myrrh. And the king thought the first forgiving thought of his life: Joachim's kin have suffered enough."

I want to whisper, Don't lie, my father, it is beneath you. But my father murmurs, "Mashiah is so close to us now. He can't reveal himself yet, but he's close . . ." *Oh, God, what gift you gave him, that he can make the rustling of leaves, or the crunching of sand, feel like the nearness of Mashiah! That warm, caring being whom none of us saw, whom we may never see in our lives.*

Meantime, I try not to think of the Roman. But I can't help it. He was so well built, so confident, and healthy. *And he turned out to be a good man, how like you, Hashem, to make a Roman good!* I smile.

Akam creaks, "So it's settled, Joachim? You'll give Mary to Shalafta?"

"To Aaron, to Aaron!" other elders yell. "Aaron's even more bloodthirsty!"

"Aaron killed my wife!" Akam jumps up, thrusting his

groin, stabbing with an invisible knife. "Stabbed her as he raped her! She had milk, she bled blood and milk as she died, and my life was taken from me—I look like I'm alive, but I'm a ghost inside!"

I think, *So don't waste your time here! Melt away, ghost!*

"I prophesize that Mashiah will make himself felt to the king," my father says. He raises a finger. The dusty palm trees are becoming the pillars of his synagogue. "Mashiah will say to the king, 'Let Joachim's clan live as part of my arrival.'"

Akam shouts, "That's why you lost your hands, and we all suffered, because you told prophecies to the king's son. You still want to be a prophet?"

"Shut up," my father says, trying to sound gentle. "Without us, there is no priesthood in Nazareth. When our cousins awoke from that rage of raping and stealing, don't you think they wondered, 'What did we do, chase away our priests?'"

The elders grunt softly. They love to think that they were missed.

"Very well," Akam says. "But Aaron and Shalafta *will* let us come back if we bond our girls to them." Now all the elders squeak, "Right, give Mary to Shalafta! And Orpa to Aaron! No, Mary to Aaron, and Orpa to Shalafta! Right!"

Like twitching, dying roaches. Orpa's father is in that crowd. He's not protesting.

I glance at Orpa. *You and I, are we going to speak up? You and I, we saw the well first. You and I, we scooped out the sludge and drew the clean water, and now they'll sell us like cattle?* But my fiery friend Orpa, who's never at a loss for what to say, guesses my thoughts and whispers to me, "We have no dowries, Mary, and we're old. I just turned sixteen." The thought of how old I am freezes the words on my lips. I'm even older—a year older than Orpa. If no one wants me as a wife and I refuse to be a bond-woman, what will I be, a beggar by the roadside?

"Now, let's not offer the girls before they ask," my skillful father says. "If they ask, we'll negotiate."

My mother shouts from our tent, "If I give my daughter in bondage, I want my house back, free and clear!" And Orpa's mother yells, "If that Roman is there with the writ, we the women will get our homes back and you men can get lost!"

I feel it. The bitterness that all our mothers and spouses stored up against our men. Priests or not, they were weak. My father was weak, too.

Akam lost his wife to the slaughter, but here, he got a mistress. She was his neighbor in the village and much younger than him, but the king's Syrians killed her husband. Loneliness does wonders. And she has a daughter, nine years old. At nine, one can be a bondwoman already.

Akam's mistress steps to the circle of men. "Who asked you to decide anyone's future, Akam? Go sleep off your drink!" And he crawls off, knowing that if he doesn't, she'll find his stash of drink and spill it in the sand.

I think, *I should've pushed Akam in the cistern last night. He was soused blind. Forgive me, God, who would have missed him?*

"Why did you deceive the men like that?" I snap at my father, moments later, in our tent. I try to keep my voice low, for everyone's right outside, everyone can hear my voice.

Through the dogs' passage, a hole in the tent's fabric, Orpa lunges into the tent. Grinning, eager to witness a fight.

I jump up and bump into my mother, who sits by the pit with rags burning in it.

My father whispers, "We have no young men, Mary, to do battle for us. If we give our girls in bond, it's to save us all."

I ask with a shiver in my voice, "You'd make me work bond for Shalafta?"

By the fire, with clean glimmers of light playing on her face, my mother says, "What's the difference who you're bonded to, if you're bonded? It might as well be someone rich. Rich men's bondwomen have it better than wives."

"When they're young and breedable?"

"You are that," says my mother, with those flames on her face.

"*Eema!* [Mother!]" I gasp, stunned. For my mother was a bondwoman to that very scoundrel, Shalafta, the richest, vilest man in Nazareth. A filthy letch, who wouldn't let a pretty woman step by him without tripping her to the ground. Shalafta worked my mother for ten years, then he sold her bond to my father, who married her, and I was born fourteen months later.

So when my father married my mother, she wasn't a virgin, but she wasn't soiled in her heart, *that I know.* Thanks to Hashem, she had no children by her owner. As for her body, one can wash one's body. But it's still sad that she said what she said. There is no shame in her eyes, but there is shame in my father's eyes, that what she said, he cannot make better. "I'm too old to protect you, Mary," he starts, but my mother cuts him off. "The women always have more to trade. And the men want servants."

"So, women are born servants?" I know what I really want to say: If I'm to be sold, I'll choose my own buyer! The Roman, for instance! But just then Hashem whispers to me. *Hush, Mary. Your parents can't do any better just now. Don't be harsh on them. It doesn't help.*

So I walk off to the tent's door and stand looking at the flickering oasis.

I feel the Roman's presence. He's right behind me.

I imagine myself sweeping the flagstones of his house. Through a window, the sky of Jerusalem drips on me—that sky more blue than anything but the sea.

Suddenly, the Roman overpowers me, and not only with his lusting body. He overpowers me with the blue of that sky, with the perfection of his house, with the majesty of the city of David. I fight, but our fight will end in a mating. God made women to be taken, God made their bodies in such a way that being taken cannot be fought off, not for long anyway. And being taken bleeds and smarts and it gets noticed and known. *Why, Hashem? Why that way?*

I'm suddenly so sad. I touch my mother's hand, which she rests on her knee. I feel in that touch our past together. As a little girl, I lay in my parents' bed on some forgotten afternoon, and Mother told me a story, then we dozed off together. If I woke up before she woke up, I studied her face, so known, yet so mysterious. Her face was my world, her presence was my life.

What's left of that now? Even if we hadn't been banished, I would have become who I am, a girl without dowry and thus without prospects. I had my first bloods three years ago already. What man will want me as a bride when we go back?

Going home suddenly feels so fraught with bad luck, I scowl at my father. "At least find a way to trade me off for our own house."

What are you saying? That secret voice whispers inside me. *Joseph is back there, he is waiting for you!* But that voice cannot be your voice, Hashem. It's my own voice making a promise it can't fulfill.

I burst out of the tent. So roughly, I tear the fold hanging over the tent's door.

BLESSED BE THOU, *Adonai El Roi, the Seeing God, I See Therefore I Am!* And I see that I'm so angry, *I am.* I snap at Orpa to wake all the boys and girls, and she snaps back, "They don't need waking, look around, everyone's up."

So I gather them and I tell them, "We have much to do, better start now in the cool of the night. Round up the goats and slaughter them and cut the meat in strips to dry in the sun to-morrow, food for the trek back. And clean the goatskins, salt them, and sew them into water skins." I turn to the boys. "You and you, pluck the wheat by moonlight, and get it in heaps for tomorrow morning, when you'll thrash it into flour. You and you, make the tent poles into sleds to carry our belongings and our lit-tle children. And you and you and you, haul everyone's soiled clothing and diapers to that purifying hot spring, wash it all, and set it on rocks to dry. Jump to it. Shimon? Why are you still loi-tering here?"

Shimon stares me in the eyes. "I'm not washing diapers."

"Then wash the clothing, we're all doing something."

"What are *you* doing? Giving chores? Who do you think you are, woman?"

Strange, it feels, not to be a woman yet, but be called one by a boy who's not a man yet. Shimon pushed me against a rock last week and tried to feel me under my shift. I kicked him in the shin.

Everyone turns toward Shimon and me, all those girls and

boys sprouting hair under their shifts and breeches. There's something dirty in the air as Shimon sputters, "I'm kind, calling you woman—you don't even know what's between your legs." He heard that from Darvoush, a Persian caravan master who got in a fight with my father.

Darvoush and my father had agreed on twenty knives to be paid for a watering; knives are our most useful tools. With his camels' bellies dragging to the ground, Darvoush went back on his word. He'd give us five knives only. I blurted out at him, "You filthy cheat, don't stop here anymore." The Persian glared at my father. "Who's speaking to me like that, Rabbi, some son of yours dressed in a girl's clothes? I'll take her to the sands to strip her and find out what creature she is—and if she doesn't know what's between her legs, I'll teach her." Then he shouted, "All of you Jews, get out of my camels' way, or I'll burn you in your tents and set my own people to run this well!"

There was a dead silence. My father had turned pale.

And I heard my lips whistling. *Whooooshh!* Dying of fright, I was whistling, and the jackal pack raced over, bristling hideously. Emboldened, my father yelled at Darvoush, "Thirty knives, *now,* or our dogs at your camels' throats, and let God decide!"

Darvoush handed over the thirty knives, then turned to me and spat. "You little witch, I'll be your shame one day."

The caravan left, and everyone raved about my craziness. Our old men assailed my father: *Never let Mary dare a man again, never! Those roaches!* And my father . . . he told me that my bravery endangered everyone, and did I want it known that I had more thatch than a man?

Shimon was there. He remembers all that. I move away,

glaring at him. Suddenly, he trips me and wrestles me to the ground. In front of everyone, by that pile of soiled clothing. On top of me, he blows in my face, grips my arm, twists it. Our feet kick the sand. With five other boys there, not one moves to help me. But the girls—Dalit, who sings well; Yorit, who is hare-lipped; the twins, Neah and Nava; and my friend Orpa—all leap and grab Shimon by his hair and peel him off me. Orpa knees him in the crotch. I hope she bruised him good. The girls throw rocks at the other boys: cowards, cowards!

I stand up and comb my fingers through my hair. I breathe hard.

And yet . . .

Thank you, High One. That our boys grew into men, even here, in squalor and starvation. That they're starting to rush the girls, that's a good thing, isn't it, High One? It's toward your command to be fruitful and multiply. Glad that I didn't scratch Shimon's eyes out, I lift a bale of soiled clothing onto my head. *Help me, Hashem!* Off I trundle, with the girls behind me under soiled clothes, to the cave with the hot spring in it.

The cave's mouth blows an odor that's sulfurous and yet clean. *Mysterious are your ways, Hashem, cross-grained and contrary. You couldn't make a hot spring fragrant and cool or make a woman ready for breeding without pain and bleeding between her legs or, above all, without fear of men! I want to be like any other woman, but not a bondwoman, no! I'd rather die unwedded!*

THE SUN RISES, hovers on high. Work goes on. The sun drifts downward. It sets.

We work 'til the dead of night, then Orpa and I collapse by the cistern. I sleep fitfully for a few hours.

As I lie awake, Orpa opens her eyes. "Where are you?" she asks.

I know what she means by that question.

"I'm in my garden of peace."

That's a place in my mind where I add good memory to good memory and soothing dream to soothing dream. No haunting questions there, no guilt. When I need respite, I step—one step!—into my garden of peace.

"Me, too," my best friend replies. For she, too, has one.

"Who's in your garden, Orpa?"

"Men. Who's in your garden, Mary?"

"Angels."

"Liar. Is it the Roman?"

She waits. I say nothing.

"He had such big boots, like he had his feet in leather buckets." Big feet on a man, the saying goes, mean a big *rod of life,* to be fruitful and multiply.

Orpa rises on one elbow, studies my face across two inches of darkness. "You *are* lying. Even if you didn't like him, you're thinking about him! He smelled of leather, even after riding five days, he smelled of nice, freshly tanned leather. And he was so stocky and strong, he seemed tall."

"It's not the Roman, and I'm telling the truth."

"Who is it, then, the one who carves angels? You *still* think about him?"

I hug her, so I won't have to speak.

Then she whispers in my ear, "Betoola, betoola," and we feel like two sisters, anxious about each other, annoyed that we're anxious, and loving each other endlessly.

"You're a betoola, too," I whisper back.

"Not by choice," she says, and I smile. Orpa's so daring with words, but if a man were here now, would she be as daring?

I have a crazy thought. "Let's get the mirror and look at ourselves."

Orpa laughs so hard, she has to bite her sleeve, not to wake the nearest other sleepers. The mirror! No one knows about our mirror!

It's not a mirror of glass. It's a big, long plate of polished copper, three cubits tall and one wide, but not very heavy—its copper was hammered into a thin sheet. A cheap object; Jibril, the Arabian caravan master who gave it to Orpa and me, kept it in a pile of junk he hadn't managed to sell. Jibril is fond of us, he brings us apples. He lets us look through his junk. When I saw myself the first time in that dusty copper, leaned up against some unsold mats, I twitched as if a mosquito had bit me on the lip. Was that me? And that other creature, was it Orpa? Glimpsing ourselves in polished metal, instead of in water mixed with camel drool?

"Take the copper, it's yours!" Jibril said. And how he laughed when Orpa and I grabbed it, one end of it each, and ran into the dunes with it, to bury it before any other girl saw it. Otherwise can you imagine the mayhem? Moments later, we walked back without it, and Jibril choked with laughter. "I'll buy you two from your fathers," he said. "As bondwomen to my eldest sons. You'll lead happy lives and have boys by my sons, and in time you'll replace their wives in their hearts."

"I don't want to replace anyone's wife," I said. "Besides, Jibril, your sons are not Jews."

"A man will be anything his beloved woman wants him to be. My sons will become Jews for you and Orpa."

"We're too young to even think of marriage."

"Go ask the mirror about that! Where are your fathers?"

We bumped him each from one side, knocking him down on the sand. We tickled him, then freed him, and brought water and washed his feet, which Jibril relished—and he agreed to make his offer to our fathers some other time.

The mirror—we hid it so well that when we snuck back to stare into it, we couldn't find it. We searched the wrong dune, then another wrong dune. At last, the sand felt hard under my foot: There it was! We dug, turning our nails inside out. It was filthy, dusty. But desert dust, when rubbed with spit, polishes copper marvelously.

"Don't scour, Orpa!" I kept squealing, stopping Orpa's hands, pulling the copper to myself, falling on my face to stroke the copper with my sleeves, ever so gently until, barely with a scratch or two from broken nails, the mirror shined against the dune. We stood before it, and I thought, *Blessed be thou who said I am that I am, Adonai El Hai, Adonai El Roi. Who is this I see in the mirror? Is this me?*

I stood full height, with Orpa shoulder to shoulder with me. Then Orpa turned sideways and the grown roundness of her buttocks didn't fit the mirror. She pushed me, and I pushed her. The mirror wasn't wide enough for the two of us!

We had grown! I was three years older. Blemished a little by desert life, but . . . My breasts and hips had filled up . . .

"You think Jibril's sons would want us?" Orpa asked.

"His eyes are getting bad," I joked.

But I was so happy that instant, so happy! And for Orpa, too, not just for me!

I thought, *Blessed be thou, Adonai, Elohim, El Shaddai,*

Hashem. That most secret name of yours, which no mortal knows, and which I love the most, because it's a secret. Bear with me, El Hai, the Living God, El Roi, the Seeing God. I see therefore I live. I am therefore I am . . . I, this girl here, I am—what?

I didn't know what to reply to him or to myself.

All I knew was, that question—which I was asking somewhere in my mind where I didn't even use words—that question was so wondrous, it was like a miracle in itself.

So, with dust on my face under the deadly desert sun and hugging Orpa around her slender waist (but just above her growing hips!), I thought joyfully, *Thank you, Hashem the Unnameable, and of course you're unnameable, you're so all-too-unusual, you could only be unnameable, so . . . let me whisper your name . . .*

You heard it?

I just said it!

Now in the dead of night, lying next to Orpa, I wondered, *Where is the Roman? Back in Jerusalem? Did he already stand before the king pleading for our homes?*

And I wondered, *Am I really going back to my village? Me, Mary-amneh bat Joachim, seventeen and as tall as my mother? Oh, God. I know that I'm no beauty, but I'm not afraid of work, be it the hardest. But, God Eternal, don't let me be a bondwoman. I'll dye like my mother, I'll even learn carpentry from my father, and I'll be happy with the poorest of husbands. I'll keep my head down and my hands toiling while my belly is swelling with our first child. I'll make half of our earnings at least. But I'll say my husband is the one who earns it all, he's my savior. I'll be so thankful to him and to you, Hashem. I'll repay your kindness. I will! And then you'll grant me a good cry?*

Orpa had set her head on my shoulder. Her breath was steady and light, she'd fallen asleep again.

I eased her body down onto the sand. I got up, put my hand inside my shift, but didn't find what I was groping for—an object as tiny as a thimble. My istomukhvia was gathered at the waist with a string tied and untied so often it was mangy its whole length. When flax clothes are new, they're itchy and hard. When they're old they're supple and soft, and my clothes were the softest. Did that little thing fall out of my clothes? Throughout the day, I had felt it sailing around my waist.

I reached behind my back. Aha! Resting against the small of my back! Come here!

I tore it free: a tiny piece of cedarwood.

I held the wood above my face, lowering and lifting and lowering it. Making its scent stronger, then faint again, vanishing, then reappearing, close, unmistakable—I've held this thing so many times, stroking its surfaces, its roundness and its leanness. It's not a key, this little thing, but it's really like the key to my garden of peace. What's it like to enter my garden of peace not drained and hopeless, but with hope?

Part 4

Mary and Joseph

Galilee, three years earlier.

The summer when Herod banished our tribe.

MY FATHER had said, "This is the last time I'm taking you to the fair, Mary, for you're a grown woman now."

Meaning that I'd begun to have my bloods. The fair was the carpenters' fair in Sepphoris, the Greek city five miles west of Nazareth.

Ljla, virginity, was like a strange weed that had grown inside me for so long, I forgot I had it in me. Then that weed blossomed, red and warm. My father, who until then took me everywhere, now avoided me, because he, too, had to show *betwlwt,* modesty, which is from the same root word as "betoola" and "ljla," a word built around that *l* sound, as in *lo*—Hebrew for "no." My betwlwt started with my parents showing betwlwt; for years they had lavished me with hugs, but now they were stingy with any kind of touch. My father didn't hand me a cup or a work tool, but now set them on the ground for me to pick up without my fingers touching his. He was a man, and his little girl had become impure in the womanly way. During my bloods' flow and a whole week thereafter, he opened the house doors with his elbow or shoulder, mumbling a prayer of cleansing, if I had gone in ahead of him.

My mother shied away from me almost as much, and she showed constant worry about my new state. When I brought in a bucket of water from the brook behind our yard, she peeked over the fence to make sure that I was alone and not in danger of impregnation. She wouldn't let me sleep at other girls' homes anymore, she forbade me to take walks by myself, and when I went with her to Nazareth's open market, she made me wear a hood with a brim of doilied cotton, which I could snap down over my face if a man peeked at me.

Since I couldn't ask too many questions of my parents, for that would be inappropriate, I walked around dizzy with my new state, which in my mind was really innocent. A spell had ripened, a plant's stem had broken through the earth's crust—so what? In every animal or plant, becoming ripe was no cause for worry. Why did simple creatures have it easy, while women, made by God and in the image of God, have it so hard?

"There are so many men at that fair, and so many are not Jews," my mother said, her voice heavy with the unseen dangers to my betwlwt.

"But I'm the elder of the fair," my father replied. "And she's good help to me, adding up my sales." I had not learned how to read because I was a girl and reading was for men, but my father had taught me the numbers, and I helped him with keeping his records. And I was quick sweeping his stall with a broom of cypress sprigs.

"Keep her next to you at all times," my mother cautioned.

So the next day at the crack of dawn, I harnessed our donkey, Ozney, "Ears" (named so by me when I could barely stand up to its knee), and packed the water skin, the brooms, and the food cooked by mother the night before into our two-wheel cart. Also, my father's *punda,* the leather purse he wore at his belt during the fair. And his sandals and my sandals, which once in Sepphoris we'd put on. After loading all that, I jumped on the cart's box and waited, for my parents were still asleep.

Sitting on the cart's box, I dozed and dreamed. About Sepphoris, with its streets of stone, and statues in the marketplaces, and throngs of non-Jewish women whose life was astonishingly loose. Such as: There was friendly talk in the streets between men and women who weren't married to each other. Sepphorian women did not cover their hair, but styled it in fanciful patterns, or let it wave freely onto their naked shoulders, for they did not wear shifts but strapless dresses. They lived with such ease and lack of stricture, those lucky women. I wanted to glimpse them for the last time. Was that a bad thing?

Then I bolted awake. My father was stepping out of the house.

Seeing me sitting in the cart, he climbed in muttering, "Before the next fair, you'll hopefully be married and with a child."

I grabbed the reins, lashed the donkey's back, and we drove off.

IN SEPPHORIS, THE fair was held in an insula with four stories and a courtyard in the middle that you couldn't see from the street. This insula was built to be rented to Romans, Greeks, and Phoenicians in passage, a beehive with holes for windows you'd think wouldn't let in enough air for a cat to breathe. But it made someone a fortune, until it burned down except for the walls and was sold to the Jewish carpenters' guild. The carpenters knocked down the charred inside and carted out the filth, dark and mummified-looking. Inside the cleaned lower floors, they put stalls made from sheets of plane wood and knocked open wider entrances for the timber to be carried in and ramps for bondmen and slaves to pad in and out.

Gradually, the odor of ashes, sour and rank like burned piss, was replaced by scents of wood, clean and damp—wood stores humidity, always. The aroma of felled cedars, spiced with spruce, cypress, oak, pine—all Jewish trees. Foreign timber such as sandalwood, sycamore, tamarind, came by caravan—thus I first heard of caravans. Setim, the acacia of the Galilean desert, was harvested right by Nazareth. When asked why we had returned from Jerusalem, my father replied that he wanted to be where the setims grew. "The setims are holy trees, Mary," he told me once. "The ark of our covenant was carved from two setims." I believed him, although he made up stories all the time.

We set up our wares in our stall. My father gave me a look when I took off my hood, but I had combed my hair fiercely and drawn it into a tight bun. He said to me, "I'm going to meet with the other wood sellers. I'll be back before you boil the noon gruel."

And off he went.

Our stall had a brazier in one corner, to which I fed kindling, never letting it out of my sight. An unwatched cooking fire that got out of control was how the building had caught fire. I cooked the gruel, put out the fire, and stepped out to sweep the passageway. When carpenters, apprentices, and bondmen with loads walked by, I, the only female around, looked down at my broom handle. When I stepped back into our stall, I saw a man on the floor, on all fours. He was rummaging through a thick, dirty pile of wood chips. He'd stirred the dust, which made me sneeze.

Our stall was very narrow. Cut-up trunks and carved product, from three-legged kitchen stools to plow horns, leaned against the partitions, and other trunks and carvings held up the partitions from the other side. The space in between was only a few square cubits. When I sneezed, he jumped up.

He was a whole head taller than I but still a boy; I saw beard fuzz on his neck and chin.

An apprentice, most likely. I knew the apprentices here, and my father knew everyone, but this boy I'd never seen. His hands were loaded with pieces of wood he'd found on the floor.

"*Boker tov,* good morning," he said, not in the least ashamed.

"Why are you stealing our wood?" Wood was scarce in Galilee; carpenters could only harvest those forests not earmarked for the king's use or for the Roman navy.

"I took only three pieces, you have enough left." Soft, husky voice. More grown than the fuzz on his lips.

"Who are you?"

"I'm Joseph, bondman to Shalafta."

Ugghh! I winced as though my teeth were aching. Because my mother had been Shalafta's bondwoman, I hated Shalafta, and I especially hated that he had a daughter, whom I knew all too well: Lanit, the most adorned girl in the village, one year younger than I, had her own bondwoman. Turning my nose up, I dropped my broom on the floor. Then I froze. Joseph had pulled a knife out of his punda.

"You want me to carve you an angel?"

"Huh?"

He plopped down on the floor and put the knife to a piece of pine.

I leaned out into the pathway between stalls, staring right

and left to see if my father was returning. I didn't see him. I lunged back in as Joseph leisurely got up.

"Here." He put something in my hand.

He had carved the angel so quickly, flaking its body with quick strikes, making its robe flutter in flight. The angel was diving from heaven like a hawk sweeping on a rabbit. Its head was a knot of wood; Joseph scraped it, giving it ruffled hair. He drilled a hole for the mouth, notched in the nose, the eyes. He put his hand in his punda, pulled it out, and opened his palm, revealing two shards of glass, smoky blue, from some broken cup.

He put the shards in. Blue-eyed, the creature peeked at me. All in three instants.

"This is the archangel Gabriel," he explained.

Good, I thought. I could talk to this boy about that, I knew about angels. And talking of angels, although with an unknown young male, shouldn't be too unbecoming. So I whispered sarcastically, "*This* is Gabriel?"

"Yes. I carve him a lot." Joseph had dark eyes, really dark-dark, very pretty. "I also carve Raphael, Michael, Uriel . . ."

I knew a lot about angels. My father had taught me that there were many heavens, not just two or three, set up in circles over circles, each higher and higher, with so many angels' gangs to each—one gang was led by Gabriel, *the hero of God,* another by Michael, *who was like God,* one more by Raphael, *the medicine of God,* and a fourth by Uriel, *whose light was God.* So there. The expert that I was, I relaxed my body, set my right hand upon my right hip, pressed my lips together just a little, to make them more shiny and more pink (a girl knows about such things!), and asked smartly, "Is this why you're stealing wood?"

"Yes. I sell angels to the Greek children."

He shifted his weight from one foot to the other. He wore thongs of plain wood soles, held over his feet with strips of tanned leather. He had wide shoulders. Usually I could tell bond-people by their rags, but Shalafta, I had to admit it, kept this bondman in clean fabric.

"I made another Gabriel last week, I gave him to two *porneioi,* two sisters."

"Porneioi"? Greek word, for sure. I didn't know what it meant, but I didn't want to seem ignorant.

"They were kicked out of their place for not being able to pay the rent. I brought them here." He motioned above us. In the cremated upper stories, homeless Sepphorians had settled in lairs of bare planks stolen from the carpenters. "I paid for a month of their rent with that Gabriel. I keep my carvings up on the roof. You want to see them?"

Oh, God. What was I to reply to that?

"This Gabriel's very wrong," I replied. "Gabriel's said to have a hundred and forty pairs of wings; this one has only one pair." Joseph leaned his head to one side, his eyes even prettier. He rounded his mouth to speak, but I didn't let him. "Gabriel might also be a she, not a he, doesn't she sit at God's *left* hand?" He smiled and I felt so strange, I didn't want to be there, yet I wanted to be nowhere else.

I peeked at his untied collar. Joseph's throat was clean, hairless.

He took Gabriel from my hand. With great precision, he cut a woman's crotch onto *her,* in one flaking strike. "Is she better now?"

"No, not at all. Now it's like she shows flesh!"

And I looked at Joseph's long eyelashes and skidded into his brown eyes.

"Where did you say you kept your carvings?"

"On the roof. You can look at the sea from there." And then, as if to reassure me: "I know your father, Rabbi Joachim. My father was a rabbi, too. You come to Sepphoris often?"

"Only to the wood fairs, with my father."

"I come with Shalafta, he comes here all the time." Without looking at his hands, he carved something else, fitting bits, taking the smoky eyes out of the angel and sticking them onto the new piece, which he showed to me. I squealed: a smoky-eyed fly, with veined wings folded tightly, looking wound-up for flight. *Buzzzz!* He laughed, put the fly on an oak trunk.

"Who's your father?" I asked, almost certain that he had lied, I knew all the rabbis in Nazareth.

But suddenly I guessed. Because it was in Joseph's eyes: His father was no more. "What happened?"

"The lightning struck him. He took our goats up on Mount Barak. He was caught in a storm." Joseph smiled, his pain was old, it didn't hurt much now. "After my father died, Shalafta took me in. Shalafta is a good man." He turned, listened to the noise of the fair. "Your father's coming—with Shalafta."

I leaned out of the stall. Indeed, my father and Shalafta were walking over, talking loud and waving their hands. Joseph had heard them before me.

"Come up on the roof. I'll wait for you."

Then suddenly, he was gone.

The fly made of wood was sitting on that tree trunk when my father and Shalafta stepped in, but they were too spirited to notice it. When I heard what Shalafta was saying, my breath stopped. Shalafta would bring Prince Aristobulus, King Herod's oldest son, to my father's stall today. The prince was looking to hire a cabinetmaker.

"You'll give me half of what he pays you," Shalafta said, which didn't feel outrageous, it felt right, if the blood prince of Israel hired my father!

My father excitedly turned to me. "What do you say? Wondrous is God's way of making things *khofef*, coincidental. Luck is shining on me today."

Indeed, I thought.

I happened to have a coincidence of my own, more modest, of course. Mine was about getting up on the roof of the building, to look at the sea. I'd never seen the sea before; this would be my first time. Joseph waiting for me up there was really purely coincidental.

Soon thereafter, Prince Aristobulus arrived at the carpenters' fair.

As usual when royalty made its appearance, everything else changed in size and outlook. Things and people shrank and became dim and dull, while a halo of light seemed to surround the fair's entrance where my father stood waiting to welcome the prince and his servants. Everyone had come out of the stalls, choking the place. You could hear a pin drop as my father wished the prince peace and welcome, to which the prince replied in a twanging voice, "Peace be to you, too, Rabbi Joachim, and to all my subjects, and I desire you to build me a cabinet, Rabbi Joachim." Which was all that the prince said. It didn't take much longer than to say "Good day."

Then the princely throng rumbled out again. Though I stretched my neck 'til it hurt and stood on tiptoe so eagerly I could've cracked a toe, I didn't see the prince; the crowds concealed him like the sun in an eclipse—which you did let me see, God, in Nazareth, when I was six!

So the prince's order was placed. One cabinet.

My father was in such a jubilant mood, I knew I could ask him for almost anything. So I told him that I didn't want to clean the stall—let the apprentices clean it—I wanted to look at the sea, which I'd never seen, from up top.

My father didn't even hear me. He was marking this and

that grove of trees in his mind: Enough planks for that cabinet, or better to add another grove?

I started up the stairs into a misty stench, past entryways charred from that fire and not shut with doors now but curtained off with rags. Most doorposts carried mezuzahs affixed to them; though horribly poor, the people here were Jews, my people. The reek from those lairs was unspeakable. A shiver of fright pricked up the hairs on the back of my neck. Drips of fear, down my back, giving each bead of my spine a frozen kiss . . . Once I was alone on the roof with Joseph, what would happen to my betwlwt? But perhaps my betwlwt was the one chasing me to the roof? I almost felt like crying, I wanted to be a child again. Waking up in the still of night, listening for angels' wings flapping, or smelling angels—a flat bland smell of air washed with water, like rain.

I quieted my heart somehow. I started to climb again, as light dripped through holes burned in the roof. The light was inebriatingly pretty. Out of breath, I bustled out onto a large, banistered, very littered roof.

And I saw the sea.

Joseph called out softly, "I'm here."

He stood against the roof's banister, which was not only bent and dented, it missed entire sections. I should be careful not to walk too close to the edge.

He was chipping at something.

Beyond him, I saw that flawless straight line of blue, drawn from the left of my left eye across to the right of my right eye. God, how did you make the sea, and out of water, too? And the azure with which you filled it! My heart was pounding. Leaning so carefully over the banister, I glanced down.

Sepphoris came into view; dirty, exhaling smoke, echoing with rough cries. Streets filled with men and women. Even from up here I could tell that the women were dressed elegantly, walked confidently, and had their hair in incredible patterns. Exactly the den of sinners where a confused young Jew like Joseph could sell images to gentiles. But beyond Sepphoris, hanging right by the sea—Joseph, still chipping, noticed my awe, and grinned—there was a white-tiled Roman port! Ah! Every house a temple! With an aqueduct striding the skyline in generous arches and golden like a golden rainbow.

The port was filled with many ships with oars in two rows or three rows. Joseph explained to me that those ships were called biremes and triremes, according to how many rows of oars they had. And so many docks and quays, and so many Greeks and Romans, like a busy paradise . . . God? Why did you make our enemies so wealthy and powerful, is that another coincidental?

"Is that Ptolemais?" I asked, guessing.

"That's Caesarea. Ptolemais is up there." He pointed to the north.

"Oh." I puckered my lips. May Israel's invaders perish; they came like locusts and took over our ancient places, renaming them after their tyrants, with strange ugly names I'd never bothered to learn, why would I?

I stared at the port's busy wharves. I glimpsed herds being led out of the ships; swine, made pretty by the distance. In one corner of that beauty, upright crosses, not loaded, rested before their next tour of duty. Then antlike Romans dragged along a tiny lawbreaker, and nailed him on a cross. The clanging of hammers and yells of pain reached across the air's transparence, one instant later. I understood what torture was, truly I did. Take a human being, force him or her to a hard post with a transverse piece on top, and see whose shape breaks, the post's, or the human's. Joseph moved and stood in front of the banister to spare me that sight.

"Look, I carved you." He held up another piece of wood. I smelled it—cedar. I started to laugh. This was *me*?

He'd carved a girl. Face turned up. Hair held back tight, like mine. Eyes scanning the sky, nose small and straight. She had no mouth yet. As if admitting that she was unfinished—forgetful boy!—he shook his head and stabbed a tiny dot to the left of my nose, a freckle. Then he handed me to me, and we laughed together, and my fear was gone. I said, "I like it," feeling very awkward.

Pleased, he called me away with his finger. In the midst of the roof . . .

There stood a strange sculpture, made of dried-up clay. A kind of hollow, like an animal's burrow torn open. Inside it, in a space that felt tight and protective like a womb, lay an infant, eyes open, sad, and serious.

That womb was large, it rose to my face, and the infant was life-size. Mothered inside the earth, he stared up at the soil sealing him in. Aboveground, angels of clay, each smaller than the baby, scratched at the hollow's top. Excited, trying to free the creature in the earth.

"Shalafta takes a cut from all these?"

"Yes, but he helps me sell them, and they go toward my bond."

I heard a clatter of shoes. There were women on the roof, walking around in twos and threes. Wearing thick-soled sandals, they sashayed, hugging each other's waists. Their faces were painted thickly, their hair was soot-black and stiff with henna. It was hot in that bath of sun; the melted henna ran down their cheeks. I winced. Some were girls, but most were hags. Their cosmetics made them all look the same age. At the far edge of the roof, I saw tents of rags and clothes hanging to dry, bright-hued and gaudy. Two women who looked strikingly alike undulated toward Joseph, bowing to him. So those were the sisters he'd given a place to live.

The sisters smiled, as if pleased that Joseph was not alone. I saw the frailness in their smiles, I saw their lack of choice. Could I be angry? I tried to smile back, with stiff lips. The painted women bowed to Joseph, whose eyes borrowed gold from the aqueduct and port.

Then they turned away, there was no business for them to do. They clattered back to their tents, and Joseph asked me under his breath, "Will you be married this year?"

"Maybe," I stammered, wondering whether to feel insulted.

He was a bondman. Bondmen were not even free to marry when they wanted.

Just days before, Jerash, the son of Aaron the gang leader, a terror with Nazarene girls, had hurled me against a fence, then hooked his arms around me, spitting in my face. Did I get my bloods yet? Meaning, was I marriageable? He was interested, you see, and I should be so flattered, he was Aaron's son. He expected me to run breathless to my parents now, to tell them he had "proposed!" I scuffled him off me, but he chased me, jeering, "Betoola, betoola!" I dived into our yard, then yelled at Jerash that I'd never lie in his bed, never.

But Joseph was a bondman, not free to marry unless allowed by Shalafta. If Shalafta agreed to our marriage, would we live in Shalafta's house, under the leather switch he whipped his servants with? I knew about that leather switch from my mother.

"I never saw you in Nazareth," I said, as a hold-all answer.

"I live at Shalafta's oil press."

So that was why I never met him before. Shalafta's oil press was by the road to Sepphoris. It was run by Shalafta's two older sisters, who were widows. Joseph was really the widows' bond-man.

The widows were very talked-about characters. The older widow's husband had been bitten by a snake that had crawled into his clothes. He died three days later and left his widow twenty olive trees. She partnered with Shalafta and with that younger sister, also widowed, and by hard work and discipline they made their oil press the most prosperous in Galilee. Shalafta took his cut, of course. I never thought I'd paid attention to those widows, but how easily they came to mind now! They shopped at Nazareth's two Greek stores, on the main street. I even remembered how they moved as they walked to those stores. Well fed, unhurried. Attractive.

Joseph! I thought in panic. *The widows! The widows!*

They were far more dangerous than the whores on the roof. They were Joseph's livelihood, and the passing of other men over them had left no traces. How could they not notice the comely bondman in their yard, Joseph?

Unaware of my turmoil, Joseph talked. "In a year I'll be twenty." An old man. How could I like him? "When I'm twenty, Shalafta will adopt me."

Shalafta had a daughter, but no sons. So Joseph might become the heir of the richest man in Nazareth.

To be truthful, I breathed easier. Because this coincidental, of

Joseph and me being married, would never work if Joseph was a bondman. Say all you will about the poor being rich in virtue and a good servant being like an angel to Adonai our God! What I feared worst about my not finding a husband in Nazareth itself was that my father would ride our donkey to ten villages around Nazareth, seeking doggedly 'til he dug up a mute, a clubfoot, a shrivel-hand whose kin had *money*. And they'd be looking for a dowry-poor daughter like me. Loving me so dearly, my father would rate me healthy for two—that's how Galileans acquired the fame of being mongrels! It would be your mitzvah, Mary, he would say, and your children will not be mute or curly-tongued, if you live a righteous life (in the mute's bed!). And since I'd never marry Jerash (I'd rather jump in a well), Joseph seemed so wonderfully marriageable now.

One year only . . . Brilliant were my thoughts. A year was a long time, but Joseph carved well, and my father was a carpenter, and he could use a helper!

"A year?" I smiled as if I meant a week. I turned over that little me of wood in my hands and smiled at Joseph. What could go wrong between him and me that I couldn't fix in a year?

Nothing!

SOMETHING WENT WRONG, though, only moments thereafter. My father showed up on the roof, looking for me. He saw those painted women, and hissed, "Mary, what are you doing here, near these *zonot*?" I guessed: "porneioi" in Greek meant what "zonot" meant in Aramaic—whores. Like dogs too starved to fear the stick, the painted women leered at my father, while God's coincidental rolled on its own track—as proof of that, who else but Shalafta then showed his broad bald head on the roof? Surprised to find it crowded, he smiled like a puppet pressed in the right spot. "Rabbi

Joachim, I thought you already left the fair. I was looking for Joseph. My bondman, you remember him?"

My father glanced at Joseph. "It's been a long time," my father said. Shalafta, Joseph, and my father nodded at once, and Joseph lowered his eyes like a child trying to escape attention.

My father took my arm and pulled me toward the stairs, tripping on some burned piece of furniture. "When is Aaron going to clean this filth?" he growled. I'd heard him mention to my mother that he and other carpenters bribed Aaron and his gangs to make the insula free of transients.

"When we pay him more," Shalafta said brazenly. Shalafta never paid Aaron.

"Let's go," my father snapped.

The apprentices cleaned our stall, while I threw out the cold pot of gruel, then gathered my father's things—his abacus, his punda, my brooms.

"That dog Shalafta," my father kept saying. "He skins everyone, then he sins with the zonot. He has a daughter that's ready for marriage. You think she doesn't know what kind of father she has?"

I thought, *I don't think that bothers her spoiled life one bit.* For I'd never seen Lanit even bring a pitcher of water from the brook. But I carried water in pails four times a day so there would be enough for my mother's dyeing, for all of us to drink, for all of us to wash before the prayers, before our meals, and each time after we eased ourselves. My hands were blanched from washing, with only three souls under our roof. And if I were blessed to be married, I'd have to wash for a horde of children! *Is that fair, Adonai?*

DRIVING THE CART out of Sepphoris, my father whipped the donkey, which wasn't like him. Ears responded by trotting unusually fast. As usual, I held my sleeve over my eyes as we sped past the nude Greek statues at the crossroads.

We slid into the road back home, and there, among rolling hills and groves of olive trees, my father stopped hitting the donkey. Peasants wished us shalom as we passed. Everyone around here knew my father. Ahead, I could see Mount Barak, its crests green with trees, its peak always wrapped in clouds. For the Nazarenes, Mount Barak was a mountain and a rain-god in one.

I muttered, sounding quite uninterested, "Tell me more about Joseph."

"He and his father took their herds up there." My father pointed to the grassy crests. "Then a storm started, and the lightning hit them. The old man died on the spot, but Joseph still breathed. The shepherds brought him down, and I dug a pit in a field and buried him in it to his neck. So that the lightning in his body would seep into the earth."

I squeaked, "You knew that would work?" I imagined the lightning seeping out of Joseph's body, dripping from his hands, from his fingers.

"I didn't know. But I told myself, If Adonai lets him breathe, he'll let him recover, too."

I felt like hugging my old father. "So he got well?"

"Yes, but very slowly. For a while, he didn't even speak. His mother took up with another man and left Nazareth, and Shalafta took him in as a bondman."

So Joseph owed Shalafta. How could he pass judgment on Shalafta's vileness? But Joseph owed my father, too, more than he owed Shalafta. Even if so many years had passed. "How old was Joseph back then, fifteen?" My father nodded. "So that was right before we went to Jerusalem?"

"Yes. He was already carving back then. He's better than I was at his age." I heard the crisp envy in my father's voice.

"He would've worked for you, had you asked him," I said, and my father blinked. This daughter of his was not stupid! "Now you have this job to do for the prince and you'll pay Shalafta half of what you make. Ask Shalafta to lend you Joseph." That way, I would see Joseph every day, as long as my father worked on that chest! Astounded with my own cleverness, I wondered how long that would be, a few weeks, maybe?

My father's working shed was set behind our house. I would have to go into the shed to bring them water to drink, and their midday meals, which I would cook myself and then carry to the shed, complaining that my chores were hard already, but now that my father had a helper, they were excruciating—brilliant! But then I saw it on my father's face. My brilliant plan wasn't working.

"I shouldn't let anyone peek at that cabinet. The prince wants . . ." He glanced around. No one was close enough to over-hear him. "I'm scared to say it. He wants a chest of setim, three cubits long, one and a half wide, and one and a half tall, with carrying bars overlaid with gold. With two cherubs with spread wings facing each other on the lid. That's the ark of the covenant! What kind of Jew is that prince," my father exploded, "if he wants the ark as his furniture?"

I shrugged, feeling that I was cleverer than my father. Sons of royalty were like that! My father raised the stick to hit the donkey. But something caught his attention; he pointed to a side road. "Shalafta's oil press lies that way."

I'd noticed that road before. I'd never wondered whose property it led to.

The road was narrow, but built of even stones with a filling of gravel, and the bushes on the sides were lush, well watered. I couldn't see the olive trees, they lay beyond, but the feeling was one of quiet, industrious richness.

"Joseph should walk away from Shalafta," my father said. "Shalafta's a copperhead snake, the air he breathes out is poison." I knew this wasn't about Joseph. Even today, my father couldn't stand that my mother had been Shalafta's bondwoman. I countered obnoxiously, "You breathe the air around Shalafta quite well."

"Mary! I would not have met the prince without Shalafta."

"I was about to remind you of that."

I felt like tickling my sweet old father, and then telling him what happened in my mind, for it was amazing. I was angry that I hadn't peeked at those Greek statues. I could have judged from their naked shapes what a man of Joseph's age should look like! By Nazareth's standards, Joseph was already old. But did that mean that he was *slow*? Did that mean he was ripening slowest in those parts I'd never looked at?

I prayed silently. *Ripen slowly, Joseph, because I'm not ready, either!*

And I put my arms around my father's neck. He was sweaty. The years had made his body soft, he had the smell of an old man. I didn't care. I loved him.

Stay like this, my father. Don't grow any older. And don't ever die.

Part 5

The Promise

W E SLEPT on our roof in summertime, unless it rained.

So goes a Galilean proverb: After dark, you get to know your neighbors.

Late spring and through summer, the Nazarenes slept on their roofs like in one oversize bed. Our homes were clumped together, for they had been built as additions to older homes by the youngsters after they got married. Houses leaned on each other. The roofs touched like sleepers in a crowded bed.

So I knew all our neighbors by the noises they made at night. I knew who coughed, who snored, who farted. I heard sleepwalkers rise under the glassy moon and trudge away—luckily they stumbled on relatives before they fell to their crippling deaths. Men and women awoke to ease themselves; the men and boys lurched to the edge of the roofs and pissed in the yards below, urine that would be cleaned by the cool dew of dawn. The women brought night pots for themselves and their daughters. Pesky little brothers stole night pots from little sisters too afraid to wake their parents, for they'd get the fatherly switch on their little rumps—the boys hurled the pots in the yard, and the sisters pouted and scrambled after the pots.

Before the appearance of what-I-should-be-so-thankful-for (my highly prized bloods), I was allowed to sleep nights with various friends. I slept on Orpa's busy roof; she was an only child, but her mother had three sisters, all married with children, all

119

sharing that one roof. Sometimes, Orpa and I slept at Lanit's, who dazzled us with a roof with a real bed (for herself; we guests slept on hay pallets). I liked it better at Orpa's, whose mother told bedtime stories, while Orpa and I giggled and whispered about *everything*, from getting married to the one true God. I taught Orpa how to close her eyes, then suddenly open them, and she would see angels. I assured her that a girl could see angels if she prayed hard enough. But Orpa just wasn't the kind to see angels—too bad. We still lay in each other's arms and talked 'til dawn, and she said again and again, "I wish we were sisters." And I said, "We are, Orpa, you're the sister I always wanted."

Orpa didn't have siblings, either (another coincidental). From then on we would feel like sisters forever—until of course, some man came along and made us betray our sisterhood, but that, too, was in the way of all flesh.

SUCH WERE MY thoughts, after we came back from the carpenters' fair. I helped my grumpy mother grill tilapia fish for us to eat. Each time I moved, Joseph's carving moved in my sleeve, scratching my forearm or pinching my elbow—not roughly, though. Making me remember Joseph's golden eyes.

My mother kept glancing at me, wondering why I was so excited as I washed the dishes and spread the bedsheets on the roof. She thought she knew why, however, when my father told her that he'd been hired by the prince. Then we all lay down, and I folded my arm under my cheek and breathed the scent of that carving in my sleeve.

My parents slept near me, oblivious. My mother with her face up, legs straight out, arms tight by her sides. Filling what she needed of the roof, not an inch more. My father slept facing my mother with one of his hands touching the crown of her head, as if craving her nearness. There was no one else on the roof.

I WAS AWAKENED by our bitch, Lintra, barking beyond our back gate. I knew her bark. She had scooted under the gate, into the wild brush with setim trees.

I stood up on the roof. The moon, just a nick before full, hovered above me.

Out in the brush, someone was walking toward our back gate, stepping with a wide step. A man. He came from outside the village, across the desert brush.

As I debated whether to wake my father, Lintra jumped at the stranger. He moved quickly, dropping to the ground, catching her and rubbing her under her chin. When he stood up again, she beat her tail against his knees. The man was Joseph! Joseph leaned onto the latticed back gate that I opened every morning to let our goats out to graze.

I gripped the branch of an acacia tree that touched our roof. I could've gotten down from the roof by using the ladder, but I climbed that acacia so often as a child, its branches were polished from my palms.

I jumped down, ran to the gate, and right away I smelled him. I'd smelled a boy turning into a man before. Soiled and spicy.

I pulled the lattice open. "You have a way with yard dogs," I whispered.

He nodded, and his eyes filled his face.

He had put on a clean shift. I could tell from its collar; it had been starched with turnip skins boiled in water. I knew how to make that starch, too. The one who'd made it for Joseph had to be one of the widows.

121

I didn't ask how he found out where we lived. I was too aware of the moon shining on both of us. Moon, woman, man. "You wanted to tell me something, Joseph?"

"Yes," he said, and both of us caught our breaths at the same time.

He touched my hand, and I jumped.

"You're so frightened."

Yes, I was frightened. Of all men, and of this man, Joseph.

So I smiled and prayed that he would say to me, I couldn't wait any longer, Mary, I had to race here in the dead of night to tell you that I'll break my bond with Shalafta and start my own carving business and marry you right away—why wait a year? If he said that, I'd wake up my parents to ask their blessing.

He said, "The prince is sleeping at the oil press tonight."

"Huh?"

"He wanted to see your father's work, so he and his two servants headed to Nazareth. But it got dark. They stopped at the press, and the widows took them in for the night. I just served him dinner. He's asleep now, but tomorrow he'll be here."

"That's what you rushed to tell me?"

"Yes. And also . . ."

He spoke with a flame in his eyes, which I found so pretty, lit up in the lakes of his eyes by the moon. "Your father has the best saws and planes and pliers and awls. I could help your father build that chest."

So, what did that mean? Did he just want to improve his carving skills? Then why had he asked me if I would be married soon—because I was this carver's daughter? But I couldn't ask those questions, all I could do was comment, as calm and collected as I could: "So you like carving that much?"

"Yes. I want to make big statues, of wood, of stone. Like the Greeks." He grinned, happy that he had told me what he most wanted. So I made myself smile. "But the widows won't let you leave the press."

"Of course they will. They do what I tell them. Oh. Yes." He had remembered something important. "The prince wants your father to build him a sukkah. He'll sleep at your house, but in a sukkah."

"But it's not Sukkot yet." Sukkot, the festival of the harvest, was one of our most important holidays. It was the celebration of the bounty of nature, a result of the earth fecundated by water. So for seven days the drinking of water became a religious duty. Children walked around with bellies swollen from slurping water with sugarcane in it, an enticement to keep drinking.

I touched Joseph's arm with one finger. His shift was tight on him.

I took my finger back. Joseph whispered, "The widow Irit asked the prince, 'You never had a sukkah when you grew up?' And he said, 'No, never.'"

"Which one is Irit, the younger one?"

"No, the older one."

Of course, I knew which one she was.

Irit was thirty at the most. And Joseph said her name with such familiar ease! What if he *does it* with her? I thought suddenly, and the thought bit my heart. Being slow was just a rumor. Perhaps he did it with both of the widows!

I lowered my eyes and whispered, "All right, I'll speak to my father about you. Go now."

"Can't I sleep here?" He pointed at the dry grass under his feet.

Our dog, Lintra, reappeared out of some fold of the night. She wagged her tail. I felt like kicking her, but instead stroked her between her ears. "Joseph . . . what's the prince like?"

"You'll see. Good night." He lunged away, into the nearest setim trees.

"*Wait.*" *So rude! When I meet the prince, he might fancy me, Joseph—would you not care?* "Joseph?" I was afraid of being heard by my parents. Joseph stepped back from those trees. I took a deep breath. "On my father's side, I come from Matthan, who came from Levi, who came from Melchi and from Jannai, from Esli . . . from Semein, Joseh, Joda . . ." Joseph stood right before me; I started stammering the names. "Z-zerub-babel, Shhh . . . Shaltiel, Addi, Cosam, Elmadam . . . Simeon, Judah . . . Eliakim, Melea, Nathan . . ." My father had taught me our bloodline, forward and backward. "All of them from"—with soft pride—"David!"

"That David?"

I nodded.

The king above all kings, his blood begat my blood.

Those were my ancestors on my father's side. On my mother's . . . Who bothered to trace them? Nameless poor folk who sold her into bondage. My dear mother, she had just sewed me a special set of clothes, *levoosh dameem,* my "blood clothes." All white. For when I would show up on the main street in clothes new and white, with mother by my side also wearing white. Behold, Nazareth, this girl is marriageable! And from David! I lingered here, *begging*—well, almost—for this boy to notice me, when everyone in Nazareth would say, as I walked in white, "Joachim's daughter? Ah, yes. Well, she's not dowry, but she's *lineage!*" And tomorrow, the blood prince will be a guest in our home! Starting tomorrow, I'll be so talked about. Which

Mary, *that* Mary? I suddenly felt so proud, I could fall in love with me, too!

And Joseph, he searched my face and asked, "What are you doing? Raising your price?"

"Me?" I marveled. "I thought you'd like to know who I am."

And I threw a punch at his strapping chest. I didn't even shake him.

He turned and walked behind a setim tree. I rushed after him, bumped into him in the dark. My face in his face, my lips near his lips. To keep his balance, he locked his arms around me, and I shivered from his arms; they were so muscled, so soothing and safe and so troubling all at once. I breathed in his face, "Are you *slow?*"

He stared at me, and whispered, "I let people think that I am."

"Why?"

He let go of me, and I shivered. "You're so afraid of men. Why?" he asked. I brushed my hair off my forehead. I swallowed the lump in my throat, wondering, was I indeed? And how plainly did that show?

And I heard myself tell Joseph, yes, I was. I'd been terrified of men since one time when I was nine, when I witnessed the ordeal of a bride found not whole before her marriage. Dragged by her hair, along that street of shame that we lived on for a year, in Jerusalem. Dragged to her death by stoning, by her own father and by a whole enraged crowd, while the bridegroom stepped along, too, yelling, *"Kesef! Kesef!"* Asking for money from the bride's clan, to restore his honor.

I stopped talking. I felt so frightened, I heard my teeth click.

Joseph took my hand. My palm twitched in his.

125

I don't know when I finally moved; maybe Joseph, among his other mysterious gifts, could make us move together without me even knowing it? I found myself sitting on the grass next to him, with my hand in his.

Had I wanted to pull my hand free, I could have done it, but I didn't even try to free my hand.

We sat facing my father's house, dark and silent, and I told him the worst of what that nine-year-old, me, had lived that day.

Everyone on our street of shame was out that day, running after that crowd, trying to guess how the ordeal would end. Would they take the soiled bride into the temple's Women's Court, and punish her there? Outside the Women's Court, a breed of gypsies, *tsoaneem,* sold stones out of their carts. Broken stones, light enough to throw, heavy enough to kill. *God, please God,* I prayed as I ran behind that screaming crowd, *have them flog the soiled bride, but not stone her! Have them feed her that boglike water for wives accused of infidelity!* Under the third marble slab of the next court, the first court of the men, there was a pit of sludge. Wives accused of cheating were forced to drink that sludge, which ailed their stomachs horribly, but only some of them died. In despair, I tripped and fell, and staggered up again.

As I did so, half hidden behind a portico's pillars, I glimpsed a man who watched that crowd, too, as it dragged that girl past him. He was young and handsome. He seemed so bitter and conflicted, perhaps ravaged by pity, perhaps kind in his heart, and yet, he didn't move to stop that crowd. The father of the bride let go of the unfortunate's hair and fell on his knees in the street. He was handed a loaf of bread. He rubbed the bread onto the grimy pavement, then bit from it. "See me, clansmen and strangers, see me eat *lechem booshah,* the bread of shame, because my daughter shamed me!" That stranger stood and watched, with the midday sun shining on his dark hair and on his earrings; as his clothes were rich, but his adornment un-Jewish, I guessed that he was part of the royal court. Hellenized in garb and customs. The father dropped the soiled bread and grabbed his daughter again, while that stranger, biting his lips, I noticed, strode away in the opposite direction, and passersby made room for him.

My sight was so blurred with tears I closed my eyes. But those three men loomed behind my eyelids, I would never forget them. The father who ate the bread of shame and beat his chest. The callous bridegroom, claiming money while the bride had less than an hour to live. (I knew what an hour was. The Romans beat a drum on the roof of Antonia once, loud and clear, at the end of each hour.) And that stranger. Why was he there? What did he have to do with that girl's shame?

Staggering up the street, across thinner crowds, I made it to our rented room.

Neither of my parents was at home. My father was working, overseeing a building team at the temple. My mother had left early with two baskets of her dyed fabrics to sell door-to-door in the upper city.

I sat on the bare floor of our room and stared at the wall, which was part of the temple's wall.

All I could think of was that ahead was the temple, in which abided the soul of our God Adonai, the only one. And our God Adonai had allowed this to happen.

Adonai, why? Adonai, how could you?

As that girl had been dragged past me, I had noticed how pretty she was. But she had a tiny disfigurement, a little scar across her upper lip. Her features were lingering on my face. I lifted my hand and touched my upper lip. My face was the one I knew. But my soul had changed in one morning, forever.

I cried quietly. *Adonai, why? Answer me, say something! Are you ever accountable, Adonai, for the suffering you inflict on people? And especially on the ones you shaped as your vessels of life, the women? Say something, do something! My father believed in you all his life, he taught the Torah with unshakeable faith, he believed in your heavenly hosts, though I know that you never showed him even the tip of an angel's wing (for he would've told me!). So for all the times you showed him nothing, show me something, now!*

And then an amazingly brilliant little creature, shaped like a child but with wings green and transparent like a giant grasshopper's, tumbled down the temple wall.

An angel, I thought. The best possible proof that I had lost my mind.

"I know," I said to the angel. "She's dead, isn't she?"

"Yes. But she's not in pain, nor alone, nor sad."

"Thank you for telling me that," I said. "What is your name?"

"I'm Armisael, the angel of births and pregnancies. I'm pleased that you are feeling better. Speak to me."

"Was the tainted bride pregnant?"

"No."

Oh, good. The thought of a second life being extinguished I found unbearable.

"She wasn't punished," he said. "Death isn't a punishment."

"Then why are people so afraid of dying?"

"They're afraid that in death, they'll forget those they loved."

"You mean, be forgotten by them?"

"Yes, but their worst fear is that *they, too,* will forget. Forgetting love, that's the worst fear. Of course, I'm an angel, I never died nor loved, I'm not speaking from experience."

"I have a question. Why did God put so much pain and uneasiness in the love between men and women?"

He thought about it and said, "What you're asking me is about God's ultimate will. And about that, only he knows." He sat on the floor, and the floor planks lit from the flesh of his buttocks, which were flesh made of light.

"Mary," he said. I shivered, because he said my name sweetly. "*You* ask God."

I gasped and jabbed my thumb at my chest. "Me? If I ask him, would he answer me?" The angel shrugged good-naturedly. "Maybe, why not?" "Am I insane?" I asked him, and he laughed. "Because you see me and hear me? Don't you have thousands of thoughts every day? You never see your thoughts. But you know that you have them."

"It's not the same," I said, though his demonstration seemed astute and simple.

"It is. Here's some proof that I exist. Hear me laugh."

And he laughed with trills. Wonderful, melodious trills.

"You must laugh, Mary, you must laugh even as you cry, for this life is all that you're given. And laughing makes your heart breathe freely. Remember that." And then he vanished like the flame of a candle snuffed out by a thumb, and I wondered what to do—Forgive Hashem? Not forgive him?—until my mother and father came home.

I rushed into my mother's arms as if pursued by ghosts, and it took my father's strong hands to unclasp me from her.

My parents had heard, out on the streets, about the end of

the tainted bride. Her wedding would have meant the union of two Hasmonean clans, which the king found threatening. To stop the wedding, the king had decided that the bride must be seduced and exposed. So she had been.

Not long thereafter, due to his own strife with the king, my father was banished from the temple and from the holy city.

WHAT JOSEPH THOUGHT, as I sputtered all that, I couldn't guess. I said it roughly, I said it with deep feeling, I said it with a kind of vengeful passion. You, too, Joseph, are of the male breed! That's what men do to women! Yet with my hand resting in his, while my passion and pain made his eyes brighten, then dim again, he was with me, holding his breath, not missing one word.

I stopped talking.

Then he muttered, "I'm telling people I'm slow, because it makes it easier. They work me less hard, they don't mind me around their wives and daughters . . ."

I laughed nervously. Why did he say that? Maybe just to change my mood?

He opened his hand, showing mine snuggled in the dip of his palm. Like a little bird. You can fly away now, you're free. I lifted my hand, and it felt replenished and comforted.

"Put all that out of your mind," Joseph said, with moon-glow on his face. "Think that it never happened."

"It did happen."

"But you weren't who you are now. Why don't you bring me a sheet to sleep on?"

I stood up. He didn't move. I turned and walked to the house.

* * *

I GROPED IN the dark for the lid of our linen chest, lifted it. I dug
my arms into the linen, perfumed with lavender flowers pressed
between the folds by my mother.

I pulled out a bedsheet and walked out again.

I walked to the setim trees. I didn't see Joseph.

Had he gone back to the oil press?

I went around a setim tree and found Joseph asleep, leaning his back against the rugged trunk, snoring. *Ppffff-brrrrr,
ppffff-brrrrr.* But what man isn't a snorer? My father snored far
louder than Joseph.

I spread the sheet. Now, how could I put Joseph on it without waking him?

I had to move him.

Of all of the parts of him I could get hold of, I chose his
head. Large and heavy and warm, too. Oh, what a nice toy a man
would be, were he powerless like this in a woman's hands! Oh,
God! I had dropped his head.

He grunted a little. But he was still asleep.

I rolled him onto the sheet, in pieces, so to speak. Heaving
at one end of him, then at the other end. Still pretty frightening,
that he was so big and robust. *Don't make me think of that,
Adonai, don't!*

So. He'd be here in the morning, and I'd get him hired as a
helper if I had to nag my father 'til he whipped me. And if Joseph
worked with zest, then I would point out to my mother and father that Joseph could make us money. So, during his apprentice-
ship, Joseph should settle in our yard—where else, poor soul,
since he was orphaned on both sides—and we'd make him a bed
in the work shed. And since Joseph was *slow*—everyone knew
that—it would be no danger to my maidhood that we suddenly

had this strapping young man around the house. And then . . . as God might take pity on a man's slowness, maybe Joseph would become *not so slow*? All of which would finally lead to our marriage? Was that unachievable? No, of course not!

Grinning to myself, I got back in the yard, climbed on the roof, and lay down, clutching Joseph's carving in my hand.

But then I set it by me on the roof. I had this strange desire to mix nothing with the feel of Joseph's hand on my hand.

God Eternal, are you meaning something for me, with all this? Hands were . . . Well, they were . . . I didn't know how to word it. They were . . .

Then I lay sleepless, and thought of that mysterious child whom Joseph had carved in that womb of earth.

I cringed. *God, don't punish me for this! I'll never think this again, I swear, but . . . that baby mentioned in Isaiah, I feel that he's the same baby, and he's reaching up to me, through blind blankets of the earth . . .*

From under me, from under our roof of clay layered over wood beams, from our home's foundations and further below, deeper, deeper still, do I hear a kind of promise?

Adonai, I know, I know. I haven't lived enough, nor loved enough. I have no wisdom, no tools, I'm not ready. But I want me to beget him, the one who will free us. The one who will come one day, the one who will lick away our pains! Me! Don't punish me, Adonai! But it's not only because I fear men (which I do), because I fear a man's flesh in my own body (and I do)—that I wish and yearn, I yearn and wish . . .

Terrified, I put words to my thoughts: *I wish you had asked Eve what she felt, what she wanted—don't strike me!—so you could improve the fate of women just the tiniest bit. Oh, Lord, my Lofty*

Lord! You made Eve in your mind before you made her from the rib!
You thought her up and then made her and saw that she was good;
but couldn't you ask her, How do you, woman, mean to live? How do
you think it's best and fruitfulest for you to live and love? Are you
angry? Hashem, are you? Speak to me, don't hold me in dire fire that
I insulted you. All I want, Hashem, is to help!

He didn't say anything.

Yet I felt that he wasn't angry.

He was quiet, attentive. He'd opened worlds and parted
skies to be able to hear what I was saying.

My tears overcame me . . . I was no one, but I was being listened to.

So I was *the one,* for a brief instant, just by desiring to be the
one. He did not turn me into a pillar of salt, he didn't even scold
me. He let me feel I was the one.

I smiled. And I fell asleep.

I woke up. Lying in a warm pool of sunshine. I peeled open one
eyelid.

Hearing the yammering of a crowd, I opened my other
eyelid.

I heard Shalafta's voice and then Aaron's voice. Both of
them sounded so insistent: *"Hod ma'alah, hod ma'alah!* Highness,
Highness!"

The prince was here!

He got up early, I thought, jumping up grumpily. I glanced
to our front gate. People, everyone in the village, it seemed, were
walking toward our yard. My mother and father stood by that
gatepost, nicked over the years with my body height. I spun
around to look at the back gate. Joseph was lifting the lattice to

step in. I motioned frantically that he should not cross the yard, but steal along the goats' path, into the street, and pop into view like he had just arrived. He did exactly as I wished.

I turned toward the front gate again. Aaron the gang leader, who was our village smith (he made the very knives he used in killing and robbing), tramped beside the prince, a young man with shiny, dark hair worn short, Roman-style. Shalafta tramped on the prince's other side. Both he and Aaron squeaked, "Stay in my home, highness! No, no, in *my* home!" Two men-servants, young, wearing boots, stepped behind prince Aristobulus, who waved his jeweled hand to silence Aaron and Shalafta. "Thank you both, the house of my servant Joachim will do fine." Down at the gate, my mother turned and glared. Where's my foot-dragging daughter? I rushed down as if hit with a rug-beater. I had to take out our cow, which we tied in the house overnight, then clean the house. Soak the floors with boiled water, then mop them, quick, one, two, three! About to dive into the house . . .

I stopped.

The prince . . .

Yesterday, because of the fair's crowdedness, I had barely glimpsed his face. Now I could see him well. He wore twinkling earrings. I had seen him in Jerusalem, hiding behind that pillar. Watching the doomed bride.

Part 6

The Snake

I SCALDED MY hands with the hot cleaning water. I mopped the floors so hard, I broke the mop's handle.

So I got down on all fours and scoured with my hands.

Maybe he had nothing to do with that girl.

My mother rushed into the room and told me to put out some fruit. Pomegranates. Had she lost her wits? Pomegranates were too dear for my father's purse, maybe we had apples. But I said yes, while my mother poured the hot water left in my mopping pail into the washbasin, then washed her face and her arms, then combed her hair and tied it. Then she put on clean clothes, moving like quicksilver. I was moving the same way.

The prince had told my father that he wanted to take his chest to Rome (where he was headed next!), so it had to be ready in two days. Joseph was drafted as a helper on the spot. My father hurried to his work shed; he was moving with pride. Armed with my father's best ax, Joseph darted off to fell setim trees.

Most of our neighbors still milled outside our gate, trying to glimpse the prince. Aaron peered into our yard through the picket fence. His face was filled with awe. How often would a thug like him get to see the king's son in his neighbor's yard? When the crowd began to thin, I had scoured the floor planks, polished the mezuzahs on every door, dusted the doorjambs and windowsills and the doorsteps. The mezuzahs, of wood, had been chiseled by my father. Every inch of wood in the house had been carved by my father and cleaned by Mother or by me countless times.

The door opened.

Prince Aristobulus walked the steaming floor planks toward me, sized me up, and his earrings twinkled just like five years ago—or was I going insane?

"Your name is Mary-amneh, yes? Like my mother's."

That cleaning rag was still in my hand. I dropped it to the floor.

"My father and king, he brought my mother to an early end. He smothered her with a pillow, until her breathing stopped. Is that known in Nazareth?"

Said without one twitch, peering at me through the steam from the floor. My shift was all wet. My hair weighed damply on my shoulders.

He moved with a kind of sideways flow, glancing over his shoulder, like a man used to watching his back. Shorter than Joseph, maybe a finger taller than I, but lean and muscled. A snake, when it's aroused, sits up on its tail, so as to strike. Why was I thinking of a snake?

He looked at the walls' tethering rings. "You keep your cattle in the house?"

"At night, yes, or they get stolen."

"Why are you covering your mouth? You lost a tooth?"

My hand was over my upper lip. I dropped it to my side.

"Senators Vedius and Asinius Pollio will be our hosts in Rome, mine and my brother Alexander's. Vedius read the book of the Jews." He grinned. "Our book, yours and mine. It's fairly well known in Rome."

"As entertainment, Highness?"

He smiled. "You're not stupid. Yes, to the Romans our book is like a bawdy tale. Who begat, and who begat, and who went into what servant. My brother Alexander does not care for the book, but I keep reading it with awe and fear. I am a Jew, as my mother was my father's one Jewish queen. Do I remember you from Sepphoris?"

"I don't know . . . I was there . . . Uh, what are the Romans like?"

"They put no worth on a woman's virgin piece, while we Jews kill if we find it missing." He leaned closer to me. "There's this fashion in Rome, they sew girls back to being virgins before marriage. Maybe that's due to our book? Find a quiet place where you and I can talk."

"What's there to talk about?"

He laughed. My mother stepped in with a dish of sliced watermelon. The prince looked at it and told her he never ate watermelon. His father said it was food for camels. "But today, I'll try it." He picked a piece, put it in his lips. My mother gave me the dish to hold for him. "With your permission, Highness."

She ran back to the kitchen. He wanted to spit the melon, I could tell. He caught himself and swallowed it.

"Your clan is from David, yes? David took Uriah's wife Bathsheba, and had Uriah killed. But what was she doing, Bathsheba, bathing naked where the king could see her? Wasn't she enticing the king? But, *ssshhh!* . . . Can we question God's ways? He made your lineage rife with *khet*, sin, Mary-amneh, yet Mashiah is supposed to come from your lineage, despite all that khet. God never punished David. He didn't punish my father for the murder of my mother, either. I have so much to tell to you, Mary-amneh. Find a lone place for us."

Through the open window, a shadow fell into the room. Joseph, carrying a string with knots to measure those setim trunks. He leaned in, spoke to me. "Your father's drawing the cherubs, you want to come see the drawings?"

"Yes."

Joseph looked at the prince, then at me, then smiled as if saying to me, "Your father's the master here, and this man's only a guest."

"Yes. I'll be right there."

Joseph bowed good-naturedly and walked off.

The prince teased one earring with his thumb. "You like him? Look, you blushed!" he cried out like a prankish boy. "He served us at dinner last night. The older widow, she got drunk and said to me, 'Joseph is useless in bed.' So don't save yourself for him, Mary-amneh. You want to be my servant in Jerusalem? You'd live a lavish life."

I saw myself in a lavish bed with a midwife raising a pretty child toward my face. His child.

I said before I could bite my tongue, "We'd live with the one who killed your mother?"

Behind his eyes, something moved. A twisted soul. He put his jeweled hand out toward me. It met a patch of steam, parted it, landed on my shoulder . . . He lowered his voice. "I'll kill my father, or he'll kill me, it's that easy. But you could help me, maybe? You're from the lineage, and you have my mother's name, isn't that a sign? You might beget a child like no other, why not do it in my palace?"

"Th-that would be a good story to tell in Rome . . . ," I stuttered.

He laughed. "Indeed. Why don't you start saying that you

received signs, Mary-amneh? That you'll give birth to a holy child. And you and your people are on my side and I deserve to be king. When my mother was killed I was ten; I slept in dread every night thereafter. I had to learn how to kill, so that my father wouldn't kill me. I had other people killed. Innocent people, Mary-amneh. So as to buy myself another year of life, and another year." He stood so close, I heard his earrings clink. "Could your father start saying that you're the one foretold? And he and you and all your kin desire me to take the throne? When I am king, I'll make your father the highest priest in Jerusalem."

That hand on my shoulder, it felt me through my wet shift.

I moaned. "That foretelling may not be for many years . . . and who knows if it will happen at all?"

"Can't your father say that it will happen during my reign, Mary-amneh?"

I turned and ran out of the room, into the yard. Over our back gate, I saw Joseph felling a setim.

Aristobulus raced out behind me, right on my heels. "What do you say, Mary-amneh? David's son Absalom rose against his father. But David killed Absalom, then lamented, 'Oh, Absalom, my wayward son, why did you rise against me?' Even though he killed his own son, David wasn't cursed in God's eyes! Is David's blood blameless in God's eyes? You're from that blood, Mary-amneh. We should be one, you and I, so I, too, would be blameless!"

I raced beyond the gate, then glanced back at him. Aristobulus had stopped. Though he was so pretty, there was something gangly about him, his short hair was tousled on his head—it looked like a scared animal's . . .

Joseph had eased his shoulders out of his shift. He wore a

piece of netting over his face, against flying splinters. He raised his arms, his ax glinted, his muscles swelled . . . I suddenly heard the tree. It spoke, just like a human. "I don't want to die, I don't want to die! Maybe next spring, I'll topple over in a big storm, when the snow thaws on Mount Barak and rushes down like a river, turning the scrub around Nazareth into a swamp. I'll die then. I want to live another year, even as a cripple. This is such a beautiful morning, I didn't expect the ax!" But Joseph gave it one last whack so mighty, I heard the ax pry from its handle. That waist of whittled wood, thinner and thinner, it broke. I gave a shout, Joseph jumped to save me from the toppling tree.

We fell to the ground. The tree fell beside us. It died.

Joseph pulled me to my feet. He held my arm, and I tottered back into the yard.

The prince had just left with his servants.

THE PRINCE WORKED the village. In the shade of our unfinished new synagogue, he met with our rabbis and told them that he'd be the best king for us, he would lower the taxes (yes!), donate land to the poorest Jews (yes! yes!), and ask Rome to withdraw its armies (yes! yes! yes!). If Mashiah arose, he would welcome Mashiah to Jerusalem, offer him the highest priestly office (amen! amen!), and even dismiss the priesthood as we knew it. Let Mashiah form his own priesthood.

Now our rabbis stopped cheering, worried that they, too, might be dismissed. They started shouting. Mashiah was not the prince's concern, he should leave that issue to the rabbis, all the prince needed to do was live as a true Jew. Just then Joseph and I walked along, pulling two donkeys to the unfinished synagogue, to load them with cut-up planks. My father's wood supply was getting low already. We passed the prince and the rabbis yelling at him. Aristobulus looked like a tomcat doused with dishwater. So I couldn't help but whisper to him, "Forget these old men, win over the women and the girls. Buy them trinkets, throw pennies to their children." Then I pointed to the nearest Greek store, and Aristobulus rushed into it.

"What was that about?" Joseph scowled at me.

I stepped on. I tried to pick up a plank and got a splinter in my finger. Joseph pulled on a pair of gloves from my father, loaded planks onto the donkeys until he bent their backs, and scowled again. "You just told me what a snake that man is, and now you help him?"

Then he sat me down and picked that splinter out of my hand. "What does he want from you, anyway?"

"What do *you* want from me?"

He said nothing.

Take me in your arms, I thought. *See what happens. You dimwit. Maybe you are a dimwit.*

He looked at me with those golden eyes he had on the roof in Sepphoris.

Then I reached and touched Joseph's cheek. He closed his eyes. *That's good,* I thought. I was suddenly full of confidence. *I'll awake you, Joseph, if I have to use that snake with earrings to do it!*

"Are we done here?" I whispered.

He handed me the gloves and grabbed the harnesses, pulling both donkeys with his bare hands. Was that to show me that he was manly?

We walked the donkeys back into the main street. The prince had bought cheap earrings and necklaces at the Greek store. He came out with those necklaces hung on his arms, and the girls and women jumped from everywhere. He chatted them up. Joseph grumbled, "Where are their husbands? Why are they letting them talk to him?" "Why is that your business, Joseph?" I countered. I felt suddenly cheerful. *Learn from the prince, Joseph. Learn from the snake.*

Aristobulus was making promises to the women. He would fund a charity for Jewish widows and mothers with more than five children. He would let Israelite women testify in courts . . . if their fathers or husbands agreed. Our law said no Israelite women could testify in courts under any circumstances. Orpa and all my other friends had ditched their duties, clustering in the street, hanging from the prince's lips. He told wives to complain to the king's courts if they were beaten at home . . . but only if their fathers, or other male relatives, cotestified that they were beaten *without need*! Orpa looked at me, and we both rolled our eyes. Orpa had two older sisters who got drubbed regularly by their husbands, yet Orpa's father never interfered. Because women, Orpa's father argued, were sharp of tongue while men were not, so men had to use their fists to defend themselves from those women's sharp tongues.

Up to this time, Nazareth's men had kept to their yards. The king's son was trying to ingratiate their wives? So let him. He'd go away and the wives would stay here, *heh heh*. Until the talk turned to wife-beating; then the men stepped into the street, calling to their wives. The babies were crying undiapered, the food was spoiling uncooked, and besides, when did a husband beat his wife *without need* in our saintly Nazareth? Don't teach us how to run our lives here, beloved prince! The wives trailed home, casting moist glances at Aristobulus. He'd tried.

Holding on to the donkeys' harnesses, Joseph whispered to

me, "I would never beat you, Mary, ever. Whether with need or without need!" And I was so touched, I rewarded Joseph with my best smile.

So, we trekked back to my father's yard, to resume our chores. He in the work shed, I in the kitchen.

Later, carrying a water pitcher, I walked to the work shed and peered in. The outline of the chest was a wonder. Reeking of sweat, my father and Joseph bent over it like worshippers, and Joseph argued with my father. "The cherubs on the lid are too small, Rabbi. Too small."

"How would you know the size of cherubs?" my father replied.

As I stood in the doorway with the pitcher, Joseph glanced up and was so happy, my Joseph, that I was there! It couldn't be—it couldn't be that he was worthless with women—he was so full of zest for working, how could he not to be zestful for *me*? Joseph, you're ready, you just don't know it. Smile at me, *now*!

He smiled, as if on cue. I set the pitcher near him, and went back to the kitchen without feeling the ground under my feet.

MOTHER MADE FOOD for half the village. With help from the widows Ava and Irit, who came over bedecked in their best and begged Mother to let them help, since they knew from last night what the prince liked and didn't like.

Shalafta was going to sit with us at dinner—who could shake him off? Green with envy that he was not the prince's host, he offered to slaughter four sheep for dinner, but I told Orpa to have her father gore four sheep and five three-month-old lambs, which did not smell of piss in their innards as grown sheep do. Then I told Shalafta, "Thank you, but we have no need." "I'll bring the wine," he said, "if you seat me and my Lanit with the prince." I took a breath, and said, "Rabbi Shalafta, you must be joking! You want your unwedded daughter at the men's table? Aren't we helping the prince catch up on true Jewishness? Not even my mother will sit at the men's table, she'll be running back and forth serving, as I will be. We need all the help we can muster. Is Lanit in the kitchen yet, helping?"

You should have seen his face!

I left him, went into the kitchen, and saw the widow Irit slaving by my mother. An attractively aging woman, light on her feet, not too chesty, and with a round face, which is good against wrinkles. She had been a fetching girl once. And she was working her bottom off, trust my mother on that. Fuming, Shalafta slithered into the kitchen, and muttered for my mother to hear. Was it not khet for the prince to show off that arklike chest in Rome? If the king heard about it, wouldn't my father be held responsible? Ah, you vile, skulking lizard! Who brought this job to my father, and who will take half the money for it? But again, I stepped right up and said, "The prince *should* show his Jewishness in Rome, and if it be with an arklike chest, it's God's will!" My father couldn't have said it better.

The widow Irit tried to chat me up. I turned and stepped out of the kitchen.

What else?

Ah, yes. Aaron, the gang master, with his son Jerash who both arrived in clean shifts and looking hungry. And Aaron asked me meekly if there was room at my father's table (which would be the prince's table) for himself and his son? If only I could have replied, *How many of our goats have you stolen already, Rabbi Aaron, so that we tether our animals inside our home at night? How many bribes have you squeezed from my father to protect his business, and he was still robbed and held at knifepoint?* With my eyes, I said it. He heard it, for he mumbled: What a lavish repast my mother was preparing, he could tell from the smell, and the tables were set beautifully. And since the prince brought only two servants and no bodyguards, Aaron's clan would ensure that we were all safe at dinner—

I cut him off. "Why, Rabbi Aaron, you're such a man of the law all of a sudden. I'll see if we have room."

I went into the kitchen. Irit tried to chat with me again. I went back out while she was still talking to me.

"We have room, Rabbi Aaron. You and your son are welcome."

Jerash, in sandals that were pinching his feet—I could tell by how he was shuffling—looked at me as if he'd never seen me before. *Did I look different, Adonai?* Jerash was ogling me, not like when he pushed me against that fence. Like he truly valued me. Wonderful.

What else did I need to do? Oh, yes.

I pulled my mother out of the kitchen—let the other women break their backs—I took her inside the house, brought a washbasin, washed her hands myself. I washed her arms and, because she still smelled of cooking, had her stand in the basin naked and poured water on her, then oil, then water again. Then I worked her with a towel. I kneaded and softened the skin on her face and around her tired eyes.

She said, "Tomorrow, if we have any time to breathe, you put on your bridal clothes, and we walk around."

I choked up. She and I walking from the Greek stores to the unfinished synagogue and from the synagogue to Aaron's smithery and back again. With my mother all in white and wearing sandals, and me all in white, too, and wearing sandals, signaling that mother was ready to listen to proposals, which she would report to my father, the master of our house and of Mother and me. Rich girls would wear jewelry and perfumed sandals on this occasion, but for Mother and me clean white linen and sandals would still look festive. I had so longed for that day. It would happen, tomorrow!

"And, Mary? The widows want to buy my dyed dresses."

"That's good."

"If I make better money . . ." She corrected herself, she shouldn't speak of herself as the main breadwinner, which she was. "If your father and I are blessed with better money . . . Mary, you'll use it on your wedding day, *only when you dress before stepping toward the canopy,* yes?"

"What? What will I use?"

"The Greek Tassos has a mirror that's cracked just a little. I'll buy it for you."

"*Ee-ma!*"

She closed her eyes, deafened by my squeal.

I kissed her closed eyelids. I was choking up. I put my arms around her neck. She gave me one of those stilted hugs, afraid of feeling too much happiness. "*Eema,* there will be this . . . boy . . . he'll come forth to talk to you about me." Her hug loosened, but mine gripped her even harder.

"He's only a bondman, Mary." She tried to undo my arms.

But I kept hugging her. *Adonai, help!* He helped. My mother kissed my cheek. "*Talk,* that he can do. You'll change your mind about him, after you get some good offers."

Never, I thought. And I was so happy!

148

I'd almost forgiven the prince (and maybe it wasn't he who snared the bride?), for had he not ordered that chest, Joseph would have not been here now, and God's coincidental would have ended. But it didn't, it went on in godly wondrousness!

THE MEN ATE in the yard, at a long table set under an overhang of wild vine. Like a vault of rustling leaves, very soothing and comforting.

I seated my father at the place of honor, in the center, with the prince to his right, Orpa's father to his left, and elders on each side, falling away in importance toward the ends of the table. I seated Shalafta at the very end of the table, and Aaron at the other end. Perfect. Aaron's son Jerash I put at the men's second table, the one for the neighbors and the more distant kin. The women ate at a table of their own, behind the men's tables, so they could jump up and serve. The bondmen and servants, who were to jump up and help, too, should have had their own table, but there was no room for a fourth table. So they would eat after the masters were done. I'd give them wooden plates, and they could sit behind the back gate, eating abundant scraps, under the stars.

So caught in making this flawless, I still found the time to fill Joseph a plate and walked around looking for him with the plate steaming in my hands. I didn't find him.

I asked my help, Orpa, Neah and Nava, Avigai and Ahuva, Yorit and Dalit, and a second cousin of mine, Elsheva, who had become a snot after she married this priest at the temple in Jerusalem. She and her Zachariah were in Nazareth to visit her mother, so of course I had invited them, and placed him at the second table, next to Aaron's son Jerash. So. Elsheva told all souls how her Zachariah was toiling to get her with child. Praying in the temple every day, then coming home and doing those prayers all over again on Elsheva's body. "I hope he's not missing the right parts," the widow Irit chuckled. "The right parts of the prayers?" Elsheva asked. "Of what else?" the widow replied.

All those women kept jumping up to do this or that, checking on the fires, stacking away the dirty pots and plates, washing plates for the next dishes, so they were all over the yard and none of them had seen Joseph.

I strained my ear to hear more ax blows. All I heard was rowdiness in our yard.

Jews who are poor seldom drink freely; when they do, they get soused quickly. The men seated with Aristobulus got drunk, and the prince got drunk with them. Shalafta shouted, "How smart is our king, whom the Romans appointed to manage the iron mines of Cyprus!" Aristobulus burped. "Yes, my father's very business-savvy, but I'll be even richer." Aaron shouted, "The king's greedy, he takes a cut on every knife I make from steel. But I'll willingly give that cut to you, my prince, if you are friendly to my kin"—meaning his gangs—"who keep peace here better than the Romans!" Aristobulus burped back. "I'll remember you when I'm king, Aaron." Akam shouted, too. "King Herod is doomsday with women, he even got Cleopatra—he plowed her good, *heh, heh*." Aristobulus glugged wine and stuffed himself with lamb steamed with olives and dill, grilled tilapia, and quail roasted on the spit. Orpa and I carried off dirty plates. Wasn't this wonderful, this gathering in our yard, wasn't it like a wedding, when Jews rejoice that the Jewish future will be replenished by "being fruitful"? Eyeing the prince, Orpa tripped. I steadied her.

"Did you see Joseph, Orpa?"

"No."

"Where could he be?"

Aristobulus's servants stood halfway toward that heap of wood planks that Joseph and I brought from the synagogue. I heard one of them whisper to the other, "With a good horse, spurred hard, I'd be in Jerusalem in two days."

"You'd need three days. And you won't find a good horse here."

"I could sneak to Sepphoris and get one there. He won't notice, he's too drunk. Are you going to lie with him in that box, and wait for the hammer to come down?"

The box was a sleeping sukkah made of joined wood planks. The prince had insisted it be set with pillows and sheets by the front gate. He would sleep in it tonight. But what hammer did that servant talk about?

The servant became aware of me. "Beg your pardon. We were speaking Greek."

"It didn't sound like Greek," I mumbled.

"Oh, yes, that's what we speak between us. Forgive us if we confused you."

I stepped away, wondering. And I heard a strange silence at the main table.

The prince was sitting tightly, and his face was very pale. Just then my mother motioned me to run to the kitchen and bring more clean plates.

When I brought the plates, the prince was even paler. Slurring, he was saying to my father, "I've paid my dues for the throne of Israel. I'm of a whole mind, I speak four tongues, I throw the javelin like a Roman. When I conquer Jerusalem, I'll put my father's seed to the sword, I won't leave one Idumean alive at the court!" Herod was Idumean, which was rarely said out loud. The Idumeans, whom the Jews had conquered, were Arabians, dirt-poor and despised. I prayed, *Adonai, bring peace to the prince's mind, and get Joseph here! Where is he?*

My father replied to the prince, "You are from the king's seed, Highness, and you won't right up your mother's killing by killing your father." Everyone at the table was holding their breath. My father spoke on. "God doesn't owe you just because you suffered. And if you rise with revenge on your mind, you'll perish of revenge, from one of your brothers, or from whoever else covets the throne. God doesn't owe, Highness, we owe to God." Aristobulus kicked his chair and burst away from under that vault of leaves. My father bolted and gestured to me. "Maryamneh! Go after the prince, make him come back to the table!"

"How?"

"Ask him sweetly. To you, he'll listen."

I ran after the prince.

Very drunk, he was staggering toward the work shed. He heard my footsteps, turned, and snapped. "God doesn't owe me, your father just said! What does your father know of my pain? The soles of my shoes, the feathers in my pillows are made of pain!"

He was shaking. My mind kept urging me, *He's the future king, find something soothing to say to him, but something truthful, too.* "Maybe God favored you already . . ." I was choosing my words. "For you, too, dealt pain to other people . . . whom you could have saved?" He raised his hand to touch that earring, and I was suddenly certain. He was the one who seduced the bride. And then, as if reading my mind, he muttered, "The king knew that she liked me. And I knew that he didn't want that wedding. I was . . ."

"Weak?" I whispered, to help him.

Aristobulus grabbed me so suddenly, I couldn't even squeak. One arm curling round my neck, jeweled fingers clamping my mouth.

"You think I'm weak?"

He pushed me behind that pile of planks, by the work shed, whose open door let out the glow of an oil wick. What fool had left a burning wick near all that wood? I couldn't even moan. I tried to scratch the prince's jeweled fingers, but he squeezed my throat harder while his other hand pulled up my shift. My legs were apart, I could be raped before I uttered a sound! He pushed between my thighs . . . Fighting, close to passing out, I saw Joseph through the shed's open door, carving knife in his hand, a sliver of bread stuck in his lips. Munching and carving . . . I couldn't scream with my mouth, but I screamed with my mind, and fell, pulling the prince with me, hitting my face on the shed's doorstep.

He flipped me onto my back. I prayed for my face to resemble the face of the dead bride, with that scar on her lip. And then Joseph lunged out of the shed, knocking Aristobulus down. He slammed his knee in the prince's belly. Aristobulus tried to sneer. "Take your hands off me, you're no one . . ." Joseph pointed the carving knife at his crotch. "I'll make *you* no one . . . Without offspring, you'll never be king . . ."

I screamed.

Footfalls drummed close. My father ran to me, as I raved at the prince. "You killed her, you killed her! She loved you, and you killed her!" Everyone was running over; Shalafta was running amazingly fast for his bulk.

Chaos seized our yard. Shalafta yelled, "What were you doing, Joseph, to Joachim's daughter?" But for once, a bad name protected the innocent. Everyone stared at the prince, everyone guessed that he was the culprit, not Joseph.

The prince got up mumbling that he was drunk, he had tripped and clung to me and brought me down. I was a fetching little piece, maybe he had pinched me . . . The old men started to snicker, but the women, I could tell how turned off they were. There was a deep furrow in my father's brow as he looked at my swollen face. My mother sprinkled my bleeding lip with flour that Orpa had run to bring in a cup. Then my father told the prince that he should spend the night elsewhere, so the prince turned and looked at Shalafta, who couldn't believe that he got his wish, to be the prince's host!

My mother dabbed the cut on my lip. I cried. I had ruined my father's hour of glory, and how would I walk in bridal attire tomorrow, looking like a fat-lipped cow?

The prince muttered that he still expected his chest. My father nodded curtly, and the prince walked out, calling for his servants. I did not hear them respond. Joseph lingered by me. Over his shoulder, I saw the shed's door, broken at its hinge. Joseph had lunged that hard when he saw me writhing under Aristobulus.

I moaned, "Why were you in the shed by yourself?"

He replied that my father had carved those cherubs wrong. He was redoing them.

Through the fence's pickets, relatives and neighbors still peered in.

I could not even face Joseph, for fear of how hideous I looked, so I stared forlornly through the fence pickets, and glimpsed the widow Irit, peeking in at us. She turned, and melted into the dark street.

I sat on the doorstep. With closed-up faces, my parents walked back from our front gate. Joseph spoke to my father. "Rabbi Joachim, if you trust me with what's best for your daughter, let me take Mary out of Nazareth. If you agree, we'll be engaged to each other. I'll take her to Sepphoris, and if no deeds of dread happen in Nazareth, I'll bring her back safe. You know enough about me to trust me." Now he looked at my mother. Despite how stunned she was, my mother motioned Joseph to sit.

Joseph sat on the doorstep right next to me.

My mother asked, "What are you really saying, Joseph?"

"I'm saying, it's not safe here for your daughter, and maybe not for anyone. The son of the king set fate in motion."

So, I'd just received my first proposal from a man, to whom my mother finally responded. "We're looking for a different kind of husband for Mary."

"I know, but you might not find him so quickly. And you might ask Mary, too, what kind of husband she wants."

"She doesn't know her own mind. And you're a bondman."

Joseph blushed, insulted. "I'll leave Shalafta and earn my living as a carver. We wouldn't hunger. Think of what's best for your daughter. If you think I'm frightened without reason, tell me so."

"I pray that you are," my mother said.

"Very well. I'll fell another tree. The faster we finish that chest and the king's son leaves, the better for all of us."

He walked toward the back gate, and my parents stood shoulder to shoulder, as if he'd cast a spell on them.

BECAUSE THE COW was tied inside again, as if the peaceful togetherness of the dinner hadn't even occurred, my mother made our bed in the sleeping niche under the roof. That niche smelled fragrant, from dried flowers sprinkled on the floor by my mother. I had such a need for being near my mother's body, I lay next to her and burrowed in her side like a child.

Sleepless, I thought about our neighbors, settling in their beds with stomachs filled and bodies tired, but with tongues not tired at all. The whole village was prattling about what had happened in our yard. Then I had a hideous thought. After Joseph fells that tree, he'll join Irit in Shalafta's yard. Why not? My parents had turned down his proposal, and I had remained silent, why wouldn't he seek comfort from her? I remembered her steps, her face. She had lingered in the street, peering in at Joseph and me.

I heard the ax. Its blows were like thunderclaps. Then my mother sat up in bed and asked, "Who's knocking? There's someone at the door, Joachim."

"There's that fool felling a tree."

"Someone's at the door," my mother insisted.

I leaped from the bed and padded to the door. Who could it be but Joseph?

I opened the door, stared at a face tanned by smithing fires. "It's Rabbi Aaron."

"What is it, Aaron?" my father asked, making his way to the door.

"Come out to talk to me."

"Why?"

Aaron hesitated. "Can I come in, then? Send your daughter away. The *rabanee* can hear, you'll tell her anyway."

My mother poked me with her elbow. I pretended to scurry toward the kitchen, but stopped and hid behind a grain basket.

I heard Aaron say, "A shepherd just came to tell me that the king's Syrians are up on Mount Barak. They're looking right down at the village." The Syrians were the king's irregulars. Wherever he sent them, to subdue rebellions or extort taxes, they left burned homes and nomadic orphans in rags.

"Is that what you wanted to tell me?"

"Yes, and there's no doubt in my mind, the Syrians are staking Nazareth to kill the king's cocky son. Rabbi Joachim, talk to your clan. I'll give you knives for how many men you bring with you, and we'll strike the prince together, and Shalafta, too." Aaron was excited. "The Syrians will be thankful to us, if we cut them enough booty. Also, Rabbi Joachim, my son likes your daughter. With Shalafta's heirlooms, we'll give our children the most lavish wedding."

There was a silence. In the dark outside, I heard Joseph's ax shattering that tree.

"No," my father said.

"Why?"

"Because, aside from committing sin, you could be mistaken about the Syrians' intent."

"Ha!" Aaron snickered.

Then he whispered hotly. Didn't the prince brag openly that he would kill his father? But the father was stalking the son, wasn't that obvious if the Syrians were nearby? And the prince's servants, where had they vanished when that mayhem occurred in our yard? They didn't show when they were called, as the prince stumbled off to Shalafta's yard. Ingenious Aaron turned to my mother. "Rabanee, my son wants your daughter so much, he can't sleep from yearning for her. Think of how rich they could be together." I became terrified, maybe my parents would bespeak me to Jerash? "Rabbi, if I kill Shalafta by myself, I won't have to share his heirlooms with you, but I want my Jerash to marry your daughter. Isn't her bloodline foretold to beget Mashiah?"

What a man of faith hid inside the worst hoodlum in Galilee!

My father raised his voice. "Aaron! Stop! I'll go warn the prince, he'll leave tonight, and Nazareth will be free of trouble."

"And the king will still kill him, and we'll get nothing?"

"You want me to share in murder and robbery? You sat at my table with him."

"I didn't know that the Syrians were on the mountain. Don't turn me down. I never made this kind of offer to anyone." Aaron's tone was not menacing, but it was not beseeching, either. "Don't turn me down," he repeated, his voice heavy with omen.

"Don't threaten me," my father said. But he didn't sound as self-assured as usual.

"Think about it, before the cock crows. Good night."

I heard the door close. I stepped out from behind that grain basket. "Go warn the prince," I mumbled to my father. When I spoke, that poultice of flour cracked, and blood seeped into my lips. "Go, Abba [Father], now."

My father reached for his shift.

But my mother pulled it from his hand. "Let them do as they wish to each other, you stay and protect your own home. Are the Syrians truly on the mountain?"

I listened, trying to hear if our yard dogs were barking. They were not.

My father said to my mother, "You're right. Maybe Aaron made it up, just to get Shalafta." He hesitated, pulled out a drawer, and started putting on his tefillin to pray. Then he tore them off.

He stepped back toward us. "Why is this happening? The king's son came to me. Why to me of all the carvers in the land? And all this talk about our lineage." I wondered, should I tell him what the prince had said to me that morning? But maybe it was foolish talk, why make my father more disturbed than he was?

"You *wish* that your lineage mattered that much," my mother snickered.

"Shut up," my father growled, but he was relieved. Mother's humbling reply was reassuring. He went back to his praying corner, put his tefillin back on.

I whispered to my mother as I lay next to her, "When the lightning struck Joseph, maybe it injured his male parts, that happens. But he may be healed by now." My cheeks were hot. I was thankful for the darkness. "He made me a proposal, you heard it."

"A man would say or do any crazy things, to get a woman to care for him."

"Then, he loves me?"

"Try to sleep," my mother begged me softly. "So I can sleep, too."

"I'll fall asleep when you do. And tomorrow, if I have to put a pound of flour on my face, we walk together, yes?"

She shook her head. I was unmanageable. "Sleep, my daughter."

How could I sleep? I could hear my Joseph making noises in the shed. Working, trying to finish that chest.

Listening to him, I fell asleep. Until the door came down with a hellish crash.

The Syrians hurled torches into the house, and then the king stepped inside. Studded gloves on his fists, studded boots on his feet.

I'd glimpsed him in Jerusalem, always from a great distance. Now I saw him close. He was so short, almost a dwarf, but so broadly shaped, his shoulders were twice wider than my father's. His bearded jaw was like the bow of a ship, and his mouth was crimson red in the curly gray beard. Everything that was pretty and elegant in Aristobulus was thick, squat, and ugly in the king. He hurled my father to the ground, jumped on my father's hands, screaming "Mashiah!" with such rage, as if he were screaming a curse. Joachim the carver would never carve again.

The Syrians dragged us outside. My father with his crushed hands held up by the Syrians, like a hideous example. My mother and I behind him, kicked at every step. I screamed Joseph's name.

Then I saw him. He was running to the donkeys still tied in our yard. He jumped on one and bit its ear. The donkey broke its tie, and Joseph drove it at the Syrians, who were knocked down. When they let go of us to deal with the maddened animal, I pulled my father toward the back gate. Maybe we could hide behind the setims. But the Syrians caught us and chased us back into the street. Joseph was still trying to fight them off. A Syrian brought his spear down on his head, and I lost sight of him.

There was blood on the ground. Our kin were being whipped along with us. A Syrian on horseback rode by me, calling out like a town crier. *"I the king, ruler of all Jews . . ."* I kept hearing screams—were they killing Joseph? *"I the king, builder of the temple . . . shall nip betrayal even from my own flesh! My son*

plotted to overthrow me! I sentence him to die! My son's host, who is
my son's accomplice, Joachim—" I stopped breathing. How devil-
ishly clever the king was. "—*Joachim, I will spare for the sake of his
lineage, mindful that it may benefit Israel! But I exile him for life,
him and his kin!*"

My father was right, this was about our lineage, in some
hideous way.

I heard the screams of Aristobulus. He was running stark
naked, chased by Syrians who had torn off his clothes. Men from
Aaron's gangs joined in chasing him, and I saw Aaron lunge at
the prince and rip off his earrings, bloodying the prince's cheeks.
The crier kept calling. *"All who remain loyal to the king . . . swear
not to allow Joachim's clan to come back! What was theirs is now
yours!"*

The Syrians thrust two wooden posts into the ground and
leaned them over each other, making them into that torture tool,
the *tselav*, the cross. Aristobulus saw it and burst into tears. I saw
the king walk up to him. As if turned off by those tears, the king
pulled out a dagger and stabbed him in the heart. As the Syrians
lifted him and nailed him onto the crossed posts, I found myself
praying, *Let the prince die from that stab, Adonai. Please spare him
any more pain, Adonai!*

Part 7

Mary and the Lightning

Three years later, at the well in the desert.
Three weeks before the Roman's arrival.

I WAS NINE years old, three times three, when my father was called to work on the temple in Jerusalem.

I was almost ten when we returned to Galilee.

And I was thirteen, three and ten, when I met Joseph.

Sitting cross-legged, resting my back against the cistern, I held up three fingers of my right hand and stared at them. Then I held up all my fingers. Ten fingers.

Wondrous was ten and wondrous was three. Three and three made six. Added to the ten of all my fingers, that made sixteen. Adding one, which was your number—one God—made seventeen.

I had just turned seventeen, and we had been at the well three years and a little.

Sitting under the date trees, I held up my right pointer finger and my left pointer finger. I turned my right pointer finger into me and my left pointer finger into Joseph.

I touched my pointer fingers.

* * *

165

THREE MONTHS AFTER we arrived at the well, I found out that Joseph was alive.

I found out from Jibril, who watered his camels at the well. Many caravans were buying water from us and spreading the story about the rabbi descended from David, whom the king had maimed and exiled with all his kin.

That rabbi had a daughter, still unwed, gifted with amazing skills. Such as: She found water in the desert, tamed jackals, spoke for the tribe as if she were its leader, and never backed down before a man. In short, she could be a witch.

But Jibril wasn't scared of the young witch. He liked her and knew what pained her. So, the third time he stopped at the well he sidled up to her and told her he'd run into Joseph in Sepphoris. Joseph had left Nazareth after the night of the Syrians. Aware that Jibril was a caravan master, Joseph asked what his trade route was, and Jibril replied, "across the desert of Jeshimon." So Joseph asked about our tribe.

I had tied a new belt woven from a camel harness around my waist that day. Now I twisted its ends and held my breath. I let go of my belt, pressed my hands on the cistern until my knuckles turned white, and told Jibril that Joseph had been my father's apprentice, and that he tried to rescue me on the night of the Syrians.

Jibril replied that Joseph had told him that already. Joseph, Jibril said, lived in a building with harlots on its roof.

I asked Jibril when he would go to Sepphoris, and he said he'd go to the Red Sea first to trade with some Jews who had taught themselves to drink seawater. Even so, they kept our law, and their men learned the Torah like everywhere else. But he would go back to Sepphoris and look up Joseph in three months. Wondrous is the number three.

* * *

THREE MONTHS DRAGGED by.

When Jibril brought his caravan in again, he waved at me, got off his saddle, and I stood by him as he grabbed his camel's foreleg and lifted it to look at a cracked hoof. He let go of the hoof, muttering that he would tar it now and cover it in leather so the camel wouldn't go lame. Then he took out of his garment a tiny bit of wood.

"That man Joseph gave me this for you."

It was a carved wooden fly.

Has a girl ever gripped more tenderly a disgusting fly?

Jibril laughed. "Joseph made this thing in less time than it takes to say good day. Such a gifted carver. What's between you? You saving yourself for him?" Words that pinched my heart. Aristobulus had told me: "Don't save yourself for Joseph, he's no good in bed."

"Did Joseph say anything when he gave this to you?"

Such as: I'll soon ride the desert to see you, Mary! For I'm dying without you. Being without you is like being without air to breathe!

"He said that he remembered you."

"Anything else?"

"Nothing."

I gave Jibril a message for Joseph. That I remembered him, too.

JIBRIL RAN INTO Joseph at Sepphoris's next caravan market. Joseph asked Jibril to a meal on the roof of that building. They ate served by those sinful women; they acted like helpers to Joseph, cleaned the roof for him, shopped for him. But Jibril had not paid them much mind, for Joseph asked so many questions about my father, and about me—how hard we, and I, were having it here.

Then he told Jibril that he had many things to take care of now—working and such—so he said, "Tell Mary I'm not ready."

I felt as if a camel had kicked me in the head.

"What did he mean, he's not ready?"

"Why don't you tell me what you really want to know?" Jibril countered grumpily. "Or tell me word for word what to tell him next time."

Oh, God. What could I tell Jibril? Maybe: Go back to Sepphoris and pay Joseph's harlots to get him drunk and into bed? And then ask them if he can do you-know-what?

"You still want news from him?" Jibril asked.

"Yes. Why not?"

JIBRIL AND I worked out a sign language, indicating whether he brought me news about Joseph or not. When he arrived, Jibril rode in on his lead camel, shouting, "Oh, *Ilu, Ilu,* mighty is your beneficence. *Ya-Ilu, ya-Ilu, Ilu-hoo!*" When I heard his voice, cracked and husky, I stared through the turning spokes, and if I spotted him raising his right hand, it meant he had news. So we looked for a quiet place to talk, such as by a cart heaped with huge incense sticks, which Jibril sold to those dwellers way by the sea.

This last time, Jibril couldn't find Joseph in Sepphoris.

I started trembling.

"Bestill yourself!" Jibril snapped, as I seemed ready to throw myself in the cistern. "He's in Nazareth. I trekked past Nazareth, and Joseph came outside the walls. Nazareth was so wracked by Shalafta and Aaron fighing their own war, there are barricades in the streets, and the population is halved. Shalafta asked Joseph to return to Nazareth and offered to adopt him as he once promised. Joseph returned but he turned down the adoption. He's carving big statues now and he's working in stone, too, like the Greeks."

My heart bounced joyfully. So he's a free man now and not poor anymore! "Did he marry anyone yet?"

"No."

"Did he ask about me?"

"He asked what you looked like."

I felt like screaming, Climb onto a camel and come see for yourself!

"He's got orders for statues from many Greeks and Romans. He's making money." I became worried. A free man making money, with so many unmarried girls around him! "Did he ask if *I* got married? Did you tell him I didn't?"

"No and no." Jibril seemed sad for me. "He's still not ready, Mary. You know?"

I felt like grabbing a stick and hitting Jibril. Here's for not saying to Joseph, That girl, she shines when she stands atop a dune, and rich traders are proposing to her *every day*! I also felt like trekking to Nazareth to find Joseph and beat *him* with a stick, one blow for every step across the desert. *If you're still not ready, then let go of my heart!*

After that visit from Jibril, I tossed that wooden fly in the desert.

But I couldn't make myself toss out that carving of me. It had lost its arms and most of its likeness, but that little nick from the knife's point, I could still see it, near my nose. So much like that freckle of mine, I wanted to cry. But I hadn't cried in so long. Maybe I would never cry again.

JIBRIL GAVE THAT mirror to Orpa and me, and he watched the ripening of our bodies. He had four sons, so he had his own designs on us. Girls who husbanded a living from the desert could be assets.

"My sons think you'd make a good wife," he told me at his next visit.

"Thank them for me," I answered forlornly.

"Mary . . ." I could tell how fond of me the old Arab was. He was watching me so sadly. "Jerash, Aaron's son, hasn't married, either. He doesn't look like a runt anymore, and he asked me, 'What about Rabbi Joachim's daughter, is she still pretty?' 'She's prettier than a gold ring,' I said."

"That's what you should have said about me to Joseph. Is Joseph handsome?"

"He is," Jibril sighed. "He put on weight, he trimmed his beard. He takes himself around in clean clothes."

I was so dejected with my fate in love, I couldn't even peek at myself in the cistern.

ONLY A DOLT like you would keep on hoping," Orpa told me, after I told her. "That Joseph might still show up before your father's tent and say, 'Here's the latest wonder from God— my-you-know-what is right and ready, under my *abrition.*'" Which were the drawers rich boys wore, made of linen, tight and fitting on the crotches, while poor boys wore nothing under their shifts but their flea-bitten skins.

"What if Joseph shows up?" I countered between clenched teeth.

"You are insane! No wonder you see angels!"

OBLIVIOUS AND STUPID, my bloods kept coming. I knew the full moon's approach without glancing up at the night sky, I knew it from the way my body became feverish and sore. When the moon added one more rim to its perfect roundness, *bang,* I was awash in fertility yet again to be wasted.

So I would purify again. I would swim in that hot spring, I would climb out with my skin creased from the hot water and with my mind aching. What was I doing, waiting? Waiting for what?

Some of our unmarried girls responded to the attentions of the camel drivers. Some got pregnant. Babies were born. Akam circumcised the baby boys, early in the morning so as not to mishap their little rods of life with hands shaky from drunkenness. He cut off the foreskins as by the law, with a chip of flintstone, yea, like Abraham was cicrumcised, and Moses! Their little tools, swollen and tender, were rubbed with olive oil by their doting mothers, bandaged in oil-swathed flax, and tied with bright red string, poor things. They munched with toothless gums on wads of cotton dipped in wine—we had a little wine now and then from Jibril. *Adonai, life you gave us, life we give back to you! Here it is, tiny and swollen, tied with red string. But what about* my *life?*

After the next watering, Jibril sat down with my parents in our tent, and my mother served him a warm brew of myrrh, good against body pains. My mother kept myrrh dry at home in Nazareth and boiled it into a brew for me the first months after I had my bloods. Jibril ached from aging, so mother brewed him myrrh tea every time he came, and Jibril thanked her. "You made this brew even tastier than last time, rabanee."

By chance, I had crawled into the tent by the hole reserved for the mutts, and heard Jibril say, after another sip of myrrh (I'd gathered those branches myself, squeezed out the yellow resinous gum, and mixed it with water), "Aaron and Shalafta are talking peace. And Shalafta asked Joseph to marry his daughter, Lanit . . ."

I felt as if a herd of camels had kicked me in the head.

"And Aaron asked Joseph to marry his daughter, Rona. And guess what? Joseph said yes to both proposals, so it will be a double wedding. With wives from both clans under one roof, war will be weeded out of Nazareth."

Carefully happy, my father muttered, "If there is peace, we should petition the king to grant us an amnesty, so we can return to Nazareth."

"Indeed, Rabbi," Jibril agreed. "Maybe the king, that blight on the face of the earth, has second thoughts about having exiled the clan of the promise." My father nodded. The last few years, as passersby kept threading that story, my father had started to agree with them, with a gently wise nod. Yes, we are that tribe. My father noticed me. "There will be peace in Nazareth, aren't you rejoicing, Mary?"

"I am."

"A double marriage. What a clever idea. God is looking after his people."

"It could be a triple marriage," said Jibril. He glanced at me quickly. "Didn't Joseph once ask for Mary in marriage? If you agree, Rabbi, I'll ride to Nazareth and say to Joseph, Ask for Mary again, as your third wife. That will make room for her tribe to return, too."

I said nothing.

My mother said: "I'm so happy for poor Joseph. He deserves this windfall." She aimed her eyes at me. "You'd still marry Joseph, wouldn't you?"

Her eyes said to me, My beloved daughter, this is not coming to you the right way, yet this is your chance to marry the one you like, and now he's a man of wealth! And my eyes said back to her, Hmm, did you forget, beloved mother, that you told him, we want a different kind of husband for Mary?

"Did Joseph truly say yes to Lanit and Rona?" my mother asked, with hope in her voice.

"He did, he did. He's so *giving*. He cares about saving Nazareth, where people mocked him, as much as your daughter cares to get you out of this hole."

Sweet shrewd old uncle, Jibril! Trying to twin my feelings to Joseph's! I glared at him. "What's your gain from this, Jibril?"

"Mine? None, I stand to lose. I wanted you for one of my sons."

I threw my arms up. "But didn't God set it up that there should be one wife to one husband?" I looked up. I could see no sky above me, just the frayed flaxen tarp of our tent, and the supporting pole from which my mother hung her rags to dry. Dirty, old, and ramshackle was everything that surrounded me. "Didn't Hashem say it's no good for man to be alone, and then he made him *one* mate? Isn't it written in Moshe's law, Don't covet your neighbor's wife? Wife, *one only!*" I cried toward the cobwebbed top of the tent. "God Adonai, why should I be a third wife?"

My mother spoke to me with her eyes. My beloved daughter, I cherish you for your daring thinking. But life is life, remember that, my beloved headstrong daughter.

My father squatted next to me. "Mary, with you as third wife, Joseph will sway Aaron to let us come home."

"Aaron's the hard one, Rabbi," Jibril agreed. "You irked him bad, at some time."

I looked at Jibril and saw it in his eyes: love for me, like for a daughter of his own. He wanted me to get married to the man I loved, and this was the best plan he could come up with. "Joseph is so giving," he said again.

"How soon is the wedding?" I choked.

Jibril shrugged. "A few weeks? Shalafta and Aaron will ask for guarantees from each other, like goods and cattle. They'll spend time haggling."

"Good," I said. "I need time to think what I want to do."

"Mary, all of us depend on you so much," my mother said.

"I know, you never let me forget it."

I was so unhappy.

But later that day, Jibril sidled up to me at the cistern. "Mary, that wasn't my own thought, for you to marry Joseph. I'm a messenger only . . ." For an instant, his eyes glowed so bright, like someone else spoke from inside him. "I'm a messenger," he repeated. "Joseph himself told me to ask you to marry him, but how else could you marry him, in Nazareth, your own home, without some peace agreement? If there's no peace, there will be no Nazareth."

"I need time to think," I said stubbornly.

"Speak to someone sensible, another woman," Jibril said. "Speak to your mother, you hear me? Speak to your mother."

"I will," I promised.

* * *

I SPOKE TO Orpa.

"Why would he want me, even just for a third of his bed, unless he was in love with me?" I exploded, trying to convince her, trying to convince myself. "Nothing forced him to add me to that deal."

She replied, always telling it as it was, with the bark on: "You think anyone cares that you'll lie in bed with Lanit on one side and Rona on the other, waiting your turn with Joseph? You should be so lucky that he can fill all three of you!" I could kill her for the way she dumped me in *all of you*! "But what if he's still not ready?" I gritted my teeth. "And the wedding's a sham for peace and money? Then you can be a strumpet—who's to judge you?—which might even be pleasing! We could both be strumpets with whoever we like!" That tough nut, her eyes brightened at the prospect and her mussed hair rustled on her head. "Lord, sentence me to pleasure! You hear me, Mary?"

"I hear you."

"That bride who was stoned, for whom you cried your eyes out, who knows what a strumpet she was."

"I hear you."

"So why do you look so grim?" She laughed so cheerfully, I forgot myself and threw my arms around her, and we swayed in a girlish embrace. She was right, being a strumpet was better than being a lemon on a shelf, drying up!

So, A WEEK after Jibril's last stop at the well, I sewed a water skin from the skin of a lamb we'd eaten and filled it. I stole some strips of grilled lamb and made some flat bread.

I wrapped the food and tied it inside my shift below my

breasts and tied Joseph's little sculpture around my neck. I lay by the cistern that night until everyone fell asleep, then got up and climbed out of the gulch, starting along the caravan trail, back toward Mount Barak and Nazareth.

I walked until the sun rose. I kept walking under the sun's furnacelike glare. I'd not thought about taking my sandals with me, as sand is soft to walk on, so I walked until my feet were broiled. But after a while the pain in my feet became numb, and I just kept walking on.

I put on a hat I'd woven myself out of wheat straw. It didn't help much.

The desert was deathly beautiful.

I took the tiniest sips from my water skin. At the end of the day, I lay down in the shade of a dune. I chewed two of my strips of lamb, sipped a little more water, wet my fingers, and rubbed them on the soles of my feet, tickling myself, and laughing. I fell asleep laughing. I woke up as the sun burned my face.

I walked again with a bath of fieriness on my head.

I finished the water.

I'd heard from the caravan masters that when they exhausted their water supplies, they gathered urine from their bodies and from their camels and sprinkled it on the sand. That cooled off the sand. They lay in that moist bed and regathered their strength until they could walk again. They dipped their headscarves in that moisture to keep them a little cooler when they headed out again.

I thought about doing the same and squatted and tried to pass water. But there were barely a few drops left in me, not enough to make a puddle in the sand.

I wobbled on. To give myself courage, I thought of Joseph.

How he had tried to rescue me from the Syrians. *What a man you were that night, Joseph. That night, even though I didn't say yes to you, I did trust you, and you trusted me. Like spouses in marriage.*

The sky was so fiery, it looked white, an incandescently white sky. Then the sun went down, the sky went back to blue, and the beauty of the desert was maddening.

Tottering and staggering, I glimpsed an elevation ahead, at first so uncertainly outlined against the sky it seemed like a mirage. It was Mount Barak.

Now I knew why I had traveled here.

To ask the mountain: What have you done to my Joseph? What have you done to his body and his mind, that he's so afraid to talk to me, he's sending me messengers?

I CLIMBED THE lower ranges, and the rocks acquired those otherworldly colors, places where lightning had hit them. Purples and light blues sprinkled with beads of black.

I climbed until the air was cold and damp. I found a dip in a rock, filled with rainwater. I slurped, crying like animals cry, heaving and keening. Then I climbed across mountain grass.

Ahead of me, a sheep's fold had burned from being struck by lightning many years before. Of the thatched roof, nothing was left. Of a wide sheep's corral, only charred bits. Of a working shed, I recognized the shapes of butter-making churns. Bones of humans, perhaps engulfed by fire in their sleep, were everywhere. Some had turned pink, blue, purple.

I sensed that Joseph's father had been struck here. Had I been able to recognize his remains—I did look around, for a belt, or tefillin, or some other personal object—I would have tried to bury him. Up here, Joseph had been struck, too, but he survived and was found by my father. *How little I know about Joseph,* I thought. But I knew who *I* wanted to be: a helper, a loving hand-maid. But for that, I had to love and be loved.

I climbed higher. The colors became even more delirious.

Then . . . I saw a shepherd.

He was walking away from me, toward Nazareth. Leading goats or sheep, I couldn't tell at that distance. He had a dog with him, but the dog did not put his nose up to sniff the air. He and the shepherd and the herd were too far.

Was the man Joseph?

I started running on my scorched feet and fell after a few steps. That man and his animals slipped over the crest and disappeared, and I thought, *It's better this way.*

This way, I would never hear Joseph say to me: Mary, how much you changed. You're so different from the one I remember. And I'm to be married soon, Mary, to two other brides. You and I were not made for each other. When I asked for you to be my wife, I did it out of gratitude, because your father saved my life.

Those thoughts made me titter with cracked lips. *What are you doing to me, Adonai? Mocking me? It was you, Adonai, who hung the full moon over my young womanhood before it ripened fully. How happy I was that night, sitting by the setim trees with Joseph. Hand in hand. Our hands married to each other. How confident I was, and how at peace with you, Adonai, after I hated you (don't strike me, I'm already almost lifeless) for the stoning of that young bride! Adonai, you were cruel to me. Adonai, you were cruel to us women, in making us so defenseless and conflicted. Giving us such power in our prettiness, yet all a man has to do to defeat our power is to knock us to the ground. On our backs, as if ready to be slaugh-*

tered, feet in the air, unable to flee. All a man has to do is hold us down, and trap our lips with his lips, while you, Adonai, bewitch our minds with that feeling beyond all feelings, that we'll give birth! Adonai, Adonai, what power you have over women, and over me! For even as I complain about you, I feel so guilty that I am complaining. So here I am, praying with cracked lips. What am I feeling, Adonai? What am I really feeling?

You're feeling love, Mary.

"Ha-aaah?" I gushed.

I STOOD UP and looked around with eyes dulled by exhaustion. I moved my hand and touched the top of a bush.

It was a myrrh plant, with small oval leaves and sharp spikes—the kind my mother brewed against Jibril's backaches.

Maybe I was not dreaming.

I looked at the sky. The sun had set, but I saw no stars.

He spoke again. *Love is the only way to know another being in his innermost core. In his body and in his soul.*

I shrugged. Did I know Joseph that well? No, not by far.

But I remembered how Joseph fell asleep under the setim tree, and that when I looked at that muscular man, I felt that I wasn't frightened of him—no, not of Joseph, not one bit. Was that part of being in love, perhaps, that lack of fear? And God made a sound that was so peaceful. *Mm-hmm.* Soft and throaty, like my father would, when he coughed in agreement. *Yes, for how can you love someone you fear?*

I squeezed those myrrh branches. What did it matter if they scratched my palms, the pain was so trifling, in exchange for hearing him speak. *Look how you gave Joseph everything. Your dreams, your hopes, your unashamed admission that he is everything for you. You didn't haggle, you didn't bargain, isn't that so?*

I nodded, ready to cry. That praise, that I had not held back my love, was so sweet, like a caress on my bare heart. If this was my last hour, as the old Jewish men say, *acharon haviv,* the last is the sweetest. So I spoke out loud, for did it matter if I showed my insanity to the bushes and the grass and the rocks?

"Give me some proof that you're near me now, and I'll believe I'm not insane."

Turn around.

My fingers pulled at that branch, and spiny tips of myrrh lodged in my fingers. The branch snapped against my hand, while . . .

I saw a man sitting on a rock top, ten paces from me. Staring down the slope.

He had the look of a workingman resting. Hands in his lap, shoulders slouched from the weight of a mature body. Then, as he tilted his head back, his breath rose from his lips, bright with light.

He spat a mouthful of stars, and they filled the bowl of the sky.

With my hair crackling on my head, I watched him stir to his feet. He looked so average, like a man who drove sheep up the mountain, a shepherd.

Aren't you coming? he said, stepping past me. He held his chin to his chest and his eyes low as he spoke to me.

His face, I thought frantically, *his face!* No one glimpsed it without being charred to cinders, at least that's what the Book said! But he had showed me the making of stars!

I inched myself up and into his footprints, and he vanished.

But not his footprints. Ahead, they had become a trail, as if he paced up here so often, he'd worn a trail in the mountainside. Footprints among grass bitten ragged by the sheep, and among stones scattered in the grass. I thought, *I am this grass, I am these stones. I'm a country girl, powerless against the passage of time, name-*

181

less in my wish to live and to matter to no one except to those I love, *but in that way . . .*

I'm the same as you, he said from somewhere ahead.

"Truly?"

Yes. He ruffled the grass tassels, as if he'd become shy.

This could not be, it just could not be . . . I stepped under stars, and I thought about them. "They are good."

I wasn't certain they would be.

I chuckled. "You mean, *you* didn't know?" For I remembered my father, reading to me from the Book: And the Lord God made the light. And he saw that it was good. And he made the heavens, and the stars in the heavens. And he saw that they were good.

I didn't know. I waited to see if they worked right, and they did.

"Did you wait long?"

No. They worked right away. So, why are you here, Mary? What do you want?

"I want to see Joseph," I cried. "If you are to end my life after revealing yourself to me, I want to see Joseph one more time. Not just the moon and the stars and all your unmatched creations. They are too big, too scary. I am small, I don't want to be scared."

Shhh. I haven't revealed myself to you yet.

"You haven't?" I felt my tears so close. Maybe he'd allow me one rich, scrumptious cry before dying.

You're not going to die, Mary. And you'll be a mother. Isn't that your deepest concern? His voice had changed, it was less heavenly, more like my own. I thought of my friend Orpa. She, she would have the guts to ask him for something now. So I pouted. "With what spouse? I have none."

You'll choose a spouse.

A haze of sweat broke out on my forehead. "*I'll choose . . . ?*"

I let everyone choose. That's my will.

Oh, God, dearest, sweetest God, may I live to whisper this to Orpa? So frightened, I peeked under my eyelids—but I still peeked! His eyes were shut. *Look how much he cares about me!* So I whispered in my sweetest daughter's voice. "May I tell Orpa about this, Shaddai?" Shaddai means "God on the mountain." Addressing him that way, I showed him my manners.

Wouldn't she be scared, Mary?

"You don't know Orpa!"

And then I felt that we were laughing together. So when he started to speak again, I urged impetuously, "Say I know her better than you, give me that little thing. Go along with me, yes?"

Yes, you know her better than I do, he agreed. *Now, about Joseph, does it have to be him and no one else?*

He turned and we were face-to-face. His hand over his forehead. *Must it be Joseph, and no one else?*

I screamed. "Yes, only him! Shaddai, your will be done—but don't shatter my hope. Your will is my will, isn't it? You yourself set it up that way, you made that first pair a pair, not a threesome, nor a foursome! So it's Joseph for me, only him! Yes?"

And at last, I blurted out: "And she wasn't a strumpet, that bride!"

She was kind, he agreed, ruffled by my passion.

"Then, *why?*"

Suddenly, his heart beat so close to mine. He'd had such a hard, godly time deciding her fate. He was sad, confused even. And scared that I guessed this about him!

He turned toward the heights. *Come,* he pleaded brokenly, fighting a godly emotion. As before, he vanished. But I saw his footprints. They were leading up the mountain.

Very well. God, take me to where I've been headed since I took my first breath—to love, *to my love*! Let me glimpse it again, let me breathe its scent, one instant if that is your wish—but make it a long instant! For you don't know how I feel, I complained to him.

But he beamed back. *I do, Mary. I know your longing and your fear. There's nothing of yours that's alien to me. Otherwise why would that feeling be in you? Pain, fear, love . . . loneliness, loss, confusion, shame . . . I know them all . . .*

Dumbstruck, I gawked at the footprints. "So . . . not just our flesh is in your image, our hearts are in your image, too?"

I felt his heart. It was so lonely!

And I felt his tiredness. So vast. Tiredness was a piece of his soul; he would never lose it again.

Time was God's tiredness—from his tasks.

T HE INCLINE became steeper. I panted. I was bone tired.

Close your eyes, he told me.

"How can I walk, then?"

Just feel the ground for my steps.

"You said you'd show me Joseph."

I will.

I had lived such astonishments in the last few hours, I should have been numb. Yet hearing that, I found some unsuspected strength inside me. I climbed on, dizzily.

The grass was tall now, almost to my chin.

A sycamore fig loomed just ahead; ripe figs had fallen on the ground, darkening it. *When I return this way, I'll pick a breastful of them,* I thought, *to take them back to my mother. We'll bake them together into dry fig cakes.* I breathed the trees. Poplars and willows. Oaks, with leaves like tiny green pennies. "How did you think up all those shapes, Hashem, or did your hands let themselves go and just *did*?"

He smiled from right nearby. *Ask my hands. They're still doing.*

I hiccuped as I bumped into a trunk. A terebinth tree. As I tottered back into the clear . . .

His hands were large, with flattened thumbs, skin broken by healed cuts, thickened by work, not pretty. They shaped tree trunks, tweaked branches, split green stuff. Leaves fell from his

185

fingers. Everything shaped differently, sized differently. He didn't plan things in detail, not from the start. He was too buoyant with creation, too anxious to fill the empty space. More trunks, leaves—veined, fringed, spiked. He tickled bark. There was that hazy feeling in the air, that tired feeling: *It is good.*

No longer lonely! He seemed to exult in his work. Busy now! And he made eyes twinkle everywhere, then rinsed his hands on the sky. He dropped them back, clean and tired, and folded them and waited.

Smiling from my own cleverness, I said, "Don't trick me. Your hands look now like my father's. But my father's hands are old. Yours are young. And how do I know that? Because you made the first man and woman in your image, and they were young . . . so, *you* are young!" Delighted, I waited for him to praise me.

Go back, he beseeched. *Seeing Joseph will be painful.*

"I don't care. I've had a lot of pain lately."

You're too dear to so many people, and to me.

I felt an emotion beyond bounds. I felt him so near me, I couldn't help a gasping sense of triumph. I'm such a woman, I have such skill to draw another soul toward me, a man's especially. *And you, Adonai, are more man than anything else, sadly so for women, but I feel it in everything you do and say. Am I wrong? When you begat it all, and me, you had a partner? I don't think so. I saw how you fit leaf to trunk. There's such longing in you for* pairing. *When you made the man and the woman, you took from him and gave to* her, *so in a way you made us fused from the start. I have the man about myself, everywhere. How could I not know him better than he knows himself?* He was utterly quiet, while I (daring me!) dallied with him: *You wanted me to understand you? Am I beginning to understand?*

Stop, he said. *We're here.*

* * *

I LOOKED AROUND. All around me, overgrown and wild, was *that* garden.

I stood in grass up to my chin.

Joseph lay on the ground, face up, breathing haltingly in sleep. Tiny bubbles of spit showed in the corners of his mouth.

I watched, with my heart in my mouth. "Why would you show me Joseph as the first man, Adonai?"

Watch.

His fingers tore out the rib, red like a ripe core of fruit. Palpitating. The future!

I gasped in pain for Joseph, but Adonai urged—*Watch!*—as if proud to show off to me. He stretched that rib, thinned the red of blood into pink of newborn skin, turned that skin tan, spread it over shoulders and arms and legs. He flipped his littlest finger at a face, flecking it with cheeks, with dimples! He tickled the eye sockets; lids and lashes! He rubbed that littlest finger on the woman's head; rich brown hair, to comb, to let loose, to swirl! (Did he foresee the countless ways in which I could play with my hair?)

I thought, *All that I was at first was one rib, one piece. But I'm from flesh and blood. The man is from dirt. His crude skin, the earth shows on it. My skin has silkiness. His hair erupts all over, his smells are from sweat clogged by dust. My smells are sweet. My markings are discreet, and wary, and lipped and leafed and budlike.*

He closed the ribcage. He wiped a bruise. He blew into Joseph's face. *Foo!*

Joseph blinked, sat up, jumped up. His eyes and mine met—gold in his eyes, gold in mine.

There was a throbbing between us. The air felt loaded, as if a nameless spice was sprinkled in it. There had been an ignition, a change.

He and I. Maybe other worlds were being made now, but we didn't care.

My host whispered to me, *If you love him so much, I'll take you both up to me, up here. You'll never be without each other . . .* I gasped, "What about my mother and my father? I'm a loving daughter, I couldn't live away from them . . ."

I'll take them to me, too.

Then I felt terrified—Joseph and I, and my dearest mother and father, all four of us, glazed in timelessness? No movement, no life? I'd have no offspring, no pain, no sacrifice to worry about? I glanced over my shoulder. That tree, where was it? That snake, did he not make it this time? I'm too frightened to live in heaven, too used to my dusty little life. Hope and expectation are part of it, but what would I need hope for, up here? *Come see Joseph, then*, he said. And without touching me, he hurled me into pricking thicket, and I gasped.

Naked, Joseph stumbled blindly in a thorny forest. Lacerated and scarred were his parts of pride and shame, crusted with blood, making me feel such pity! *Joseph! Joseph! I would deal with anything just so that we were together. I would heal you. Just give me a chance, High One! I would cradle what the lightning numbed between my breasts! I complained about you, Joseph, and about you, Adonai. I'll complain no more! I'll warm you up, Joseph, cool you off, toil for you, water you with my tears, and feed you my flesh, my beloved!*

Joseph was rambling in a thicket; his stare was one of madness. He pushed himself against a tree and raped it dryly, groaning and crying. *"Lama ze, Adonai,"* he moaned, *"lama ze?"* Why this? And kept thrusting and bleeding—maybe the pain would awaken his flesh . . .

I screamed. The vision of Joseph vanished.

I fell on my knees in the grass. "Why?" I wailed. I cared nothing that Hashem would be angry. "Why would you make Joseph with life in him, only to deaden the seed in him? What were you trying to prove, what were you finding out? Your self-ishness is hideous! And you can't say you know what Joseph feels!"

But he answered, so close, he froze the air on my lips. *I know! I was like Joseph. I was him. Wandering in dry, sterile alone-ness . . . I was unable to decide, unable to bring anything into being, and I felt alone. I never want to be so alone again.*

Then I felt I glimpsed his riddle, but it was even more puz-zling than I had imagined. What had really happened, between him and us? He made us, so as to free himself from aloneness. But when we disappointed him, why was he not done with us? For obviously, he was not!

I tore free from the thicket and ran down the mountain, stammering, "You who made all from nothing, it was you who set me up in the garden. It was you who gave speech to the snake. It was you who made me want the fruit. Had you shown me any other way to be a mother, I would have accepted it. I'm nothing but what you made me. But you, Hashem, you've been holding back from me. You showed me how you fitted star to sky, leaf to tree, and fang to beast with parts that fit. And me to the man with parts that fit. *You* were the one who set it all up. Then how could you punish me?"

I started running down the mountain harder and faster, with the stones in the grass crippling my feet, jolting my thoughts in my head as I stepped on them. I was so angry, and so sad, too! *You left us together, having set up everything between us, and came back and had my husband tell on me! Then you sentenced me: From here on, in pain you shall bear your children, and your man shall be lord over you! Oh, your cruelty to me back then hurts me greatly. I say to you,* I still, still love you, *but with this mind you gave me, which wishes to understand you, I ask, Was there something you didn't think through? Something you couldn't predict or failed to fathom?* At the peak of my revolt, I was running into thinning darkness, dawn was near, and I tripped, and fell.

Terrified, I waited.

There was dawn in the eastern sky.

I felt that by not answering me he was answering. Something had escaped him, something had turned out different. But, maybe he, too, had suffered from what he had not expected, he, too, was sad and abashed and clumsy. That I knew. I'd heard him speak. He was so like me!

I waited. A new day had broken.

I waited.

HE ARRIVED BY my side again, stepping gently. I felt how he hunkered down by me. His breathing swayed the grass tops. With his silence, he asked if there was something he could do for me.

"Yes," I said. "Let him be a father."

He spoke. *Very well, Mary. One day, Joseph will be a father. What else?*

I wanted to add, But . . . will he be the father of *my* children? But I was too afraid that he would find me greedy and become angry and take his gift back! Insincerely (for would you believe it? I was still angry at him!), I murmured, "Hashem . . . can *I* help you with anything?"

He smiled, unseen. *Yes, Mary, you can. So be it.*

So be it? But I was too worried that I might upset his promise about Joseph. Leave well enough alone, earthly girl. *So be it.*

Go back, he said. *Step in my footsteps so you won't get lost.*

"It's daytime," I said. "I won't get lost."

Then run down your own path, he said, as if defeated by my stubbornness.

And I started down.

But I couldn't help it, I peered back.

He was watching me out of every leaf and blade of grass.

I FOUND THE caravan trail and followed it back toward the well. I walked a long time, out of time. I collapsed.

I WAS FOUND lying right by the caravan trail. Muscular arms lifted me up, the arms of Jibril's sons. They felt like Joseph's arms.

They put me on a camel with an umbrella made of men's shirts over my face, and I was brought back to the oasis like the queen of Sheba, twisting in my saddle.

I awoke again in our tent, and my mother was crying beside me. "Don't vanish like this again, Mary. No man is worth chancing your life for him that way. And without you, my heart would die."

Then my father sat by me and said, "Jibril just brought us word that Joseph's marriage to Lanit and Rona is in two weeks. Mary, is there word from you, for Joseph?"

I contained my crying.

"He's very noble, Joseph. If he said he wants you as his third wife, he feels pledged. So he sent Jibril to tell you. His word is your word now."

I saw the old Arabian, standing in the door of the tent. He paced over and sat by me, too, and was so moved to see me alive. I remembered that Jibril meant "Gabriel."

So I whispered, "No, Gabriel."

Jibril leaned forward, as if he hadn't heard well.

"God made one spouse for Adam, not two or three."

There was a silence.

My heart was tearing, one little piece at a time.

"But El Olam had promised me that Joseph would be a father. About that, will I be happy, Gabriel?"

Gabriel, in the shape of the old Arabian, watched me carefully.

I said, "Whoever will give me a child, I'll do my duty, I'll be the handmaid. God's will be done. That much you can be sure of. So, don't play with my heart, like Joseph did while he thought that he was being so giving."

"What shall I tell Joseph? What is your reply?" Jibril asked.

I shook my head. "No, Gabriel. That's my reply. For I, too, want to give, but I want to give happily, and just now my giving isn't happy."

I had expected the man looming in the tent's door to be Joseph, not Jibril. If Joseph had told me, All of me is yours, Mary, even if some of me is stunted—I would have followed him anywhere! I would have learned the ways for him to give me a child, even if they were hard or disgusting. But he hadn't come for me. So what was I to do?

I would not be his third wife.

Jibril left. To tell Joseph something, to tell him nothing, I did not care.

I slowly healed from that thirst and exhaustion. Amazing is a young woman's body. A week later, I was walking under the date trees, and after another week I started working at the well again.

And shortly thereafter, the Roman man arrived, with the writ of forgiveness.

* * *

BELIEVE IT OR not, I had not told Orpa what had happened on the mountain. I kept that to myself—for one whole day!

Then, still languishing in bed, I whispered it all to Orpa. She was so curious about Joseph's man parts being fried by the lightning. Yet, had that been Joseph? Maybe, delirious from hunger and thirst up there, I saw some crippled vagrant and made up all else?

I told her I didn't make it up. I asked her, "You're not scared of this, Orpa?"

"Of what? You came back from that mountain still unopened, sadly enough. Jibril's sons could have had their sport with you when you lay senseless in the desert, but . . . they didn't. I almost wish they did, it would have been a way out of your quandary. What's to be scared about?"

I threw my arms around her. Oh, Orpa. Orpa.

Orpa, you're my dearest friend and such a tough almond, no wonder you're named Orpa. Your father told me once how you were your own girl from the start, when you spat the tit your mother tried to soothe you with, but hunted for it with your tiny pink gums when *you* wanted it. They planned to name you Ruth, but your father said, She's no Ruth, this girl, she's no submissive servant. She'll be no one's follower.

So they named you Orpa after Naomi's other daughter-in-law, who wouldn't stay with Naomi as Ruth did when both of them were widowed.

The widow Orpa said farewell to Ruth and trekked alone back to her native land of Moab to start a new life, most undutiful!

I so love you, Orpa, my tough almond from the desert!

* * *

SO. JIBRIL CAME with his caravan again, and the Jews of the Desert waited for him strung around the lip of the oasis, making Jibril wonder, *Did someone die?* But my father called out to him, as I had coached him, "We're going home. The king forgave us! And the well is for sale!"

"Praised be Ilu, but the well's not yours, it belongs to everyone that rides by!"

Said my father, as I had coached him, "Then we'll ask Darvoush the Persian to take over the well, you think it will still be everyone's? This is your chance, Jibril, and the price is eight carts and eight donkeys—a steal."

Jibril's four beefy sons clicked their tongues to push their camels closer. They bowed to my father, but gazed at me and the other girls. Like hot steel tempered in water, was how they gazed at us. And Jibril said, "Sell the girls, Joachim, and you'll have all the carts and donkeys you wish."

I stepped up by my father like a young sprig of cypress by the old cypress. The beefy sons converged their glances on me, the wind stood still, and I said, "We worked the well from silt back to clear water, it's ours to trade if we want to. What you'll give us, Jibril, is really no loss to you, and you get the well, and you're a good man in God's eyes. Don't you like being that way?"

Jibril smiled sneakily. He anwered toward my father, "Has she agreed to marry Joseph?"

"I don't know. She has her own mind about that."

"Then never marry her off, never! She's your good luck charm from Ilu. Whoever she's around, she blesses. Let her be *my* bondwoman, I'll set her up in my home in Etzion by the Red

Sea. She'll wash my feet, that'll be her only chore. I'll bring her back in a year, still unopened. I swear by *Ilu*! And I'll buy the well now. Name your price!"

"I can't sell her," my father said. "Who'll take care of my own old days?"

There was a silence.

Then the older of Jibril's sons talked to Jibril in Arabic, and I guessed his meaning, Arabic and Aramaic being not that far apart. "You sick old dog, father, sick for any bitch's tail raised up and juicy underneath, we'd rather get none of these girls than you acquire the betoola. For she'd be the end of you! Hear me, kin of Joachim, we'll buy the well, at your price!" And Jibril's sons flogged their camels to look for carts to give to us. Because they felt it, my urgency. Give, for love is giving. Giving without fear. *I* say so, *I,* the betoola. Feel the beating of my heart.

Then I looked away. That day happened to be particularly clear. Far to the west, the mountain outlined itself, barely a shade darker than the air, but I could see it.

Love is knowing someone in his innermost core. *Yes, Adonai?*

And love is knowing without fear.

One day I'll know you *without fear and in your innermost core. Yes, Adonai? And now, say nothing. Submit to me for once. Agree with me, by saying nothing!*

And he said nothing.

Part 8

Pilate

The Galilean coast, one week after Apella's visit to the oasis.

H E COULD have requested a driver at Fortress Antonia, but he decided to drive the rapid two-horse Roman *cisium* himself, knowing that the exercise would clear his mind.

Whipping the two horses along the coastal highway to Caesarea, Apella glanced over his shoulder. His assigned escort, four mounted legionnaires, galloped hard behind him, but they were no match for his handling of horses.

Being in advance of his schedule, he was happy to have a day to himself in Caesarea, to spend it at the local army brothel, or in an extended dinner visit with the Velleni, a family of Roman colonists, whose patriarch worked in the tax collection office. The Velleni were always happy to have him as a guest. They lived behind thick walls, had no contact with the locals—their own servants being Greek—and like all resident foreigners they relished gossip from Herod's court.

Unexpectedly, Apella had to pull on his reins. Ahead on the road, a mounted centurion *primipilus* was signaling him to stop. He brought his steeds to a clattering halt. The soldier saluted with outstretched arm, and reported that sped by good winds, the *Tyrenia,* a fast ship from Brundisium, Italy, had been in Caesarea two days already. Among the arriving passengers was Doctor Aulus Celsus, a distinguished surgeon from Rome.

"I was just heading to the port, to welcome Doctor Celsus and take him to Jerusalem," Apella replied.

"The doctor was called to the army hospital," the primipilus reported. "He was asked by the army doctors to repair some soldiers of ours, whom the Parthians sent us back as part of a prisoner exchange."

"I see," Apella replied, suppressing a grimace. He knew what kind of repair those prisoners needed after having been held by the Parthians.

"Was my mail boot on the ship?" he inquired. The "boot," a round trunk of leather, inside which were sewn letters from Italy, was his own personal link to Caesar. It was always marked *magni momenti,* "of great urgency," on its sides and top.

"It was. I thought I'd bring it to you, but the doctor held on to it and took it to the hospital. So I rushed to inform you, as your correspondence must be important."

"You did the right thing. Drive me to the hospital."

The soldier jumped from his saddle, threw himself in the cisium beside Apella, and picked up the reins.

The four legionnaires caught up just then. One leaned from his saddle to grab the bridle of the horse of the primipilus. Apella turned to the oldest legionnaire. "Ride on to Casarea's marketplace and ask for Xilos!" He had sent Xilos ahead with a catering cart to buy fresh fish, bread, and fruit at the market so that Apella could welcome the doctor with a *prandium frigidulum,* an al fresco lunch.

"Have Xilos wait for us outside the city's east gate," Apella added.

The legionnaire nodded, turned toward the port, and clattered on. The cisium and the three remaining legionnaires sped down the highway toward the Roman army hospital.

APELLA HAD HEARD about Doctor Celsus when he was still working at Marcias's riding school. Celsus restored the sexual vigor of dissipated Roman aristocrats. His book *De Medicina,* a treatise about how to enlarge and reshape the male genitals, sold well. Celsus had dedicated *De Medicina* to Augustus himself.

Who exactly he would be treating in Jerusalem, Apella did not know; the commander of Herod's personal guard was the rumored patient. But Apella expected that the beneficiary would be Herod, typically testing the treatment on someone else first. Herod planned to marry again; his intended was a young princess from Petra.

It might help to befriend Celsus, Apella reflected. But first, he should read his mail.

That feel of cold leaves, that brush of fear, swept down his spine again. What was happening in Rome? Was he still in the emperor's good graces?

Apella had left the palace without going before the king again, to ask for the return of the homes of the Joachimites. He didn't want to give the king the slightest chance to reverse his first writ and reinstitute the banishment. The tribe was trekking back already. He would convince the doctor to travel via Nazareth—an interesting ancient town—hopefully reaching Nazareth at the same time as the tribe.

And then . . . his heart quickened. He would see her again.

She was a spell, that girl.

Just before leaving Jerusalem, Apella had written to Ascanius:

> *Carus magister,* dear teacher,
>
> Virginhood never leaves my mind anymore,
> after being so immersed in the old Jewish writs. What
> is in virginhood that makes us men so fascinated with
> it? Is it from respect for our mothers' purity, that we
> wish they hadn't brought us out *inter feces atque*
> *urinam,* from between shit and piss? Do you
> understand, magister? I don't. But I so wish I had
> more time here.
>
> How is the emperor's health? How are Tiberius's
> conspiracies affecting our timetable?
>
> I wish that there was one god. Yes, one only, so I
> could take my confusion to him, like the Jews do, in
> prayer and humility. When are we Romans ever
> humble in prayer, even standing before Jupiter
> Tonans, Maximus, all forty feet of gilded marble? But
> who knows the right way to have faith (maybe the
> Jews?). With hope, your devoted pupil,
>
> Pilate

The army hospital and the army brothel lay side by side on the shore, separated by a wire fence.

Pilate had never visited the hospital. The brothel he had, and often. He left lavish tips and graded the women in a ledger kept in the anteroom. Atria from Damascus, sixteen, tells filthy stories: *mediocris.* Carmen, from Ebusus, seventeen, dances naked: *saluber, commoda.* Hypatia from Rome, twenty-six, attended Caesar's sexual parties until struck with an ugly skin rash: *optima.*

The place made him feel as though he were in Rome; closing his eyes, he could be in a Roman street, among red-blooded men who drank, gossiped, raced dogs, gambled, eased themselves side by side in the latrines, and talked about Rome's future. The solidarity of common fighting men, wasn't that Rome's moral virtue? *Hmm.* That brothel should have some Galilean girls, too. Preferably with cute freckles, tanned, with shiny eyes . . .

He glimpsed the adobe buildings of the wards and a heap of burning wood set right on the beach. The soldiers who died here without specifying where and how to be interred were fed to the pyre. Apella spotted whores crowding the wire, peering into the hospital grounds. He heard their voices. *"Surgite, sanescite!"* they shouted. Get sewn up, and heal! The whole brothel seemed to be at the wire.

Puzzled, Apella realized that the women were watching men lining before a potbellied individual Apella had never seen before. The visiting surgeon.

Doctor Celsus had gaunt cheeks, at odds with his body's plumpness. His eyes were dug deep in their sockets, brown and piercing. Chatting with the soldiers, he bit his lip, as if in compassion. All the men were bandaged around their loins. The Parthians had cut or crushed their genitals. Celsus turned to a soldier who opened his bandages, revealing a halved manhood. At the wire, the whores shrank back, mute with horror.

Apella gritted his teeth. Just then he noticed his mail boot in the arms of an orderly. On its side, the initials MM were clearly visible. *Magni momenti.*

Someone opened a gate. He walked in. The orderly with the boot recognized Apella and hurried over. Celsus turned, guessed who Apella was. "*Salve,* Eques. I've heard a lot about you."

"Salve. Any hope for these wretches?"

Celsus lowered his voice. "No. The Parthians didn't leave me much to work with. I'm giving them a little hope . . . and acquiring rights to their bodies. Most of them will die within the week from bleeding and infections. But the skin from their bodies, I can use it for grafts." Celsus turned back to the mutilated man. "What is your name?"

"Lodus," said the soldier. He was young, one of the few with a fit, muscular body.

An orderly scribbled the name on a tablet. Apella guessed. *You'll become graft for some rich Roman, Lodus.*

"They left me enough to rebuild you, Lodus. I shall operate on you when I return from Jerusalem. With skin from your own belly, and veins from your own legs. March aside. Next."

"Thank you, Doctor! May you be the earth's happiest man!" Stumbling away, Lodus glanced at the wire with women. Which whore sobbed louder for Lodus—that mature madam? That shy new recruit? They all cried. Purified by compassion. *Ite me dei,* who's putting such thoughts in my mind?

Celsus addressed the remaining soldiers. "I'll examine the rest of you when I return from Jerusalem." A moan of disappointment swelled, but Celsus waved his hand reassuringly. "Back in a week. I'll do my best for all of you. Let's go, Eques."

They paced away. The doctor's tone was relaxed. "So, you're a legend in the high circles. Agent of history, Ascanius calls you. How's the hunt for prophesized virgins?"

"Slow," Apella mumbled. Why would Ascanius confide in Celsus? "What's new in Rome?"

"Tiberius snuck in from Germany and tried to kill Augustus. Augustus captured him and would have killed him, but his wife, Drusilla, intervened, and Tiberius was sent back to Germany in a kind of perpetual exile."

"*Dei boni!* When did that happen?"

"Just before I left. Only a handful of people know."

Apella breathed deeply. In Rome, the power had almost changed hands. He spoke slowly, choosing his words. "The emperor was wise not to kill Tiberius. Showing restraint will benefit him."

"True. But Rome is in such a crisis. Real estate is tumbling, there are slave uprisings every day, and the rich are even deeper into magic and sex. Which is not bad for me, I charge five thousand aurei for an enlargement and twenty-five hundred for sculpting the tip. Want your *acro-posthion* sculpted?"

"My acro . . . ?" Apella mumbled, trying not to sound stupid.

"As in 'acro-polis'? The tip of your man-tool? I might be useful to you in your marriage to Octavia. Are you not supposed to marry her soon?"

"I am, and she hasn't complained about my shape."

He took the lead, walked the doctor out of the hospital grounds, back to the road, into the cisium. He pointed the direction, toward Caesarea's east gate, and the primipilus whipped the horses.

Celsus stared at the well-kept Roman estates on both sides of the road. "Where are the Jews, Eques? Everyone I meet—officials, soldiers, doctors—they're Greek, Roman, Phoenician, Arabian. Where are the Jews?"

"Farther inland. We pushed them into the hills and the desert."

"Out of view, in their own land?"

"Precisely. We turned this sea, from Spain to Palestine, into a Roman lake."

"Is that a Jew?" the doctor pointed.

The catering cart, drawn by two horses, was coming out of the city's east gate. Sitting with dignity on the box, in a gray shift and a black head-cover, a young man with earlocks steered toward the cisium. Red-faced and crabby, Xilos sat behind the driver.

"That's one," Apella confirmed.

"The breed in its own habitat. How long do you think the Jews will be around?"

What the hell's he twaddling about? Apella wondered.

"Are you hungry?" he countered.

He waved at the cart.

Xilos recognized Apella. He barked orders at two Greek boys, kitchen assistants, who busied themselves with pots and baskets of food. The cart driver pulled by the side of the road, stepped down. Apella had seen him work for Xilos before, his name was Hillel. Hillel pulled pita bread, dried olives, and an apple out of the sleeve of his shift, then sat by the road with his back turned to the cart and ate.

In an instant, the Greek boys had prepared a very nonkosher meal of grilled prawn and crab beaten in its shell and steamed with dill and garlic. Xilos opened a flask of white wine, warm, bubbling from the cart's movement. While the food was spread onto a cloth on the grass, the doctor strolled over to Apella

206

and said softly, "Don't be cagey with me, Eques. I know every-thing that happens in Rome. Not to speak of who my real patient is in Jerusalem."

"So it's the king?"

"If my treatment is successful, I'm sure the king will avail himself."

"I'm due in Nazareth," Apella said. "I'm in charge of reset-tling a tribe. The caterer can take you to Jerusalem." He walked to the cisium, grabbed the mail boot, took out his pugio, and started chipping at the boot's clasps.

Celsus approached the cisium. "I'll go to Nazareth, if it's on the way."

"It really isn't. Why did you take my mail off the ship? Did you try to open it?"

"Of course not. I just deemed it convenient to bring it with my luggage. Ascanius wants us to be friends."

"I'll decide who my friends are. Don't ever try to bully me, even if you are the emperor's doctor." Those accursed clasps gave way to the pugio. "I saved the emperor's life."

And that was utterly true.

THERE WERE THREE letters in the boot.

He recognized the seal on two. They were from Ascanius.

He did not recognize the seal on the third; it was of clear plain wax without letters or other symbols. Worried, he opened it first. It was very brief:

> *Pilate, my niece Sabina Octavia Minima accepts*
> *you as her husband.*
>
> *Caesar*

Aha. That tart got herself pregnant at last.

He noticed a few words scribbled at the bottom of the page. They were in a different hand, small and cute:

Quidnam venatio virg.? How's the hunt for the virgin?

He guessed who wrote them. Octavia. Maybe she and Caesar laughed together as she added those words. Apella remembered the musky scent of Octavia's wolf fur.

He was excited. His instructions to sail back to Italy should be in one of Ascanius's letters. He would be needed as bridegroom!

He opened the first letter.

It recounted Tiberius's attempt to seize power. In the dead of night, twelve days before, Tiberius had led a strike force into the villa in Colli Albani, to kill Caesar. But Tiberius's mother, Drusilla, was sleeping in Caesar's bedroom. She threw herself in front of Tiberius's sword and begged him not to kill Caesar. Then she turned to her husband, agog and disheveled, and pleaded that he should designate Tiberius as his successor, while Tiberius should swear not to set foot in Italy before Caesar died naturally. Caesar would hold Drusilla hostage against another attack from Tiberius.

But as Caesar almost agreed to the deal, Ascanius surrounded the villa with an army of vigiles. Tiberius's men dropped their weapons and begged for their lives. Caesar pressured Tiberius to divulge his supporters' names, and Tiberius gave them away. The most important of them turned out to be Senator Textor, who ran Rome's taxation office.

Then Ascanius ended his letter:

I'm off to arrest Textor. Was Drusilla involved in
the conspiracy? I don't think I'll find out. *Sic transit
infamia,* thus infamy comes to pass. Congratulations
on your marriage to Octavia!

A.

Apella stared at the letter's final line. Marrying Octavia
would inextricably tie him to Caesar.

Should I quickly sail to Italy? he wondered. *To court
Drusilla, just in case? If Tiberius was allowed to go back to Germany, then he's not finished in politics. What could Tiberius's
mother be like? Still healthy, still open to a young man's advances? I
used to be good at that game . . . Maybe I should let Celsus embel-
lish my acro-posthion . . .* The prawn he'd barely tasted came up
in his gut.

Breathing slowly, he calmed down. Caesar's not dead, and
marrying Octavia won't hurt me in the least.

He glanced over the top of the papyri. Celsus was strolling
with Xilos. Two beggars with long earlocks approached them.
Xilos shouted them away. The cart driver, Hillel, tried to appease
Xilos, but Xilos shouted at him, too. Hillel made a disgusted face
and stepped away. Apella opened the second letter.

Carus amicus atque discipulus, dear friend and
disciple,

Lucky hag, Drusilla! Caesar declared her *Mater Patriae,* Mother
of the Nation, and will dedicate her a temple.

We caught Textor. We'll keep him under house arrest
and poison his food a little bit every day 'til he dries
up on his feet. The others, we'll throw them off the
Rock.

Now Caesar was shattered by all that. Tiberius
grew up in his palace. He sent for me and cried on
my chest. "Who can I trust?" I didn't have the heart
to reply, You can trust no one, power and trust are
self-exclusive.

Caesar summoned three doctors to examine his
health. One for bones and joints, one for breathing
and digestion, one for urination and sex drive; that
doctor, you guessed it, was Celsus. Celsus told Caesar
that he has the bladder and genitals of a twenty-year-
old! Caesar told him about the theophany and about
that baby king born to a virgin. He got drunk with
Celsus and me and raved, "Could we bring that girl to
Rome, and have her give birth in Circus Maximus?"
So now Celsus is in the know, watch yourself, puer.

Bizarre discovery at Textor's mansion. Textor
and Tiberius had drafted a plan that if Tiberius
becomes emperor, Rome's Jews should be banished
from the city. Too influential, too numerous,
according to Tiberius and Textor.

So I asked Textor, What do you really hold
against the Jews?

And he replied, Their notion of God. The deities
from Mount Olympus are depraved and childlike.
They never laid down laws, their word was never
gathered in a book. The God of the Jews is so grim
and shrewd, intense and cryptic. Forever putting the
humans to the test, forever holding out a promise.
How could that not be scary? Besides—and now he
looked me in the eye—you're a Jew, Ascanius, and

Augustus is under your spell. You're the Jew who rules Rome. That cannot be. Rome is for the true Romans.

I said, My ancestors came here with a Phoenician ship, two centuries before yours, Textor. How are you more Roman than I am?

Rome is Roman, he repeated. Roman means Roman only, not Roman *and* Jewish. There's the difference.

Can you imagine, puer? I have lived here as a Jew, feeling that this was my home. The Romans would never try to erase the Jews, like the Assyrians and the Egyptians before them. Now I wonder. Can you tell that I am sad, puer?

Celsus told Caesar that he's off to Judea, to massage Herod into one last good erection. Caesar was amused. "Ah, Herod, my best *rex socius,* client king. When I was fighting Mark Anthony, Herod was tetrarch of Galilee and Anthony's ally. I told him to betray Anthony, and I would make him king. He betrayed Anthony. Always trust a traitor. Now I'll send Octavia to Judea when she starts showing, she'll marry Pilate in Judea, but *he's not excused from bringing in the theophany,* and it better be one I can replay in Rome, or it's the Rock for your pupil! I promised the Romans the best show on earth!"

So, it's on you, puer.

Now—tear this up after you read it—you might succeed Augustus, for I and the vigiles will never support Tiberius. I'd rather pay off the plebs from my own purse to get them to clamor: Pi-late . . . Pilate . . . In the Forum, in Campus Martius, in the temples, on the steps of the Ara Pacis: Pi-late, Pi-late! Do your utmost, Pilate. And write soon.

Your loving teacher,
Ascanius.

P.S. If you save Rome from chaos *and* Rome's Jews from exile—what a joke on God, Big-boned. You, the ultimate non-Jew! Good luck.

Folding the letters, he stared ahead, at the cart carrying Celsus and Xilos.

Tonight, I'll destroy the letters, out of the sight of those snoops.

Or maybe I shouldn't destroy them!

Jolted about in the cisium, he thought soberly, *I could be the next Caesar. I'd have to wrest Rome from Tiberius's supporters, but I could be the next Caesar.*

But how can I stage a theophany in Rome? My own theophany?

Let's see . . . The stadium of Julius Caesar had a flooding mechanism used to stage naval battles in front of thousands of spectators. The army engineers could flood it, while I would rise above the waters, pulled up by ropes, commanding the flood to subside. The waters would be sucked back into drainage pipes. Again, using Rome's drainage, I could part the river Tiber. Or I could make day into night, by filling Rome with smoke from smoke machines, causing utter panic, until, suspended above the chaos, I could yell for the smoke to subside. I'm saving Rome, I'm bringing daylight back! I, Caesar-God! And the vigiles, strategically placed in every key spot, would intone, Pi-late, Pi-late!

He choked from fright and excitement.

He bit his lip, stood up straight, stared at Xilos and the doctor in the cart ahead. He forced himself back to reality.

"Drive alongside the cart," he ordered the primipilus.

The man brought the cisium next to the cart. Celsus and Xilos were in deep conversation.

Xilos was complaining to Celsus that he was born with *lipodermos,* the condition of having a very short foreskin. Could Celsus lengthen Xilos? "Easy," Celsus replied. "Two thousand aurei. You should stop drinking, wine inflames the blood vessels and the urinary tract."

Xilos sighed: "I could pay a thousand . . . But what's life without wine?"

On the cart's box, Hillel was listening in, his eyes bulging in surprise. He noticed that Apella was staring from the other vehicle. "That man really stretches foreskins?" he inquired incredulously.

"Yes. The world is made of crazy quirks."

"Xilos told the doctor that all Jews are witches or thieves." Hillel spat in disgust.

"Don't work for that drunk idiot again. Where are you from, Hillel?"

"From Nazareth. But there was a clan war in Nazareth. No work, the harvests went to waste . . . Now, finally, one Nazarene is to marry girls from each clan, to make peace. Put it all in one bed, you know?"

"Is he that man who carves angels?"

"Yes," Hillel smiled. He liked this Roman, he felt no distrust for him. "Joseph, the no-good with girls, who gets the best girls." He pointed with his whip. "Nazareth is that way. We'll be there by late afternoon."

The road was paved the Roman way, with flagstones set in an even layer over a bed of limestone concrete, with the curvature of the top raised, so that rainwater would seep down the sides. The best Roman engineering. "Look at what we gave the Jews," Xilos grumbled. "The best roads! Are they showing gratitude? Nah!"

The cisium and the cart moved at a fast trot.

Farther inland, a column of Jewish convicts repaired the road under the whip of Syrian overseers. Now Celsus saw Jews in good numbers, the convicts were easily a hundred. They worked naked. They had full beards and earlocks.

"Barbarians, when will they learn how to shave?" Xilos belched.

"What did they do?" Apella asked Hillel.

"*Ha-kol*, everything," Hillel replied sarcastically.

In the blink of an eye, a revolt started. The convicts grabbed a guard, knocked him to the ground, dropped a road flattener on his face, blood splashed out. They ran off toward the hills—not chained, Apella noted. The Syrians ran after them, speared a few, caught two alive. Crossed poles were planted upright by the road in no time; the rebels were shoved onto the poles, and nailed . . .

It was over. The traffic moved on.

TIRED AT LAST, he closed his eyes, nodding his head to the horses' trotting.

Mary was near him. Live, vibrant. So close, he could touch her.

Would you help me? he wondered. *And I'll help you, too, as best I can.*

She nodded. Her innocence was so natural . . .

He opened his eyes. "Drive easy," he ordered the primipilus.

He scoured inside his travel sack. He brought out his stylus, a writing board, an inkstand with fluid ink in it. He searched for clean papyri, but found none. He pulled the top sheet of Ascanius's message out of the boot, dipped the stylus in the ink.

In large Latin letters, he wrote the grant of the Jews' homes on the back of Ascanius's message.

> *I, the king, ruler of all Jews, hereby grant the homes*
> *of the kin of Joachim ben Ahaz ben Matthan back to*
> *their original owners, upon their return to Nazareth.*
> *Such is my will.*

He signed in thickly drawn letters: HM for Herodes Magnus.

I promised to get you a writ for your homes. You see? I keep my promises.

She thanked him with her brightest smile.

FIELDS OF WHEAT began to line the road. Oak groves animated the landscape. Two women, minuscule, toiled at an olive press. Beyond the oil press, he saw Nazareth's walls and sun-baked streets.

The village swarmed with people. Men mended the roofs of their houses. Children ran in and out of the walls.

"Getting ready for that wedding," Hillel explained. "They're so looking forward to peace, you'd think everyone's getting married."

"Who owns those?" Apella asked, pointing to two grain silos made of mud bricks that rose within the walls of the city.

"The smaller one belongs to Aaron, who runs the gangs.

The larger one belongs to Shalafta, who's been pushing for that tribe to return."

"Why? Wouldn't he lose property that he plundered?"

"He'd make up for it. And why is this Rome's business?"

Apella explained that the Romans had become interested in the faith of the Jews. He expected Hillel to react flattered. Instead, Hillel rolled his eyes. "Woe to the Jews, when the goyim take a liking to their faith! Is that why you were sent here?"

"Yes. If your Mashiah arrives, we're trying to be prepared."

"You are prepared. You have legions here, and catapults, and crosses."

"Don't worry, Hillel. The Jews have nothing to fear from me." *Spoken like the next Caesar,* he told himself. And then he gritted his teeth. *Get ahold of yourself, puer!*

Hillel looked away and whipped the horses.

The mountain of lightning was now in full view.

It suddenly seemed taller and greener. Above the peak, one cloud flashed lightning, like a winking eye.

Then out of that single cloud it rained, and the rain turned to hail.

The hail stopped as brusquely as it had started. Men and women hurried back to their tiny fields. With harnesses around their shoulders attached to plows, they cleared the fields of rocks.

Celsus asked Hillel, "Don't you people have oxen to pull the plows?"

"The oxen we sell to pay the Romans' taxes," said Hillel in passable Latin.

In a farmyard, sparrows caught in nets flitted their wings. A housewife gathered the sparrows and clamped dry raisins in the cleaned nets to attract more sparrows.

216

"That's for the family pot," Hillel explained. "The chickens we give to Aaron, to help us with the Romans."

"Does he help you?" Celsus asked, beginning to seem interested.

"Like coughing helps a headache," Hillel replied.

The cisium and the cart passed a circle of boulders set around the village. Hillel was not sure how ancient they were, but Apella had checked his history. The boulders had fortified Nazareth against the Greeks of King Antioch, who had tried to force the Jews to give up circumcising. The Jews fought the Greeks off with pitchforks and hoes, and when the Greeks broke into Nazareth, the Jews fought them even with circumcising knives.

The Greeks had defeated the Jews and burned Nazareth, sparing only a handful of survivors.

Then the Romans had chased away Antioch's Greeks and conquered Nazareth and all of Israel more thoroughly than all invaders before them.

They had brought Roman peace and progress—roads, taxation, crucifixions.

Apella ordered the vehicles to stop outside Nazareth's east gate.

"All of you wait here. Come with me, Hillel."

He strode toward the gate, with the driver scurrying after him.

Two steps from the gate, he took out the forged writ and pushed it into Hillel's hand. "This is the order that Joachim's tribe must be resettled in their homes, unharmed. You'll take it to Aaron. I'll be right beside you. You tell Aaron that if he touches one hair on them, I'll have him on a cross 'til his bones are picked shiny." The Roman had talked in a controlled manner. But Hillel seemed afraid to touch the papyrus. He shuffled his feet.

"Get going, Hillel."

"Y-You don't know Aaron, you'll only make him more fierce . . . ," Hillel stuttered. "He'll slaughter them *because* you told him not to do it."

Apella spoke patiently. "Listen to me. I'll be the protector of your land. I'll be the procurator of all Syria-Palestine, I will clean out the gangs, and I will exempt the Jews from taxes they can't pay."

Behind them, Xilos, his assistants, and the doctor had stepped out of the vehicles and were walking now toward the gate. Apella turned and snapped at them. "I said, stay back and wait!"

"Where are you going?" Xilos asked. "The Jews will jump you and kill you."

"Do as I say."

They drew back, perplexed. Bearded faces were showing on the village walls—men, most of them old, some armed with spears and pitchforks.

"This is not the king's hand, you wrote it," Hillel whispered, crumpling the forged order.

"Give it to me, then." He took it from the driver's hand.

The village gate was being repaired; whole beams and panels were missing from it. The men nailing wood planks over the holes gawked at the Roman. Some seemed to recognize Hillel, though no one spoke.

Apella pushed the gate open. He moved his pugio to the front of his belt, at the ready, then looked up the street. He had a full description of Aaron: short, bowlegged, his skin parched red.

He saw a blackened hut with two smokestacks. A smithery.

He walked toward it.

The village looked like a war zone. Barriers with sharpened spikes surrounded the houses. Ramparts of clay were built in front of house doors. Boys with spears stood watch. Everywhere, dogs snarled.

As Apella advanced, the windows filled with faces, and the yards and side lanes filled with men and women.

Hillel caught up. By the time they stopped before the smithery, Hillel reached for and took the forged order from Apella's hand.

A short man in a sooty leather apron stepped out. He looked at Hillel in surprise. Then he looked at the Roman. His face was red like metal in a furnace.

Hillel handed Aaron the forged order. Other men in smoke-stained aprons, helpers and apprentices, stepped out and fanned behind Aaron, who held the papyrus, pretending to examine it.

He obviously could not read Latin and very likely could not read at all.

Apella crossed his arms over the platelets of his tunic. *Aaron looks like Herod,* he thought. The same hardness of features, the same rage in his eyes, old, stayed, and empty. A man who forgot that he could act gently, or be patient. Apella's trained ear picked the sound of a bow being tautened. *They won't jump me, they won't dare.*

Aaron asked a question. Hillel said something in reply.

One of Aaron's men held a set of pincers. He suddenly lifted a red-hot chunk of iron in its jaws. "Put that down," Apella said in Aramaic. Like lightning, he thrust the pugio toward the thug's face. The man dropped the pincers. The red-hot blade splashed into a tempering bucket. The sizzling of the metal in cold water broke the deadly tension.

Aaron folded the papyrus, stuck it under his apron. He nodded to Hillel.

"What's his answer?" Apella asked.

Hillel read the silence. "Be on your way, Roman. You told me."

Aaron stepped back into his smoky shop. Apella turned and left with Hillel following. They reemerged outside the walls, walked back to the stopped vehicles.

"Where's a place to spend the night?" Apella stammered.

Hillel pointed. "Up behind the widows' oil press there's an inn."

Apella waved at the primipilus. The man dashed over.

"Get on your horse and ride back to Sepphoris," Apella instructed. "By tonight, I want you back with all the legionnaires you can find, at least two *manipuli* [platoons] with horses and rations for a week. Emperor's orders. One manipulus will camp by this gate, the other by the inn." He turned to Hillel. "Go back to the village. Talk to the people and be back at the inn by dinnertime, to tell me what they're saying. Understood?"

Hillel replied in Aramaic. "I wasn't hired by you. But I'll do it."

"Then turn around and go. We'll be at the inn."

T HIS BOX contains seven different measures of the *pondus Judaeus,*" said Doctor Celsus. "I invented this implement and I'm the one who officialized the name. I named it the Jewish weight because, as I explain in my *De Medicina,* the pondus was from the beginning *plerumque ad usum Romae nobilitatis Judaicae,* most often used by Rome's Jewish aristocracy." Pushing away plates with leftovers, cups, and decanters of gravelly Galilean wine, he placed a wooden box on the table.

Apella glanced back at the curtain that separated the inn's dining room from the common room. A child's hand pulled up the bottom of the curtain, and several little boys peered in. Orphaned little beggars. The doctor lifted the lid of the box. Five pear-shaped bronze weights of different sizes nested inside in gray velvet. The doctor took out the largest and the smallest weights.

"They're brand new, never touched by a man's parts." He chuckled drunkenly, pulling out chains with clawlike cleats and hooking them to the weights. The chains were thin like horse hairs. "These upper claws are hooked into the skin, and the weight hangs from the patient's tool, pulling its skin and elongating it."

"Ouch," gasped one of the kitchen boys.

"The pain is bearable. Try this weight." The kitchen boy picked up the smallest weight. "It's only half a *mina,* about two hundred and fifty grams."

"How long does the patient wear the half mina?" asked Xilos.

"If he wears it one hour every evening, he might progress to a full mina in a week. Not everyone lasts a full treatment." He picked up the largest pondus, handed it to Apella. Apella weighed it and winced. "Two pounds?"

"Maybe a few fractions more." Celsus smiled proudly. "My procedure is becoming so popular, there's a name for my patients. *Recutiti,* the reskinned. In Greek"—he grinned at the Greeks at the table—"they're called stretched men, *epispastikoi.*"

"Epispastikoi, epispastikoi!" chanted the urchins peeking under the curtain. Xilos threw an empty cup at them. "Who are you going to fix at the court?" Xilos asked the doctor.

"Maybe Herod's sons by Queen Malthace? They're athletes, but how can they compete in the Olympic games if they are circumcised? Olympic athletes are examined for mutilations before being allowed to compete."

Xilos twitched. "I don't think I could take your treatment, Doctor . . ."

"Give it some thought." Celsus grinned at the kitchen assistants. "Young ones? Interested in being sculpted?"

The Greek boys averted their eyes. Celsus shrugged. The men's lack of refinement in this colony was deplorable.

"I'm going to turn in," Apella announced. He lifted the curtain and stepped out. The smell of grilled mutton wafted toward him in the cavelike cellar.

Hillel appeared in the entrance. He looked tired and gaunt, as if he'd run back and forth all over the village.

He spotted Apella and walked toward him, past a line of prostitutes.

"Your legionnaires just arrived." He spoke so softly Apella had to read his lips. "Don't run out there, they're only three. There was an uprising on the coast and the troops were rushed to put it down. Pretend you're choosing a prostitute." Apella glanced at the girls; they corrected their slouching posture, and pinched each other's cheeks to look less pale. Hillel kept whispering. "Don't speak, the men in this cellar are from Aaron's gangs. They're watching and listening. This one with the dimpled cheeks? Give me two aurei." Apella pulled out two aurei. Hillel handed them to the girl.

"Buy us two cups of wine and come outside," he said loudly to the girl. Then he turned and headed out with Apella following him.

The legionnaires had tied their horses in a patch of willow shrubs. Their bronze-plated tunics glowed from the lights of the inn's windows.

Hillel hurried away, but Apella caught him by the elbow. "Where are you going?"

"I want to see if anyone followed me." He rushed to a tall rock ledge, climbed it, and stared back toward Nazareth.

Apella ran to the willow shrubs. The oldest legionnaire, a gray-haired veteran, patted the mouth of his horse to stop it from neighing. "Everything quiet here?" he asked Apella.

"Yes. Where's the primipilus that I sent for you?"

"He rode on to Ptolemais. He said to tell you that he'll assemble a larger force, and if we can hold here by ourselves, they'll be back tomorrow by sundown."

"There's nothing to hold. I called you here as a precaution; I'm accompanying a guest of the king."

The veteran took off his helmet, combed his hand through

his matted hair. "Blessed be the gods. So you're the Roman who serves at the court?" Apella nodded. "I was stationed in Jerusalem five years ago. I put down the march of the pots and pans."

Apella had heard of that uprising. During a terrible drought, starving housewives had marched on Herod's palace, banging their empty pots and pans.

"We ran down those unarmed women with our horses. But if the uprisings start again, this time it won't be so easy. We'll be up against *everyone*. I thought this was the beginning of it."

"On the contrary, I think we might enter a peaceful spell."

"May the gods hear you. Where shall we camp?"

"Get out of the shrubs, you're not supposed to be hiding. Set your tent right by the inn's door. I'll have hay and water and food and drink brought out."

He ran back to Hillel, who was descending from the rock ledge.

"I didn't see anyone sneaking up," Hillel whispered. Just then the girl with dimples stepped out of the inn, a cup of wine in each hand. "Don't spill that wine," Hillel called to her.

She nodded, unsteady in her thick-soled sandals that were dyed red, advertising her trade. "You new?" Hillel asked. Under her rouge, the girl's face was young. A victim of Pax Romana. Hillel took a cup, swigged hard, and whispered, "The village is in an uproar over Joachim's return. Everyone's awake. Shalafta locked himself in his house, claiming to be sick. He's not sick, he's waiting to see how the people's mood turns."

"What about Aaron?"

"He's going around saying that Joachim and his daughter are witches or they couldn't have survived in the desert."

"And the people?"

"They don't know what to think. What are *you* going to do?"

"I don't know," Apella admitted.

"You want to believe that this is from God? Then, *believe!*" Apella was tempted to reply, That's precisely what I'd like to do. But he muttered, "I'll try bribing Aaron. I'll offer him a hefty bribe to let the tribe return in peace." He knew how to get the money. Any Roman who found out that he was about to marry Octavia would lend him money and never press him to repay the loan.

"I hope he takes your money. Aaron could kill Joachim *and* Shalafta. He may do it at the wedding and make his daughter a widow before she becomes a wife. He would plunder everyone's homes and cattle, and then . . ." Hillel pointed his finger at Apella, "he would bribe *you.*"

"I'd never take a bribe from him," Apella said with repulsion.

"You're so clean?" Hillel mocked. "Aaron could even use the *tsoaneem,* those vagrants that Alexander the Great dragged here from India. Aaron's chances are better than yours now. Good luck to you and your three legionnaires."

"Shut up. When is the wedding?"

"In four days. I asked in the village."

The prostitute stood before them, offering the other cup. Apella took the cup. Hillel held his cup for the girl to drink, too. She took a shy slurp.

"I'll lie with her behind that rock," Hillel said in Latin, "but I'll claim that I drank too much and lost my urge. Otherwise she'll wonder what's going on." He patted the woman on her arm. She smiled; any friendly gesture was welcome. "Think about what's best to do, Roman man."

He led the girl away, thrashing his feet in the grass to scare the hiding snakes.

"So," said Celsus. "Now we can talk quietly."

Apella dropped his cup. The doctor had stepped out of the inn without making any noise whatsoever.

Apella picked up the spilled cup. "What do you want?"

"The Greek passed out. His boys carried him to an upper room."

"That's not what I asked you."

"I'd like to understand you, Eques. It seems that the Jews are your card . . ."

From behind the rock came muffled voices. The girl sounded scared, and Hillel tried to appease her. Then the men from Aaron's gang stepped out of the inn.

They stopped dead in their tracks. In front of the steps, the Roman soldiers were raising a military tent.

Aaron's men turned and stole away. Apella breathed.

He turned to the doctor. "You were saying?"

"I was saying, Caesar is sixty-three and sickly, but he might last another ten, perhaps even twenty years. That could mean twenty years without Tiberius, which means the Jews will not be exiled from Rome. That will take us down one road in history, instead of another."

"And what's your road, Doctor?"

"I'm a Roman, I'm practical. I'm speaking of you, Eques. Isn't it wiser to use the Jews' lore, but . . ."

"Without the Jews?"

"Cyrus the Great defeated the Jews, then he rebuilt their temple. Had Cyrus foreseen history, he might have killed the Jews and kept the temple."

"So, shall we kill the Jews and keep their books?"

"Are you a believer in God?" the doctor asked. He let himself sink onto the dry grass. The drunkenness had left his voice. "Centuries ago, philosophers like Epicurus and Democritus posited that there were no gods, that we humans made them up. Why should we submit again to something not believable?"

"Maybe something in our souls wants it to be believable?"

"I'm a shallow man, Eques. I know myself well. I could never have a mystical belief."

"Right. Shallow men know themselves well, the bottom is close." Apella pulled the doctor to his feet. "Go to sleep. Don't let me kick you to your bed. Go willingly."

"Pilatus. The warrior with the pilum. What's your mystery, Pilatus?" the doctor mumbled, stumbling into the inn.

An instant later, Hillel walked back from the rock with the girl. At the inn's entrance, he patted her arm and pushed her inside, then looked around.

The Roman stood staring into the night, listening to a feeble braying. Tinkling their bells, a small herd of sheep were approaching from the direction of the oil press. Six or seven heads at most. Herded by one dog and one lone shepherd, tall, wrapped in a big shift.

Knowing their direction, the sheep started across the scrub, toward Mount Barak.

Hillel stood beside Apella, watching the shepherd walk toward the mountain.

"What can he see from the mountaintop?" Apella asked. He had guessed who the shepherd was.

"He can see the tribe returning. The caravan trail runs right by the mountain."

Apella rushed to the soldiers' tent. The gray-haired veteran had taken the first watch. He sat outside the tent, spear in hand. He jumped up when Apella started untethering one of the horses.

"This man"—Apella pointed to the Jewish cart driver—"is my lieutenant here, and I'm making him a vigil Asiae. You'll help him any way you can. Hillel, go back to the village tomorrow and tell everyone that if they welcome Joachim, they're exempt of taxes for five years, *fides Romae*. The doctor and Xilos are not to move from here 'til I come back with troops and money." He was already up in the saddle, gently spurring the horse. "Come on, boy. Come on."

The horse moved tiredly, its belly low, having just been watered and fed a big bucket of oats.

But he'd be good for trotting, at least a few hours. At dawn, Apella could be in Jezreel, where the Romans kept horses. He'd get himself a fresh horse and gallop on, to Jerusalem.

Part 9

The Mountain of God, 1

Mount Barak, later that night.

*T*READ SOFTLY, Joseph whispered to himself. As he did every time he climbed the mountain.

You're entering the place from where your father departed. Tread softly.

As they climbed the dry crags, the sheep smelled the rich grass ahead and hurried into the moonlit night. There was no way to tread softly. Joseph thudded after the herd.

Again and again, he had told himself, *Next time, I'll climb here by myself.*

But every next time, he'd taken his animals with him. Their noises, their smells took his mind off his pain.

When a sheep snagged a hoof in a crag, the tinkling of its bells warned Joseph, who ran to free the sheep. When noontime approached, the drooling dog bumped him with his nose, asking to share his midday meal. Joseph could pray even as he cared for the herd. *Tread softly.*

Those words had become his prayer.

Many times, he had stopped on the heights, peering down into the chasm below, thinking, *One slip, one tumble. Ripping through moaning wind. Crashing down. And then . . . relief?*

But he had stepped back from the edge. Feeling that his carvings had called him back. If he stepped back from death, they smiled, warm and caring. Live, Joseph! Let us be in your life, Joseph! You're safe with us!

True all, except for that unusual girl. She had not turned into a statue in his heart.

She was alive in his heart. Not a statue.

Tread softly, he told himself, becoming aware that his words were not about his father now. They were about that young woman.

Joseph had turned twenty-three. The girl in the desert should be seventeen now.

Tread softly.

SHEEP WENT WHERE the grass was, and grass was where the rain fell, and there was no rain without lightning. "Even a woman's mind should be able to make peace with that," Joseph's father said every time he and Joseph prepared to take the herds up. Words he meant as a reassurance. Yet, hearing them, Joseph's mother became insane with fear and yelled at Joseph's father. "I shall make you a cuckold. I'll have other children by whoever won't put my children in harm's way on that accursed mountain."

How can she be so insanely fearful? Joseph wondered. *She's married to a rabbi, who knows the ways of God, and God watches over good people.*

To Joseph, the mountain was paradise. When people barely had enough to eat in Nazareth, sheep and goats foaled madly up on the mountain, and meat, milk, and butter were in amazing plenty. Other food filled the water, the trees, and the air: Wild trout jumped in brooks, honeybees nested in trees, birds winged in the sky, as if asking for the shepherds' arrows. Bushes glittered with berries, red, yellow, black, God loved them all!

And there were other wonderful things a boy could play with: whips to herd animals, cord to tie tents, scissors to shear wool, knives to whittle with.

And his father had given him the best advice for his safety: Say your prayers.

Rains started brusquely on Mount Barak, out of that one cloud forever hovering around the top. Pouring sheets of rain flowed out of its belly, lit by dazzling lightning.

Joseph stared at the lightning. Feeling safe with that certainty of young manhood, trusting its own indestructibility. Others may be hit and perish, not me.

THAT SPRING, THE cloud behaved amazingly. It parted into countless smaller clouds, a whole fleet of them that encircled the tops and plateaus on which the shepherds kept their sheepfolds.

The shepherds were careful of the sheepfolds, with their sleeping huts built stone on stone without mortar. They planted spears on the heights, to lure the lightning onto the spears, away from the slaughtering tables, the butter-making churns, the scales, skim pots, tools for shearing wool, and shepherds' beds. God be praised, those folds had everything. The shepherds had everything they wanted up here—except women.

Joseph had not been with a woman yet.

Instead of treading softly, he ran now. He chased and kicked the herd. They reached the pastures, but he didn't let the sheep graze. He sicked the dog on them, higher, higher, faster. The sheep brayed, hungry, but he did not care. He ran, torturing his feet on the crags.

The lightning that had struck him was so pretty.

A flash of lightning always had a lead stroke, a beam of fire that came down straight, while the rest of the lightning zigzagged behind it in steps.

When it touched down, the lead stroke stirred the fire in the earth, fire from countless flashes that hit the earth at earlier times. A counterstroke flashed up, making one with the downward stroke, like seeds homing in. Out of that core, the lightning ramified, into fantastic multibranched trees of light.

Seven years ago, the rain started falling at dawn. Joseph and other youngsters were bringing the filled butter churns out of the fold's basement. One day every month, the wives climbed up from the village with their donkeys to bring their husbands and sons flour and olive oil and fresh flat bread that would be hard when they got to the top. They would take back the butter and cheese to sell. It was that day today.

The married men and their wives would go off behind boulders and bushes. They would come back rolling their shoulders and stepping fully. They would sip gravelly wine later, after the women left, and scoff at the married men who had had no visitors. Were they being cuckolded by their wives?

There was gossip about the fold master, Ovad, that his wife was cuckolding him.

Joseph's father expected Joseph's mother to come up. He asked two shepherds to go down with him with mats of rattan and blankets to meet the women halfway and save them from the bone-chilling rain. Ovad told Joseph's father to stay at the fold and work, women didn't get sick from sheer rain. Women had the devil's rib in them, which was the one that God freed from the man, Adam, and made the woman from.

Joseph's father replied that they had finished the work. The filled churns were lined outside, sealed with lids and covered with tarps. Nothing to hold a man from going down to meet the women.

Ovad said no again. Let them trek in the rain, it will cool the devil in them. And he, Ovad, was the one giving the orders here.

Joseph's father gathered his bedding and told Joseph to do the same. He said to Ovad that they'd be looking to sleep in another fold. Other men who didn't like Ovad's tight fist started to grumble, too, and Ovad yelled, let them all leave, but without beddings or tools. "Your wife's a whore like mine!" he blurted at Joseph's father. "Look at the man leading her donkey when she climbs up, he's putting his seed in her, that man! My wife, I have a mind to kill her when she comes, and the man who leads her donkey. But first, I'll make her put her lover in her, in front of all of us!" His bloodshot eyes rolled in his sockets. "Which you should do also! We'll watch them sin, then it will be easy to kill them!"

"You're insane, and I'd rather chance the lightning," Joseph's father said.

"You should punish sin!" Ovad yelled. "The women are the living sin. When they're twisting under us, it's the snake that's twisting. Twisting in our beds in the village, when we're away! I'll watch that snake twisting, before I crush it under my heel."

Joseph's father looked at the other shepherds. He said to them—so soft, so different from Ovad's grinding voice— "Lightning is from God, even if it strikes at random. But when a man speaks like Ovad, that's not random. Come away, all, before he spills blood."

Beside him, Joseph felt a man's body trembling. A young shepherd, engaged to be married only a month before. He trembled from Ovad's words, thinking of his betrothed. She was coming up the mountain just now. A man, the young shepherd's neighbor, was leading her donkey. Was that man her lover?

The young shepherd didn't care for words of reason. A dark light kindled his eyes as he rushed from the fold.

Joseph found himself rushing after him, out into blinding rain.

He gripped the shepherd by the edge of his cloak and tried to stop him, but the man slipped from Joseph's hands.

Below, a file of women and donkeys were advancing on a tortuous path, the women slogging through the rain instead of riding, to save the donkeys' strength for the trek back. As in a vision, Joseph saw a young woman wipe the rain from her face, and the man leading her donkey let go of its bridle. The man brought up his sleeve and held it against the rain, over that young wife's face.

And the wife smiled.

Joseph stumbled.

He stopped, as his eyes scoured the climbing file. He prayed for his mother not to be among the women bringing up the flour and oil. Even if you're with another man right now, even if you're sinning, may God forgive you, and may my father forgive me, but I want you alive, Mother, alive!

He didn't see his mother among the climbers, nor did he see Cheba, Ovad's wife.

When he looked skyward, thankful that his prayer was heard, the fiery speartip of the lightning was upon him.

Huge it looked, that load of fire, larger than the load of a catapult.

The light blinded Joseph. As the giant fieriness hit him, all his senses blacked out except for smell—he smelled singed hair, his own, and the singed fabric of his cloak. After striking Joseph, the lead stroke broke into those ramified trees of fire. One branch lashed at Joseph's father, who was racing after him, crying his name. "Joseph, my son, wait! My son!"

Other branches of fire curled down the incline, hitting the climbing women.

Joseph's blood stopped in his veins. His mouth, his gums, the rims of his eyes, the inside of his armpits, the fork of his legs, all that was naturally damp in him felt dried-up. Dryness dark and bitter, inside his brain, too.

The sheepfold had burned. Dead shepherds and sheep were strewn all over the mountaintop.

HE FOUND HIMSELF crawling. He tottered up, stepped on his father's body, jumped back. He held himself above his father's face, which was light blue, the color of certain flowers of the heights. His feet were light blue. His hands, his palms, his fingers. The blood that seeped from his nostrils was dark blue, like ink. Joseph knew the tint of ink, because his father wrote letters for the illiterate Nazareth peasants. He also wrote words from the Torah for mezuzahs nailed on doorposts, for which the peasants paid him paltry money.

Joseph managed to tilt his head back, opening his lips, letting the rain fill his mouth. He could hardly taste the rainwater. But he put his face over his father's face and spat the water into those blue lips. A twitch, from muscles perhaps dead already, then no more movement. He tried to breathe into those lips, he kissed them. He massaged them. But that heart beat no more.

Joseph rolled down the incline, away from the horror of his father's death. He fell off a crag's edge and passed out.

He awoke being undressed roughly by a gang of boys.

He was so weak, he could not fight them off. He could only utter groaning gasps.

The rain had stopped; there was sun on the pastures.

Fingers pried his body. "Are his privates burned?" someone wanted to know.

Joseph recognized the voice. It belonged to Jerash, the son of Aaron.

The thugs were all sons of friends and neighbors from the village; he knew them all.

Aaron had roused his gang to search the mountain, and they'd found every dead victim, and Joseph last.

The boys found two melted knives on Joseph's body—on one hip, Joseph had a deep festering burn from the liquefied smaller knife. When the lightning had struck him, its fiery power had been sucked into those blades. His larger knife was two feet long, the kind used against sheep robbers. When Joseph collapsed, the larger knife stabbed into the wet ground, drawing the fire out of Joseph, into the earth.

The thugs whooped, realizing how badly Joseph had been hit. It was a wonder he was breathing. That made them even more curious.

"His *zayin* don't look burned," Aaron's son Jerash said. As if he were sorry.

"But they feel dead," someone else said, pinching Joseph's parts.

"Bring that girl," Jerash said. "Let's see if she hardens him up."

And they brought the young wife who had marched up through the rain wiping raindrops from her face. She was dead, her face burned, her hair burned to clumps that made it fleecy in a horrid charred way.

They had undressed her and raped her.

"We made her warm for you," Jerash snickered. So unafraid of the sin he was doing and saying!

They rubbed her onto his body. He was not responding.

"Let him be, he can't even moan," one boy said, and Jerash spat at the sissy.

"You want to know if you're still a man?" Jerash asked Joseph. "Put it in her or you'll never put it in anyone again." The fright that seized Joseph's mind was bright like the lightning, and it split in countless branches like the lightning.

"Do it," Jerash yelled, as he and the others lay the girl on her back, and forced Joseph onto her openness. Joseph thought, *One day, Jerash, I will kill you for this.*

Then a boy who stood apart as a lookout whistled in warning. Someone was coming.

Cursing, the others threw the torn clothes onto the girl. Joseph they left almost naked, and told the arriving grown man that they had searched Joseph for burns, which had revived him. The man, Rabbi Joachim ben Matthan, ruled that Joseph should be carried down, he had life in him.

What would that life be like?

* * *

HE WAS CARRIED into the village on a stretcher, face up. People kept darkening the sky above his face; the whole village wanted to peer at him.

Rabbi Joachim, who oversaw the bathing of Joseph in lukewarm water and his anointment with oil, told him that his mother had not gone up on the mountain—people had seen her in the village during the storm. So she had to be alive. Joseph was overjoyed.

There had been nine giant flashes, the villagers said after watching God's wrath from the safety of their backyards. Five men, including Joseph's father, and two women and more than a dozen sheep had been killed.

Joseph's mother never showed up. Later, people found out that she had left the village. Ovad's wife, Cheba, had vanished from Nazareth, too.

When Ovad came back from the heights, he marked his house as a house of khet. He nailed the entrance door shut, tarred the walls, killed the guard dogs, threw them in the well, and tarred the well's lid, condemning the water in it. Then he went back to the heights, where, people later reported, he built another sheepfold, a tiny one, and lived like a hermit because other shepherds would no longer work for him.

Joseph was nursed in Joachim's yard. The rabbi chased off the villagers and the children, including his own little daughter. They had no business gawking at Joseph's misfortune.

At the end of the week, as the rabbi had predicted, Joseph regained his working strength and Shalafta offered to take him in as a bondman. He could use a new bondman. Joseph was still mending. Shalafta asked his widowed sisters to care for him at the oil press.

* * *

TREAD SOFTLY NOW . . .

Joseph herded his sheep along a narrow path with a steep incline to the right and a chasm to the left. Cold air swirled above him, gusts wheezed below him, and the echo of his footsteps was so acute, it went on forever: No one, no one . . .

He crouched down on that terribly narrow path. He covered his face with his hands. He said to the one he had not seen in three years, *I love you, Mary.*

You are the one creature I haven't turned into a statue in my heart. Into an image I could hold at a distance, bringing you close, then pushing you away again.

You became very pretty, the Arabian man told me.

It's you I wanted, always. For you, I'll face that most terrifying fear—loving you and chancing that I could lose you.

Could I let love come back into my heart, like touching and feeling once came back into my hands?

Help me, Mary.

He uncovered his face and found that he had crouched under a large piece of ice—old, striated, from snow that had survived the thaw of spring. It hung from a crag, right above him.

Warming the air with his breath could detach it, causing it to crash down on him.

He told himself to run forward, but knew that footfalls could loosen the ice, so he slunk carefully under it. Finally, he stepped onto open heights. The sheep reached the tall grass and started eating hungrily.

Joseph, my soul, a voice said unexpectedly, *you want to feel desire, and hope is desire.*

Yes, he agreed, trembling.

Don't think of your father, the voice said. *Or of your mother, she was too scared to face her son being brought back from the disaster on the mountain. You are stronger than your parents. Think of that girl. Trust that girl, for she knows desire,* the voice said, astonishing Joseph. The voice sounded loving of the girl, and of Joseph, too.

She knows desire, the voice repeated.

She knows it? Joseph wondered, incredulous.

More than you as a man can fathom. She can feel the desire in you, faultlessly. So go ahead, step on toward her, Joseph, my soul.

Yes, Joseph promised, overpowered.

Then there was silence.

He heard the frothing noises of the sheep eating the grass of the heights.

IT WAS MIDDAY when he arrived on the crest from which he could see the desert.

He sat down and broke out food: dried cheese, grilled lamb, and flat bread. He shared with the dog, while the sheep cleaned the ground around them, then moved farther away and ate some more.

He lay down on his stomach and gazed at the desert's uniformity until a moving rash of people appeared, far off across the brown skin of a dune.

He focused his gaze while his temples pounded.

The dark rash stopped advancing.

He guessed that they were setting up camp after marching at night. They would rest during the heat of the day. They would start marching again at nightfall.

He laughed. Who else would be on the move in the desert

but *her* tribe? He jumped up and danced. He grabbed handfuls of dirt and threw them around, then pinched the nose of the dog. *She* was returning. He remembered holding her hand that night and smelling her nearness: young female, a scent impossible to describe. Too deep, too basic, too hungrily wanted by that man sleeping inside him! His senses lived their own mirage. He could smell her now, across miles of desert.

Joseph laughed loud. He was going insane! Enough!

He had so much to do, before descending into the sands, to meet the girl's tribe.

He left the sheep chewing in the shade of the trees; they were so heavy with grass, they barely moved when he walked past them. He whistled for the dog to follow him. He was worried that Aaron had posted lookouts on the mountain, to spot the tribe and rush back to inform him. If Joseph ran into a lookout, he'd gag him and tie him to a tree. If the lookout chose to fight him, he would kill him.

He wondered if Aaron's son Jerash might be on the mountain now. You and I have some unfinished business, Jerash!

Well thought out, the voice said.

JOSEPH FOUND NO lookouts.

Part 10

The Mountain of God, 2

The oasis in the desert, one day after the well was sold.

I SLEPT, AND I dreamed the sweetest dream ever.

Our tribe had just arrived in sight of Nazareth's gate. Father and mother and I at the fore, and all of us on foot and dusty, but with our nursing mothers in carts drawn by donkeys like queens. And the wedding canopy was set outside the east gate, and Joseph was about to step under the canopy to be married to Rona and Lanit.

And I felt no bitterness in my heart, none at all!

I was a little tired, but joyful in my heart. I didn't mind Joseph marrying someone else, not at all. All I wanted was that Joseph see me. *I swear, Adonai.* He could have his accursed wives by his side, as I trekked in with saintly composure, leading my kin. I wouldn't even peek at his wives. Well . . . Once, under deeply lowered eyelids, to appraise Rona and Lanit. They would look plain, overadorned, and *stupid*! But then Joseph's eyes would bulge out. Who's that, Mary? My, has she grown! My, is she pretty! Amen, selah! How did I miss out on such a pretty girl? Aaaahh, his lips would twist bitterly. While Mary-amneh bat Joachim, I, me, no other, walked past Joseph, toward the Roman man.

249

And of course, the Roman was right there, on his fat stallion, for this was a dream.

I acknowledged the Roman, with a smile not too wide or too tight, just right. Here we are, Roman!

Meantime, Joseph was about to cry from his realization: I lost this girl forever. Through my own stupidity! Embittered I shall be for the rest of my days. Amen, selah!

In my dream I wondered, *Was this a lot to ask for?*

Then the Roman turned his fat stallion around and led us all through the gate, toward the first home to be returned to its rightful owners, *our* home.

My mother was stepping next to me, and she was smiling! She had lost that frown between her eyebrows, born of fatigue and worry and hard work; from her hard work alone, I could have built Jacob's ladder and hung it from the sky.

I glanced back at the water girls. And I saw delightfulness! Dusty and pale and sweating from the trek, they still looked gorgeous. I felt their souls inside me, all of them, as they babbled happily, "Amen, selah, and no small thanks to you, Mary!"

Aaahh, due praise for something I truly earned, what could be sweeter?

"Welcome to your home, people of the promise," the Roman said, astounding me that he would call me that. And our yard was so wide, it seemed endless. Past the nicked post, all of our returning people stepped into my father's yard.

Suddenly, a big *whoosh* of silence fell outside in the street.

All eyes turned to stare out through the gate or peer through the picket fence back down the street.

Joseph was hurrying to catch up with us. All alone he was. He waved at me, but I was not sure what his waving meant. He opened his mouth. I was dying to know what he would first say to me . . .

But I woke up.

I lay among the other water girls, on the sand of the gulch, under the date trees. With rays of dawn beginning to tickle our faces.

We had yet to return to Nazareth.

I jumped up and yelled at the girls to wake up. We had work to do.

Now, ARE YOU sure the Roman will be there with the writ for our homes?"

"Of course I am!"

I felt that pagan paw of his, squeezing the writ.

We were trampling toward the hot spring to wash the last little stitch of everyone's filthy clothing. For I had decided that as we rounded the mountain's spur, coming in sight of Nazareth, we, the tribe, would peel off our dusty garb, put on fresh linen, and march smartly toward home and toward the Roman on his horse.

Oh, High One. I would endure the touch of his paw, to see us all settled back at home! Don't strike me!

"I'm so sick of washing men's soiled clothing," moaned Yorit.

I said, "Aren't you looking forward to having children, boys in particular, who are the messiest? Come on, I have a treat for you girls, after we clean this filthy stuff!"

"What treat, what treat?" they chirped. But before I could reply, Akam the old drunk ran after us. "What a great husband my nephew Shimon will make for you, Mary!" he slurred cheerfully. And I replied, moving faster, "Are you soused this early, Akam? When did Shimon become your nephew?"

"Shimon's late uncle, who died from a wasp that stung his tongue, which clogged his throat and choked him, was a third cousin to me. So when Shimon's parents were killed, I became Shimon's closest kin. I'm going to ask for you, Mary, in Shimon's name! I'll run to speak to your father!"

"Don't waste your breath. My father doesn't like Shimon. He loses sheep in the desert and wets his bed. The proof of it is bundled on my head."

"Blessed be El Hai, that's the juice of life he's overflowing with, with which he'll fill you! Don't be so picky, you're a spinster." I ran full tilt, and couldn't believe how well he kept up. "Mary, your lineage is *the* lineage, which is why that scoundrel who sits on David's throne let us live in the first place! And you're that girl. But we have to bring you back pregnant! Shimon can't wait to give you a boy, he had five brothers, the Syrians killed them all." For an instant, my heart broke for Shimon, God had tried him too hard.

"Who had this amazing thought, you, or the other old roaches?"

"Me alone! We'll trek home slowly, so you and Shimon can have time together! And when we get before the village, you miss your bloods, it's God's will, and no one will touch us!"

I glanced around, dreading to glimpse Shimon and the elders marching from around a dune with a makeshift canopy and a winecup to break!

Yet I didn't feel angry now, I felt bewildered. So I murmured, "Thank you, Akam. I'll think about it."

"Good. Shimon is ready."

Orpa pulled my sleeve. "Ow!" I cried. That feisty, dark-faced elf had pinched me hard! I lunged after her, and she tripped me. All the girls fell on top of us.

"Tell us the truth," Orpa panted, "you really said no to Joseph's proposal?"

"No. I mean, yes. No."

"Then, why can't you choose the Roman?"

Now all the girls yelled at once. "Become his servant, Mary! And the Roman will be our protector! And your children by him will be Jews, as by our law, since the mother is Jewish. We'll come to visit you in Jerusalem, and the Roman will show us to his friends . . ." That prospect made them throb with anticipation.

"Girls! It's not being done, it's not to be!"

"Why not?" Orpa asked. "Choose the Roman, Mary, and I'll go to Jerusalem with you as your maid."

"The Roman would gag with joy," Dalit said. "I peeked when you served him that food. He would have eaten out of your hand."

"And if your first man is a Roman, that little door into you won't care," said Nava.

I blushed red-hot. Orpa daydreamed. "He'll take you to Jerusalem in a sedan chair."

Just the thought of that—a sedan chair. I'd never been in one.

So we all squealed, and hugged, and ran to throw the rags into the boiling-hot spring. And then I told them, "Girls, Orpa and I have a mirror, and we're going to show it to you!" And then the girls squealed so loud, my teeth ached with the racket they made!

Then we couldn't find the mirror.

Where had we hidden it last time?

"How stupid could you be?" Yorit said. "Not to stick a marker next to it?"

"We did," Orpa wailed. "Where was it, by this dune or that dune?"

Who could tell one dune from another?

I kept throwing myself at this spot and that spot and digging with my fingers 'til I peeled back my nails.

Adonai, help me. I enticed the girls here to give them some confidence before they climb onto the auction block of marriage without a dowry. What am I going to do now . . . ?

Hush, Mary, the mirror is right under you.

And my fingers hit the brass, deep inside the sand.

You MIGHT HAVE thought we were being slaughtered, the way we yelled.

Like a table of the law was the way the old brass looked when we raised it out of the ground with sand filling its tiniest cracks, making those cracks look like unreadable hieroglyphs. We rubbed it with water from the spring and with spit, and with the hems of our shifts, 'til we made it look honey-warm and deep. And then the girls peeled off their shifts and gawked at their scratched knees, skinny thighs, shoulders tanned brick-brown, breasts with nipples like goose bumps. And navels like tight little knots.

At the door of death, the water girls had grown into women!

So now that they looked better than they had expected, they were done with the stayed old homeland! "We'll go to Jerusalem, what's in Nazareth for us?"

"It's home," I pleaded. "We have to give it a chance!"

"Mary's in love!" Orpa snickered. "She's dying to see her carver, though she won't be third on his pillow!"

Yorit threw her arms up. "You want to see him marrying two other women?"

"Forget him! You waited for him three whole years! You went looking for him on that mountain and nearly died! Isn't that enough?" Orpa wasn't snickering anymore, she was wailing her indignation.

Big shivers worked my body. "I can't do otherwise! I don't know why! I'm afraid to love, but I want to love, and maybe the same is true of him? But how can I find out, if I don't see him?" And then I remembered something else. "We left the men's clothes in the hot spring! They must have boiled to shreds!"

Jibril had counted wrong. He had left us one cart too many.

So I told my father, "Mother and I will pull that cart, and you, Abba, will sit in it."

"Am I that useless already? I'm too heavy. I'll walk."

I laughed. "You're so thin, our rags are heavier than you. You'll hold the water skins between your knees, make sure they don't spill."

I made him feel useful. He agreed to travel in the cart.

So we packed our junk, and he said to me, "Come here, Mary."

He dug up a tied prayer rug from a corner of the tent. He untied it with his maimed hands, wincing. He revealed an armful of knives, large, small, all kinds. Caravan drivers had lost them by the well. He had picked them up.

"Give one to each girl, Mary. And take the best one for

yourself. You are strong, Mary. With a knife, you can frighten a man."

I grabbed the edge of the rug, folded it back over the knives. "If we are attacked, we're done for, Abba, you know that."

"No one knows that," he said, choking. "If we are attacked, you and the young ones run for the mountain. Tell the young ones, Mary."

"And leave you to be killed?"

"Yes. We walked the earth, we had our lives. Don't speak, shut that clever mouth."

And I shut my clever mouth.

It was cold in the desert at night.

Our tamed jackals trotted behind us. The female who led their pack was one that I had tamed as a pup. She caught up and rubbed against my leg. I tried to push her aside. She wouldn't go away. I thought to myself, if the jackals followed us to the village, the Nazarenes would think, Those witches brought jackals, they're intent on revenge. They would come out with knives and pitchforks.

What could we do about the jackals—throw stones at them to turn them back?

But I didn't bend to pick a stone, and no one else did, and that female clicked her teeth, shiny against moonrays, and led the pack on after us.

Our scouts were six girls and three boys. They walked about a hundred paces ahead, on both sides of the camel trail. I trusted the girls better than the boys. They were lighter on their feet, less likely to nod off, and they had sharper eyes. Before we left, I had stepped around the camp and looked at the girls and at the boys.

The boys were scared, they packed with jerky movements, broke things, argued. I stopped a few fistfights. The girls were quietly efficient. I saw them smile. They had hope.

I had hope, too.

My mother and I harnessed ourselves to the cart, and we rolled ahead.

Lord, let us return to Nazareth in peace.

Panting against the harness, I glanced around. Everyone carried so much junk! Bundles, bags, tied tarps, cooking pots, mats, blankets, water skins . . .

And guess what? Our women wore their adornments. The cheapest, humblest, most touching homemade adornments. Combs, hair slides, necklaces of painted wood. *Oh, Adonai. When we get home I'll cry, yes? When I glimpse that gatepost of ours, nicked with my growing height?*

Hush, Mary . . . Let's get you home first . . .

OUR MEN CARRIED the broken masts of the tents. Around those shafts of wood, we had lived. To each tent pole, a family.

I wondered if any of our pregnant women—we had three in an advanced state—would give birth on the way.

If a child were born en route, my father had instructed that a tent mast should be raised up, tied with a bright red rag on top. We would rush to gather water and food for the mother, praise be El Hai, she should eat and drink to make milk for the newborn.

I smelled a fire somewhere ahead. It tickled my nostrils. I stopped the cart and woke up my father.

IN AN INSTANT, our scouts were running everywhere. I ran with them.

We climbed on the nearest dune tops. Moon brightening our faces. The scouts carried some of the knives my father had saved. They seemed so ridiculously ineffective.

Mount Barak loomed to our left and seemed so close now, maybe only a day's trek away.

To our right, there was a rocky hillside, which I didn't remember from three years ago, when we crawled behind every rock and burrowed in every hole, while the Syrians kept chasing us, poking their spears at anything that moved.

That long spur of rock was lower than the mountain, and strung with big jagged boulders. The boulders were lean and uncracked, and they reflected the moonbeams.

I heard footsteps and jumped. The roots of my hair crackled from fright.

It was only my father stepping around a dune, toward me.

"You remember that?" I pointed to the rocky ridge.

"No," he replied. "But if the mountain's so close, then Nazareth is right behind it." He pointed to where the trail wound between the rocks and the mountain.

We looked around.

The night breeze ruffled the dune tops.

I kept hearing sheep bells.

My father and I walked along the caravan trail, looking for sheep droppings. We found plenty, but they were dark and hard. "They're old," my father said. "No one's stalking us."

I whistled loud, a signal for all's clear, and led my father back to the cart.

Mother and I were about to slip our shoulders in the yoke, when Shimon walked over and said, "I'll help you pull, Mary."

I didn't want him around, yet I wanted my mother to rest,

so I nodded to Shimon. As soon as she climbed into the cart, my mother lolled her head onto my father's shoulder and sank into sleep.

Shimon and I pulled the cart. Shimon pressed his shoulder on mine. I leaned away. He leaned closer. I gritted my teeth and suffered his touch, trekking and staring away at those boulders reflecting the moonlight.

Shimon pulled harder than I did, jolting the yoke. I stared at him to slow down.

"Your father owes my uncle an answer."

I laughed. "*That* uncle? Here's the answer: My father doesn't want me to marry you."

He pushed the yoke against me, almost knocking me off my feet: "I could've had you, when you and I herded sheep. I could've been inside you before you were done screaming for help."

I said nothing. I pulled as hard as he did. The cart was going fast.

"I had some of the other girls, you don't even know."

"Stop lying, who would look at you?"

He pressed his shoulder on mine again. "You smell nice."

I smelled of sweat and of frankincense. My mother had traded her best cooking pot to a caravan man who had given her a tuft of dried frankincense. She crushed a little piece between her thumbs, rubbed her thumbs between her breasts, then rubbed her palm over my cheeks and over the dip of my throat. Shimon sniffed me; maybe he thought he was putting me in the mood.

I stopped the cart. "Thanks for helping. Go away."

"If Aaron's thugs strike us, I'll hand you to them," he promised under his breath, then he trod away.

I watched him a while, ahead of me, splitting the night defiantly. Not quite a man, but already angry, quarrelsome, bitter. I pictured him jumping Orpa. Had Shimon raped Orpa, would Orpa's father have killed him? I pictured Shimon as a little boy, tearing off the wings of a bird, will it still fly? Wringing its neck, will it still be alive? Knowing a secret, by tearing it open. *Adonai, you endowed man with curiosity, look how he thanks you for your gift.*

The trail went down. I could pull the cart by myself.

I panted down the trail littered by caravans and thought, *I want something clean in my life.*

I want to walk on clean floors. I want to smell a freshly whitewashed house.

We walked 'til dawn, then stopped and ate cold grilled lamb and flat bread. We set lookouts on the surrounding dune tops. We raised only four tents, huddled in them, and slept with each other's shoulders and sides as pillows.

We woke up during the worst of the heat and sipped water. One sip, another sip. We were almost out of water.

But no one was sick, thank heaven.

At sundown on Friday, we lit rags and prayed. Then we trekked off again although it was Sabbath. We were walking on Sabbath. We were walking for our lives. God would forgive us.

MOON RISING AGAIN.

The mountain seemed so close, if I broke into a good run I could make it to those rocks painted by lightning, and then farther up to the trees and the pastures.

The mountain seemed to nod to me: Come closer, closer, it's safe.

But we were exhausted. Voices grumbled that we should stop sooner.

My father jumped from the cart, walked up and down to assess how fatigued everyone was.

Up on those forested heights, the mountain jackals started to howl, and their voices sounded well fed; they feasted on deer and wild hare. Our mangy jackals heard the mountain jackals and bounced up the rocks. Orpa chuckled. "Our mutts found their own Nazareth."

Akam grabbed a lanyard, caught a jackal, dragged it back, and tried to tie it to his cart. "For protection!" he foamed. His woman, panicked that the jackal would gore him, hit Akam over the head with a cooking tray.

Then I thought I was hearing sheep bells.

So, are you ready?

I shivered. What did I hear?

Sheep bells! I truly heard them, so close now. From behind the next dune.

I raced around the dune, while the rocks reflected the moon back at me, and—

I was face-to-face with Joseph.

He was walking toward me, but he had no inkling that I'd spring before him. We both stopped in front of each other, dumbstruck. Four sheep tottered to a halt behind Joseph, and a dusty sheepdog gaped in surprise, and . . . Joseph wore a big burka of camel hair, hood on . . . He peeled back the hood.

I wanted to turn and run away. But my body wouldn't move.

He looked dirty and ruffled. He had slept in the desert.

When he spoke, his voice was rocky and parched. "Mary . . . ?"

I was less than an arm's length from him.

I still expected him to melt into thin air.

His face was frosted with sand, his cheeks gaunt, but otherwise he looked strong. His beard was trimmed very light, barely enough of a beard for a man his age. He held himself confidently.

Well, no wonder. He was the village heir now.

Yes, he seemed to really be here. He took me in.

I had changed, too. I was grown.

My mouth was dry, my ears hummed, a night bug hit me in the face . . . What was the right thing to say? You were heading to our camp, Joseph? Stupid, where else would he be walking in the desert?

I said, "Joseph . . ."

He said, "Mary . . ." His voice had grown, too, it had a nice manly resonance.

I looked in his eyes . . .

And I saw *me* worrying about him. Those nights by the well, tossing on the sand . . . Waking up, touching that piece of wood, rubbing it until it lost all likeness of me. Wondering, was he alive?

And all the days when I carried that piece of wood in my sleeve or my bosom, and found a nick of time now and then to pull it out and stare at it. Tell me, little image, where is Joseph? Did he survive? What happened to him?

He cleared his throat and asked—so hoarse, he barely spoke—"Mary . . . *kkhhh-what* did your father decide?"

I heard the jackals' howls. Our pack was greeted by the mountain pack.

That tiny cleft above his upper lip, sweet and unhairy. I remembered it. His one babyish trait.

I said, "It's been three years."

He tried to touch my arm. But he stopped himself. He cleared his throat. Painfully gruff and husky. "You . . . have someone?"

Ah, thank you, Adonai! Feel unloved, Joseph, as you made me feel! That feeling, which I know so well! Thank you, Adonai, so much! But Adonai did even better, he made Joseph's eyes goggle out of his head. And I knew why—he was dumbstruck at how I looked. Pretty! Like nothing when he had first met me! I saw in his eyes that glint of male admiration that any girl can recognize. If I wanted to torture him, now was the time!

So, I nodded my chin toward the camel trail. As if to say, Yes, behind that dune, among that rabble of people, someone might be my pair. Yes, why not? Such is life. Don't you have two brides already, Joseph?

What a nice twist of the knife.

But I simply couldn't get those words out.

"Mary," he mumbled.

He shuffled his feet. "Mary, I came to tell you . . . that . . . Lanit and Rona, they're nothing to me."

Aaaaahh! I had wanted to hear those words! And now I did, but they passed so quickly and felt so light!

"My wedding is really for Nazareth, Mary . . . The village was so ravaged . . ." He touched my arm, and I didn't pull away. Did his touch trouble my thinking the instant it happened? I suddenly thought, *There will be two more women in our house. Too bad, but there are always plenty of women in a rich man's house! I can be the mistress over all of them! What should I care what the village says?*

Meantime, Joseph still didn't know whether another man had

263

claimed me. He didn't know how to guess my mood, either. He didn't know what else to say. He fretted, he seemed in pain. "Someone had to save the village, Mary. Shalafta came to me, and *bowed* to me." He made me feel the miracle of that bow, from Nazareth's most vainglorious man. "He begged me: 'Save the village, Joseph.' So"—a little glow of pride lit his eyes—"after I said that I would, Shalafta and Aaron came to an agreement, and the people tore down the walls from around their homes . . . Mary . . . If the village had asked you to make peace, what would you have done?"

I?

I had gotten lost in that little glow of pride, which warmed his face and made him so handsome.

Waking up, I tried to remember. When was a woman bespoken to several husbands, in order to save a nation?

He breathed tightly. "Lanit and Rona . . . I barely know them . . . I spoke with Lanit maybe once or twice . . . I never once spoke with Rona."

"Yes . . ." I found it in me to chuckle. "David the king owned forty wives and mistresses. Surely he never spoke to many of them."

"What?" he asked, looking lost.

I said, softly, for it hurt me to say it, "No, Joseph."

"No, what?"

Something dripped down my face. I brought my hand up and wiped my face.

I was crying with regular tears.

Finally, I was crying. My chest was heaving, my throat was aching, and I was remembering. *Yes, this is what crying feels like.* Tears kept rolling down my cheeks, I wiped them with my sleeve, and they kept coming.

I gave up. Streaming with tears, I cupped Joseph's hand in both of my hands.

That feeling, of his hand in my hand, I had dreamed of it. I had wondered, would the skin of my palm remember that touch, which had happened just once, that night under the setim trees?

I had dreamed of how our hands would fit, of how our bodies would match perfectly, as if made to order by Adonai. My fit to Joseph's fit, and to no other . . . I had dreamed lush, unclear dreams that made me wake up with hot cheeks.

And Joseph . . . Joseph . . . *Oh, how many times would I have to kill Joseph, Adonai, and then beg you to resuscitate him (and you would!), so I could finally forgive him for being such a dolt.* For finally, finally, he seemed . . . worried that I was crying. He tried to put his arms around me!

But I pressed my palms on his chest and pushed him away. I could hardly speak. I was mewling ridiculously. "Why didn't you-oo . . . trust me, Joseph? I didn't care what people said about you. I was so in love with you, I would've been . . . so *patient with you* . . ."

I hadn't meant to insult him. Just to tell him how deeply I felt.

But he ground his teeth behind his tightened lips and averted his eyes.

I felt like laughing. What did I say, what everyone else said about him? But instead of laughing, I sobbed. "I went up on that mountain." I turned now and pointed to the hirsute crest of Mount Barak. "So I could understand what happened to you." He stared, astonished.

Then he said, without one speck of pride, "Mary, you and I can bring peace to Nazareth . . ."

I cried.

"What about peace under your roof? What do you want me for, to help you rule over Rona and Lanit?"

I would have liked to say, David, the king, was a selfish, flesh-loving, unrestrained man. But he was a man, of that there was no doubt. Can you father my children, Joseph? (And alas, Rona's and Lanit's, too?) But maybe that question showed on my face, because he stuttered, "First wife."

Huh? Had I heard right?

"You can be my first wife."

He eyed me beseechingly and smiled. He had made me an improved offer!

He reached for my hand. I pulled it away, but he reached for it again. "Where is your father?"

I pointed with my chin, beyond the dune. "My father's right there."

He lurched in that direction. The dog nudged the sheep in their sides, and the sheep trotted after Joseph, bells chinking. I had no choice but to rush to keep abreast, while I said between my teeth, "You think you can buy me with four sheep?" I could hear Akam, and the other bitchy old men: Even Shimon can match that! And he babbled, "They're just a gift of food for your father."

No. Thank you, but no. I cannot chance it all, my future, the future of my offspring, on four sheep and *peace*! That's what I should have told him.

But instead, I pointed toward the camel trail and said as coldly as I could, "Herd your sheep that way, by yourself. I won't walk by your side. Good luck."

He walked toward the camel trail, his shoulders drooping.

Glumly, I told myself, He's not taking me for granted anymore. I stood my ground, I showed dignity.

And now, what? For I had just made a decision, hadn't I? That it wasn't to be.

I ran after him and grabbed his arm.

Man, woman, dog, sheep, we all ran to where my kin were making camp. My mother was beating a tent picket with a mallet. She saw us; her fingers opened, and she dropped the mallet.

The water girls were up, and Orpa was up, too, of course. Even Akam was still up. He saw us and screeched, "Who's that I see? Jo-o-seph? Shimon! Shimon, come here, Mary's got another bidder! Come fight him off!"

All this happened in an eye-blink, while I rasped to Joseph: "I'll give you *one chance,* to tell my parents and me what my marriage with you will be like!"

It was that hour before dawn: gray like a jackal's hide. I sat on a rock top, about twenty paces from Joseph. He had made his improved offer to my father. I had told my father that it wasn't good enough. Twice already, my father had walked to where I was sitting, to present the offer again. Twice already, I had turned it down again.

My mother sat beside me. After I said no the second time, she leaned into my ear and reminded me that I was seventeen and not getting any younger.

Meantime, our old men milled around Joseph, asking him how much money he was making by carving images. Which was forbidden to a Jew, but Joseph's status was so enhanced now, our elders found an excuse for the carving. He was carving for goyim, not for Jews, and he was saving himself from poverty, which could be viewed as saving his life, a duty for Jews and for all human beings.

I sat with dignity on my rock top, while the girls fretted around me, clearing the path when my father trod over again, to try to convince me.

My father was angry, from exhaustion and worry. And yet, he was impressed with me! I held on so staunchly to how I wanted to be treated.

"Are you still sore about third wife?" he whispered to me.

I replied to my father, "Please, Abba. Who knows if Joseph

will treat me as a first wife a year from now? If he doesn't like me in bed, if he wants a son and I give him a daughter, if he thinks I'm a nag, or just because love wears out . . . I can lose my first-wife status anytime!"

I knew what I was saying, I grew up among women whose status was never clear, whose importance and their children's importance shifted with the birth of other children, from other wombs. I was like all brides before me, mind you, but like so few before me, our strange circumstances allowed me to haggle and fuss!

"Joseph loves you, Mary."

"If Joseph loves me, why doesn't he marry *only me,* and drop the two others?"

"How could we have peace then?"

"What kind of peace are we talking about? Nazareth just got weary of fighting, that's why they're talking peace! Have they returned our homes of their own will? Hardly! But we have the king's forgiveness." I gripped one of his maimed hands; it hurt me to feel how crippled it was, so I held on tightly to it, and whispered fiercely, "Joseph should marry me only, if it's me he really wants. And I'll be the cleverest, most helpful one wife!"

The girls were not missing a word of this. Under their breath, they issued a deep approving hum. Mary just said it. Meantime, my father gritted his teeth. "I never would've put up with this, in the village!"

"I know," I replied quietly, making him shake his head, and wonder, Did I just make her even more stubborn?

Back home, a woman was property. Her father's property, until she became her husband's property. If her husband died, she was her elder son's property, yes, that's how women had been written into the law. Thou shall not steal thy neighbor's house, oxen, asses, plows, stones of weight and measurement, nor his manservant or maidservant, nor his wife! Yes, that was me: I came after asses and stones of measurement. I was the property to pass from hand to hand, from father to spouse and then to elder son. Only if I were bereft of father *and* of husband *and* of sons would I cease to be a man's property and become my own property (the widow Irit flashed up in my memory; maybe widowhood was not that bad?). Aside from being property, the other choices for a woman were to be a slave, a beggar, or a whore.

"You're driving Joseph insane," my father moaned. "And me."

"She's making great sense!" Orpa shouted. "Joseph should drop the two others!" A murmur of approval went around the girls' crowd. That hard nut of the desert spoke truth!

"Let him marry you here and now, Mary, or else you won't know if you have anything," cried Yorit. And the girls cheered, "Amen, selah!" and chattered busily, "A wedding here, what fun!"

"What about the wedding in Nazareth? And the two waiting brides?" My father was desperate.

"Why is that your concern?" asked Orpa. "Those two are not your daughters."

He had no reply.

"If he marries her here and now, with four sheep as bride price," Orpa said with a mow of disdain for the four sheep, "we'll send Shimon to tell Shalafta that Joseph is married. If he still wants his Lanit to be *second wife* to Joseph, let him pay for that, let him buy us assurances that we won't be attacked. And then . . ."

My father's eyes popped wide open: Orpa was an even

fiercer haggler than I was! Meantime, among the old roaches, Orpa's father rolled his eyes: El Olam, where was I looking while this pipsqueak grew up so dangerously smart? I'm in trouble in my own house, my daughter can whip me with her wits alone!

I tried to speak softly to my father. "Why are you acting so bereft, Abba? What are you learning that you didn't know? Once is a woman powerful, once only, before she gives in."

A little crowd of elders trundled toward us. I was so wound up from hunger, fatigue, and emotion, I could hardly speak. "Tell those old men to stop right there, Abba, they won't soften me, this is about my life!"

My father waved at them to stop. They stopped.

"Is there more?" he whispered.

"Yes." The girls cheered my yes. "And if you're my father, you should've thought about it yourself." I had never spoken to my father so firmly before.

Joseph had pounded a pathway in the sand. He turned toward me, tripping because he did not look where he was putting his feet.

My mother walked to him. She started talking to him. She made him sit down on his own rock top. Then she looked at me. I heard her heart saying, I love you, Mary, my feisty, strongminded daughter, for I know that you're hardworking, selfdenying, and devoted. You would be Joseph's best compass in life. If he marries the other two also, you, not he, would make that foursome work! So I understand, Mary. But I want the best for you, and, alas, the best for you is before you, so bend and pick it up!

I wondered, had my mother, not my father, acted as gobetween, would I have said yes already?

I looked over at Joseph. At the touch of my eyes, he jumped up. I saw the veins bulging on the side of his neck, he looked so tortured.

I'm sorry, I thought, *but I haven't decided the women's fate in this world. One time is a woman powerful, before she gives in, and all a woman wants is to give in with love . . .*

I hardened myself, and muttered to my father, "I want my children's rights to be first when it comes to inheritance. If I die and they get to be raised by Lanit and Rona, I don't want them disowned. I want their rights upheld"—I took a deep breath— "and I want them larger than the other children's."

"You want that, how? Written into the *ketubah?*"

That was the name of a Jewish marriage contract. Often, the ketubah was the only piece of writing a Galilean woman became familiar with in her lifetime.

"Yes, Abba. Exactly. Tell Joseph that."

"He's coming over," my father said. I turned. Yes, Joseph was walking toward us, fast, kicking the sand. Handsome he looked, and bone tired.

Instantly, a worried hum went around the girls' little crowd. What if Joseph said to Mary now, Forget it, Mary, you're too hardheaded, you'll never submit to me, you'll never obey me. So I don't want you! They were worried; if this whole thing fell apart, that would be worse for them, who had no offers yet.

He was in front of me. My father told him what I had asked for.

"Come on," he grumbled. "Who would dare disown your children? Anyone can guess who would be the mistress in our home."

I became disgusted with myself. *What have I done, haggling*

so hard? *Sweet Lord Adonai, shouldn't love be our only contract?* On
the other hand, I felt very insulted, as I knew myself to be weak,
wavering, and unauthoritative! "Rona will be twelve on her wedding day," Joseph added, "do you think she'll ever stand up to
you?" Being reminded of the wedding (not to mention that he
knew Rona's birthday!) made me so angry again. I snapped, "I'm
deeply sorry, but my answer is no. My own kin don't need this
wedding anyway, the king's man is waiting for us in Nazareth."

"The king's man will come and go. We'll be left with
Shalafta and with Aaron."

"And with each other!"

He looked as if he hated me just now.

But then his eyes showed that golden tinge of yore. It
seemed less pure now, more tired. But it was still that glow,
earthly yet innocent, and I felt that my heart was melting. "You
want our children's rights spelled out? They'll be spelled out."

He said, *"our children."* His eyes and mine met. I couldn't
help it, I gave myself to his eyes. He and I.

I said, "Maybe I don't need anything spelled out, if I know
that we agree."

"We agree."

So, I thought. *I won't have him just to myself. But there's no
other way I could marry him, and Joseph is doing his best, and the
people deserve peace. And . . .* suddenly the High One whispered to
me, *He's a good man, with such amiable commonsense.*

I replied, *I know, I chose him.*

*Ah, Adonai, you made me so responsible, so dependable and
guilty, if this marriage collapsed before it even started, I'd feel so
miserable! Avinu, our father, why did you make me like this? Besides, if this ended just now due to my hardheadedness, I'd be so*

lonely—All three of us would be lonely, Avinu whispered back, astonishing me.

So at last, exhausted, I nodded to Joseph. "Yes, Joseph, it's yes!" Then I smiled at my mother. I couldn't fight anymore, it was done.

There was an ovation from the girls.

My mother rushed to hug me, squeezing me to her with joy and guilt. Forgive me, my daughter, that you couldn't have a better match!

Orpa gave me a glance that said: You haggled well. Yorit gushed, "Now make the Roman take us to Jerusalem, Mary. No one says no to you."

"I'll do my best, Yorit."

I thought the bluntest thoughts of my life. I had agreed to not being the only wife, was that weakness on my part? Was Bathsheba weak for being ravished by David and then added to a harem of forty? Or was she strong? For she couldn't prevent the killing of her husband, Uriah, and being part of the harem came with being queen, and at least she did her best for her offspring.

I decided Bathsheba was strong. What fate dealt to her, she made the best of it.

"So, we'll be married right here?" I said to Joseph.

"Yes. But in Nazereth, you'll stand under that other canopy, too."

"No." I tried to sweeten my voice. "Joseph, please . . . I love you . . ."

"All the more, then . . ."

"Oh, shut up! Did Shalafta buy a fancy canopy?"

"Yes, he bought it in Sepphoris. Gorgeous it is, with silver *rimonim* [pomegranates] adorning the tops of the four posts. He had it carried to Nazareth in an open cart. Everyone from Sepphoris to Nazareth gawked at it as it rolled by."

"So, he's making that wedding into a show already." Just thinking about that made me angry again. "Why does he crave you so much as son-in-law?"

He smiled proudly, and told me why.

A few months back, Syria's procurator, Ventidius Cumanus—known for "arriving poor in rich Syria, and now Syria is poor and he's rich"—had visited Sepphoris and seen Joseph's wares. Ventidius had paid Joseph two thousand silver shekels to carve his likeness.

I noticed how polished and confident Joseph's speech had become. He was a dashing, worldly Jew with ties to mighty non-Jews. No wonder Shalafta wanted him. I got worried: How would I measure up?

I took Joseph's arm. "You want to get away from this noise, Joseph?"

I pulled him gently across the camel trail, toward those rocks that glowed with dawn's pink.

My father ran after us, to tell us that the elders were breaking the tent posts, to raise a wedding canopy. I smiled, I was happy! "Find something to write with, Abba, so I can have the children's rights written down."

He threw his arms in the air. "We have no ink, Mary."

"Maybe you could mix water with ashes from the fire and make ink?"

"We have no scrolls. Don't you trust your husband?"

"Of course I do! Write the ketubah on the back of the king's scroll. Put in it everything I mentioned."

Joseph muttered, "Uh, Mary . . . how much inheritance did

you have in mind for *our* children?" Finally realizing that by favoring his children with me, he would prejudice his children with Lanit and with Rona! *Oh, God, don't let this fall apart!* "I want a third of everything for my children only, and the remaining two thirds shared equally by *all* the children." My heart was beating hard. "Yes, Joseph?"

He shrugged in defeat. I had only meant to be fair.

"I'll be so good to your other wives' children . . ." I heard my father say to someone, "Bring water and scoop ashes from the fire to mix them into ink." I started crying again.

And Joseph stared in confusion. Had I not gotten all I wanted? What was wrong?

I felt like telling him that I should be so lucky. For even that written ketubah guarantees me nothing. *By our law, Joseph, you can divorce me anytime. If you say to me in the presence of two witnesses that I displease you and thus you divorce me, by the Jewish law, I would have to walk out of our yard with only what I could carry on my back. My children would stare tearfully through the picket fence, but they would not be allowed to bring me back, or join me. Oh, Adonai, how greatly did your daughter Eve disappoint you, that you saddled her with such a fate? What did Eve really do? What did all women go on doing, that men have such contempt and fear for them? Ever wonder about that, Joseph?* But I knew what Joseph would reply. None of that crossed my mind, Mary. I'm a man.

Choked with tears again, deeply misunderstood, I stared away . . . That cloud that usually hovered on the top of the mountain was creeping down the mountain's shoulder.

Rain pattered on the sand, and on the top of my head. The girls danced excitedly in the rain.

Somewhere behind us, Akam was still belching. "Shimon?

Mary's other bidder is taking her away! Don't let him! Face off with him, break his bones! Where are you?"

Shimon did not reply.

I asked tearfully, "Do you know what happened to our house, Joseph?"

"Your cousin Elsheva lives in it now."

Oh, yes, Elsheva! Who told everyone how her Zachariah toiled on her body.

"Elsheva is three months pregnant. When they found out that she was pregnant at last, Zachariah was so struck with wonder, he became mute a while. Even now he speaks like he's got a cork in his throat." I could tell that Joseph wanted to put his arms around me; but he was uneasy, everyone was staring at us. He whispered to me, "I love you, Mary, I wanted to buy you an expensive ring, but I was afraid that if I brought it with me, I might get robbed."

I jumped. "Did you buy rings for the other brides?"

"Uh . . . Shalafta said he would buy the rings, and I said I'd pay for them. He bought the rings."

"Pretty ones?"

"I didn't see them."

I managed not to burst into tears again. Through what twists of fate I got to have you, Joseph! I lifted my hand and touched his lips, enjoying the soft, rugged tickle of his skin on my palm. I was still choked by the injustice of women's fate, and yet . . .

I heard squeals. Joseph's sheep were being slaughtered for my wedding feast.

That cloud rolled down from the heights. The morning's chilliness was unusual.

Something ripped the air right by my face.

A stone tumbled on the sand a few steps away. I spun around to see where it came from.

On the other side of the camel trail, the rock tops were studded with faces.

I froze. It couldn't be . . . Who else but Shimon was peeking from between two rocks like a scout leading an invasion? And beside him, short and red-faced . . . Aaron's son Jerash, grown, his chin dirtied by a knotty beard. A satchel of stones strapped on his shoulder. He put another stone in his slingshot. "Jerash!" Akam moaned, as if waking up. Joseph shoved me to the ground, pulled out his knife. He yelled, "To the mountain, Mary! Run to the mountain!"

More stones crashed near me. Akam went down with a wail . . . Like a whip cracking, a stone hit Orpa in the forehead.

A throng charged toward us. I recognized boys I knew from the village. But they were few, most of our attackers were strangers, young, children almost, hard-eyed, in rags. "Up on the mountain!" my father yelled.

Akam writhed on the ground. Orpa moaned. Her forehead was bleeding.

I wanted to run to Orpa, but I was knocked aside by women and older men running toward the mountain. One old man picked up a stone, wanted to throw it back, but it fell from his hand. My father called to Jerash, whom he had known since Jerash was in his mother's arms: "Don't do this, you'll have to live with it!" Orpa's father ran stiffly toward his daughter. A stone hit her in the chest. Orpa let out a throttled cry and fell.

Then Joseph's last sheep, spared from the slaughtering knife, ran into a rain of stones. Our attackers kept pelting. When they crushed the sheep's skull, they cheered. Joseph started toward

Jerash. Knife out, not even ducking the stones. My father felt Orpa's cheek with his unfeeling hands. A stone hit me in the back, but I almost did not feel it. I lifted Orpa.

Orpa tried to speak. I yelled at her to live. She nodded and bubbled a word I didn't understand. Then she said it again, "The mirror . . ."

I shook her, damning myself for being rough with her. I laid my face on her heart, I wanted to hear her heartbeat.

"The mirror . . ."

I stammered, crying in fear and pity. Her forehead was a puddle of blood. "Yes, Orpa . . . the mirror . . . ?"

She rolled her eyes back.

She drooled blood. I wiped it off, kissed her lips before they filled with blood again. I lifted her in my arms and ran to lay her behind our carts, to find shelter from the stones. But our attackers were there already, setting a cart on fire. *Adonai, take my life, but let Orpa's life come back to her. Restore my sister, Orpa, to life, I beg you, Adonai!*

Our older people shouted from the mountain, "Run, girls! Run, Mary!" Breathless from climbing, desperate that so many of us were still down here.

"Shimon . . . Shimon . . ." Akam writhed on the sand. His eyelids blinked spastically. His mind was dying.

Shimon stabbed Akam. Akam moaned. "Shimo-oh-onnn . . ." Maybe he wanted to ask Shimon why. But he stopped breathing.

I was thrown off Orpa's body by two urchins, ragged and dirty. I remembered those strangers who sold stones by the gate of the temple. Tsoaneem. Those unfortunates whom Alexander the Great had dragged out of Asia. Who lived in homes of garbage, in Ge Hinnom, the Valley of Hell. *Am I in hell, Adonai?* They pulled Orpa's shift over her bloodied face, baring her breasts. They tried to part her legs. I screamed like a beast being slaughtered. *Adonai, did you not speak to me on the mountain, did you not reveal your kindness to me, but above all, your* knowledge *of us, of me? Your care and joy that I* was, *as Orpa was, and all of us are the proof that* you are? *You made me believe in you as I never did before! What am I to think now? Are you filling me with hate for all my days to come, are you filling me with evil?* Screaming at those ragged apparitions, I uncovered Orpa's face and wept onto it that word she had sputtered with her last breath: "The mirror . . ."

Jerash was suddenly by me. He looked at me with curiosity. I was not bloodied and I was alive.

He glanced at Orpa, lying on her back, breasts bared.

Joseph ran to us. I thought, *Stab Jerash, kill him!*

Joseph yelled at him to call back his horde. He begged, "Don't make me kill you, Jerash!" Jerash lowered his slingshot, as if undecided. *Adonai, you who give life, how can you take life back?* Raindrops, large and slow, fell on Orpa's breasts. I wanted her to sit up, to wipe away those raindrops, to say, And now let's hop around at Mary's wedding! But she wouldn't sit up! She wouldn't speak! Jerash was calling his urchins. So malnourished, so gaunt, seemingly unthreatening. But there were so many of them. Orpa's parents lifted Orpa, her mother rubbing her under her left breast, tapping her on the side of her heart. Orpa seemed so innocent in her nakedness; strange that a body so innocent could stir urges. I mingled my hands with her mother's hands. Orpa was warm from our hands. And then I knew. She was gone.

I realized the horror of putting her in the ground. Covering her up, walking away, letting the nameless dirt settle over her face, over her hands and feet, chin, throat, and lips.

I screamed. I scratched up sand and ground it onto my face. *See me, High One, and do the same, up in heaven! Didn't you tell me that you felt my pain? I want to feel your pain, and I want your pain endless! Guilty forever, I want you to feel the injustice of your decision, its rashness, its error. Oh, its error is as endless as you are! Strike me now, for I won't stop judging you, most harshly! I won't stop screaming,* "Aaaaaaahhh, Orpaaaaaaaa, my heart, my soul, my sister, my sister!"

Maybe my screams stopped those killers from reloading their slingshots. I was screaming so loud, they began to shake. My cheeks were bleeding from the sand. *Are you hearing me, Adonai? Are you grieving and acknowledging error?*

Lightning, like a tree of fire, flashed above me. Its branches reached downward.

Four branches of lightning, jagged and blinding, blackened the sand and blew it to specks, while Jerash opened his mouth . . . and seemed to inhale that fiery charge. A steam of flame came out of his lips. He raised his hands to his throat and collapsed. I wailed, "Do it again! Again!"

Jerash did not move. *Do it again. Feel the thickening of my heart, feel the freezing of my soul. Strike the traitor Shimon, too, strike him, too!*

That roar of thunder blew my hearing away. Deaf, I watched how lightning from above stirred up lightning from below. Fire stored in the ground, from earlier storms, bolted to meet the fire from the sky. That tree of fire—its branches met the branches from the earth in awesome silence. But I saw with more keenness than ever. Fire added to fire, fire piled on fire, blinding clarity, nothing shaded by nothing. The light split the skies and us, these specks of living dirt. I raised my hands, and paths of light peered between my fingers. World made of light. Light of God, merciless God, merciless light.

Aaron's son Jerash lay motionless, a few steps from Orpa.

And the rain fell.

Part 11

The Mountain of God, 3

My father knelt near Jerash and felt his face, then his chest.

He got up and gestured; there was no life left in Aaron's only son.

My ears had unplugged; I heard myself scream at my father to get away from where the lightning kept striking. I'd lost Orpa, my sister in my heart, I couldn't afford to lose him, too!

But my father stepped up to those dirty boy-men, who had dropped their stones and were cowering now. My father asked them how much Aaron had paid them to kill us. They wailed that they got no money from him, but Aaron had told them to take whatever we had, that we'd be easy sport. Loose your stones at them and don't miss the girl, she's the witch. It dawned on me that they mistook Orpa for me. Facing toward Nazareth, my father said, *"Aaron, mekoolal atah,"* cursed be you, Aaron. For some odd reason, his words made me a little less angry at God. I'd never heard my father curse anyone before. Then he told Joseph to take me away, to make me safe somehow, and I squirmed and hollered. I didn't want to be safe, I wanted to die. Then another tree of fire struck down. Yelling in terror, our attackers scattered into the desert, while two of our women rushed to untie the donkeys, kicking them 'til they raced toward the mountain, faster than donkeys ever do.

My father called out that we had to bury Orpa and Akam.

And Jerash, too—we couldn't leave him to the vultures. The kindlier we acted, the more certainly God would notice our selflessness and come to our help. And we should bury the dead on the mountain, for down here their graves would be lost in the sand. Then, we should gather on the crest by the sheepfolds and decide if we should continue on home.

I thought that he was raving mad.

Maybe I fainted. When I woke up again, Joseph was carrying me in his arms, and my mother walked next to me.

JOSEPH SET ME down under trees dripping with rain, near three freshly dug graves. The three bodies were put in the ground, and the earth was pounded over them.

We mourned. Almost all the mourners gathered around Orpa's grave, while only two old men and Akam's woman wept over Akam's grave, and Jerash lay alone until earth was kicked over him. I wished that the rain would lay him bare to the jackals. Joseph picked me up again, and I tried to fight him as he carried me with my face in his wet burka, sheltered from branches that slapped my shoulders and back.

But I was too weak to fight, and he climbed fast, through the wild forest.

I let my face loll onto his shoulder, and glimpsed my mother behind us, helping my father, who could not cling to crags and tree trunks. She bumped into a donkey tangled in a bush and called to the other women to look for our mothers with suckling infants. Two of them could ride on that donkey. It was amazing that she was so together, while I felt so insane. I could hear my mother's thoughts: Pain is bitter, Mary, pain is sad, but it has its place in life. Death begets new life, Mary . . . Don't turn away from God, Mary, even as you lose someone so dear to you. Don't turn your face from him, please . . .

The streaks of rain looked green from the green leaves they were falling on.

I had not helped Orpa.

I had stroked her chest, but not long enough, I had blown my breath into her lips, but not patiently enough. I had not brought her back to life.

Then I realized that she was killed by that first stone that had torn the air in front of my face. She did not collapse right away, but her life was already wrenched from her. I could have tried to revive her again and again, but it wouldn't have helped.

Finally, I regained some strength and walked with Joseph holding me, his arm around my waist.

It was raining hard. He mumbled that we would find shelter in one of the sheepfolds. Everyone would be looking for shelter there.

One of our jackal mutts appeared in the rain. It ran off, ahead of us.

I kept thinking of Orpa's tiny body.

I had a vision of the endless time ahead. Hundreds of years, thousands of years after I was gone, other clans would rise, other kingdoms would be at war. Other bloodlines would be mixing and multiplying and then draining and drying up.

It all came to death in the end.

Death was the carrier, the channel, the vehicle.

Death?

I wondered what my tribe would do once we found each other on the heights and counted how many of us were alive. Go back to the well? If we returned to the well, I could end up as a bondwoman to Jibril or to one of his sons. I'd live among strangers and have children with strangers. Then I told myself that I was not alone, I was with the man I hoped to entrust my life to. But had I lost what I never thought I could lose? My trust that Adonai was watching over me? My belief that I was, because *he was*?

Despite my pain, I begged him to whisper to me, *I am. I still am.*

He was not speaking.

I cried inside my heart. *Now I know—it was always a fairy tale—to believe that you really have any knowledge of me.*

He said nothing.

I listened to that depth inside me, that narrow echoing valley where I had first heard his voice. *Say something! Show me something, anything! Lure me back, in any way possible!*

Joseph stopped walking. He set me down and looked at me. *Did you make Joseph stop just now?*

"There," Joseph said, pointing.

I saw a lopsided hut of stones fitted together without mortar, with a roof of thatch and woven branches. There were holes in the roof; puffs of steam rose out of them.

"Who made a fire? The shepherds?"

Joseph smelled the air. "There's no fire. The air inside is warmer, when it rises above the roof, it steams up."

"Where are the shepherds?"

He knocked on the hut's door.

There was no reply. He peered in the storing sheds. Not a soul.

He told me that if the shepherds had taken their sheep to new pastures, the fold would remain empty 'til fall.

We were close to the peak. The air was strong. Old and broken, the darkened corrals twisted among the tall shrubbery of the heights.

"We're ahead of everyone else," Joseph whispered.

I thought, *I should enjoy that Joseph is with me, for who knows if he's really here? And if this dream ends, too, I won't miss much, will I?*

And then the voice said, so stunningly close, it pricked up my skin, *Do you want death instead of life? Answer me. That question, only you can answer.*

I barely breathed. I felt that the pores in my skin had become eyes and ears.

Meantime, Joseph walked to the lopsided hut. Its door was shut with a wooden latch. Joseph moved the latch. He pushed the door with his knee. It started to swing open on hinges wet from the rain. Then it got stuck.

Instead of busting the door open, Joseph felt the lower panel. He found the spot where the panel was jammed against the threshold. He pressed it skillfully, while pulling the latch up with his other hand. The door opened all the way, and Joseph gave me a look, as if wanting to be praised for his gentleness.

"Come in," he called, and stepped inside.

Just then Adonai thinned the rain. He stabbed a dagger of sunlight sideways across a cloud, hitting the trees flat against their trunks.

Beyond that cloud, the sun was very low, ready to set.

The edge of the mountain was a few steps behind me. If I walked backward, I wouldn't even know when my feet would lose ground. One step off, I'd sail into the void.

And then I felt the nearness of the High One. He shuddered that I might step into the void and he made me dig my heels into the ground.

The man you want is waiting for you, he pleaded.

I stayed where I was, utterly silent. Breathing and listening and feeling that he was very worried, but with every instant that passed, he was worried a little less.

For I knew now, and he knew, too, that I would not hurl myself into the void.

Then he asked, *What do you want, Mary, power? That comes with loneliness. Mine is the greatest loneliness. You don't want that.*

I tried to think about what I really wanted.

I thought, *You in the Highest, listen to me. This is me, a mere womb. That's all I have to sell, all I have to trade. The road to it, between my skinny legs, a man could become tired of it in one night. That's the way between men and women. But let me ask you, when was it decided that it should be that way? When you and the man were alone in the garden, and he still had all his ribs? And how was it decided? Did he say, Yes, Lord, my rib goes to her, but,* all else *goes to me? Yes, Lord? Did you reply, Yes, that sounds fair, First Man. Done. And now lie down so I may put you to sleep, to get that rib out of you. Won't take even a whole day of creation. You're asleep now? I'm tearing you open to take* her *out. Are you here, First Woman, all packed in one rib? Pay attention, I shall recite your rights: Be second to the man, and when you have children, be second to them, too. Yes? Yes, Adonai, yes, how right that sounds! How generous! Also, First Woman, you could be thrown out of your nest at any time, by being handed a get, a bill of divorcement, which no woman can fight, no woman can reverse, if she displeases the Man! But I'll never displease him, or you, Lord, never ever! Good, you're appreciative, Woman. But keep remembering that your husband has that get written up in his mind, while my approval for it is on my lips, anytime it's needed! Yes? Oh, indeed, yes. How wonderful all this is. And it's wonderful that you spent time alone with the first man, and you looked him over proudly, and chuckled to yourself: He is good, the man! But you never spent time alone with me, the woman, though I, too, am your creation. No wonder You do not understand me. But never mind, never mind, wonderful is my life and all that comes with it. I'll never ask for a better deal. Yes, Lord. Yes, Man. Yes, yes!*

I took a breath. Was that the way it all happened?

How simple, how easy what I wanted was! I wanted to put words to what happened. I wanted to understand and be understood. It was that easy.

Do you have anything to say to me, Hashem?

He coaxed me gently. *Go inside. He's waiting for you.*

Joseph made loud noises inside the hut. I gripped the fence with both hands. The fence pickets were so old and saturated with rain, they couldn't have been flimsier.

Joseph stepped out of the hut. He was combing his fingers through his wet hair.

"There's a table inside. I can break it and make a fire."

"Make a fire, then."

Awkwardly, he touched my hand clutching the fence, and I felt his fear. *What if I don't fulfill you?* his fear said. *This is the place where the lightning struck me. And though it was years ago, and I desire you so deeply, I'm still so full of fear. Will I become whole with you?*

He looked at me, without hiding his fear, and I felt naked in Joseph's eyes . . .

I snuck a glance at my arm, covered by my drenched sleeve.

I glanced at my feet—they showed just as they should under the hem of my shift. Bare and scratched, and my shift was so heavily stained with mud and squashed leaves.

Though I had my clothes on, a kind of inner nakedness was coming out of me, I felt it opening under my wet clothes, I felt it opening inside my heart. That undress of the soul, which made me so uneasy, and yet . . . *Uneasiness, abashment of my body— that's what you want me to feel, isn't that so, Adonai?* My heart of hearts was baring itself, and it was like a bud of nakedness—so secret, so unknown—it had never been glimpsed . . .

I tried to look Joseph in the eyes, but Joseph's yearning was so overpowering, and he was so desperate that he might not fulfill me. But if he failed, I would still be what he most wanted in life. Because I was the woman and I could cause desire, yet my desire couldn't be without the man causing me abashment. *And that makes me the woman. Yes, Adonai?*

And Adonai, blessed be he, seemed to stutter. He, too, seemed abashed. *Ssshh, I know what you feel, Mary. I know abashment. I am the shyest of all.*

And that is why I made you just like me. I gave you no easy path—yours is the hardest.

But that's why you're so astounding in the undress of your soul.

Oh. I beamed. *Am I really so astounding?*

The feel of his praise was so delicious that within a fold of my heart I teased him, quick and breathless: *I can't be! Flatterer!*

And then he for whom no human is a match stared out of Joseph, at me.

He stared out of Joseph's golden eyes, those eyes he had swept me with on that roof, against the endless sea. Just for an instant, we peeked at each other. I felt the loneliness he showed me that first time he had talked to me, that loneliness that touched me yet terrified me. Is that why he's calling people back to him, is that why he's ending lives on earth before their time? So he wouldn't be so lonely?

Might we die, my husband of a few hours and I, if I follow him into that hut and become his?

And he hurried to whisper, so worried I might not trust him, *No, no, you have nothing to fear, everything that will happen will be your choice! Trust me! But now, take Joseph's hand. Take it. Someone must make the first step.*

And I felt his worry and loneliness. I felt it so deeply that I took Joseph's hand.

GOD IN THE Highest, I used to wish, I used to dream about how I would breathe the scent of Joseph's skin, when he would be kissing me.

And I prayed that he would smell manly, yet clean.

Adonai, why are your smallest gifts the best? Perhaps because they're not that small? How often do women gasp for their lives in the bridal tent because of the reek of armpits! Men's bodies do stink, and I'm not talking about gaminess that would put a woman in the mood! So, Adonai, you pleasured my wish of cleanness. Joseph, washed by your rain, smelled pure.

He kissed me now and was so awkward kissing me that he bit my lower lip, and I could tell that his teeth were so healthy. And that lovely haze of sweat on his forehead and cheeks! Just right! Could things so small matter so deeply? Well, they did! I had dreamed of how, when he would take off his clothes, his skin would glow, for he'd have as little hairy growth as possible. Thank you, again! The rain was pelting so hard on the roof above us that Joseph stopped kissing me and started tearing off his clothes. He bundled them up and stopped up the leaking roof with them.

So the hut was plunged in darkness, but around the edges of those bundled clothes, the lightning flashed outside, and Joseph was lit on and off as he became more naked.

I burst out laughing. He wore so many layers of clothes! Truly, a rich boy's clothes! Underneath his burka, he wore a thin fitted *haluk,* long, with long sleeves. Under it, he wore a flaxen *kolbur,* short, with short sleeves. Tied to his kolbur's belt was his punda. A rich boy's punda would be large and embroidered. Joseph's was large and embroidered, and it clinked with coins.

And now . . . he was bare chested. Not hairy. Wonderful.

But he still had his *subrikin,* his trousers, to take off, and then his *empiliot,* his long stockings.

When he took those off, his legs were still covered with white abrition, knee-long drawers that young rich Jews took to wearing after the Greek fashion.

From inside his punda, he brought out a flintstone. "I'll make fire."

With his bare hands, he broke up the table. He crouched on the floor, gathered twigs, chips, sawdust, piled them in the middle of the room. He sparked the flintstone. He made fire.

"Give me your shift," he said.

I took off my shift. It was heavy, soaked with water. He wrought the water out of it, spread it by the fire like a bedsheet. It would warm up from the fire.

He gestured to me to go to him. I stepped across the darkness and sat next to him.

He put his arms around me, and his skin was burning. He pushed me onto the floor.

I let my hands furrow his wet hair, then I laced them behind his neck, where his skin felt soft. With teeth clenched, I kissed his lips, hard. We gasped for air at the same time. He whispered, If things went bad in Nazareth, if the death of Aaron's son turned the clock back to war, Joseph had a way to save us, my mother, my father, and me. He would *buy us:* We'd be his property, untouchable by God's commandment—Thou shall not steal.

While saying all that, he kissed me.

I kissed him back. "If we're not good slaves, will you sell us?"

"You're sweating." He felt my palms, my arms. "You're so strong! A woman shouldn't be as strong as a man. Don't toil hard when you're in my house, the servants will resent you. Mary . . ."

"What?"

"If Aaron thinks that I killed Jerash, he'll want to kill me. If I'm killed but you carry my blood already, that will be better for you. If you are still a betoola, Aaron will drag you into his yard. If you're not, he won't care. Mary . . ."

"What?"

"I've always wanted children."

He was trembling. All the suffering of the Jews, all the strife of Adam's seed, they were in his eyes, lit by the smoky fire.

I was so touched. I stroked Joseph's heart with that hardened palm of mine. I got a knot in my throat, though I could have laughed. So you are ready now, Joseph? That's all it took, being alone with each other, in a rainstorm, on a mountaintop, after so much strife and misery? Aahh, but he was so happy, my Joseph. I couldn't utter a word of all that, for he was kissing me like a madman and his heart was beating so hard. I saw his heartbeat twitching in his throat and I glimpsed it in his eyes. So I closed my eyes, and I went deep inside me. To where Hashem waited. I asked him, *You're in Joseph, yes?*

He could have replied, Yes, I'm inside him, I'm inside everyone.

But . . . he didn't reply at all, he was silent, silent with such overwhelming nearness to us. Joseph held on to my body. I closed my eyes, but glimpsed the hands that shaped the trees of the first creation. Now those hands were young, otherworldly young. I opened my eyes again, and I saw Hashem's own undress of the soul. It was in Joseph's eyes, telling me, *I'm here.* Only for me to know. *I'm not a thought, not a prayer only. I'm truly here.*

I thought, *Joseph knows nothing about this.* And the voice countered with the deepest gentleness. *But he does, in a way. For even the first time he met you, he was so stunned by you. For who is like you? So, he knows.*

Hashem's eyes in Joseph's eyes caught the glow of the fire. All glow. As if, across the peacefulness of Sabbath candles, a path had become open. I still wanted to ask why me, but couldn't. I had wished to be the girl of the promise with such strength, with such desire that it had been noticed. I peered back, along those pathways of eyes, into the garden.

And then I understood.

Back in that garden, the instant that she had opened her eyes, Eve knew her future. Which astonished Him, and his crafting hands, and his soul which had just marveled, *She is good.* He, too, knew her future, but she knew it even better than he. And when he decided to remove her from the garden, she left *him* in such loneliness, he missed her with such heartache.

For it was she who mattered more—as one might have guessed—since he punished her harshest. Don't we punish harshest the ones we love most? So, from then on, lonely he was for the man he had made, but he was lonely much more for the woman . . .

Joseph didn't fight me. I took him in my arms. I had dreamed so many times how we'd make love, face-to-face, eyes upon eyes, we'd forget we had bodies; our bodies would fulfill their fate, while we watched love's workings in each other's eyes. Yes, oh, yes, Ruth had uncovered the feet of King Boaz in his sleep. And yes, she was the one who drew the man to her, and drew his seed into her. But I, I just held Joseph, until I felt a touch, unspeakably easy and simple. Soul to soul.

I LAY ON the floor, hearing the rain drip right near my face. I kept lying there, until drops fell on my face. They were heavy and strangely warm.

I sat up.

Joseph had tilted to one side and closed his eyes. A puff of exhaustion came from his lips. Like a child, he was asleep. So charmingly and endearingly tired. *Look, Adonai, so did Adam sleep afterward, so innocent. So did Eve sleep afterward, so innocent. Your children whom you loved so much, how could you banish them?* I asked him, dizzy with the freedom to ask him anything just now. Then Joseph's clothes, weighted from the rain, dropped from the roof with a soaked plop. Then a sheet of rain came down, rinsing my sweaty face. *Even this caress of rain felt like your caress, Adonai.*

I squinted, trying to see if there was red from me, bleeding onto our makeshift bed. But the flicker of the fire put red on it, so I couldn't tell what was blood and what was fire. I touched my shift, but it was wet from raindrops and from the water building on the hut's floor.

Everything was wet, lukewarm, soft, like a womb, everything felt so fertile. Within me, seed was moving, homing in. Then, with one blow, it broke into its matrix.

I was speechless, and he said nothing.

IN THE open crack of the roof, I saw the night sky clearing. That stubborn storm sailed away, leaving one long streak of cloudiness, very thin, very high.

Pushed by a breeze, it floated, so sheer and shiny, it caught the starlight and looked alive . . .

The hut's narrow window was covered with a goatskin.

A gust of wind. The goatskin was blown away.

I tiptoed to the window and peeked out.

Glittering shapes squirmed in the wet grass.

Snakes, scores of them! Crawling up the mountain! Their scales shined. Their movements were sinuous but slow, exhausted. Below the heights, the downpour was so much worse, the snakes had crawled up to escape the rain. Some twitched one more time, then grew inert. They wouldn't wiggle into the hut, we were safe.

I padded back from the window, and stood under the open roof, looking at that thin cloud. Sailing slowly in a wide circle. I felt that it was made of souls.

Orpa, Orpa, I'm down here.

I feel so selfish to even think this, but I think it, I could become a mother, and soon . . .

Orpa, you, the one who lay with me in my secret garden—and we talked of men and of angels. I have a man. Adonai healed Joseph, Orpa . . . Unfortunately, he'll never heal my sadness from losing you . . .

I didn't want to cry again. I wanted to give Orpa something of mine, but I was down here and she was up in the sky, so what could I give her, what could we share?

Be in me, Orpa, when I grow seed inside me. Have joy with me. And forgive me that I'm alive, while you are not . . .

I feel that I know why you had to go, Orpa. It was so that I could stay . . . How can I thank you?

She said nothing, my friend. She sailed slowly in the sky above me.

And Adonai said nothing, because my loss was so painful. But he made me feel it again, that undress of my soul. He made room inside me to receive everyone, so I could carry them all, for I needed them all. My mother and my father and Orpa and Joseph. And the one who said nothing, but I felt him inside me. Adonai.

Part 12

Magnificat

THE FIFTY Roman soldiers, half of a *centuria* unit, were marching toward Nazareth. They had been marching three days already, eight hours a day with a few minutes of rest every two hours, and a half hour for the midday meal.

Paulus Arsinus, the officer who commanded them, had reacted curtly to Apella's request that they reach Nazareth at the end of the third day. "Four days might be feasible, if I order them to force-march. But if they force-march, they'll be worthless for battle when we get there."

Force-marching meant stepping flat onto the sole of the foot, maintaining constant speed, while the column advanced with that discipline unique to the Roman army. Roman soldiers claimed that they could sleep while force-marching. They held on to each other's arms, closed their eyes, and dozed off, in lockstep.

"How many rebels are we supposed to face in Nazareth?" asked Arsinus.

"None. I need a show of presence, to make smooth the relocation of a tribe. King's business. That's all you need to know."

"If there is an uprising in Jerusalem while we are away, the king might be gone when we return," Arsinus countered. He was a commander risen from the ranks, straightforward and well liked. He had been *aquilifer,* bearer of his legion's eagle-shaped insignia, in the last Parthian war.

"Fifty Romans, the other half of the centuria, will still be in Jerusalem," Apella countered, aware how meager fifty troops sounded. The agreed-on policy had long been to keep only a hundred Romans in Jerusalem. Neither Rome nor the Jewish king wanted Jerusalem to look occupied.

"Plus, the king has his Syrians," Apella added.

Arsinus spat scornfully. "The Syrians are good for terrorizing unarmed civilians. Faced with desperate throngs, they'll turn and flee. The news from the north is that the uprisings are spreading."

Apella lowered his voice. "I know. The king is very unpopular. Maybe one of his sons by Queen Malthace is behind these uprisings?"

The soldier remained silent, but his eyes darted from Apella to the open window and back to Apella. Through the open window, they could both see the king's palace.

Very good, Arsinus, Apella thought. *Look how easily you believe that there's a conspiracy in the making. Rome is letting go of Herod. Rome is removing half of its force from the capital, rushing it to a godforsaken hamlet, making it easy for one of the princes to seize the throne.* Apella wished that such a conspiracy existed.

Maybe I'm actually starting that conspiracy, all by myself?

"Judea would have fewer problems if it were a regular colony," Arsinus said. "Under the rule of some able Roman like yourself."

"I just suggested to Caesar that the army's pay should be increased," Apella said, making a mental note to include the suggestion in his next report. Arsinus relaxed in his square garrison chair and winked at the liaison man.

"Very well, Eques. I'll order my men to leave Jerusalem in

groups of ten, through several city gates, to make the movement seem benign. We'll assemble in a marching column up the road, by the Ramah spring."

"Excellent. I heard about your bravery in Parthia, Arsinus."

"And I heard that you'll be married to Octavia Augusta. I'm sure you two won't set up house in this wasteland. Will you take me back to Rome with you?"

"I wish I could. I'm staying on here, it seems. But I'll help you get a transfer to a quiet garrison in Italy."

"Many thanks. You look worn out, Eques. Sleep tomorrow, and catch up with us in Galilee."

"That was my plan. Can you spare some cavalrymen to ride with me?"

"Yes. You can have three."

HEADING BACK TO the palace, Apella was stopped in the street by two Roman jewelers, who were worried about the uprisings. They offered to pay Apella if he made some legionnaires available to guard their shops.

He burst out, surprised by his own rudeness. "You could afford your own private armies, that's how well you fattened yourselves here from Jews and Romans alike!" He walked on, leaving the jewelers nonplussed.

I've become so daring, he thought. *It helps, being Octavia's future husband!*

He arrived at his suite in the royal palace, where a servant told him that a madam from the house of joy in Kidron Valley was waiting for him, and she had brought three girls for his inspection.

He gave orders not to be disturbed, then took a look at the

girls. All brunettes with hazel eyes; one had freckles. He chatted with that one, then dismissed them all, and told the madam to keep looking. He wanted someone with more innocence. Also with a will of her own, natural cleverness, good repartee, and from a religious background. The madam commented that if he was looking for someone he'd already met, he should give her a name or a place. He told her that he'd never met that kind of girl. "But keep looking." He gave her some money, and she went away shaking her head.

He lay in bed and slept deeply, exhausted. He awoke the next morning and heard from his servant that Herod had inquired whether the Roman surgeon had arrived. Apella sent word to the king that he would depart for Galilee today, to find out what kept the doctor.

Ordinarily, he would have rushed to the king, to ask for orders in person. Now, feeling wonderfully untouchable, he bathed, ate lunch slowly, then rode to Antonia. The fifty men with Arsinus at the fore had been gone for twenty-four hours. The three horsemen assigned to Apella were ready and waiting, with weapons and food packed in their saddlebags.

Moments later, all four clattered out of the Syrian gate, so named because it opened to the road to Damascus and Antioch. They galloped up the road, northward.

THROUGH THE DAY and the next day, they galloped, changing horses at En-gannim, the dusty little border crossing from Judea into Galilee.

Soon, beyond the border, a thick rain awaited them.

Then travelers coming from the north informed Apella that the uprisings had been quelled in Caesarea and Sepphoris, but were continuing in other coastal towns. But the rain, miraculous for this time of the year, doused the wrath of the rioters, who were gathering in the local synagogues and settling down to write petitions to the king.

No one had specific news about Nazareth.

No news was good news. Relieved, Apella led on his mounted escort, heading north.

The road rose into the mountains, but it was still a good, passable road. Galloping in the rain, Apella came in sight of Arsinus's troops. Not marching now, but scattered on the road, staring up at a nearby mountain.

A cloud hung low on the mountaintop. Lightning flashed through a rift in the cloud, like an angry, blinking eye.

Arsinus had spread out a map. He was examining it under a shield held by a soldier to shelter the map from the rain. Apella stopped his horse next to him. Arsinus reported that the column was advancing, dozing in lockstep, when the soldiers in the front rows awakened to lightning flashing ahead.

It was flashing in such a regular pattern, that the soldiers marveled and stopped. Some of them began to panic.

Others controlled themselves and counted the flashes out loud. *"Unus, duo, tres . . . quatuor, quinque . . . sex, septem!"* For Romans, seven was a magical number. No one had ever seen lightning flashing seven times, and again seven, and again seven.

"Look." Arsinus pointed his gloved hand toward the peak.

The lightning ceased, as if taking a breath.

But then it flashed again, and the soldiers counted . . . four, five, six, seven.

One soldier cried, releasing pent-up strain.

Arsinus reported that the night before, as he ordered his

men to pitch their tents, a legionnaire had reported lightning flashing in threes at the edge of the horizon. This mountain lay in that same direction last night, though it was much farther away. The lightning flashed regularly: one, two, three; one, two, three—like a signaling system. No one had heard of a Roman signaling post perched on that peak. Arsinus ordered his fatigued men to place their spears, shields, and other metal tools outside the tents, in case the lightning struck closer. The soldiers ate their dry rations and turned in.

This morning, they marched on until the front rows noticed more lightning. Now it flashed seven times.

Apella wondered what Ascanius might have said about the symbolism of seven. Seven hills supported Rome? God needed seven days to make the world, six for creation, one for rest?

"I need to give my men an explanation," Arsinus said. "You come up with one, Eques."

Apella gathered his thoughts.

He asked for a drum to be brought over, stepped up on it, and clamored, "Soldiers of the Terdecima Centuria! That phenomenon out there is a theophany, a direct manifestation of God! As Caesar's representative here, I am overjoyed that fifty Roman citizens are witnessing it!"

His impetuousness had an instant effect. The soldiers packed the space around the drum, while Apella went on to explain that a theophany foreshadowed renewal. Rome was on the brink of an amazing renewal, and its protagonist was none but Caesar, who showed signs of divinity. *Caesar aequat Deus,* Caesar equals God, he trumpeted at last.

Then he told the soldiers that all they had to do in Nazareth was to patrol and make sure that the locals were quiet and the roads safe. No battle. Relieved, the soldiers shouted *ave,* and Apella got down from the drum, motioning Arsinus to bring him the map.

"Excuse me, Eques . . ." A youngster with the insignia of an army scribe on his chest blocked his path.

"Yes?" Apella responded, friendly.

"No disrespect for Caesar's divinity, but the regularity of that lightning is just too perfect not to be man-made. Our army's catapults can fire burning pitch. Maybe fire catapults are being loosed on that peak?"

Apella smiled. "How many catapults should be lined up there, to be hurled out in so many series of seven?"

"Then what is it?" the scribe asked. "If it's some military secret, tell us that, Eques, and I won't ask more. But nature is never so regularly predictable."

"That lightning looks godly to me." Apella pointed to the mountain. It blinked again. One, two, three . . . The soldiers intoned four, anticipating the fourth flash, and then they gasped from fifty chests. The lightning stopped at three, like an eye that had closed.

The soldiers burst out laughing, but their laughter was broken and nervous.

Again, the lightning flashed. One, two, three.

"He's playing with us," a legionnaire muttered.

"He?" Apella asked.

"*Deus ignotus,* that unknown god," the man muttered.

"That's Caesar," a legionnaire shouted. "Caesar, blinking at us from the mountaintop!"

He'd meant it as a joke, and everyone laughed and hollered, and the mood swung to joyful. Only the scribe seemed upset.

"You should tell us what's going on, Eques," he muttered angrily. "Our military can put on a light show. The question is why?" The soldiers gathered around Apella and the scribe, jeering and laughing. "Go to it, Lodus Geminus, let's hear your argument," they shouted. The scribe was obviously a character in the unit. Lodus Geminus replied with distress in his voice. "Men, hear me! If we are to give up our republic for Caesar's rule, we don't need stories about Caesar's divinity, we're not children. We should have a referendum of the citizens, and agree to live in tyranny if our families are cared for and our bellies full! But why should we pretend that Rome's change is God's will? It's Caesar's will, and that's all there is to it . . ."

"Fine by me," a legionnaire cut in, "as long as Caesar increases my pay."

"I've been asking Caesar to increase the military's pay by a quarter," Apella interjected, and Arsinus loudly joined the cheering.

But the scribe still protested. "What if I don't believe in God? Would that make me a traitor to Caesar?" He turned to the other soldiers. "When death fells a soldier, do you think that God knows, or cares?" But he had made a mistake. "God is a soldier's best friend," yelled a legionnaire with all fingers missing on his left hand. "Jupiter looks out for us," others shouted. "Caesar-Jupiter! Caesar-Mars! Caesar-Deus! You're a scribe, Lodus Geminus, when we go to battle, you hide in the food wagon, with your records!"

"I have a fighting twin who was gelded by the Parthians, how did Jupiter look out for him?" Lodus Geminus asked miserably.

Apella started; he remembered the other Lodus, the injured soldier in the hospital in Caesarea. Yes, that man and the scribe looked alike.

"I'm sorry for your brother," he told the young man. "Your feelings deserve respect, and you are not less brave for being a scribe." He patted the young man's shoulder, then raised his voice to all the legionnaires. "When I enter politics, I'll make you, Rome's fighting men, my priority!"

And they hailed him again—"Ave! Ave!"—as he stepped toward the map.

ON THE MAP, *Nazaria,* Nazareth, was marked halfway between sea and desert as a jumble of flat-topped houses and tiny vineyards and gardening plots.

Against its east gate, a mountain bristled with trees under a cloud with jagged lightning glaring out of it.

Mons Fulminis, the Mountain of Lightning, an army topographer had written near the drawing.

Putting his thumb on the map, Apella measured where they were: less than a day from Nazareth.

"Let the men eat their lunch already," he told Arsinus. "Give them double rations."

He walked around as the men ate, telling them not to jump to attention when he stopped. Through full mouths, they shouted "Ave" again, and applauded him, his simplicity and optimism were so reassuring. They asked him questions about the theophany, and did not find the notion too farfetched, not in the least. They also asked about Rome, which most had not visited; they were Roman by blood, but born in the colonies.

Apella was very satisfied. Fifty Roman citizens could testify that they'd witnessed the rain out of season and the unusual pattern of the lightning. He invited the soldiers to observe a moment of silence for their fallen comrades. Lodus looked to the ground with all the others, while rough voices called the names of fallen comrades. His brother's name would soon be added to the death roll, Apella reflected. A surge of sadness gripped him, but he controlled it, looking away to commander Arsinus: Let's go.

The blinking eye over the mountain kept blinking.

It started to rain again. Light, but persistent. The air was cool. The soldiers advanced easily, rounding the mountain until the setim trees appeared, and then the village.

Apella strained his tired eyes.

Seen through the drizzle, Nazareth's walls seemed unmanned.

And then Apella bolted in his stirrups. Dead bodies hung over the crest of the walls.

What's this? Apella wondered, horrified. *And where's the girl?*

He had expected the girl and her tribe to be waiting at the gate, while the village would be humming with preparations for that wedding.

He saw that the gates' panels were unhinged and broken.

Two voices shouted at once: "Eques! Eques!"

Hillel and the legionnaire he had left in charge were running toward him. Hillel wore a Roman helmet over his rabbinical headdress and long hair.

Exhausted, interrupting each other, the two reported that Aaron and Shalafta had fought a regular battle the night before. Nazareth's streets were filled with dead from both sides. Shalafta had won; he had taken Aaron's wife and daughter hostage, and barricaded himself at the widows' oil press. There were still survivors in the village, hiding in basements and cellars. As for Aaron, he had escaped into the desert . . .

"Where is the girl?" Apella asked. He gripped Hillel by the shoulders. Squeezing his horse with his knees, he lifted Hillel off the ground. "Where is the girl?"

"Half of them came back already . . . over the mountain . . . this morning . . . Joachim and Anna are at the inn . . ." Hillel squeaked, more frightened of the Roman than of that vision of death straddling the walls of the village. Apella set him down and ordered him to tell his story again, slowly. But Hillel was so shaken, Apella barely made out that the Joachimites had been attacked, though not by Aaron but by his son Jerash. In the ensuing fight, Jerash had died.

"And the girl?" Apella rasped.

Hillel shrugged. He did not know.

I cannot be feeling like this, Apella told himself. *Not about a woman I only saw once.*

But what *am I feeling?* he wondered.

"Go into the village," he ordered one of the horsemen. "Tell whoever's alive to come out of hiding, they're safe."

The man spurred his horse, and charged over the unhinged village gate, shouting, *"Pax Romana! Pax Romana!"*

Faces, pale and emaciated, started appearing above the village walls. Old men and boys. Looking like ghosts, they waved at the Roman saviors.

Where is she? What happened to her?

He could not think of anything else.

The inn's yard was a mess of prostrated silhouettes in muddied rags. Some slept, from pure exhaustion. At first, Apella could not recognize anyone.

Then he spotted Joachim and Anna, huddled in each other's arms.

Joachim saw Apella, staggered up, and called out to his kin. The Roman who had brought them the king's forgiveness, he was here. Those ghosts came alive. Crying, they banded around Apella, who raised his voice to tell them firmly that he was here now, and they were safe.

Doctor Celsus was setting a man's broken ankle in splints improvised from sticks.

A woman from the village, young and pregnant, walked around giving people cups of goat milk. Xilos, more sober than Apella had ever seen him, went around behind her, handing out bread.

Swallowing the knot in his throat, Apella asked Joachim and Anna where their daughter was.

"She's still on the mountain with her husband," Anna replied.

Her husband?

He stepped away and called Hillel back to him, and learned

314

from Hillel that Joseph, the carver of images, had met the tribe in the desert and had proposed to the girl. Joseph and Mary were still trekking down from the mountain. Reassured yet irked by the news (*A fast mover, that slow one!* he thought), Apella asked who the pregnant woman was. Hillel told him that she was a cousin on Joachim's side, her name was Elsheva. She and her husband had been living in Joachim's house.

The doctor stepped up, wiping sweat from his forehead. He told Apella that he had been straightening sprains and twisted limbs for the last few hours. Apella snickered. "You can be a real doctor sometimes?"

Celsus smirked. "Sometimes. So, you'll report this to Caesar as a theophany?"

"Yes, and you'll confirm under oath that it happened."

Celsus shook his head, went back to caring for the moaning survivors. Apella ordered Hillel to the oil press, to tell Shalafta to release the hostages, or else he would be arrested and charged with rebellion. Shalafta should also provide food and drink for the Romans and for the survivors.

A FEW HOURS later, Apella stood inside Joachim's yard, facing the gatepost nicked with the growing height of Joachim's daughter.

Elsheva and Zachariah had received Joachim and Anna with a great display of joy. They ran to milk the cow and catch and slaughter chickens. Then Elsheva and Zachariah rushed to the grimly thoughtful Roman, assuring him that they had kept Joachim's house in good shape, though some furniture and work tools were missing, stolen by neighbors.

Elsheva had pimples on her chin, at odds with her ripe look and her melon-shaped belly. Apella wished her a healthy pregnancy. Perhaps because he had spoken in Aramaic, she beamed and hummed that "the angel Gabriel" had announced to her that she would be with child. "Zachariah and I had lost all hope. I'm twenty-six if I'm a day." Prematurely bald and very sweaty, Zachariah smiled and nodded as Elsheva hummed on. "The angel Gabriel is coming for Mary, too."

Apella asked, "And what does an angel look like?"

The two of them looked at the Roman with such earnest conviction, and tried to explain, interrupting each other. "Angels," Zachariah stammered, while Elsheva waited for his laborious utterance, "are humanlike creatures with wings, whom God sends out with good news." "But maybe," Elsheva ventured, "God *himself* is inside those angels?" Which made Zachariah squinch his face uncomfortably. Almost swept into the issue, Apella overheard a commotion by the work shed.

He turned and saw Joachim, wincing as he tied strings around the folds of his shift while Anna tried to stop his maimed hands. Anna looked at the Roman for help. Apella rushed to the old man. "Don't climb back on the mountain, Rabbi, I'll go looking for your daughter myself. I can't push my men to go just now, they've been marching for three days. But if you're so worried, I'll go find her myself."

"You don't need to go," Anna said. "She's with Joseph. Joseph knows the mountain."

"If they spend another night up there, they'll drown in the rain," Joachim insisted.

"I'll climb up there," Apella assured him. He looked to where the last rays of the sun stabbed through the cloudiness. The night was on its way. "Settle in, Rabbi. Listen to your wife."

Then he walked back toward the front yard. By the gate, two middle-aged women, dressed demurely, whispered to Xilos. The older one, whom Apella found quite fetching, seemed very anxious. He strained to hear her what she was saying.

"Joseph," she whispered to Xilos. "His name is Joseph."

They must be those widows, Apella realized. They're trying to hire the Greek to go look for Joseph.

As he wondered if Xilos would agreee to help and how much he would charge, Apella found himself out in the street. He smelled grilled meat. Loaded bondmen were approaching, with lamb on the skewer and baskets of flat bread from Shalafta's yard.

He passed the village gate. He found himself by the tents that the centuria had raised outside the gates. He motioned to commander Arsinus, who rushed over. Apella gave him his orders. The Nazarenes should be kept inside the walls. The doctor and the caterer should not be allowed to leave on their own. Whoever made trouble should be arrested on the spot. "That's all. Now give me your coat," he concluded. Arsinus peeled off his big military cloak, whose hood was already soaked with rain. Apella draped it over his shoulders.

"What are you doing, Eques?" Arsinus asked. "Where are you going?"

"Never mind. I'll be back at cock's crow."

He walked on.

TIRED, HE TRIED to maintain his energy by giving himself a mental task.

He thought of that part of the Book called Creation, which

he and Ascanius had lingered on during those nights of studying.

He remembered how he had challenged the story, with the candid logic of an uneducated Roman.

In the garden, after surrendering his rib, the first man had awakened to the first woman. She was so beautiful and so differently shaped from him, his curiosity knew no bounds. Who was this creature, what kind of companion would she be to him?

But the curiosity of the first man seemed overwhelmed, Apella had reasoned to Ascanius, by the curiosity of the Creator himself. Far more astonished and confused was God by what he had created—and anxious to keep this new creature in his power.

For God had made the woman in his image, yet not in his likeness at all. Being a Roman man, Apella could only conceive of God as a male. God's names were male. His attributes were male. His wrath felt male.

So, the male God had created a female.

And he became instantly fascinated with her, and anxious about her unexpected intentions, some of which, most shocking to God's own mind, he could not easily guess.

So, keeping her in his power seemed essential, and God explicitly forbade her to do her own knowing. He forbade the man, too, yet the man, at least so it seemed to Apella, was never very obstinate about knowing. Altogether, God placed his highest creations in a garden endowed with fruit and with a speaking snake. And then God wandered off! Wasn't God's claim to be surprised thereafter hypocritical? Wasn't his indignation unfair and out of proportion with the crime?

In short, had God set up the first humans?

But why? What was the true meaning of that ancient tale?

Ascanius could not answer those questions. He confessed his own puzzlement, then he commented about the forever uneven relationship between man and woman. What a seesaw for the heart! When one was up, the other was down! When they were without each other, they missed each other terribly, but when they were together, they quarreled. Men feared women. Women dreaded men.

And yet, whenever either was alone, they cried for the other, with passion and dreamy hope, because in the absence of the other they did not feel alive. But in the nearness of the other, they did not feel safe.

Why did God set it up that way?

What an incredibly delicious enigma.

With the village lights dimming behind him, Apella found himself at the foot of the mountain.

And then he could not advance one more step. Tiredness weighed on him like the mountain itself. He unsheathed his pugio, meaning to lift it and wave with it, to catch the legionnaires' attention, so they would rush to carry him back to the tents. But he couldn't even lift the pugio.

He sat down on the ground and wrapped the cloak around his body and face. He wanted to sit just a few moments and rest.

T HE NIGHT was over. It had felt like the blink of an eye, and yet like a month of nights.

I had slept, fitful and worried, bolting upright a hundred times, then settling down again.

When I smelled the morning, it smelled heavenly.

I felt so proud of myself. I had endured. I hadn't lost my patience or my hope. I had waited for this, and it was worth waiting for!

I awoke again, lying on Joseph's chest.

Joseph was snoring.

I said a quick prayer of thanks. *I glory in you and I magnify you, Adonai, with my whole soul. I knew that I would be seedworthy, if you only helped Joseph and me the littlest bit. So you glanced down onto me, and now, I feel seeded to capacity! Me, the handmaid, the humble. Yes, humble I am, submissive and obedient and cooperative and docile! I know, some people couldn't tell that I was obedient, but I know and you know—or else, with what could I have moved your heart? Now behold, I am blessed. Thank you! You sated my hunger with your goodness, and other great things! Your mercy, which was so amazing, was on those who feared you, one of whom was I, and another is snoring in my arms. And your wrath is on the rich, the swindlers, the tightwads, the sinful. Aaahh! Let me peek at the world after you fulfilled my one great wish!*

I peeked.

The rain had flooded the hut.

The floors were underwater. Rippling wall to wall. Almost creeping into Joseph's mouth.

Now I remembered: Through the end of the night, Joseph had held me above his body, so I wouldn't drown. So tired I was, I had slept as he held me on his chest and on his joined hands. I had gotten a crick in my neck from lying on his clenched fists. *Adonai, how you tested Joseph for all those times when he wasn't ready! But here he is now, fulfilled, so as soon as he unglues his eyes, his prayers, like mine, will gush with gratefulness.*

Joseph and I were almost floating on our bed of bundled-up clothes.

Quick, I clutched my *klanidja* and pulled it on, all soaked. Joseph sneezed from the water bubbling into his nose and mouth. I grabbed his soaked punda, pushed it under his head to raise it, then waded after his drawers, and wrung the water from them.

A loud screeching of birds started outside.

Joseph sat up and gaped at me. I was bruised, my hair was like a wet mop, I was so fetching. Then he smiled, for this was the first moment of the first day of an entirely new life for him. *Thanks, El Olam.* As I most sweetly smiled back to Joseph, I heard footsteps!

Outside, someone's sandals were miring in mud.

"Joseph! Who's outside?"

An unknown man leaned his face, a red craggy face, into the hut's window. He vanished as quickly as he had appeared. A man alone, it seemed, for I'd heard only one set of footfalls. "Joseph, see who's outside!" Joseph got up, scowling like a brand-new husband being intruded upon. He splashed loudly across the water, burst the door open, and lunged out, armed with his bare fingers only. I got so frightened for him, I lunged out right after him.

That unknown man stood by the hut, ankle-deep in the snakes. I could tell that most of them were dead. Harrier eagles fed on them, picking out their eyes and tongues. Harriers are noisy birds, but just now, busy picking, they didn't utter one caw. But the stranger was afraid some snakes might still be alive, and when he saw us in the doorway, he called out, "Throw me a rope, a plank, a stick, anything!" He was perhaps fifty, ugly, not a Jew, for his hair was cut too short. I'd never seen him before.

Joseph reached back inside, pulled out his soaked burka, and threw it to the stranger. He stepped on it, treading heavily, to make sure the snakes underneath did not move. Then he asked to me, "So, you're the *parthenos*?" Whatever he called me, I didn't understand. I don't speak Greek. He was round-eyed with curiosity.

He hopped on the doorstep, right next to us. Then he announced that his name was Xilos, and he had arrived with the Roman, whose soldiers were now resettling my kin. My parents were already in our old yard, said the one named Xilos, and I cried out, "*Aaaahhhhh,* hosanna, amen, selah!"

"Aaron's climbing the mountain now," the Greek pursued. "He's looking for Joseph and you. You want to put on my clothes, parthenos?"

I looked at him. "Why would I want to do that?"

"You put on a man's clothes, you can run past Aaron, into the village."

And he started undoing his shirt, while ogling me through my frayed klanidja.

"Will you pay me a thousand shekels for saving your life? A

thousand shekels for one life? Maybe two lives." Grinning, he pointed to my belly. "Maybe you're filled with seed, *parthenos*?"

Joseph started to clench his fists. He glared at me, as if to say, *You're married now, you better not answer this fool. I'm the man, I'll handle it.* Then he growled at Xilos, "What are you raving about? Where's Aaron?"

"Down that crest," Xilos pointed.

"Come," Joseph said to me, and he clutched my hand. He looked for ground without snakes, and trod heavily, away from the crest. I pulled on Joseph's arm and stopped him. I looked around, and could not believe what I saw.

The mountain . . .

The storm had changed the face of the mountain. All the smaller peaks and lower ridges had caved in and become craters. Scores of trees had been uprooted. Dead creatures lay everywhere, and all the pathways were gone.

We heard the panting and cursing of men. They sounded like they were climbing on both sides of the ridge with the hut.

"This way," Joseph decided, and the Greek jumped to stand in our way. Joseph shoved the Greek. I turned and was seized by such fear, I ran to the edge of the crest.

I felt Adonai, rustling along, sweeping like a shadow next to me, worried for what I might do. I thought, *Aaahh, you're so like a man, Adonai. Had you been more like a woman, taking care of all the hanging little bits, you might've stopped Aaron, too. But I'm not complaining, I'm not! As long as you get us out of this!* Joseph was running after me, yelling that I should not show myself on that crest, but which crest was safe? He ran after me, and Xilos ran after both of us, yelling about money, until I heard a flat, thick blow. I looked over my shoulder. Joseph had plowed him down.

I peered down from the crest.

Across devastated trees, about a dozen men climbed, slogging through the mud. Aaron was at the fore. I saw him with amazing clarity, the air was free of even one mote of dust, as the rain had washed it so thoroughly. Aaron stepped on a snake, live or dead I could not tell, but Aaron jumped and shouted in fear.

The Greek shouted, too. "I'll talk to Aaron, I'll turn him back. Two thousand shekels?"

Aaron saw me and started running up toward me. I saw everything with terrifying clarity, as I did on that day when the bride was killed. I saw all the way down the incline, to Nazareth's plain and to Nazareth. So I saw the Roman, too. He was climbing up by himself, a good piece below Aaron and his gang. Climbing slowly, as if barely awake and finding his bearings. Looking upward, he saw Aaron and his men.

He pulled out his sword and started running up.

Joseph clutched me and tried to drag me behind the crest. Aaron saw Joseph from below and yelled at his men, there's my son's killer, stone him! I thought, *No, Adonai,* no, no, I won't have anyone killed in front of me again.

Then I heard the rumble of the moving earth.

With deafening noise, Mount Barak cracked its side, springing two new ridges.

They rippled down, away into Nazareth's plain, like giant arms. Covered in giant sleeves of quaking dirt and chipped rocks.

I was knocked off my feet.

When I was up again, I was so scared, I knew that I was crying out, but who could hear me against the earth's rumblings? I was looking around for Joseph, and he was not near me. Then I saw him. He'd been knocked down, too. And now he was tumbling, as those twin ridges kept advancing toward Nazareth, rippling the dry valley below. Joseph stopped tumbling. The quaking, like a huge rippling wave, rolled under Joseph and went ahead, chasing Aaron and his men. They ran for their lives. The earth kneaded itself like putty right under them. They were mowed down and knocked to their feet again. I saw Aaron stumble. He fell, he got up, he ran on . . .

I ran down, blinded by clouds of dust. *Joseph?*

Joseph had collapsed onto his face. I wanted to turn my eyes up *(You won't take him, Hashem. I won't allow one more death, not even from you!).* But I was too frightened that he'd die right before me. I pounded my fists on Joseph's shoulders. He staggered up. And then the second rippling of the earth started. Huge it was, endless in its might. Joseph and I clung to each other, his mouth split in shout, mine, too. We could hear nothing but the earth moving. Joseph's face was a mask of dust. He threw his arms around me, frail shelter. The mountain, with its whole being, was hurtling forth toward Nazareth, and in one spot below us, the earth churned even more angrily, near the Roman. It engulfed the Roman. I saw him look up, concentrating, figuring that if he moved up, he'd get free of that churning. *What a man,* I thought in spite of myself, as he stuck his sword in the ground and pulled himself up with it. Stuck it in the ground again, higher, and again, higher, swimming strangely against the earth's angry rapids.

The mountain was barreling over Nazareth. I no longer watched Aaron and his men, I watched how the shaking was approaching the Romans' tents. The Romans were all outside, some with their spears turned toward the village walls, some locking arms with others to hold themselves upright when the earthquake hit them. On the walls of the town, the Nazarenes gaped now just like the Romans. *Hashem, no! Hashem, feel what I feel, be in my heart, I can't lose anyone anymore. Not one more soul! I've lost enough people. I've lost Orpa, and that unfortunate bride, and my relatives clubbed and speared in the desert, and Akam, even him! And the prince, even him I lost! You took them, Adonai, you left me crying and bleeding for all of them! Not again!* I stood up above the rumbling mountain and opened my arms wide, as if ready to jump.

That seed—I felt it in me, but as priceless as it was, I wouldn't give up, I had lived with enough pain and enough guilt! *Do you hear me, Hashem?* Where are you? I closed my eyes. I told that seed, *I'm your bearer, your mother. You can't do without me. Stop the death and the pain.* Stop it, now!

Then I fell one more time, as all that motion suddenly turned to stillness.

Mount Barak had quaked back, somehow.

And it stopped moving. I heard rocks settling and air puffing up from cracks in the ground, but otherwise the quaking was over.

I heard noises from the village below. People clamored. Dogs barked. Donkeys and horses neighed. Creation cried, swelled with being alive.

APELLA STOOD UP, blinking. His eyelids were loaded with dust. Wiping his eyes, he lost his balance from not having to fight to stand up. He straightened himself, then looked first, with that trained Roman reflex, toward the Roman troops.

The earthquake had thrown their tents upside down, but the Roman soldiers stood as a unit, arms intertwined.

Peering over them, Apella saw that the Nazarenes had swarmed out of their homes like ants from a destroyed nest. Onto the village walls, peering at the mountain that was ready to collapse onto them, until—so close—the shaking stopped and the mountain remained intact. Those giant armlike ridges froze, while the wind and dust raging on the heights spat out Joseph and the girl at the foot of one ridge and Aaron and his gang at the foot of the other.

Aaron screamed like a wild man, until he became aware of his own voice, and stopped.

Apella had bitten his lip and felt warm blood trickle down his chin. He wiped his chin, wiped his eyes again. One instant before, the girl had stood on the crest, arms open like Moses, sending shivers down his spine. He would have sworn that she would jump to her death.

Now she was emerging from a cloud of dust, helped along by the carver.

They stumbled toward the village gate, the panels of which had sprung from their hinges.

Apella tried to have ordinary thoughts. So, this is the famed carver. Strong, young, muscular. Slightly taller than the Roman. *I could take him on,* he thought for no apparent reason. He noticed how the girl craved the carver's nearness; she clung to his arm and bumped into Joseph as they stepped along together. *So he'll be your husband,* he thought, feeling a bizarre jealousy. Well, I just resettled your parents in your home. That should give me some merit in your eyes.

He made his face smile, and he walked toward her, noticing how dusty and ragged she looked, with leaves and twigs caught in her hair. And yet . . . he yearned for her to look at him.

327

She closed her eyes.

The carver held her by the arm.

Apella watched the girl stepping between the gate's splintered panels with her eyes still closed. From yards and homes, people were rushing to join Mary's arrival. The sounds of the crowd seemed subdued, as if filtered.

Apella found his strength. He ran after the growing crowd.

When he was abreast of the girl, he saw her cousin, Elsheva, and her husband, Zachariah. They walked behind her. Elsheva closed her eyes, too. Zachariah peered at the ground. Behind them, other people started closing their eyes as they all walked toward Joachim's yard. Of course, all of them had walked that street since they were children. They could walk it in their sleep.

Apella was trying to assess his feelings, but as he could make no sense of them, he kept staring at the girl who had enchanted him at the well. He kept watching her. She would open her eyes now.

But she still did not.

He tilted his head back. Above him, the sky was pure and blue. And God roamed in it. *Perhaps God danced in it,* Apella thought, fleetingly remembering fragments from the Book that Ascanius had read to him. This Roman, who hadn't read one page of the Book a year before, wondered about what he was witnessing now. This girl . . . what was she doing, what was she thinking? He remembered her carved face, which the tesserarius had brought to him in Jerusalem. That hurried, unfinished carving. He remembered the feeling of it, the mysterious power of a female so aware of what happened inside her.

She had so much mystery in that carving, as she did now, walking at the carver's side.

The carver was talking to her. But she was quiet. She raised her tanned hand, to rub the dust from her eyelids. Her eyelids fluttered like butterfly wings weighted by a dust storm. But still she would not open her eyes. Not until, crying in relief, her parents surged out of their home, and ran toward her. And then she opened her eyes. She stood there amazed.

And everyone cried.

Four months later. Ptolemais, on the Galilean coast,
Rome's key military harbor in the Middle East.

THE SHIP lay at anchor outside the port's jetties, in rough swells. A large ship, without flags or pennons of rank. What gave away its status was the number of its oars: one hundred and sixty, set in four rows, making this vessel a *quatuoreme*. Starved slaves were not good enough to row this ship, which sailed the sea twice as fast as a trireme. There were less than a dozen quatuoremes in the whole Mediterranean, and they were all Roman and manned with professional mariners.

The ship was being resupplied by rowboats bringing food and water, string and timber, canvas and rope, live goats and chickens to slaughter. No passengers had set foot ashore.

Arriving on board by rowboat, Apella glimpsed the ship's extraordinary security measures. All over the deck, armored and helmeted troops stood ready to spring on an attacker.

The door to the captain's quarters opened. A tall old man with a tattoo on one cheek stood in the door. "Puer! At last!" Emotional yet tense, Ascanius hugged his disciple, after which, Apella was frisked for weapons. Then, leading the guest inside, the old advisor asked worriedly, "What are you going to tell him?"

"What I wrote to you," Pilate replied.

"You shouldn't, it's a mistake. Reconsider."

"What shall I tell him instead?"

"Any trifle. Show concern for the empire, that's all you need to do. I'll be here to help."

Ascanius acted differently when the master was around.

In the plain cabin with unpainted partitions and fixtures, a washbasin was being taken away. The emperor stood with arms stretched up, while servants shrouded him in a plain white toga without one stitch of embroidery. He waited as they tied its complicated folds. Then he turned and sat on a plain wooden chair.

The servants withdrew. Ascanius positioned himself behind Caesar, both of them facing Apella.

So here he was. Pinprick Eyes.

"Welcome, Caesar," the spy greeted the emperor.

Pale from the voyage—he was notoriously given to seasickness—Augustus replied, "Welcome to you, too, Pilate." He smiled, his eyes as piercing as ever. "Octavia is as round as a barrel. She's living on her packed trunks, waiting for me to send her to you. I'm meeting with the Parthians' secret envoys in Egypt tomorrow night. But I stopped to meet you first, as you requested. What do you have to report to me?"

Apella tried to speak, but he had a lump in his throat.

From behind Caesar, Ascanius chatted helpfully. "All's well in Rome, the theophany occurred without a hitch. In time, we'll reveal to the nation how much you did, Pilate. Caesar is very pleased with you."

"Speak, Pilate," the emperor urged. "You want to sit? More chairs, Ascanius."

Ascanius hurried to the door to call for more chairs.

Apella was breathing hard. *Why am I so fearful?* he wondered.

"The success of your deification enthralls me, Caesar. Tell me how it went."

Augustus brightened like a child being reminded of a birthday party.

"Exceedingly well. As per the plan you sent me, I turned day into night by lining Via Appia with smoke machines, which the vigiles set off at noon on a day with a good southerly wind. As the smoke covered the sky and the plebeians panicked, I galloped to Triclia catacomb. As per your plan, our engineers had felled the pillars of Triclia in advance; now they loosed the pillars. Northward and southward, Via Appia shook for miles, right at my feet. The earth bucked and churned, while trained vigiles threw themselves to the ground and jumped up again as if knocked back on their feet. Then I waved my arm, and . . ."

Apella was nodding and smiling. The quaking of Mount Barak had inspired him with the quaking of Via Appia. The mechanics of sinking Triclia he had thought up when he and those fifty Roman soldiers were still camping outside Nazareth's walls. Listening to Augustus, he felt like a playwright who had missed his own opening night.

A knock on the door. A mariner stepped in, carrying two wooden chairs. He set them down and left.

Caesar started to hiccup. High-strung and feverish, he gestured to Ascanius to tell the rest.

Ascanius intoned, as if reading poetry: "So, as Via Appia bucked and churned, Caesar yelled, 'I, Caesar-Deus, command nature to be still!' And the quake stopped. At the same instant, five hundred slaves were being crushed under Triclia's falling pillars, one could hear their screams to all ends of Rome. The vigiles yelled, 'That's hell down there! That's Hades filled with doomed souls!' Then Caesar yelled at the doomed souls, 'Die and have peace!'

"So the screams stopped. Then we turned on hundreds of wind machines, to clear the air. Through thinning clouds, lowered with cables, Caesar descended into rescued Rome."

Apella exhaled. Five hundred slaves. Paltry price. The show had worked.

"So, Rome recognized your divine powers, Caesar?"

Ascanius replied, "The crowds chanted for days: 'Caesar, deus! Caesar, theophany!' The collapse of Triclia will be inscribed on the Ara Pacis. Oh! We'll find a way to put your name up there, too, Pilate." Augustus was still clearing his voice. "Shall we go out on deck, Caesar? You'll breathe better."

His glance said to Apella, This went well enough. Now bow and withdraw.

The emperor shook his head, pressing his fists on his chest. He had small fists.

He said, his voice finally whole: "I'm well already. Pilate, I decided to groom you as my successor. Getting you married to Octavia is the first step." He walked up to Apella, examining him amiably. "But you'll marry Octavia here. And don't try to sneak back into Rome, I'm taking no chances with a second Tiberius. You'll stay here for as long as I see fit, and if I become immortal, that's your luck! Although I know you won't kill me. You had your chance but you didn't have the guts. Tiberius is a beast of a man. You, Pilate, are soft. Which is why I choose you as successor. Rome needs a softer man, after me."

From deep within him, from deeper than the desire to blurt

out, You're a clown, Caesar, I've seen the true theophany! Apella swelled with anger. He clutched the edge of the chair with his hands. But instead of fastening himself to the chair, he dragged it on the cabin's floor.

He growled. "I don't want to marry Octavia. That's why I requested this meeting."

"It's not your decision. That's already settled."

"It's a sham, and I'm not the father, and I'm needed here for something more important." Then, as the man with pinprick eyes froze before him, listening in silence, Apella spewed his prepared speech. Amazing things were happening in this land, a swelling of expectation and renewal that the Romans were not aware of. But King Herod was well aware of it. The old bastard was being decircumcised by Doctor Celsus. Week after week, with Celsus by his side, Herod wore heavier and heavier weights, so that next spring he could share the imperial baths with Caesar. But, wincing from the weights, getting grossly drunk to endure the pain, the king kept obsessing about the girl who made a mountain quake and then made it quake again.

What am I trying to say with that? Apella wondered. *Why don't I say what truly festers in my heart—that I hate serving this man who murdered my parents?*

Caesar interrupted him. "I know the old fox. I've known him for twenty-five years. Have you become naïve, Pilate? Herod's faith in God fits inside my thumb. Herod is entirely my creation, even his claim to Jewishness was made possible when I and the Roman senate gave him the mines of Cyprus to run. Which made him rich, which in turn allowed him to finance the new temple. Now, in his old age, soaked with the blood of the wives and sons he has killed, he fears—what? That from some obscure girl's womb, a holy baby might be born? So what?"

"Caesar, you yourself showed interest in that story—"

"I did. And then? The manifestation, the act of God that matters—we did it already in Rome."

Apella kicked the chair as he sprang from it. "Very well. Then you can end my mission."

"I have no such intent." While Apella's voice had thickened threateningly, Caesar's was rising to a shrieking, cawing pitch. "You'll marry Octavia and continue on here, whether the Jews' fairy tales come true or not. It's not about that anymore. Rome is safe in its faith in me, and in you serving me!"

Thrusting a swift glare at Apella, Ascanius moved between Caesar and the spy.

"Caesar, Pilate is utterly loyal to you," he said, while behind his back he balled up his fist, as if to signal to Apella, You imbecile, you want to die this morning? "But he's afraid to tell you that these new events could interest Tiberius. Pilate wants to stand guard here, against the possibility that Tiberius starts courting that tribe, and that heiress of theirs. Pilate knows Nazareth *and* Jerusalem, minutely." That was true, in Nazareth the people trusted Apella, and what better tool could a spy use but the people's trust? As for Jerusalem, after a year of bribing right and left, Apella was offered information by everyone. Besides, every guard or servant of the king was at heart a discontent, therefore an informant.

Even prudent, practical Celsus was informing Apella now. About what the king said when he sat with the pondus on while Celsus fawned, "Your Majesty, you're growing back so fast! Your Majesty, you have the skin of a twenty-year-old!"

"I say, we make Pilate procurator here, instead of Ventidius," Ascanius pleaded. "He has what it takes for this long, hard duty. But if he wants to be free in his bed"—Caesar frowned at the word "free"—"why can't we find Octavia another suitor?"

"She likes him," Augustus snapped. He turned his pinpricks to Apella. "It's you she wants as a husband, and I committed myself to get you for her. She never told you she liked you?"

"Caesar, I'll serve you as a soldier, as a statesman, as a secret agent, anything you wish. Why can't I be free to choose my own wife?"

Caesar minced over to him, lowering his pinpricks to Apella's own eyes, big, round, and blinking with astonishment.

"Because *I* wasn't!" he yelled in that cracked voice. "Besides, freedom is *despair*! Had you been desperate, you would have stabbed me in Triclia! Or strangled me right here, as soon as Ascanius let you in! If I had died, the guards might have not killed you, they might have been awed by your cruelty! Now think about this: *I*"—he thumped his small fist onto his narrow chest—"I sleep with Drusilla, who plotted my death with her son, Tiberius, and she's alive. And Tiberius is alive, too! I am not free. Nor is Ascanius, nor is Octavia, nor Tiberius, nor Drusilla. Wait 'til you sit on the throne, Pilatus. Emperors and procurators are not free men. Nor are husbands or fathers! Octavia is ready to wrap you in her chains! Choose life with Octavia, without freedom but at the peak of power, or I'll throw you in the sea!"

He'd spoken so close to the spy's face, he'd spitten on it.

A power larger than anything took over Apella's mind. It twisted his lips into a smile that hissed, *"Sum."*

I am. Short for, I am the emperor's servant. I submit.

"Thank you," the emperor replied, with tired sarcasm.

"I gave you your life," Apella whispered, strangely aware that he could say anything now.

"And I'm giving you yours, again. Thank Octavia. Without her, who would keep you around as a witnesss?"

He turned to Ascanius. "Prepare a decree to send Ventidius to Hispania, or some other place he can rob. Judea will have a new procurator."

"WE KILLED ALL of Tiberius's supporters," Ascanius informed Apella, as the two of them sat in the rowboat that was returning Apella to shore. "Two hundred of the most influential magistrates, military commanders, and merchants. Textor drank hemlock, like Socrates. He died cursing me and all the Jews. See what kind of orb you are entering?" Apella said nothing. He leaned over the side of the rowboat. "I thought you had destroyed my whole work."

Apella looked at the seawater, into which he could have been hurled, tied at the ankles and wrists and weighted with a drum of stone.

"Then," he asked slowly, "all those talks of ours, all our quests for answers in the Book . . . Your yearnings for God, even Caesar's amusement at the Jews' stories . . . What was all that?"

"Talk," Ascanius replied.

He added, "Now power is here, and power is not talk."

It was hard to look at Ascanius now. From that face of a sage seeking answers, it had turned into a lion's face. Grim, bronze faces of lions with their mouths open to receive anonymous denunciations were scattered all over Rome. So-and-so was an enemy of Caesar. So-and-so had mocked his deification. After ten denunciations (some said five), the denounced person would be arrested and tortured and pushed off the Rock.

"Between you and me, you *are* soft," Ascanius said to Apella. And for the first time that day, Apella laughed.

He thought, *I shall prove that I am not soft. I shall show you all that I can be as beastlike as Tiberius. I'll laugh just now. I'll kowtow, in the most deceiving manner. I'll bide my time.*

So the spy laughed, and the world's second most powerful man laughed with him.

"So now you're stuck with Caesar as God," Apella said, in a light tone. And the old slave replied, as if joking, too, "When I die, I'll stand before the true God, not before Caesar. Until then, I choose to live."

The rowboat bumped into the harbor's wharf. They both stood up.

"Good luck, puer. Now I shall embrace you, for Caesar's watching from the deck, and everything must look in order." The slave hugged the spy stiffly, and the spy squinted as if his eyes were blurring.

"In Rome next time? And no more delusions of freedom?"

"*Certo.*" Apella's voice was as optimistic as ever.

They turned from each other and parted. Apella walked to the harbor.

What am I doing, what am I choosing to do? he wondered. *Why am I faced with such impossible choices? Could I still be useful to anyone, outside Caesar's orb? Is that even possible?*

He felt a sadness that was so poignant and real.

He arrived at the dockside's army garrison, from whence he could choose a horse or a cart to return to Jerusalem. The garrison overlooked the harbor.

He sat on an empty bench and faced the sea.

In the outer harbor, the oars of the imperial ship were moving, popping out of the water, held parallel to the sea level. Then, again with a beautiful homogeneous motion, they were angled upward, tested for maneuverability, before sailing off. Apella could not see inside the ship, but he knew that the mariners were inspecting the cleats now, pouring warm oil over them, to make the rowing easy and smooth.

The oars were lowered again, splashing like one into the rippling waves.

The ship would be sailing in moments.

"I'm not soft, Ascanius," Apella said toward the ship preparing to depart. "I'm not soft. I didn't kill Caesar, *twice*. That's bravery." The ship's oars moved again, sideways now. On the deck, bustling sailors were tying down the fresh supplies; everyone was active, everyone had his duty. *How can you live like this, Ascanius?* Apella thought. *How can you be a wonderful teacher and friend, yet in the presence of power you are a servant and a puppet and nothing else?*

Augustus would have tied my ankles and wrists and thrown me to the saltwater crabs. What would you have done? Would you have tried to fight for my life?

No. But you did try to get me out of there before I had my pitifully brief rebellion.

I wish you could hear me say this, Ascanius. I know that you, too, want freedom. That you're yearning for dignity, and for revenge. Revenge is human, it's healthy. How can you pretend to love what you hate? Is it because you're too old?

He remembered talking with Ascanius, at night in Colli Albani, as they walked together on the gravel of Caesar's gardens. With the glitter of Rome beyond crests and forests, far, and yet close.

Always aglitter, forever awake—Rome. And Ascanius's voice, taking on inspired inflections. He had behaved like more than a teacher, he had given Apella the patience, kindness, and protection of a substitute father.

"Father of mine, the one who really fathered me? Where are you?" Apella moaned. He was still sitting on the harbor bench. Ahead, Caesar's ship shuddered from its entire hull. The anchor, ripped from the bottom, rose dripping mud, and it nested in the anchors' dip at the prow. The ship turned, one broadside with oars dipping quickly and precisely, while the other broadside held its oars above the water, to help the ship turn. *Father of mine, mother of mine, where are you?* Apella thought. His father had been pushed off the Tarpeian Rock. *Mother of mine, dutiful and frugal with your caresses as a Roman matron should be, where are your bones?* She had been pushed off the Rock. *I, your son, can I rise in history regardless of your deaths?*

What did I do to your memory, father and mother of mine? And what did I do to myself?

He had transferred to Ascanius the affection he owed to his mother and father. He had lived a bond of kinship with him, perhaps a strange bond, but strange did not mean shallow. He could not help it. Just now, he felt cruelly abandoned by Ascanius.

Meantime, he had never tried to find his parents' bones. For how could he have done it? After they were killed, he, the last Pontius, was on the run. Loose in Caesar's Rome. Had he been caught, he would have been pushed off the Rock, too.

Could I still find and bury your bones?

That whitish gravel of bones, heaped below the Rock. It was many feet deep . . .

* * *

AFTER SOME TIME, images of Mary flashed in his mind. Usually, they were full of life and encouragement. But this time, remembering how connected she was to her family, how inseparable from her parents and her people, he resented her. She had never betrayed herself.

He stared around. The sun was high, the fall weather was mild. Beyond the port, Galilee lay subdued, with the harvest in, the people tinkering in their yards, the rains on their way.

Soon, he would rule this land. In that thought, there was comfort.

He might even encounter love. Of course, he would have to support Octavia in style, but she would have her own life. He did not believe that she liked him past a selfish, superficial preference. Another woman, perhaps, true love, perhaps? But what was true love? That which could not be described? A mire of emotions that poets made a living from? Women's stuff?

Perhaps I shall find out. He managed, out of sheer will-power, to feel optimistic. *Audaces fortuna juvat,* he told himself. Fate helps the ones who dare. *Audaces, Pilate, fortiter!*

And now, up! I know what my next duty is.

He glanced one last time at the sea. The ship was sailing south toward Egypt. The oars had found their rhythm. Dipping, they moved in such unison that the ship's body seemed still while some amazing breath of the sea, puffing into the oars, blew the vessel ahead. Faster, shrinking toward the horizon. A dot of strength, streaking the blue.

AFTER THE harvest was in, and I was entering my fifth month, Joseph and I and my parents and all of Orpa's kin went up the mountain, to dig up Orpa's grave and rebury her in our cemetery.

I had sewn up a big sack of flax, the size of Orpa's body.

All by myself, not allowing anyone to help me, I crushed frankincense and myrrh and gathered from our home chips of wood that smelled sweet. I lay the sack of flax on the floor of our home, and beat it with a mallet, and then trampled it with my feet, to make the flax soft.

What difference would the softness make? I kept asking myself. Orpa wouldn't feel it, would she? But I still pounded and softened it until the sack felt smooth enough to wrap a baby in. Then I scattered the frankincense and the myrrh and the perfumed wood inside the sack and folded it and took it to Orpa's mother. Two yards away from ours.

She and her sisters were preparing food, which we would carry up the mountain, wrapped in fresh leaves, to have something to eat after we found that mound of earth. We might find it quickly or not so quickly. I bowed to Orpa's mother and spread myself on the ground in front of her. She quickly pulled me up so I wouldn't put pressure on my growing womb, and asked, "What is it, Mary?"

I presented the sack and requested that we bring back Orpa's body in it.

Her mother said, "Let this be her shroud, then."

AT DAWN THE next day, we trekked up the mountain.

We found the grave easily, before midday.

I had walked all the way, even though we had brought two donkeys. My mother and Orpa's mother had kept glancing worriedly at me, pleading with me. "Get on a donkey, Mary, you're straining the infant inside you."

"No," I said stubbornly.

Finally Joseph lunged and caught a donkey by its mane. He pulled it over by sheer strength.

He said firmly, "What are you doing, Mary? Get on the donkey."

"No."

And I kept walking.

Everyone was acting so worried. We had left my father in our yard, and that, too, had been a cause of worry. Would he be all right by himself? He looked as if his daughter and the grandchild inside her and his son-in-law were leaving him forever, not for one day. He did not act so worried that my mother might collapse from fatigue, but for me he was so worried, and even for Joseph! He had started to depend on Joseph so much.

In short, everyone around me was acting unnerved, and I

felt like tilting my head back and shouting at the sky, Adonai, what's this new fright you're putting in everyone? I see it in their eyes, I hear it in their voices. What are they sensing? What other trial are you preparing for us?

But we made it up to the crests. There were so many of us, we looked like a long host climbing the mountain as if it were a big green ladder leading to the sky. Without one sprained ankle or one sting from a wasp, we made it. The wasps rushed at that time, looking to find new nests before the rainy season, and they were at their fiercest. But no mishap.

And then we found the spot.

The men dug it up.

Orpa's parents and I, with my growing belly, lifted her out, still wrapped in the ragged clothes we had buried her in, when we were on the run. I had expected to cry longer and louder than Orpa's mother but I didn't.

I felt a low, quiet sadness that was almost sweet, as memories of Orpa crowded my mind.

Orpa, we are here. Your mother is here, and your father, and all the girls from the well, and all the boys who pestered and harassed us so often, and your kin, and my kin.

We are all here, and I am here! Now lie softly in this sack that I made for you. How I wish you could smell the frankincense and the bits of cedar and pine!

We sewed up the mouth of the sack. We lifted the body onto one of the donkeys, and since I would not go back any other way than walking, my mother sat on the other donkey, as we returned.

From what I could feel when we had lifted her out of the ground, Orpa's body hadn't broken. Maybe because the soil was

clayey and moist and had sealed up around her, airless, and had
not given off smells that would attract animals.

I walked behind her, as the donkey followed the mountain
path down.

Can you see me now, Orpa? Can you hear me?

*I am married and filled with seed! And we are all at home in
peace. The gangs broke up. Aaron vanished from Nazareth, and his
wife and daughter moved to another village.*

*The Roman soldiers kept their tents outside our walls a whole
month. Only when they were sure that the peace would last did they
leave. After the Romans left, Shalafta crept back into the village, and
with money to this neighbor and that neighbor, he hushed the ones
crying revenge against him one by one. He spared no money, and now
he's back in his yard.*

But it doesn't matter. For me, it's as if he's not there.

*Joseph is wonderful to be around. And everyone says that he'll
be a wonderful father.*

What else would you like to know? Ah, yes.

*That Roman envoy keeps stopping in Nazareth. Hillel the cart-
driver, who took over Aaron's smithery, is friendly with him, so we get
to learn tidbits about the Roman. Such as, his emperor is sending
him a wife of his own, from Rome!*

And now, as I had told Orpa all that, I could imagine Orpa
asking me in that teasing voice that I would give half my life to
hear again, just once, *What? He's getting his own wife?*

As it should be, I would have replied. *A good man should not
be alone.*

You let that one get away, Mary? He was the best one!

I am so glad for him, I would have said. Which, had she
been alive, would have earned me a hard poke from her elbow.

You little trollop, you don't care at all? I might have even blushed. *Ah, Orpa, my sweet hard almond!* Such talk would have been so like her, and so like how girls are. A girl would nettle her best friend about a man, but if she herself liked that man, you'd never hear the end of it!

So, by the time our tired convoy got back to the village and the cemetery, it was late at night. We lit torches, and we put Orpa in the ground again. When we lowered her in, the sack with crushed flowers and perfumed woods smelled even more fragrant, for it had been heated by the sun when we walked down the crests, and now it was freshened by the cool of the night.

While we pounded the ground over the new grave, I thought about the Roman man. I thought of him as I never had before. Maybe I thought of him with Orpa's thoughts?

From the cemetery, I made it back to our yard carried in Joseph's arms. I could not have taken another step.

THE NEXT DAY, I awoke hoarse and coughing and sore all over. My back ached terribly.

My mother rubbed me with myrrh, covered me with blankets, fed me fresh milk, and sat by me 'til I felt a little better. Then she told me angrily, "A girl in her fifth month shouldn't have such back pains, not with her first child." Like she herself had dropped a litter of ten! Which I rudely told her.

My father showed his worry in his own way by dragging tools and wood planks out of the work shed and starting to fashion doors for a room that we were adding to the house. A room for me and Joseph and the baby. Grabbing a hammer and a peg, my father brought down the hammer, missed the peg, and clobbered his thumb.

He cried out in pain. So I ran to wrest the hammer from him, but he tugged it back.

From the porch, watching us through the cooking fire, my mother yelled at him to still himself. He snapped at her and lifted the hammer again.

Joseph walked in the front gate, carrying an armful of sun-baked bricks that we were building with and that had to sit for weeks to dry so they would not shrink or crack. So the walls of our room went up at a snail's pace.

My mother gave Joseph a glance. Old men, her glance said, they become like children.

Joseph nodded. Very at ease with his mother-in-law, whatever she said.

He hunkered down by my father, held his palm open, and my father surrendered the hammer.

I looked at Joseph. He was the only one who understood me!

Joseph told me to go to the front of our yard, stand on tip-toe, and cling to that nicked-up post, it would ease the pain in my back.

Having children was exhausting. Even before they arrived.

I LOOKED AT the front gate, which only came up to my waist now. Joseph had torn out the top panels, to replace them with new ones. But he hadn't done that yet, he was too busy building the new room.

Staring up the street, I could see bits of colored wool on a fence. Yorit's fence. Left over from her wedding. She was the first water girl to get married, to a camel driver who had already had eyes for her when we lived in the desert.

Then I thought I was dreaming. The Roman man was standing in front of me, and he had stolen up to me so smoothly. I hadn't heard him, I hadn't glimpsed him. He was suddenly there!

It was close to candlelighting time, so there were hardly any people in the street. The Roman man had pulled his horse along, hand on the bridle. The horse, well trained, clopped the dust of the street quietly, making no noise.

"You want to speak to my father?" I asked, putting my hands on what was left of the gate's lattice.

He shook his head.

You, his chin indicated, I want to speak with you.

He looked as usual. Strong and handsome. Behind me, I heard my mother say something to my father. I wondered if Joseph was aware of the Roman's presence, and then I told myself that Joseph had walked to the back, to work on the room that we were adding on.

The Roman was staring at me with a strangely determined gaze.

"Very well," I whispered. "I'm here."

"I wanted to tell you . . . that you taught me a lot."

That's all? I wondered. But I thought, *No, no, he was the one who had taught me a lot. Especially, that good people can be of all kinds.*

I felt such a desire to keep him in my life somehow. But how? All I could stammer was, "Are you going back to Rome?"

"No. I've just been reappointed here."

He was looking at my belly, I noticed, and I leaned against the lattice, hiding it from his eyes. "I'm glad. I think about you often." I was allowed to tell him that much, wasn't I? "I trust you. Didn't you tell me in the desert to trust you?"

He nodded, as if remembering. "Listen," he said. "I don't

want to scare you, but I have to warn you about something for your own protection."

I nodded, with my heart in my mouth.

And he told me what he had to say.

At the end, he said, "Don't think of running away. If you do, the king would have you followed, and it would be more difficult for me to protect you. I have to ask you to do what's hardest. Stay here, until the child comes. Behave as if I told you nothing. I will protect you."

I leaned toward him, I knew that I did, for the light of the setting sun moved on my face. "I have to tell Joseph about this."

"Oh, yes. Him, you should tell."

All I could think was, *What's this, Adonai? Strife again? Fear again? Why, Adonai?*

I managed to mumble, "Do you think that if I give birth to a girl, the king would spare her?"

"I don't know." He reflected. "Most likely not, because she would be from your lineage, and she would most likely marry a man of your lineage, just like you did. But it doesn't matter. I'm the only one who can protect you from the king. I mean, all three of you. And I will, just trust me."

I had no choice. I trusted him. That, I realized on the spot.

But I could not hold back my words. "I have paid a lot for what I have now. What do I have left, to repay you for your kindness? If you help me, one day you'll tell me to pay you back for what I owe you. What will I do then?"

He did not reply. I felt that my heart was tearing up.

"And besides . . . why?" I stared at him, not to miss even a squinch of his face, not to let even a twitch of his mouth bewilder me, as to why he was doing this.

He still did not reply.

He stood in front of me, dark, handsome, with rich curly hair, with that strong nose of his, like a ship's prow. All of him so strong and dark, and born under alien stars.

I would be frightened if he spoke and frightened if he didn't.

"You'll find a way to repay me, or you won't—it doesn't matter. I must do what I decided to do."

He reached for the horse's bridle.

"Even the wind would fall in love with you," he said suddenly, smiling as if he liked how he had said that. Then he turned and led the horse away. Walking slowly. Had he jumped onto his saddle and raced off, a crowd of neighbors would have popped up in doorways and windows. What's that pounding? Who goes there, boisterous like a storm?

But he was so in control of himself. Walking evenly, not turning once, with strong, quiet steps.

I HEADED BACK inside and found my parents in the yard.

Joseph was by the wall of the back room, adding on new bricks.

My mother instantly hurried toward me, and I just could not find the patience to tell her who had stopped by and why. So I begged her to throw on a fresh shift, and take my father's arm, and go to Orpa's parents' yard, where neighbors and friends were dropping off gifts of food. Just until the stars came out, and then my parents could return home. I needed just enough world around me to breathe and to sort out my thoughts . . .

Maybe she understood, for she did change her shift and

combed my father's beard and hair, and they dawdled out of the yard together.

"Maybe we should build our own house," Joseph said, interrupting his work.

He was setting the fresh bricks with a big flat trowel. "Your parents are wonderful people, but maybe we should have our own place. We can afford to build a house, not just one room."

He waited. "Don't throw anything at me now," he teased me.

"I won't."

"Don't cry. Or cry, if you like."

I took such a deep breath—it felt like the deepest breath that I'd ever taken—and stopped my tears.

The sunset was red and warm, and I tottered alone toward the back gate, praying that my heart would stop choking.

I stood there for an instant and then stiffened.

"Jibril?" I whispered, noticing that the old Arabian was sitting behind the back gate.

I recognized him by his garb and by the way he held himself, tired and stooped, as if in need of my mother's brew.

I opened the lattice and stepped out. He raised his hands to shade his face against the sunset's last rays.

"I just stopped here with my camels," he said, from behind his hands.

I looked around, among the setim trees, and beyond, at the scrubby waste leading to the mountain.

I saw not one camel.

Then I looked at the old man's raised hands.

At the same moment, something moved in the landscape around me. Something transformed the sight and the distance.

Time and space seemed to enlarge strangely, while not changing even one inch or one shade of glow. I peered at my feet. Inside the ground under my feet, I saw all of time and space, blinking and swarming, but . . . when I stared up again at the nearest setim tree and at the tired man sitting in front of it, nothing had changed. Yet it had.

I heard a big, rich rustling and rippling of trees and grass.

As if I were up on the mountain again.

As if God's garden floated about the world, surrounding it from all sides.

Against that rustling, Joseph hurried out of the yard. He had followed me with his glance, when I had walked past him. Now he ran through the open back gate and stopped right by me. He was still gripping the trowel he had used to level those bricks. He flung it to the ground.

Look around, Mary. Look around with eyes drunk with love, Hashem said to me in that voice beyond voices.

Don't be confused, for you feel love. Let yourself feel it.

All you ever felt is love, and love is never khet, if it is true. And yours is true.

I have learned from you, Mary.

I have learned that although you were good, as I saw from the start, for I made you good, I did not know how good. I had doubted my own creation.

It was, it is *better than I knew, and in that, my heart rejoices greatly. And we are together again, all three of us.*

Behind his raised hands, he faced toward Joseph, making it obvious that Joseph was included.

He stood up. That old man's tiredness seemed to have vanished from his body. But he still held his hands up, covering his face.

I looked aside at Joseph. Joseph was dumbfounded, and yet instead of running away, Joseph stepped closer to me, until his shoulder, strong and comforting, touched mine.

From his touch, I found the courage to utter a reply to the High One. Although I could not tell if I was speaking words, or thinking, or dreaming with my eyes wide open.

I said to him, minding my manners, too, because I felt much compassion for the High One, "I'm so very glad that you're not as tired and lonely as when I saw you last."

I'm not, he said. *I'm not tired,* because *I'm not lonely.*

And he spread those fingers that covered his face, he spread them the slightest bit, as if to enjoy the sight of me.

Joyful I am, he said. *Joyful I am for my own son, who is ripening inside your womb, Mary. My own son who will please me well. And he shall be born, and we shall protect him. We shall be his guides, and we shall be his doting parents, his scared and awestruck parents.*

We shall raise him together, and we shall see that he is fulfilled.

Trust whoever I send to you, Mary.

"I shall," I said, although my mind was still trembling, my heart was trembling, all of me was trembling.

I leaned against Joseph, and felt that he was there.

You have given me so much, Hashem said. *And I am glad that I allowed your gift.*

I wanted to turn and stare at our house and at the roof I'd once slept on, with Joseph snoring innocently below among the setim trees. The roof on which I had dreamed that I was the girl of the promise. I wanted to glance at our roof, for it proved that I had earned that dream. But had I earned it yet? Was there more trial ahead? What lay ahead?

For the briefest instant, I stared back, and I gasped. Our yard was filled with faces. Orpa stood right at the lattice, looking at me. Seeing her, I ached and twinged so badly, I leaned on Joseph, who steadied me.

I felt so overpowered that I thought, *God, Adonai El Roi, Adonai El Hai, Hashem the Name, what did you just say to me? If any of this is true, how will I live from now on?*

And how will I? he joked.

As the sun slipped over the horizon behind us, to light the other face of the world, he headed into the setim trees, reminding me of when he had headed up that path on the mountain and then he had become his own footsteps, and I had stepped in them.

I watched him among the setim trees.

He walked with a vigorous step.

Then the thickness of the trees hid him from our sight.

But he had left his voice behind him, and it hummed in my ears. *Never fear, Mary. Never fear.*

For I will be with you from now on.

So look around, Mary. Look around with your eyes drunk with love, with your heart drunk with love.

With your eyes drunk with love.

With your heart drunk with love.

Drunk with love.

The End.

Magníficat ánima mea Dóminum,
et exsultávit spíritus meus.

Acknowledgments

Girl Mary was written over several years, but the research for it took the better part of a decade. I deeply thank the people who helped me. Some of them were scholars. For my concept of how to portray Mary, I got wonderful support from Jeffrey Siker, chair of theological studies, Loyola Marymount University, who also lent me some useful books; and from Patrick Nichelson, chair of religious studies, California State Northridge, who also corrected my Latin. For the psychological aspects of the liberal theology, I am indebted to Dr. Richard Miller. Two Romanian-born scholars, Lucian Herscovici, expert in Israeli antiquities, and Radu Ioanid, senior researcher in Holocaust history, helped me with the theme of Jewish survival. Several people who read my Romanian work before I wrote in English liked *Girl Mary* so much they told me they heard our native language in it—thank you, Juliana Astalis, Sorin Zarnescu, Florin Lupescu, Grigore Arsene. Many others helped my resolve at various stages of the work. In loose chronological order: Blake Bailey, Adam Simon, Cassandra Austin, Caldecott Chubb, Ferdinand Hauslein, Lori Scott, Robert Barron, Julian Johnson, Joyce Rappaport, Joey Perlmutter, Gwynne Evans, Lloyd Evans, Steve Wagner, Mary

Acknowledgments

Stone, Alex Rotaru, Carl Della Badia, Stefania Magidson, Gabriel Braniçteanu, Ann Marion, John Silbersack; thank you all so much.

And thank you, Marysue Rucci, my editor at Simon & Schuster, who trimmed this book into a super love story. Thank you, Ginny Smith and Sophie Epstein, who aided in the process. And thank you, David McCormick, my firm and stoic agent. You all believed in this book.

About the Author

Petru Popescu was Romania's best-known young dissident before he started to write in English. His novel *Almost Adam* was a *New York Times* bestseller, and he received high critical acclaim for his memoirs *The Return* and *The Oasis*. He lives in Beverly Hills with his wife, Iris, and his children, Adam and Chloe.